If you want to create wealth,
it will help to understand,what it is.
Wealth is not the same thing as money.
Wealth is as old as human history.
Far older, in fact, ants have wealth.
Money is a comparatively recent invention.

—Paul Graham

Praise for Dance Like You Don't Need the Money

A carnival's rich stew of honky-tonk music, swirling colors, flashing lights and friendly fraud are the backdrop for this story...whispers of Faulkner haunt this prose as the young reporter Cliff prevents the hiring and exploitation of a terribly disfigured girl found living on a farm and sent to the carnival by her parents. You can see the colorful train as it pulls into town, laugh as the elephant trainer creates havoc with his elephants to make the front page of the paper, and hear the grinding roar of motor-cycles racing inside a barrel. This story beautifully captures the intrigue of the carnival's crusade across the country.

—W. B. Park, writer & artist for *The New Yorker*

I didn't know if this was going to be a book I could get into. What a surprise! ...A wonderful, incredibly engaging tale with characters that come to life before your eyes and capture your soul. You will cheer for some and want to smack others to get their lives together. As you admire Katie's focused determination...belief in herself and...dreams...beyond the carnival...cry for Joan's parents who struggle with the decision to let their disfigured daughter go with the carnival...you will be warmed and joyful for Joan as she finds a love of herself and a life that she could never have dreamed of. All woven through the eyes of a young newspaper reporter who drinks too much, because that's what reporters do...absorbing the rich details of a community of misfits, emerging stars, freaks and con men...he will intrigue you with his notebooks crammed full of sterile facts that he's determined to assemble into a major work of fiction. This story is a wonderful roller coaster ride of real life and real people.

—Jack M. McGuire, Professor of Psychology & Associate Dean, University of Central Florida

In Dance Like You Don't Need the Money, *novelist Allen Thomas allows us the opportunity to lose ourselves in that "what if?" experience. The story takes place in the 1960s, a time when carnivals and midways were decidedly not politically correct. Up through the 60s what were called "freak shows" —people physically deformed in one fashion or another—were commonplace in carnivals. The story's characters, each searching for something, look to the carnival for answers: A small-town newspaper reporter wants to write novels that would remind his readers of Hemingway or Steinbeck; a young woman who is called to dance bravely uses the traveling carnival as free transportation to New York and Broadway; these and others in the novel are characters that Mr. Thomas obviously cares about. And so does the reader. Some of his characters see the carnival merely as a workplace while others view it as an escape opportunity for reinvention and a second act. Don't run away and leave school or your job, or the kids. Do read the book.*

—**David Malham,** Retired Grief Counselor and Owner, 8,352 Books

Cliff follows his heart and joins the carnie world of misfits, "lost souls," and freaks. In this raw and cynical environment of hustling the "marks," fixed games, and strip shows that reflects much of the disgusting parts of America's worship of money by any means contrasted with a dancer's passion for her dancing. Cliff meets Katie, who follows her passion with no doubt that she will achieve her goal of dancing on Broadway, and a disfigured young woman who finds the love and happiness her parents knew they could never give her. Cliff mistakenly falls for the lure of money, generated by the ultimate evil of the snake show. But finally he learns from Katie to let life come to him. What Allen Thomas has written is a love story—he reveals the golden thread of love and community that emanates from our source and connects us all.

—**Ron Naff,** Principle—Focused Money Advisors

I grew to anticipate my nightly readings with that eagerness that comes when we've gotten our hands on a good book whose characters we care about and whose story engages us so much that we welcome our next reading like a treat, a reward at the end of the day when we get to escape into a world that's real enough for us to believe in and care about. We get to be there when the carnival train rolls into town...we'll hear our own questions asked, face choices we, too, must make, and maybe even see things we've never seen before, such as "freaks" who teach us to look more deeply into our own fears and prejudices so that next time we encounter someone very different, we'll no longer be gawkers but will know what we're looking at and be more ready to shake the hands of the odd ones and accept them as fellow flawed dancers.

—Debby Bogard, Lecturer in Fiction and Writing, Montreat College

Dance Like

You Don't Need

the Money

Allen Thomas

Thank You, Good Friends

Alan Edwards, eager to join me in taking many grandchildren to various fairs and carnivals. And eager to read, read, read with sharp eyes locking in on the wrong usage of language—is it it's or its; you're or your?

Sharon McGuire, for throwing up her hands in frustration because I wanted to act like Faulkner and say, "Here's a whole damn page of commas—stick 'em anywhere you want."

Roberta Binder, excellent editor, unafraid to tell me I had to cut fifty percent here and there and when I did, her comment was "I wish some of my other authors would do what I tell them."

Cousin Sarah McNaught, another sharp, sharp set of eyes and authority on a certain small town in Indiana where her father and I were both born. Surprised at some of my youthful antics and giving extensive consideration as to whether or not I'm still allowed to attend family events.

Business partner and very old friend Don Barnhart, who read early drafts and knows some of the characters, real and fictional, as well as I do and who shares an interest in the stranger side of life and, at one time, collected significant news events that were brought to the public's attention by exulted publications like *The*

National Enquirer and *The Star* but—more importantly—were plagiarized by Don.

Steve Foreman was responsible for my foray into the carnival world; responsible for my joining AA; responsible for being the best man at our wedding; and the list goes on, as it does with many others.

And David Malham, who cheered me on and inspired me with his powerful ability with words and who left us much too early. David brought joy to many—I was fortunate to know him.

Jim Strates and his family, who carry on their three-generation tradition of providing entertainment for the fairs that continue to thrive and grow in this age of social networking, online entertainment and games and race cars and the other addicting digital forces that keep us isolated from each other and away from the tragedy and the joy available at reasonable prices on the fairgrounds and midways across this country.

Try it — you'll like it.

Acknowledgments

My wife Jan was with me when I started this work over forty-five years ago in a small room on the coast of Spain. Married a little over a year, she agreed with my idea of quitting our jobs, selling a car, giving up our apartment and moving to Europe to get it out of our (my) system before it would be time to get serious about life, including children, careers, mortgages, the whole deal.

My plan was to finish this book in a year or so, which would put us on the path of publishing more books, etc., etc. Jan said she was down with the plan, never dreaming the book would take forever. But miraculously we've lived through a long siege of me chasing dreams, raising two children, moving ten or fifteen times, flitting from one career to another, and now enjoying retirement and the book is finally a reality.

My love goes to Jan for supporting this effort and for reading it, over and over and over. Please understand that you are involved with a major work of love and perseverance and a living example of dancing like you don't need the money.

Thanks!

"We dance for laughter, we dance for tears,
We dance for madness, we dance for fears,
We dance for hopes, we dance for screams,
We are the dancers,
We create the dreams."
—Albert Einstein

"Life should not be a journey to the grave
with the intention of arriving safely in a pretty
and well-preserved body, but rather
to skid in broadside in a cloud of smoke,
thoroughly used up, totally worn out,
and loudly proclaiming 'Wow! What a Ride!'"
—Hunter S. Thompson

Part One

off your life, you'll think you've gone through the pearly gates. If that don't work, I'll read you a story. Come in here with me, we'll make up our own story."

Steve made an exaggerated motion for her to join him in his bed. She shook her head, blushing, then turned, stopped, turned again and walked back to her wet laundry. She stood over the basket, twisting her foot in the dirt.

Steve rested his arms on the window ledge. *Pretty woman, worn out before her time, trapped in the weeds and wet clothes. No one invited her to bed for a long time. Never hurts to ask.*

The train suddenly jerked forward, and he slammed his head against the metal frame. Steve fell to the bed, then to the floor, as blood spilled from a cut in his scalp. He shouted to himself, "Damn— won't I never learn?"

Gripping the pipes under the sink, he pulled himself to a sitting position, reached for a towel and shoved it against the gash. Blood soaked the cloth and slid down his neck. The room spun from the blow.

When he looked through the window, the train had moved away from the woman and he closed his eyes as he waited for the blood to stop, cursing the man at the throttle.

No more, I said it before, no more train, no more, the thing's going to kill me.

CHAPTER 2

This Train Is Out of Control

"A long time, we might be here a long time."

Cliff didn't care how long; he knew the gift would be worth it.

He and Franklin had waited for gifts before. Now that they were official newspaper reporters—a writer and a photographer, back home for a short time, they hoped—the waiting was a good break from the boredom of being back in their hometown.

They had waited to finish high school, waited for a girl to say yes, they waited for the license office to open to take the test so they could drive the cars they'd been impatiently working on for months, so waiting for a train carrying carnival rides and food stands and dancing girls was a great way to spend a Sunday, waiting for a gift they had a week to unwrap.

They watched a boat drifting on the Wabash River. Franklin took a picture of the fisherman as he cast his lure through the morning mist. Piles of trash filled the entrances to the abandoned warehouses. Skinny cats slunk in and out of the shadows.

Cliff said, "Take more pictures, don't let that good camera rot. You know *The Great Gatsby* could come out of my typewriter if I knew how to use it as good as you use your camera." Cliff searched the tracks. "Damn, they've got to get here soon."

Franklin moved closer as he took pictures. Cliff saw his words…
*skinny drunk smacks injured man in the face, red blood, splattered
patterns on the side of the yellow and blue train and a fat man on
crutches with stiff legs swinging like clappers in a bell.*

Steve poured vodka on the towel and pressed it to his head.
The alcohol stung; his eyes watered.

Jack crawled from under the train and managed to stand up
and swayed and stumbled, uncertain. "Bad cut, bad cut. See a doc,
sew it up? Keep it clean, clean. Bad cut."

Pagan Smith and two other strippers, with their hair piled on
their heads, walked beside the train. For the benefit of the men,
they swung their hips with each step. When Pagan saw the blood,
she ran to Steve's side, her full breasts heaving. She pulled the towel
away and winked at the camera.

"What happened? It looks bad. Does it hurt?"

"Hell yes, it hurts." Steve let her inspect the cut.

"It might need stitches."

"Jack just said the same thing. Hug from a pretty girl is better."

"I'll get you a bandage, no hugs."

"Just a little hug…that's all. I don't want to lay you on the street."

"Sweet. You know how I like to get laid on the street."

"I'll take the bandage."

"That's all you'll take." She stepped away from him. "When
you were drinking, you tried harder."

"When I was drinking, I never got cut."

"How did it happen?"

"Dumb. Don't want to tell you."

*She would laugh at him for making a pass at a woman hanging
up laundry and underwear.*

"I'll get some tape."

Pagan told Franklin she couldn't stop for pictures. "Not right now, honey, have to bandage my patient. Give me fifteen minutes and we can take our time, a lot of time." She licked her lips, emphasizing *time*.

Spectators stared while Pagan cleaned the wound and placed a bandage on Steve's head. "Too bad it didn't cut off the other ear, balance your head."

"Last time I'm riding the train," Steve said. "I ain't riding no more." He shouted, "If I have to ride a bus, I ain't riding the train."

Pagan put her arms around him. "You said that last week."

Steve motioned for Cliff to step closer. "This is Pagan Smith, a real big-deal broad, had her own joint on Baltimore's block, porn movie star."

Pagan pulled away. "Don't listen to his bullshit." She pointed toward Steve. "This is Steve Lanning, used to be the star of the Ringling Circus, featured on the Edward R. Murrow show, a real big-deal bum."

They laughed at each other. Steve said, "You're a reporter, job is to find out who's lying."

"Do I look like a reporter?"

Pagan answered, "You look like a piano player I used to work with."

Steve asked, "For what?"

"Some of this, some of that." She winked at Cliff. "Add that to your job."

CHAPTER 3

The Front Page Is Where You Want to Be

With the red and white bandage taped to his head, Steve Lanning led the elephants out of the boxcar, his chin tempting the camera. The wooden ramps swayed under their weight, the elephants blinking at the metal hook. They balanced on the narrow boards, lifting and falling with each step.

The crowd murmured—*will the board break, will an elephant go wild, swing its trunk and pick the man up and smash him against the side of the boxcar?*

The farmers thought, *look at the awful size of them, must eat a barnful, could they pull a plow?*

Franklin took pictures of the yellow tractor pulling wagons and Pagan, her red hair, and the elephants. Steve adjusted his hat over his torn ear and posed.

"Get my good side and the broad. You won't have to write much, pictures tell it all," Steve rasped. "I get paid for pictures."

"We don't pay," Cliff answered. "Which side is your good side, with or without the ear?"

Steve shook his head. "Put either one on the front page and the Man will pay you. Reporters get the run of the lot."

Cliff said, "This is the most excitement we've had since they tore down the school. There's a good chance you'll make the front page. How do you spell your name?"

"Lanning, Steve L-a-n-n-i-n-g. Come to my school at the fairgrounds. Learn things you won't learn no place else—on-the-job training. You ever ride an elephant, screw a sheep?"

Cliff laughed. "That's a ridiculous question. Who are you? What happened to your ear?

My boss wants to know if the games are fixed."

Steve offered a package of cigarettes. Cliff took one and struck a match for both of them. Steve blew a stream of smoke and asked Cliff, "Does your paper come out on Wednesday or Friday?"

"Which do you prefer? You haven't answered my question."

"If it don't come out until Friday, it ain't gonna do me much good. What question?"

Cliff ignored the jab. "Daily, every day. You're in Morganport, the big time, news every day. I'll personally bring you a copy tomorrow. Try to have the correct change. Ten percent discount if you order five copies. Did you pick the prettiest sheep?"

Steve said, "You're all right, kid. Don't knock it till you tried it. Walk with me. Show me this big-time town. I forget how to get to the fairgrounds."

"Are the games fixed?"

"Don't ask me about games," Steve snapped. "You a troublemaker? One of those reporters that stirs up shit?"

Cliff challenged him. "Come on. You're one of the insiders. Tell me. I'm writing a book. I want to stir the pot."

"Inside what? Not the games. I'm just a dumb bastard outside collecting the money. That's it. But if I did know…I'd tell you. I'll tell you who to talk to."

"You live on the train and you can't tell me how the games are fixed?"

Steve lit another cigarette and stared at Cliff. "I don't know, I don't want to know. I don't give a shit. You need to know this. I been here five years, first three bad drunk, last two, not drunk. I don't want to know anything except how much is in my moneybox at the end of the day. Jack back there might could tell you if he ever sobered up. Don't count on it."

"What about my questions?"

"Ask someone else. Ask the Man. He won't tell you either. You're after secret stuff. You can get answers, but it ain't gonna be easy. There's better answers, anyway. Let Milt tell you about jumpin' out of an airplane without no parachute. I know the answer to that. Marks know they can't win; they don't care."

"I do want to hear about that. I see why he's on crutches."

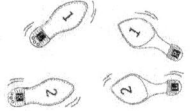

In the newsroom, Cliff and Franklin stood in front of John Stoneman's desk as they showed him eight-by-ten glossies of the elephants, and a tight shot of Steve's bloody bandage and the traffic jammed up behind the parade. There were three pictures of manure piles and six of Pagan's chest.

Stoneman picked up a magnifying glass to make the images bigger. Cliff and Franklin exchanged glances.

"Okay, here's what we do," Stoneman said. "This might get picked up by the wire. Traffic was backed up. Find out what happened to his ear. At least you got more shots of the boobs than the crap."

Cliff wanted to say…put the stripper on the front page. But that wouldn't happen. *Pagan Smith and her tight shirt, the elephants and the fat man on crutches and the skinny drunk, something outrageous, worth thousands of words, something to talk about better than the new street sweeper or the mayor's re-election. It's summer, the circus is in town—let's sell the stove and go.*

Cliff was grateful for the way the day was going. It was a lot better than the usual routine of city meetings, police reports, and senseless, empty gossip.

"Good stuff. Promote the fair." Stoneman paused, then smiled. "Elephants on page one—better than another wire report about getting our butts kicked in Vietnam."

When the reporters moved to the door, Stoneman motioned for Cliff to wait. "Franklin, you go on, get shots of something besides elephants; farm kids brushing sheep, quilts, cherry pies, local stuff."

Stoneman closed the door and sat next to Cliff. "You're getting better and better, but you have a ways to go. I told you earlier I'll recommend you for my job." He stood up and pulled a calendar out of his desk drawer and showed Cliff a date circled in red.

"I've decided to retire in ten months." Stoneman pointed to June first of the following year. "So your best bet is to stay on top of things, don't get distracted, cover Public Works...city council budgets...the police. Show me you can do it right and you'll be the next editor. You have what it takes. I want you to start laying out the pages, checking copy. It's all in the details."

Stoneman picked up his blue pencil. "I know you hate this pencil, but you have to make me stop using it. It's up to you. Tomorrow morning, Mr. John Mastras arrives in his private airplane. You meet him and welcome him to town and ask him to buy more advertising. It's part of the editor's job, I'm sorry to say. I know they didn't teach you that at IU."

Cliff shook Stoneman's hand. "Thank you for giving me your schedule."

He closed the door and thought...*ten months until you wave goodbye and head for Arizona with a gold watch on your wrist and the blue pencil stuck up your ass. We party tonight.*

CHAPTER 4

She Doesn't Keep Her Library Card Under Her Skirt

By late afternoon, the sun dropped low and cool, and when the shadow from the Masonic Lodge glided over the office window, Cliff put away his work and covered his typewriter.

A few good words today, ripe train, flying blood, stumbling drunk, epic invasion of Morganport. Sundown, beer time, Stoneman's leaving time.

Cliff turned down Fifth Street and Franklin stopped. "Where you going? No beer that way."

"Let's see how the empty train looks in the sunset."

They detoured two blocks to the rail siding. Franklin took pictures of the empty boxcars and coaches. "Like a poisonous snake hiding in the shadows."

Cliff agreed. "Do you think it's deadly?"

"I know it is." Franklin looked at Cliff. "What did Stoneman want?"

"He told me he's retiring in ten months."

"And you get his job? I work for you?"

"Together, we'll work together. Both get famous."

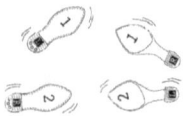

Cliff, Carolyn the librarian, and Franklin claimed their usual table and the reporters laughed when they both said "Page one" at the same time.

The waiter greeted them by name. He knew almost every customer and repeated the same drill. "I know I don't need to check, I remember when you had fake IDs." He shook his finger at Carolyn. "You never did, did you?"

"Of course I did, but not here—small town."

All the usual discussions were replaced by the county fair. The three friends were joined by others; they drank and danced and talked about the train. They had all seen the painted cars, but Cliff and Franklin were the ones who had talked to the carnies.

Carolyn said, "The characters in my library books are shallow compared to the real thing. They look bad, probably smell worse. Words don't smell except in my imagination."

"My imagination's fueled way up," Cliff said. "I love Morganport, but it can be so dull." He thought for a minute. "Truth is, there are people in town just as weird as the ones on the train, but I can't put them in the paper: Whistling Paul lives with his mother and fifty cats.

Carolyn said, "That train, the people, all week, I couldn't take it. I don't know how you do it."

"Thank God for the week," Cliff hugged the librarian, "one big out-of-control week. You're right. I'm ecstatic, orgasmic; they're here—for one week. Books aren't shallow. *You* know they aren't. Faulkner isn't; shallow didn't win him the Nobel Prize. Kerouac?

Fitzgerald? Flannery? No, none of them. It's not shallow out there, not when you dig. I'm spending this week digging. What I have to do. There would have to be a murder for Stoneman to keep me away. He told me to cover the fair; it's a filthy job but someone has to…gets to do it."

They decided to leave early so Franklin could go to the fairgrounds for set-up pictures. Cliff was okay with leaving the bar. He had other plans with Carolyn.

They stood on the sidewalk, letting the air clear their heads. Cliff held Carolyn's hand, soft in his. He said to Franklin, "Take them all night to set up. You'll get some good shots. How long you going to stay out there?"

"Don't know. See how it's going, how I feel…I hope how she feels."

Carolyn slapped his arm. "Franklin Acton you leave those girls alone; don't feel them."

"Don't you think I should go with him?" Cliff started walking with Franklin. "Come on, Franklin. Let's you and I go to the fairgrounds." He took a few steps, then stopped and returned to where Carolyn was standing.

She took his hand. "You're staying with me."

"You're right, I'm staying with you. I'll see enough this week."

She excused herself. "I'm going back in to ask Nancy something, just take a minute."

Cliff pulled her close and kissed her. "I'll wait right here."

When the door closed, Cliff told Franklin, "I'm glad you didn't say anything about Stoneman retiring. I want to surprise her."

"Don't surprise her by knocking her up."

"How would I do that? She's a librarian, too smart to let that happen."

"You slide your hand under her dress looking for a library card?"

When Carolyn returned, Cliff said, "I bet he gets some good pictures tonight, more than the girls."

"What else would he take pictures of? That's what you wanted me to ask, isn't it? You think I'm silly worrying about him, or both of you, around those people?"

"No, not silly. But it's a good thing you don't know what we did in the Navy. Then you'd really worry."

"Will you ever tell me?"

She had written both of them over the years they had served on different ships: Cliff in the Atlantic and Mediterranean, and Franklin in the Pacific. Franklin answered her letters, describing beautiful Pacific islands, Japanese ports, and the energy of Hong Kong. Cliff tried to explain his feelings about the career officers and sailors, and their contentment with living by a book of instructions. She enjoyed the letters from both of them, but when he wrote, Cliff was more open with his thoughts.

Cliff changed the subject. "Let's walk to bed…I mean home." He put his arm around her shoulders and they laughed as they stumbled against each other. They stopped in the shadows of Bailey's Department Store to share a kiss in front of a display of beach umbrellas and two-piece bathing suits.

When Carolyn ran her lips over his, Cliff whispered, "Carolyn the Barbarian Librarian," and he slid his hand over her breast.

She pushed against him. "I like that."

"I like you in brief bathing suits."

They walked arm in arm, and Cliff asked, "What do you think about Franklin wanting to leave town?"

"Is he going to?" Franklin's future wasn't what Carolyn wanted to talk about. "Is he really going to leave?"

Cliff knew Carolyn wasn't too worried about what Franklin did.

She's worried about what I do. If I don't get the promotion, I might leave, too. She's planning her life as the editor's wife, a leading couple in Morganport. Our children will grow up in a safe town with the benefits that come from the library and the newspaper, not a bad plan, but different than the one I've had. Plans change.

Carolyn and Cliff had never discussed these details. He suspected her plan, but was glad they hadn't progressed to the point of real conversation.

Cliff asked, "Do you want to stay in Morganport?"

Her apartment was two blocks from the main street, a short walk to her job. Cliff thought the location was convenient for her but he also saw it as confining.

She kicked off her shoes. "I want to stay here, not in this apartment, but I love my job."

He said, "I know you want to stay now, but forever? What if you got a chance to be the head librarian in Chicago?"

"I don't think that way. Do you think about it?"

"Tell me again, do you think...I can write...write a book? Make the words smell like the hot grease and sausages and onions, cow manure, vomit on a ride seat?" Cliff had asked her the question many times. "That's what I think about."

"Write like you talk." She lifted his arm, slid under, pulled him down and kissed him and lifted her hips to his.

They laid in bed with their arms around each other. It was a routine they'd followed for a few months and Cliff wondered if this would be their routine for a long time. Her feelings for him were easy to read, but his emotions toward her hadn't progressed past lust.

"Okay, smart librarian expert, how many books on your shelves explain the secrets of carnival con artists? Stoneman wants me to uncover the secrets that are only disclosed to those who sign in blood."

"I'll see what I can find."

"Thank you. Stoneman wants answers before the fair's over." He dropped back to the pillow. "How about this, Stoneman wants me to ask the carnies hard questions about how the games are fixed, if they're fixed; how the sword swallower swallows without slitting his throat; if the strippers turn tricks after the show closes. How about this: You ask them for me. Carolyn the librarian will have a better chance of getting answers than Cliff Walker, the gung-ho reporter."

"I can't do that. You spend time with the carnies, make some friends, and they'll give you answers."

"I can." He heard himself say he could, but it scared him. He didn't believe it. "Do you want to know why John Stoneman wants the answers?" He didn't wait for her answer. "He told me this is going to be his last fair as editor; he's retiring in ten months."

Her breath came in short spurts. She pulled him to her and kissed him, gasping at the same time, swallowing deeply so she can speak. She put one hand over her mouth, then both hands, then hugged him again and whispered, "He told you, really told you?"

Cliff nodded. "In person, today."

"Congratulations! Oh, my God, Cliff—congratulations! You're going to be the new editor. And you're going to be a great editor, one of the best. Imagine Cliff Walker, editor-in-chief of the Morganport *Pharos Tribune* newspaper."

"Easy, easy. That's not cast in stone. If everything goes right, he said he'd recommend me—but it's not for sure, not yet."

Carolyn didn't accept Cliff's statement. "I know you're going to be the next editor. You're the best choice. I know it's going to happen. And you'll be great and you'll make Morganport famous. And you'll write great novels. I know it."

CHAPTER 5

The Airplane Is a Lot More Comfortable Than the Train

The gray and silver twin-engine plane dropped through the low clouds and in the growing light, Jim Mastras stared at the neat rows of corn. The pilot circled the south side of town, knowing he had to line up on the runway and drop fast to stop before he overshot the end of the paving where solid cornstalks stood in a green wall.

While Cliff sat in his car waiting for the plane, he could still hear the excitement in Carolyn's voice when she had continued talking about him being the next editor.

It does sound good, Editor Walker, an important man in Morganport.

His attention was drawn to the silver Mercedes driving through the gate. The driver brazenly steered it onto the runway and waited for the plane to stop. Cliff wrote, *they act like they own the town—they do.*

When Jim Mastras stepped down, he looked at the two people standing at the edge of the runway. Eight months earlier, there was snow on the ground, when he signed the contract to bring his carnival to the Capp County Fair.

Cliff didn't move until his breathing slowed down, then he stepped close and offered his hand. "Mr. Mastras, I'm Cliff Walker with the newspaper; welcome to Morganport. Do you mind if I ask you some questions?"

"Certainly." Mastras shook Cliff's hand. "Thanks for meeting me. Did you see the train come in?"

"Yes. You must know what kind of thrill that gives the people. I met Steve Lanning yesterday." Cliff waited for a response.

"No surprise there. Everyone loves the elephants. They wouldn't love Lanning if they knew him."

"He had a bad cut on his head." Cliff didn't want to waste time. "He told me the train was a dangerous way to travel."

"It can be; yes, it can. What else did he tell you?"

"He told me he didn't know anything about fixed games. Are they?"

John Mastras tried to hide a quick frown, but Cliff saw it. "Fixed games are called flat stores and I don't allow them. My dad used to, a long time ago, but no more."

"So anyone can win?"

Mastras laughed. "I didn't say that. They're not fixed where the operator can control who wins, but they're almost impossible to beat, and you can put that in the paper. It won't change anything. It happens a lot. A paper will print a story that the games are impossible to win, but the people still play. The guys want to win a pink bear to impress their girls. Or they get mad at Bozo and spend their money trying to drown him in the water tank. But they don't win much."

"No, thanks," Cliff replied to Mastras' offer to ride in the Mercedes to the newspaper office. "My car's here."

The driver held the door for Mastras, and Cliff said, "Thanks for the info on the games. I'll keep it in mind. Can I ask another question?"

Mastras leaned against his car. "All you want."

"Do the strippers sell their favors?" Cliff waited. *Will he answer? He was open about the games.*

"Favors… Do you mean are they hookers? They're not hookers that I know about, but like most girls they sell their favors, a kiss for a steak. No one does anything for free." The carnival owner's eyes told Cliff he was a man comfortable with himself.

How does someone get that way, Cliff wondered.

"Besides, from what I hear, Morganport has enough whores down on the river to take care of your horny men. Do you put them in the paper?"

"No. One of the many facts about Morganport that don't make the front page—any page." Cliff was impressed that Mastras knew about the red-light houses on the wrong side of the tracks. "But most of this part of Indiana knows about them, adds to our reputation, them and the insane asylum. Thanks for answering my questions."

"You're welcome. Thank you for meeting me. I'll tell the mayor you're on top of things." The car started to pull away, then stopped. Mastras leaned out. "Ask one of your salesmen to look me up. We need to run more ads. And come to my office if you need a place to rest. I'd like to talk more."

"I'll be glad to."

Why was I nervous about meeting him? Just because he rides around in a private plane, owns a train, has a chauffeur, millions of dollars, calls mayors by their first name, what's intimidating about that? And he invited me to his office to talk. I might throw up when I get there.

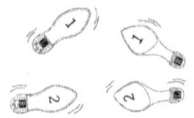

When the Mercedes appeared at the back gate of the fairgrounds, a man waved the car through and saluted Mastras.

Mastras returned the salute and when the car stopped, he walked away, moving through the jumble of tents and rides. His long strides let everyone know he didn't want to listen to their complaints or requests for better locations.

Steve Lanning saw Mastras approaching the animal menagerie.

He liked to take one turn around the midway to see if the set-up is on schedule. Everyone knew the Man had arrived. The King was in court.

Steve got out of his chair and yelled at Jack to tighten the ropes around the front stakes. "Pull the slack out. What the hell you been doing?"

Mastras stopped next to Steve. "I hear you made the front page."

"Yes, sir, I…we did, we sure did."

"Wasn't the rock this time?"

"No sir, it wasn't, not this time, didn't have to pull that stunt. We caught a break."

"Like you always say, doesn't matter how—as long as we make the paper."

Steve drew on his cigarette. "That's it, any press, better than nothing."

"I just met the reporter."

Steve crushed out his cigarette. "He'll be back. Real ambitious kid, that photographer wants another good look at Pagan."

"She'll give him plenty to look at," Mastras said. "Check the kid out. I might try to hire him."

CHAPTER 6

Elephants Will Poop on the Street

The chairman pointed to a jagged bar graph. "If we don't do it now, it will just cost more later. We can't keep paying overtime whenever the streets need to be cleaned."

The Republican members of the board agreed and nodded their heads while the opposing members sat rigidly in their seats. The windows on the third floor of City Hall offered a view of the street, where dark stains marked the elephants' sizeable deposits.

The chairman looked at Cliff. "Walker, you listening?"

Cliff turned the page to hide his drawing of an elephant. "Every word."

The same gibberish...and before...and before. Can't wait to hand this to someone else; some green new graduate excited about putting words together in correct form.

The chairman asked, "Do I hear a second? Is there any more discussion?"

"Second call for the question." Earl Shoop looked at his watch. "I've got to get back to work."

"All in favor? Like Ralph said, it will cost a lot more later."

He counted the raised hands. "Motion passed. We'll buy a street sweeper. Put it on the front page, Cliff. Tell the public we're cleaning up elephant crap."

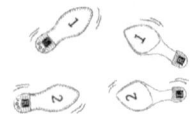

John Stoneman looked up when he heard Cliff stop typing. "What have you got?"

Cliff rolled a clean sheet into the carriage. "One more paragraph."

"Hurry up, we're almost finished. Don't make it a major production."

Cliff kept typing and, in a few minutes, handed the sheet to Stoneman. The editor read the copy and nodded his head. "Okay, this is good. What's going to happen next meeting?"

"I'll be there. I don't want to miss a word." Cliff had missed most of the discussion, thinking about the carnival train. "Aren't you going to miss this excitement when you retire?"

Stoneman rubbed his head. "No." He laughed. "Clean streets. Get me more about the sweeper; I need an editorial. Facts are my life—my grandkids say I need to get a life."

Cliff agreed. "So do I."

Stoneman turned away, hiding his smile.

CHAPTER 7

Strings Will Make Puppets Dance

A crowd stood behind a yellow ribbon blocking the entrance to the fairgrounds while the marching band warmed up; trumpets, saxophones, flutes, and drums collided under bright banners.

While Cliff questioned a young blonde girl, Franklin snapped three pictures of her red sash proclaiming her MISS CAPP COUNTY 1967.

An official car stopped next to the yellow ribbon. Mayor Hal Wertz stepped out, shook hands with Cliff and several of the other citizens waiting for the fair to open. The mayor lifted his hands in the air.

"Sorry I'm late. Let's get this ribbon cut so we can all enjoy this Free Day. Are you ready?"

June Tilsoner adjusted her red sash and walked toward the mayor with exaggerated swings of her hips. She displayed a sweet smile. "We're ready, Mr. Mayor."

"Do you have the scissors?"

June looked confused. "I'm Miss Capp County." She adjusted her tight shorts and thrust out her breasts at the mayor.

"I see that on your sash. Do we have some scissors? Can't cut the ribbon without scissors."

"No one told me to bring scissors."

Someone handed the mayor a knife and he cut the ribbon. The crowd pushed through while Franklin took pictures of June and the mayor and the army of children screaming through the gates, their nerves on fire.

Cliff whispered to Franklin, "One of the words I'm going to use for Miss Capp County is bewildered. We better warn the dairy barn…regular milking machines won't get it, need a large capacity industrial model to milk those jugs."

The mayor shook Cliff's hand. "Please write how the increased street budget and the sweeper will decrease the potholes. I'm tired of hearing about the wear and tear on the public's tires."

The mayor moved closer. "Remember this…I'm supporting you for the editor's job. And it's time for you to take over…past time. What was that editorial on street cleaning about? Stoneman's losing it. It's time for him to put away his typewriter."

Cliff and Franklin joined the crowd hurrying through the gate. "What did he say?"

"He told me he's recommending me for the promotion. And he thought the editorial about the street cleaner was stupid, should have been about his re-election campaign."

"You can't miss, Cliff, you're the next editor, done deal."

"Maybe, maybe not. I might not like the strings that go with it. The mayor wants his hand up my back, me on his lap."

"If you're the editor, you pull the strings and have the mayor dancing for you."

"Don't know if I want to play that game. Don't know if I can."

CHAPTER 8

Alive, Live, Live...
They're ALL Alive
on the Inside

Free kids' admission on opening day had the same effect as pushing dope through their veins; hot fuel, the thrill of the midway, an out-of-control world pulsating inside the main gate.

A small boy pushed clouds of cotton candy in his mouth and licked the sticky sugar from his fingers. He wiped them on his white T-shirt and wiped again until the shirt was streaked with blue and pink stripes. When the ticket taker on the bumper cars told him he couldn't ride while holding candy, he stuffed the rest of it in his pocket. The spun sugar melted and welded the nickels and dimes and quarters together in a gooey mass that he couldn't retrieve. He dropped to the ground in tears—his day ruined.

Franklin aimed his camera and took shots from different angles as the boy tried to hide his tears. Cliff handed the boy three dollars. The tears disappeared and the boy ran to catch up with his friends. Then he turned and shouted, "Thank you," and ran again.

They walked with the crowd, buoyed by the music. The midway hadn't changed since Cliff was twelve. "I love it!" He slapped Franklin on the back. "LOVE IT!"

"I hear you." Franklin moved away from his shouting friend. "Everyone hears you."

"Let's find the elephant trainer."

Franklin agreed. "Get him out of the way while it's still light. It'll be better if we see the girls after dark, hide their scars and wrinkles."

Cliff chanted, "See wrinkled Wanda the worn-out wonder woman woo and wow the willing marks. She wiggles her wrinkles—wide, wasted, and worn."

"Stoneman will need a new blue pencil."

Banners stretched across the front of the animal menagerie. A cartoon painting of a dark swami wearing a white turban leading a herd of elephants through the jungle, a midget horse ridden by a tall man with his feet dragging the ground, a humpback bull, a lion, and a hippopotamus, each canvas painted in bright colors. The loudspeakers cut through the noise from the competing rides.

"Alive, live, live…they're all alive on the inside, see the elephants, friendly friends of Tarzan. Dimes or dollars…takes you all the way through and the show never stops. See Old George the blood-sweating river hog—big as a truck and lonnng as a whale; takes a boxcar to lug him and a freight train to tug him." Steve Lanning's voice on the tape recorder doesn't stop, over and over. *"See the midget horse…so tiny…so smallll…a silver dollar makes a perfect shoe, a… ten-year-old boy can hold it in the palm of his hand. See the sacred cow of India. All alive on the inside."*

Over the entrance to the tent, they saw the front page of the morning paper taped to a piece of cardboard. The crude sign hung in contrast to the painted banners, crooked letters drawn by a shaky hand:

See the Famous Front-Page Elephant—
Free on the Inside!

By Cliff Walker

Photographs by Franklin Acton

"Not the way we want to become famous, our names on the front of a sideshow tent."

Franklin said, "Mom would be so proud."

Inside the tent, filthy air blanketed the cages holding the hippopotamus and the chimpanzee. Three llamas stood behind a rope as they shared the space with a one-humped camel. The elephants stood in the back of the tent—a weaving wall of searching trunks.

Jack was shoveling manure. He pushed against a thick leg as he forced it out of the way.

"Queen… Move, move your leg, move!"

Cliff and Franklin watched the small man as he worked between the legs of the huge animals, oblivious to the danger as he scooped up piles of manure. He stopped shoveling when he realized someone was watching.

Cliff asked, "Where can we find Steve Lanning?"

"An' juss who wan's to know? Never heard of him…Lenny? Ain't no Lenny."

"We're with the newspaper, saw you yesterday, downtown—where can we find Steve Lanning?" Cliff was surprised the man was sober enough to work.

Jack swayed against his shovel. "In back. We're on front page. Welcome, greatest show on earth, 'Merica's finest midway."

Cliff handed Jack a paper. "Here's a copy. Who put up the sign out front?"

Jack's glazed eyes rolled over the story. "I did. I'm advertising." He pointed to the back of the tent. "Follow me."

Cliff remembered his parents' warning: don't go behind the tents. Be careful. There are bad people at that fair. *But Dad, the best part is behind the tents.*

The elephant trainer was sitting alone, reading. He closed the book and when Cliff read the title, he decided the trainer looked like one of Hemingway's characters.

Steve signaled Jack to wait. He gestured to the men and asked Cliff and Franklin if they'd like to sit down and have something to drink. He motioned to the chairs. "Coffee, beer?" They asked for beer, Steve nodded, and Jack walked back inside the tent.

Cliff said, "Hemingway would like this. *The Old Man and the Sea* on a carnival midway, like one of his safari camps."

"Not many big words, an old man catching a big fish. I get it, he don't give up."

"What else?"

"Don't know nothing else." Steve lit a cigarette. "Thank you for the press, best I've ever had. Saw it first thing this morning. Front page, big time, making me famous."

"We saw the sign out front. You're making us famous, too."

Good thing it's Morganport—won't hurt us too bad.

"You're making me money, better than famous, a lot better. I've been famous, ain't much to it. You boys look pretty good today, party last night?"

They accepted the beer from Jack, and Cliff nodded his head. "Not hard to figure that out. Doesn't take much in Morganport. I need this." He drank from the can.

Jack stared at the drinkers, eyes pleading. Steve motioned him away. "Check back, see if these boys need refills. Go finish those stalls." Jack saluted and marched inside the tent. "Pitiful, used to be one of the best game agents out here, now he's a shit-shoveling drunk, graduated from college, too."

Cliff listened and wondered how long they'd been working together—and why. A hopeless drunk, a man who wouldn't be tolerated anywhere else—but Steve Lanning put up with him, accepted his drinking and got some work done. Cliff wanted to know the rest of the story.

Steve lifted the book. "Hemingway was a big drinker. Met him once, when I was still drinking," Steve shut the book. "I got an idea for a story for you. This book's the same size as a bottle, something to hold, pass the time, not hard on my liver. Doctor had to test mine with a hammer." Steve shifted the book from one hand to the other and then dropped it. "They oughta change the name, liquor store to library, check out a bottle."

Cliff worked to control his voice. "You met Hemingway? Where?" He wanted to know the details, the facts. *Is it true? What can I believe from a man with a cut head, living on a broken train?* "Liquor in the library...a good idea. I'll ask the librarian."

"Bar in Key West. He listened how I got my ear shot off in Italy. He was there before me, the first big war. They said he's the best. Hard for me to know, only got through the third grade. He don't use big words."

"Were you performing in Key West? What was he like?"

"Ringling Show, elephant act, center ring. I wish I knew, I was drinking heavy, so was he. A blur and I ain't sure it was really him, but I think it was. Makes a good story, don't it? The press likes it. Your business goes for some—," he paused as he heard someone coming. "Goes for some strange shit. I was a little famous...famous drunk. Here comes the real famous one."

Milt Hinkle arrived on crutches, jerking from side to side. When he took a step, his leg caught on a rut and he tilted in a half circle. Jack came out of the tent just in time to catch him and guided the big man to a chair. Milt's eyes were loose, spinning.

Cliff objected to the man's arrival because he interrupted the story about Hemingway. *Pick it up later in the week.* A surge ran through him. Maybe Stoneman would agree to a feature on the elephant trainer because he met Ernest Hemingway.

Steve said, "Strange as they come. This man was really famous, made the front page in old Mexico. When he was on top, he made the front page everywhere he went. Meet the one and only Mr. Milt Hinkle, Mr. Rodeo, in person."

Milt swung his crutch, pointing to Cliff. "Mr. Walker, pleasure, real. I Mil…Hinkle."

Cliff is surprised the man knew his name. "I saw you yesterday. What about Mexico?"

Franklin snapped pictures, then put the cap over the lens. "I'm going to keep shooting, you're the listener."

Steve raised his voice and told Jack to take Milt back to the boxcar. "He's about to ruin me with the press, start blowing about his trunk. He's got a trunk full of good shit and you should—you will—get a look at it, but not now. Go away. Look at the girls, take pictures, do your jobs. I got to take the money out of the box before the help steals it. Come back later. Come back anytime."

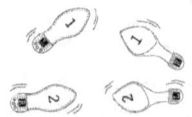

Three girls looked up at the Ferris wheel. They grabbed the hands of three boys walking past, and voiced their requests to buy tickets to the ride and one of the boys says "no," but the other two say "yes" and they push each other toward the ticket box. The boys wanted to ride with the girls. They shifted their shoulders and tried not to look eager.

"Let's ride it now before you chicken out." The leader of the girls taunted the boys. "Are you afraid? It's just a little Ferris wheel."

"Afraid of nothing out here."

The girl flipped her hair. "I think you're afraid of me."

"You're right about that. Afraid of cooties."

"You said that yesterday, get something new."

The three couples didn't see Franklin as he took their pictures while the wheel revolved past him. He saw them in the viewfinder and the sequence of shots changed—from the boys and the girls sitting apart through a revolution, sitting closer on the next revolution, then an arm around her shoulders through three turns until the final turn when her head was nestled against his shoulder. And they walked away from the Ferris wheel arm in arm, and looked for the next ride so they could sit together.

The Tunnel of Terror attracted them, with its dark track where they could neck. They didn't hesitate to buy tickets and Franklin told Cliff it would be a real score if he could find a way inside the dark ride. "There's going to be some hot making out in there, no front-page pictures."

Instead, Cliff and Franklin turned to the row of games: pop a balloon, score a basket, knock down the milk bottles, ring a plastic duck, roll a ball, ring a bell, shoot out the star, hit the fuzzy cat.

Cliff watched the faces of the contestants as Franklin took their pictures, hard work to win a cheap prize that looked valuable. Breathing hard to slam the hammer down and adoring gasps when the bell rings. Wild embraces, the hint of more to come, a pink bear was handed across the counter to the clutching hands of a girl who idolized the boy.

Cliff scrawls a note—the fix is simple; odds favor the house, big-time.

The question: Does the operator control it and how am I going to find out? Is anyone going to spill the answers? John Stoneman wants to know; my new job might depend on it.

CHAPTER 9

A Free Peek at
the Promised Land

"Enough, enough! We've done our duty; let's see the girls. These passes are burning my pocket."

Franklin's long strides led them toward the Broadway Review tent. The sky was planted with growing seeds of light, red and yellow, blue, green, blinking against the night. The transition from day to night changed the midway to a painting on black velvet, hiding the scars.

A free peek at the Promised Land. The drummer bounced on his seat, his foot punching the bass drum, hands whipping thin sticks and ringing cymbals. Two guitars and a saxophone brought the melody together and the girls spun, showing patches of bare skin as they pulled the marks closer.

Cliff's hands and feet joined the music. His nerves matched the beat of the bass drum.

Ace King strutted back and forth as he barked into a microphone.

"The hottest, the wildest, the sexiest show on the midway, the reeeal thing. Inside this tent is where they let it all hang out. They're gonna show you guys what you dream about. Come in…have a good look…believe me, the looking's good, real good, better than good, as good as it gets. The next show starts in just a few minutes. Get your tickets now, still a few seats left on the front row, up close and reeeeal personal!"

Men nodded at the reporters, self-conscious at being caught.

Ace King jumped to the ground. "We take care of the press." The morning newspaper had made its way around the lot, and the reporters were on the midway.

"You want to interview the girls? How about our star, Pagan? I turn this tip, I'll take you backstage."

"What'd you say, tip?" Cliff understood *girls*, but not the rest.

"Turn the tip—change these marks to customers. No good to me 'til they tip, buy a ticket."

"Where'd 'tip' come from?"

"Questions, questions—where'd *you* come from? Get your camera ready. You're gonna get some close-ups, real close up."

Cliff and Franklin followed Ace to the stage.

A pretty dancer looked at Cliff, smiling, her eyes boldly fixed on his. Her short blonde hair swept across her forehead as she swung her body to the beat of the drums.

Who was she? How did pretty girls end up in seedy strip shows? No creases crowding her eyes; no folds blurring the corners of her mouth. What's her secret, who was she? The homecoming queen?

He couldn't imagine any of the Morganport girls—Carolyn—strutting across the Broadway Review stage. Impossible. The young dancer didn't fit, but there she was with a real smile. Her joy was startling. She was wearing briefs, but she looked like she was on her way to the beach and when he turned away, he saw that the other faces in the audience were watching her and no one else.

Another eye exchange grabbed Cliff. He wanted to put his arms around her.

Ace King grabbed his arm. "The real show's inside. Follow me."

Cliff and Franklin followed the announcer past the ticket takers and down the side aisle to the backstage. "We want you guys to see everything."

Backstage, strippers adjusted their clothes and checked each other's makeup. Honey Dew and Holly Wood rested on folding chairs as they waited for the show to begin. Thin scarves covered their colored hair and they pulled soiled robes over their shoulders and smoked cigarettes, bored with the evening before it started— another show in another hick town in another long season.

"Who you got, Ace—VIPs?" Honey Dew lit a new cigarette; lipstick stained the filter.

"Where's Pagan? Reporters. I want you to take care of them."

"Both of 'em? Before my number? Can't Holly take care of one of 'em? She's got more energy than I do. My feet hurt."

"Where's Pagan?" Ace didn't want a discussion.

"In the trailer. She was cold."

Holly adjusted her scarf. "Can I have the tall one?"

Cliff and Franklin were embarrassed by the conversation, but they could tell the girls were kidding.

Pagan walked out of the dressing room, wearing a sheer robe split wide between her breasts, held together with a strand of cloth. She was showing what her sweatshirt covered when she taped Steve Lanning's head, clearly the star of the show.

Ace King kissed her hand, "Pagan, as always, you look beautiful. Meet the press."

"Hello, boys, so handsome... I'm delighted to see you again." She dismissed the announcer. "Go sell tickets. I'll be more than happy to entertain these good-looking men...even if they didn't put my picture in the paper."

Pagan moved toward them, smiling. Her hands and fingers combed through her hair and her long bare legs showed when the robe opened. "If you stand over here—behind this curtain—you get the good view, the C-note seat."

She put one arm around Franklin's shoulders and rubbed his camera with her hand. "I bet you're a good shooter, aren't you? You stand where I show you and I'll give you plenty to shoot. Even if it won't make the front page."

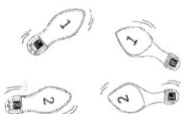

Inside, the audience stomped, clapping their hands and cheering when the girls appeared. The older strippers moved with forced enthusiasm. The three younger girls danced in unison, kicking, turning, as they merged with the music and the crowd.

The blonde offered her shoulders, arms, and legs. She was clearly the best dancer of the group. She drew in the audience, giving them no choice.

While he stood in his assigned position, Franklin had a clear view of the stage. He snapped pictures as Honey turned toward him, kicking her legs and shaking her breasts.

Cliff watched and wrote: *backstage strippers, seedy show, half-naked women, worn-out props, flashing lights, glitter, drummer knew their moves and underscored every step. Plenty of men would pay one hundred for Franklin's seat.*

While Honey was doing her act, the other girls rested backstage, but the blonde continued dancing, unable to sit down. She couldn't stop while the music played.

Cliff clapped to the driving rhythm and she moved her feet toward him, three steps forward, two back, smiling as she stalked her prey. Her glowing eyes shone against the grungy curtains and Cliff motioned for Franklin to take her picture. He wanted the photograph so he could take his time studying the details. Maybe he would find something in her high cheekbones and soft lips that explained what she was doing there.

"Will you dance with me? I can tell you like the music," she asked while Franklin focused on her face.

"I don't dance very well." Cliff was drawn to her smooth steps. The floor vibrated and he looked at Franklin. They had departed Planet Morganport. Her fingers felt soft entwined with his; shock moved up his arms and down his legs, until his feet slid toward hers and he realized he just might be able to dance with this girl.

She laughed and gripped his hand, contented to dance with a partner whose feet stuck to the floor.

He asked, "Don't you need to rest?"

"When I go to bed, not now." She spun under his arm, floating, bobbing to the drums—her gentle moves pulled Cliff with her, surprised that his feet matched the rhythm. Movements, rhythm, music, an intriguing girl, and Cliff floated above the floor.

Franklin took their picture, then turned back to the main stage. When Honey finished her act, the blonde and Cliff bowed to each other while they laughed at the applause.

She said, "Thank you. Let's dance again. You've got the hand-holding under control, your feet need a little help."

"You make anyone look good."

When Honey exited the stage, the chorus girls filled in until Ace raised his hands to the audience. "You want more? I know you want more, a lot more. For those of you that have been here before, you know there's more—give a big hand to the star of the show—the Pagan Lady!"

A lithe animal, moving with jungle drums, bending, twisting, and spinning, until she had the audience stomping, clapping, and cheering for more.

Franklin took picture after picture while Pagan played to the camera, legs and arms and thighs harmonized in sexual fantasy, pure desire glowed in her eyes and when it seemed like she should stop, her movements grew faster and faster while she built to the big finish. The audience jumped as she brought them to the climax of her dance, ecstatic twisting hips, hands hovering up and down her thighs, then a final spin with her arms and hands extended as she returned the audience's intense applause. The marks on the front row knew she smiled directly at them, inviting them back for the next show and the next.

The performance ended and the audience blinked in the light as they scrambled out of the tent, confused, their focus lost with the last slam of the drum.

Pagan walked backstage and kicked off her shoes, a cigarette between her lips, bottle of beer in one hand; she rubbed her bare feet with the other.

Franklin took more pictures and asked, "Can we buy you a cup of coffee, a drink?"

"No coffee, food. Two more shows. Meet us at the train at midnight—in the Pie Car. I'll buy you a drink."

The blonde smiled at Cliff, "See you later."

His feet sought the right steps, wanted to move next to her.

"Later."

Later and longer.

CHAPTER 10

Let's Interview
the Limber Ladies

During the drive from the fairgrounds to the train, Cliff talked about the blonde, about her beauty and her dancing. "Never before, never seen anyone like her, have you?"

"No."

"Never before. I can't believe she's dancing here, at Morganport's fairgrounds. It's like a brilliant diamond has been discovered on the muddy bank of the grimy Wabash River."

The tired carnies straggled into the Pie Car for steak, eggs, hamburgers, and beer. The light threw a circle around their car. Cliff and Franklin parked next to the tracks and saw the girls through the window.

"I don't know if I can eat in there," Franklin said.

"The beer will be safe." Cliff walked to the side of the train and waved to Pagan. She blew him a kiss. He gripped the bar and swung to the first step. "Let's go interview the ladies, what we signed up for, we're getting paid for this."

They made their entrance and quickly took seats facing the women. Holly and Honey had changed into tank tops, their flesh bulged over the top of the tight fabric. Pagan had added baggy pants to her open-necked blouse, and her red hair waved over her shoulders.

"Ain't this cute, boys on one side, girls on the other. Don't work; change with me." She stood and waited for Cliff to switch seats, which left Franklin between the other two strippers. They noticed his red face, and they leaned against him and made soft moaning sounds.

The blonde arrived, wearing a striped T-shirt, blue jeans, and sneakers. She pulled a chair from another table and sat across from Cliff.

"Sooner instead of later."

"Works for me." He made himself turn his head, to stop as he stared. Beautiful face planted in the middle of where it wasn't supposed to be. *A regular girl on a date ordering a Coke and a hamburger, looks like a nice girl in a bad place, her eyes resuming their investigation of me, mine matching hers.*

Seated two booths away, Steve Lanning was reading as he ate soft eggs. Milt was drinking beer. Steve looked up and nodded to Cliff, silently congratulating him on being with the girls, then returned to his book.

How does he decide what to read? Introduce him to Carolyn; she can give him a library card.

Cliff asked the girls if this was what they did every night.

Pagan answered, "We go to other spots. We're usually invited to go somewhere."

"And you're invited again. The Rendezvous makes the best hamburgers in Indiana." Cliff could envision the turmoil that would start when Pagan strutted through the door.

They ordered and the food was delivered on paper plates. They ate quickly and lit cigarettes and slipped low in the booth, relaxing as the feeling returned to their feet. Cliff thought it would take a wad of money to prompt these girls into bed, but he knew how money talked.

"You ain't finishing that toast?" Holly asked Pagan as she chewed her last bite of steak.

"You can have it. I'm cutting back, had trouble getting through the last show. My butt felt like a sack of mud."

Franklin said, "You looked good to me. Used a lot of film."

Pagan patted Franklin's hand. "You had the best seat in the house. When can we see the pictures?"

"I'll have them tomorrow. Can I bring them backstage?"

"You can come backstage any time you want."

While the girls laughed, Cliff excused himself to go to the bathroom. Franklin followed, and when they finished, they stood on the open platform in the fresh air.

"Are we where I think we are?" Cliff exhaled a stream of cigarette smoke. "How did two Indiana farm boys with cow crap on their shoes have the good luck to be sitting with strippers on a carnival train? This is unbelievable."

Maybe someday I'll know what to do with it. I know now; sit at the typewriter and stare at the blank page until blood runs from my fingers.

"We are here, we are definitely here." Franklin couldn't stop smiling. "I don't know how you write it—I need a wide-angle lens to shoot it."

"This can't be real—is it real? It's a hard job, but someone's got to do it. You'd have missed this if you were gone."

"Don't start on that." Franklin led the way back to the women.

The seat was comfortable. Cliff shifted his legs on lumpy padding and swallowed cold beer thinking about the old railroad cars, when the passengers had been tourists, salesmen, families, preachers, honey-mooners… *Who sat here before me? Bare spots in the carpet, chipped paint, layers of smoke and grease, still good enough to carry carnies from Florida to Morganport, Boston, and back.*

Cliff touched his pencil, then pulled his hand away. He knew the scene would remain, impossible to forget—drinking with strippers and an elephant trainer.

When I'm ready, the words will be there…why aren't they here now, not the time to write, time to dive in, soak it up.

He shuddered, his attention pulled to the face as it entered the Pie Car, like a screwdriver rammed in his brain. He couldn't turn his head. Afraid to close his eyes.

Cliff was shocked by the horrible face, unable to move, unable to run.

Not here, not where they serve hamburgers, not in the same space. Please don't come any closer. Oh God, please, NO.

A long-repressed memory floated into his head…

He was twelve years old, finished with the bumper cars and merry-go-round. He and his friend Johnny had decided to spend their last twenty-five cents to look at the freaks.

They had watched a man hammer a spike up his nose, looked at a woman with elephant feet, but when the man wearing a hood jerked it off and the bright lights brought his twisted face into sharp focus, Cliff had to look away, stare at the ground. It was the most terrifying thing he had ever seen; he couldn't inhale, his breath shut off, choking.

And he hoped it wasn't real—it had to be makeup, please let it be makeup but it wasn't makeup…

Cliff kept his eyes averted, glanced up and listened to the man explain how he was born deformed and the only way he could exist was to work in sideshows and sell pictures.

Sell pictures? Who buys a pictures? Why? What do they do with them?

Cliff had run out of the tent and waited for Johnny and then begged him to go home, even though it was before their curfew. He needed the safety of his bed. The face had followed him all the way home, floating into his thoughts when he closed his eyes.

Now there wasn't a hood. Eyes peered out of pockets of mangled, folded flesh, a shattered face ripped and disfigured. An eye moved, one almost on top of the other, twisted skin where lips should be, a mouth, a horrible, repulsive mistake. The side of the man's head bulged, pink skin stretched transparent over bone. His nose was an open hole, shiny and wet. The face was too close, horrible; shouldn't have been allowed near other people. The freak held the arm of a woman whose skin earned her the name Alligator Lady. They chose a booth and sat as they waited to order.

Cliff's eyes flooded with tears. He felt dizzy, like the seat had disappeared, falling, falling. A foul liquid filled and burned his throat, his stomach heaved. He knew he was going to be sick. He looked at Franklin for help, but his friend was laughing with the strippers, his back to the brutal face.

Cliff wanted to squeeze his eyes shut until he knew it was safe to open them again. It would never be safe. A burning stream forced its way into the back of his throat.

"Gotta go."

Cliff jumped out of the seat. If he didn't leave the car, vomit was going to spew across the table. He shut the bathroom door and dropped to his knees, retching. The mixture swirled and twisted, and Cliff saw the torn face as it floated in the bowl. When his stomach was empty, he leaned against the wall, waiting to breathe.

Don't look at him. Maybe he's gone. Can't sit there, not in the same seat, maybe he'll disappear if I keep my eyes closed.

Cliff forced himself to return to the booth. He sat with his head turned away from the face. He rinsed his mouth with beer, the whole bottle; the alcohol burned his tongue, then another beer.

How many would it take…?

"Have a good day, Steve? You got some good press, didn't you?" the three-eyed man asked in a muffled voice. The words roared through Cliff's head; hearing the distorted sounds was as bad as being able to see the twisted eyes, his presence crowded the dining car.

Steve answers, "Not bad, not much long green in this town. Another day tomorrow, ain't it, Bill? Might be better. You saw we made the front page?"

"They're mostly the same from where we set." He smiled, a contorted twist. "Don't never make the front page." The Three-Eyed Man patted his wife on the shoulder.

Pagan whispered to Cliff, "At least they got each other. More than we got."

He drank his beer, then ordered vodka. He wanted to know, but couldn't bring himself to ask. If there were answers, he didn't want to hear them. Nothing could explain something so awful.

They weren't real people when he was young, it wasn't real, couldn't be real. But now the people sitting across the aisle were too real. *Were they human? Their exteriors made them look like monsters. Monsters didn't eat in restaurants, but they could eat in the Pie Car.*

Cliff swallowed vodka when he heard Pagan as she spoke. "They've been together a long time. After you been around them awhile, you get used to it. Bill's a good man, Ruth's got a big heart, do anything for you. You should interview them, they *are* the real thing."

He knew his job was to report the facts, but not these facts. If he could somehow find the right words, they would explode, injuring the readers—and pictures would start a fire. He drank another vodka.

Pagan hugged his shoulders and rubbed the back of his neck. "We love having our pictures taken." The blonde moved her chair so her face filled the space in his view.

Cliff understood; his face was broadcasting pain.

Steve Lanning walked to the booth. "I'm buying a round. These Notch Broads ain't gonna do nothing for free. Put Pagan on the front page and see what she gives you…more than vodka."

The blonde's beautiful face, her warm smile, comforted Cliff. Three more glasses of vodka blurred the freaks; he found his voice again. It was tired and weak, but as he made sounds, he brought himself back to the girl across the table.

"Pagan on the front page will never happen unless she robs a bank or seduces the chief of police. If I had my way, we'd do a whole issue on the Fair. People want to read something besides weather, police reports, the price of corn, and basketball scores."

Pagan asked, "What's the chief look like, maybe I'll do him in the back seat of a cop car." The blonde looked away, then back at Cliff, frustrated.

The women posed and winked at the camera. Franklin walked up and down the center aisle and Milt tipped his hat back, turning his face to the light. The posing and the click of the camera became acceptable.

Three-Eyed Bill and his wife nodded, uncomfortable, but they consented to the pictures.

The vodka did its job and Cliff watched the proceedings through a new filter. He enjoyed seeing the people smile as Franklin moved from booth to booth, asking permission without speaking, like picture day at school.

Franklin's calm reaction to the carnies didn't surprise Cliff. The photographer grew up on a farm with weird animals. He knew what to do to get the right pictures.

We're a team. Two outsiders accepted into this strange society, different than anything in Morganport, but not that different, not when I look at it through an open lens, a lens with a thick coating of vodka and beer.

When the cook announced closing time, Pagan kissed Cliff and Franklin on the cheek and told them they were expected backstage tomorrow. "Bring eight by tens."

Outside, Cliff's legs wove over the uneven ground as thoughts rippled up...*read all about it*... "How do they do it, eat with him?"

"Who are you talking to?"

Cliff heard a response. The moonlight wasn't bright enough to see clearly, but when she spoke, he knew her voice. Her face was open, and her eyes were doing what they did best. "I thought Franklin was behind me."

"He's inside still taking pictures. They'll pose as long as he has film."

"You don't want your picture taken? How about another dance lesson?"

"I wanted out of there, too." She reached for Cliff's hand. The touch of her fingers linked him to safety. "It's too late to dance. Let's walk. How about we introduce ourselves? I'm Katie Flanagan."

He nodded his head, face flushed. "Clumsy-footed Cliff Walker, let's take the five-dollar tour of downtown. Is Katie Flanagan your real name?"

"It is. My own tour guide would be wonderful."

The fresh air and her fingers erased the deformed face. They walked past displays of refrigerators and washing machines; pastel dresses with matching shoes in Rowe's Department Store that women bought for dances at the Elks Club. They had the street to themselves.

He looked at Katie's clean white tennis shoes. She looked like a co-ed, not a chorus girl. Katie put her hand on his arm when she stopped to look at the display. "My mother has a dress like that."

"Where did you learn to dance? You're better than Pagan... with your clothes on."

"I watched *American Bandstand* every day, danced with my girl-friends. We copied everyone. Danced in church, with my mother. I dance in my dreams. Want to hear a funny story?"

"Yes. What's it about?"

"How I ended up in a strip show on a carnival midway."

"You must read minds. That's something this reporter really wants to know. Can I write about it?" *Nothing Stoneman wants to know, but I do.* "How's that funny?"

"I don't know. See what you think. I've never gone out with a writer before. How did you learn to write?"

"Not a writer—a trained monkey with a pencil. I'm a secretary, a mechanical robot; anyone can write what I write. I take notes at budget meetings; type them up for the editor to color with his blue crayon. Not real writing…someday, someday I'll get there."

"Like me, this isn't my kind of dancing, not what I'll do when I get to New York." Her destination was definite. "It's sure not what I thought I was going to do. They lied about this job. Made it sound like I'd be dancing in the grandstand shows, not in a midway tent with tough-meat strippers. That's the funny story."

"You didn't know where you'd be working? Who told you? That's not funny, nothing funny about that. 'Tough-meat strippers' is pretty funny. But don't let Pagan hear you say it, she is real tough meat, the kind you have to beat with a hammer. Who lied to you?"

"A slimy agent in California told me he could get me a job with a touring review. I wasn't getting anywhere in Hollywood without real experience and this agent found me at an audition where I didn't get asked back…again. That's how he operates. He hangs out at auditions waiting to see who doesn't make it, then spins this great offer of touring state fairs. He bought me a bus ticket to Atlanta where I met the train." Her laugh surprised Cliff. "He put me on the leave-the-driving-to-us bus—you should have heard my dad when he found out about it."

"Your father? I can't imagine what he said." He stared at her. How could this be funny?

"He wanted to ride the bus with me. And he meant it." Her smile grew to laughter and Cliff found himself staring at her mouth and eyes.

"Are you kidding? If I had a daughter, I wouldn't let her ride a bus by herself."

"He would have gone with me, but he couldn't be away from the church that long. It's too bad. We would have had a great time. Wasn't bad by myself, but with him there it would have been a joy."

"What does he do at the church?" Cliff tried to imagine this laughing girl's father.

How can she think it's funny? A cross-country bus trip to a midway strip show, based on a half-truth. Laughing girl, who she is, what she does, someone to know, know real well.

"He's the…" She held up her hand as she tried to catch her breath and said, "He's the pastor."

Cliff couldn't help but laugh with her, couldn't help himself when he heard the delighted tone of her voice. "Is this a joke? It must be a joke. He's not really a minister, is he?"

"He is." Katie understood Cliff's doubt. "And listen to this." She looked at him, those warm eyes. "He used to be a Catholic priest, now he's a Presbyterian and he loves bus rides, loves the strange characters on Greyhound, invites them to church. He's going to meet me when we get to New York. I want him to meet Pagan, the others."

Cliff reached for his notebook, then stopped. Katie reached for his hand, her eyes still wet with laughter. "It's a little easier to understand if you know he's originally from Ireland and had—as he says—a wee bit of a drinking problem. That's why he's a Presbyterian. He also wanted to marry my mother. You might have guessed he was Irish, with the name Flanagan. The Irish have a different way of living—at least my dad does."

"The church puts up with him?"

"They love him in California. He's the reason I can put up with this until I get to New York."

"Oh, that explains everything. Now I understand why being lied to and riding a terrible bus cross-country is funny—your former-celibate-priest-minister-drunk-father is Irish. It all makes perfect sense…in California, sure not in Indiana."

They stared at each other, a long look and Cliff lifted her chin and kissed her. Katie takes his hand in both of hers and says, "I don't know what we're starting. You're the first nice guy I've met in a while."

She tilts her head back, closes her eyes and invites Cliff to kiss her again, returning the embrace with soft breathing. Then she pulled back and stayed in his arms as her hands rubbed the back of his head, the warmth of her arms, his breath through her hair suspended them from time.

Cliff didn't know what to say. He wanted to agree with her, but no words came out of his mouth. They walked arm-in-arm while Cliff goes over her story. "Let's go back to the lying agent."

What I really want is to tell her I agree, we're starting something.

"He didn't really lie. He promised I'd be dancing in big fairs—Boston, Philadelphia, New York. He made it sound like we'd be with big names like Count Basie, the Beach Boys, Supremes. He gave me a one-way ticket and said I'd get the return at the end of the season. I didn't tell him I didn't want the return; I'm leaving when we get to New York."

"What does your minister father think about New York?"

"You ask a lot of questions."

"I am a reporter. Tell me about dancing. How did you start?"

"I've always been able to dance. My mother dances, taught me. She says I'm blessed with a real talent. Just mother talk."

"Don't you think you are?"

"Maybe. I don't know. I just love it and always will."

"You know how the audience watches you, don't you? You're the only thing they see, and the only thing I could see. So good you own them, blinding them to anything else."

"Yes, but not just me. Especially not when Pagan's on stage."

"She's unfair competition. She's mostly naked." Cliff took her hand. "You're better, much better. I don't know much about dancing, but I know you're good, great. I'm going to watch you every day, twice a day, bring my friends, put your picture in the paper, buy you dinner because you're so good…and beautiful."

"When?"

"Tomorrow night?"

"Yes."

Cliff scratched a few words and Katie tried to see what he wrote, but he folded the notebook shut.

"What did you write? Let me see."

"Scribbles, you'll have to wait till the story's finished."

"It's about me; let me see the scribbles."

"Too dark out here, why don't I show you in your room?"

Turning the corner, they could see the train at the end of the street. Most of the rooms were dark, but the painted cars glowed against the black buildings.

Katie gripped the bar and put her foot on the first step, then stopped and leaned back and kissed Cliff. "Before you ask again, I'm not letting you into my room. Not tonight. My dad's in there, waiting."

Cliff dropped his arms to his sides and hung his head. "Wouldn't expect you to, not a girl who dances in church. You don't want to see my scribbling? It's the start of the great American novel."

"Normal, you're normal. But I will teach you to dance. Tomorrow night."

"Is that all we're going to do?"

Katie climbed the steps and said over her shoulder, "Seven shows a day. I need to save my energy. If you want sex, talk to one of the other girls."

"They don't interest me, all that tough meat. Franklin's probably taking care of them."

"I'll see you tomorrow. Sleep well." She put her hands together and raised them to her lips, and whispered, "Goodnight, thank you for the tour. Thank you for the compliments, the kiss."

Cliff watched her go through the door.

I have more questions. We have more to talk about, a lot more.

CHAPTER 11

The Man with Three Eyes
Is Out of the Question?

John Stoneman sat at his desk, scrubbing blue lines through the words and sentences that made the white paper look like a child's coloring book. He glanced through the window, then quickly returned to the task and when he finished, he slapped the paper down.

"Walker!"

Cliff turned toward the editor. "Yes, sir?"

"Take out this crap about the elephant trainer, Hemingway, the strippers. This reads like you were drunk when you wrote it. Were you?"

"A little. We had a few drinks with some of the carnival people on the train last night." Cliff was relieved when the editor cut him off.

"Go back out there and interview kids with prize pigs, sheep, the biggest bull. Whose apple pie is going to win this year? How do you know this elephant trainer's in the Circus Hall of Fame? He tell you? Bring me something about hay bailers and combines, the newest thing in milking machines. They advertise all year. That carnival is here one week. And remember…how much money do they take out of town? It's all I hear at the Elks Club. Save this for your great American novel, save it for toilet paper—has a better chance of being used."

"Then I guess the man with three eyes is out of the question? Franklin got some good shots of him." Cliff's stomach twitched as he recalled the ruined face.

"News. It's a newspaper, Cliff. Not a literary magazine. And I'm not turning it into a tabloid. Get me the local merchants. Imagine you're the Chekhov of Indiana." Stoneman took a deep breath. "It is good writing; good words. I wish we could run it. I like it. But we don't have the space. Send it to *The New Yorker.*"

"Franklin's developing the film from last night, and he's got pictures I know we can't print. Hemingway wrote for a newspaper."

"Why don't you use that weird imagination to make the street budget interesting? You can do these wild stories after I'm in Arizona, far, far, away."

At least he's aiming high...Hemingway, Stoneman thought.

"We'll send you a free subscription. Thanks for the compliments."

"I still want to know about the strippers' after-hours business."

"I don't think it's what you think. They were pretty tired last night."

If they're hookers, they hide it well. First time he said it was good writing.

John Stoneman reread Cliff's blue streaked copy, folded it and added it to a file in his desk drawer. He remembered his dream to become a creative writer. Maybe Cliff shouldn't accept the editor's position because it could destroy his spirit.

Stoneman told himself that just because it had happened to him, it didn't mean Cliff Walker's dream would die. Cliff didn't have to accept the lie that facts were more important than fiction.

He looked through his window at downtown Morganport. His ghostly reflection appeared superimposed over the brick buildings constructed in the 1800s, old crumbling buildings.

I'm an old, crumbling man and it's time to pass it on and hope they don't fall down on Cliff Walker—hope he doesn't fall off the cliff.

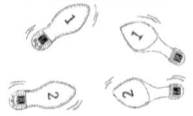

The waitress asked Cliff if he wanted his usual, and stopped writing when she heard Steve's rough voice as he asked for the same.

She aimed her cold eyes at Steve and snapped, "No sugar?"

"No sugar, no sugar in the coffee. Someone sweet's looking at me." She flipped her order pad closed.

Cliff's entrance with Steve Lanning drew surprised stares from the morning regulars. They stopped talking to be sure of who it was, the guy from the carnival, the front page, missing ear, mustache and tough face, twisted wrinkles around his nose and lips. Cliff was aware of the force of Steve's personality.

He asked the waitress, "You know who he is, don't you? Picture in the paper with the elephants?"

Sally replied that she knew who he was. "I saw the paper."

Their plates arrived and Cliff asked Steve if they served breakfast in the Pie Car. "They do. I don't eat there, bad for my guts."

Cliff took his time spreading butter on his toast.

What does he want? Walked from the train, guessing he could find me. More publicity? He hasn't asked.

Cliff ate his bacon and eggs as he waited for Steve. He knew it was a contest, but he wasn't sure if he could outwait the animal trainer.

Steve put down his fork and lit a cigarette. "Farmer asked me to look at one of his animals, thinks I might want it for the show. I told him I'd look and buy some hay. Thought you might want to go with me…see what he's got."

When she finished picking up their plates, Sally asked, "What happened to your ear?"

"Lion bit it off. I switched to elephants."

A little smile played at the corners of her mouth as she nodded her head. Her eyes shifted to Cliff, then back to Steve's face.

He returned her smile. "What kind of flowers do you like?"

"Don't do that. But I'd like to hear more about your elephants."

When she was gone, Steve asked Cliff if she was married. "Nice lookin' broad. I bet she gets it on in the back room, something in her voice."

"I want to see what happens if you take her flowers…will you do it?"

"I might, sometimes it works. Worth a try."

Carolyn was standing on the sidewalk as she waited for the light, deep in thought, and unaware of Cliff and Steve as they left the diner, aimed in her direction. Then she heard Cliff's voice and flinched, startled to see the two men.

Cliff kissed her on the cheek. "Carolyn, this is Steve Lanning. Steve—meet Carolyn the librarian."

"I'm glad to meet you, Mr. Lanning. I hope you can visit the library while you're in town. Just ask for Carolyn the librarian for a personal tour." Her voice was soft and gracious with a pleasant frown aimed at Cliff when she repeated his phrase. She was aware of her nickname, because the children giggled when they said it, but they were reading more than usual, so she was happy being Carolyn the librarian; it was certainly better than "Carol the barrel," like she had been called as an overweight teen. "I can give you a temporary library card if you'd like to check out some books."

Steve removed his hat. "Thank you, not much time with the fair open. I would like the tour and the card. Never had a library card."

"Cliff tells me you like to read."

"I do, but don't get much out of big words. Hemingway ain't bad, the one about the old fisherman. I told Cliff here I met him once, think I did. We were both drunk. He's famous for writing and drinking."

"I hear you're famous for your elephant act."

"Maybe a little, more for being a famous drunk."

"I bet not."

"You would lose. Ask the old-timers, they'll tell you I was disgusting, drunk, slept with the pigs, animal and human, beg and steal money for vodka…you're a nice girl and I shouldn't be talking like this, but I am, and I don't blame you if you walk away."

Cliff reached for Carolyn's shoulder, but she moved away. "I'm all right. I've heard worse, read a lot worse."

They talked for a few minutes more until Carolyn excused herself, explaining she had a meeting at the school office.

Cliff said, "I'll call you later." Guilt stopped him from knowing what to do next. He sensed an attitude from Carolyn but it could just be his guilt, or it might have been Steve's candor talking about his sleeping with pigs and stealing money for vodka.

But underneath, Cliff thought about Katie Flannigan.

Cliff thought about her every minute. Her hand in his, her coaxing him to dance when he didn't dance, but he had danced with the support of her smiling energy, her pure joy in dancing for the sake of the dance. He was captivated by the girl's singular focus that carried her through the muck of the midway, determined to do what she had to do to make her goal and she did it gracefully.

CHAPTER 12

The Woman with the Alligator Skin Was His Wife

As the truck crossed the bridge over the Wabash River, raindrops smacked the windshield, then increased to a downpour, and Steve downshifted into second gear. On the other side of the bridge, they followed the river past quilted patches of plowed dirt and weathered farm buildings. Rain fed the sprouting seeds.

"That librarian any good? She ready to walk down the aisle?"

"She wants to. Is it that obvious?"

"She's falling in bed looking at you. Did I put it on too hard for her?"

"Why did you?"

"What I do. Put on a little show. Helps show business."

Cliff didn't want to talk about Carolyn. He tried not to compare her with Katie, library books, or flowing turns and sparkling eyes.

Carolyn has been a wonderful friend but she's a librarian. And Katie's a dream, a dancing spirit riding a train to New York, a force that has entered my life just when I'm about to let the force of being an editor, in charge of the daily chronicle of small-town life, set my course. This is a big fork in the road.

"I should follow my own advice and not let my dick make my decisions."

Steve said, "Librarians like it, too."

"I wasn't talking about her." Cliff was uncomfortable talking about himself. "I was surprised by Mastras. He wasn't what I expected. He told me he sent you to the VA hospital to dry out." Cliff wasn't sure he should ask, but it changed the subject.

Steve didn't hesitate. "He did. I'll say this, no other boss I ever worked for would 'a done it. Not twice."

"He looks like a stockbroker or a lawyer. Did you know his father?"

"No, died before I got here. The old-timers talked about him like he should 'a been president of the world. They didn't give the kid much of a chance, but he's done all right with the show, not like the old man, maybe better."

"Why did he bother with you?"

"My wife asked him to."

"Wife?" Cliff's question is abrupt. "You're married? Where is she?"

What kind of woman would be married to Steve Lanning? Have to be as rough as he is.

"She's running a pony ride over on the Royal Show this season. We got a trailer in Florida, winter quarters. We ain't married."

"So, you must have been a bad drunk."

"Bad as they got, so they tell me. Doc told me stop or die, wasn't no third choice. I finally got the message."

"Must have cost a lot of money."

"The VA's free. I paid him back for the airplane tickets."

"Didn't cost Mastras anything?"

"Nothing. My wife made the arrangements. He fronted the tickets. He did enough. He let me come back to work."

"Not a lot of elephant trainers knocking on his door?"

"That's right. He needed me. Sober. Does the library lady know where you were last night?"

"And tonight—part of my job. Pretty dancers don't show up in Morganport every day."

"She is a good-looking broad, won't stay on the show long."

"Have you seen her dance?"

"No, but I hear—ain't no talk unless it's real good or terrible. Do you know where this farm is at?" Steve asked, holding the crude map so Cliff could see it.

"My dad was born out here," Cliff said. "I don't need the map. Young America, little crossroad town. Nothing there anymore, wasn't much there when there was something there. My great-great-grandfather was one of the early settlers. My aunt still lives on the old homestead, been in our family since the Civil War."

The road followed the section lines of the farms, turning at right angles where the land had been divided after the Indians were paid to move away. They followed the old wagon track and Cliff told Steve where to turn.

Then he asked, "Did this farmer just find you and ask you to come out here? Doesn't sound right."

"He come around last year, sold me hay."

"You remembered him?"

"Him and his wife, hard to forget some people."

"Why?" Cliff hesitated. "Who, what, where, when and why? What I get paid for. Why were they hard to forget?"

"You can be a smart-ass, can't you?"

"You invited me. What about them?"

"What, what, what. Okay, how about this: Don't look like the rest of the marks, that's what. Look like they don't never leave the farm, work boots, patched pants, faded dress, real plain, never see 'em riding the merry-go-round. They look at the elephants, the llama, the hippo—it's free and asks me if I need any hay and asks me to come to the farm, got something they want to show me. There's your what, your where, when, and why."

"Can I quote you?" Cliff paused. "Pretty weak on the why. Why do they want to sell you hay?"

Why do they leave the farm to see the fair? Why do they want to be farmers? Why do they stay with each other? Why do they want to live ten miles from town in an old house that sways in the wind and lets snow blow through the cracks? Why?

When they saw *Ryerson* on the mailbox, they waited while a man opened the gate, and then they followed the narrow lane through thick bushes and stopped at the farmhouse where a woman opened the door and looked at the car and stared at the clothes hanging in the rain, her arms folded. The farmer stood in the doorway of the barn, waving them forward. When Steve pulled the truck near, he directed them inside. The smell of wet soil, manure, and milk cows filled the dark barn.

"No cutting hay today, but thank God for the rain." Ryerson talked directly to Steve. "Give the corn an extra six inches by August; should have a good crop this year. Rain ain't good for you, is it? Don't guess the fair does much business in the rain. How much hay do you want?"

Steve said, "If your price ain't too high, I'll fill the truck."

Cliff guessed the two men were about the same age and they shared the care and feeding of animals. As he listened to Steve talk, the farmer looked at Cliff, then turned away. "If you take this calf I got, I can cut the price on the hay."

Calf? Cliff wanted to see it.

Steve sensed Ryerson's concern about Cliff. "Cliff's the newspaper reporter, did the story about the elephants."

Ryerson shook Cliff's hand. "I don't read the paper much; the missus does most of our reading. She told me about the cars backed up, said it was a good reason to stay away from town. What brings you here?" His voice was too loud.

Cliff answered, "My dad's Howard Walker, you might know him, used to live a little south of here, Poplar Grove. I'm just riding with Steve today, show him the way."

Ryerson nodded his head. "Don't know your dad too good, but I know who he is. Know his sister a little."

Cliff thought about his aunt living in the tiny house built by his great-grandfather.

At least Dad got away. Not far—twelve miles, but seemed like a thousand when he did it. Morganport's not New York, but I could have been one of these farm kids, no library, no movie theaters, no restaurants, tiny school, baling hay, might not have gone to college, no Navy ship sailing the Suez Canal…twelve miles in the country is a long haul, used to take three hours with a horse and wagon.

Ryerson called to the man who opened the gate. "Bob, we need to load some hay." The hired man slipped his thick fingers under the twine and lifted the bales of hay like he was lifting pillows. His hands and fingers were thick with calluses and Cliff compared them with Steve's hands, years of working outside, handling animals.

Where do hired hands come from? How long has he worked on the farm, does he sleep in the barn like Milt and Jack in the boxcar? Does he fool around with the farmer's daughter?

When the bed of the truck was full, Steve told them it was enough and handed Ryerson a stack of passes.

The farmer looked at the tickets and counted them and handed two of the books to Bob. "Appears to be four tickets in each one. Eight should be enough, don't you think?"

Bob kept his eyes on the floor, holding the passes in his hand before he pushed them into his pocket. "Be more than enough if I go, expect I will with these. Ain't seen an elephant in a long time. Thank you." Bob turned and walked through the rain without looking back.

It was quiet in the barn as wind and mist blew through the open door. The farmer said, "Let's look at the calf." He spoke to Steve. "You know me and the missus like your animals, elephants—and them llamas, pretty animals."

Ryerson hesitated and stared at the rain cutting furrows in the soft ground. "Years past we went to that freak show. That fellow with the three eyes is a pitiful thing, ain't he? The missus was real bothered by him, his face. She worries he has to live like that. Wants to know how he gets along."

"He's okay. Bill gets along all right, better than some. Sets up the tents, makes his own money. Got a wife. They ain't in the show no more, boss don't want freaks, too many complaints."

The farmer interrupted. "He said that, when he was telling his story. Said the woman with the alligator skin was his wife."

"They been married a long time." Steve didn't say anymore and the farmer stared through the mist toward the house while he rubbed his face with a blue handkerchief and felt his skin as he made sure it wasn't deformed.

The farmer's voice was a whimper. "It's terrible someone has to look like that." He cleared his throat and offered chewing tobacco. They declined and watched while he tore off a handful of brown leaves and pushed them into his mouth and chewed for a short time, while he decided what to do next.

"Calf come early, only has three legs, thought you might be able to use it."

"I don't need nothing else to feed, but let's take a look." He looked at Cliff and shrugged his shoulders.

They followed Ryerson to the back of the barn and looked at the calf, alone in the pen as it hopped with an interrupted gait as it shifted its weight over the missing leg.

Cliff didn't think it would be much of an attraction.

Why would anyone want to look at an animal with a missing leg or watch a man shove a straight pin through his cheek?

"Do you think you can use it, Mr. Lanning?" the farmer asked.

"If it was next year, I might be interested. I'm changing to a freak animal show. Might fit then, not now."

"Why don't you take it, so you have it ready."

Steve shook his head. "I'll be honest with you. I can't afford it. I don't know how much you want, but any's too much. Got to feed it, move it, and I don't have room for what I got now. Like to get rid of some. How much did you think you wanted for it?"

Cliff listened to them, back and forth, as they negotiated a price for a calf with three legs, like buying a used car without a motor.

"It ain't like I can make anything with it right now; it's just going to cost me."

"Well, I usually get them up to three hundred pounds and take them to the auction when the price is good. Don't expect I'd get much with that leg gone, he won't gain. Might get fifty dollars."

"You'd have more than that in feed."

"Feed 'em grass. Don't cost much."

"Like I said. If it was next year, I might be able to do something. Not now."

Ryerson sat down on a bale of hay and motioned for Steve to sit across from him.

Cliff wanted to take notes, but knew it might ruin the deal. He watched the two men; Steve just sat and smoked his cigarette, while Ryerson chewed his tobacco and spat every now and then.

Cliff understood it was Steve's ability to stare and not blink, no emotion, which made the farmer nervous.

The calf grew bolder, moving closer to the side of the pen, interested in its future.

Cliff felt the tension. He listened as he thought it was time to wrap it up and get out of here into the fresh air. *Split the difference, do something. Twenty-five dollars for an animal doesn't sound like much even if it was missing a leg.*

"All right, here's what I can do," Steve offered. "You keep it and when I get back next season, I'll give you twenty-five dollars. That's the best I can do."

Ryerson stood up, spat his chew in the dirt and locked his eyes on Steve. He stared hard while Steve avoided him, looking at the calf.

"Give me more passes and you can have it." Cliff was surprised at the farmer's decision. "I don't want it, so you just take it—now. You're damned hard to deal with."

At least Ryerson got the chance to swear at Steve; the passes were worth something.

Cliff would remember: An offer, a counter, a standoff, agreement, done deal, done and done. Spit, shake hands—done.

How about some swampland in Florida? A used car with sawdust in the transmission?

After they loaded the calf in the truck, they stood on the back porch. Mrs. Ryerson came out of the kitchen, carrying a pitcher of iced tea and three plastic glasses, and smiled at Steve while she poured. The woman was nervous, wiping her hands on her apron. The plastic glasses had matching patterns of yellow daisies, bright against the dark liquid.

"Good the rain stopped." She motioned to the clothes hanging on the line. "We like the fair, the elephants, the pretty quilts," she said. "That poor man with three eyes just breaks my heart." She refilled their glasses and stood quietly, holding the pitcher.

"Mr. Lanning says he does fine, not in the sideshow no more." Ryerson spoke directly to his wife. "He and the alligator lady been married a long time, take care of each other."

"It's nice they found each other. Do they have any children?" Mrs. Ryerson moved her eyes away from her husband, looking at Steve when she asked the question. Cliff was surprised by her intensity.

"No, they don't."

"Oh, my." The woman put her hand to her mouth, then brushed her fingers over her hair. A small light appeared in her eyes like she has surfaced from underwater, welcoming the fresh air, a doe kicking away snow to find clumps of green.

They finished their drinks and waved to the couple as they drove away from the house. The wet clothes would dry quickly in the bright sun.

Cliff thought Mrs. Ryerson didn't wash as often as most country women; either that or there were more people living on the farm than they saw that afternoon. "Maybe she does Bob's clothes. There's enough wash hanging on the line to dress two families."

A mile away, Steve said, "Dumb-assed farmer, I'd paid fifty if he held out longer." He hit the steering wheel with the palm of his hand. His rough voice soared over the rattle of the truck. "Farms like that are strange places."

"Strange? Compared to the midway?" Cliff asked. "If you wanted strange, you should meet my aunt."

"Nothin' much different about the calf, three legs ain't nothing. They're strange people. Don't get out enough. Animals born like that all the time."

"What?" Cliff didn't understand what Steve said. "What are you talking about?"

"You heard him, wanting to know about Bill. Strange people attract strange people."

"I think you smelled too much manure; it's making you hallucinate."

"I have smelled a lot of shit, grew up on a farm, ran away when I was fifteen, been smelling shit ever since. Don't make me strange."

"Why?"

"Oh shit, you and your why. Don't you get tired of it?"

"No."

"You can't do nothin' if you find out why, why ask?"

"The only thing that matters to me. Facts are too easy, way too easy."

His Life's in the Trunk and He Gave It Away for One Bottle of Vodka

Franklin squinted and blinked when he came out of the darkroom. Cliff asked for his help. "Got to carry Milt's trunk; are you finished in there? We both have to do this or the thing will fall apart."

"How'd you get it?"

"After the farm, we took the hay to the boxcar. Milt was there so I asked to look inside his trunk. Lanning told me how and it worked. The poor bastard would've given me anything for vodka, never seen anyone that bad, makes you think. His life's in the trunk and he gave it away for one bottle of vodka. Lanning told me to hold back the bottle until I had the trunk, not just a few pages, said Milt would want another bottle for every piece in there so that's what I did and it worked. I think we're onto good stuff; the price was right."

When they got to their apartment, they covered the kitchen table with fragile, yellowed paper. The smell of decaying pulp filled the room, rodeo posters and brittle glossy pictures and crumbling newspaper clippings. Franklin sorted through the washed-out photographs while Cliff read about Milt Hinkle, the last of the cowboys.

"This *True* magazine story's the best. It would be worth more, a lot more, if there were pictures...just one. The drawings aren't bad,

but if there was just one real photograph of him jumping out of the plane. According to this, he really did it…without a parachute, landed on the back of a bull, killed it, smashed both of his legs, and he's been crippled ever since. I'm going to hear this story before they leave, hear it in his words. But it won't make it true."

Cliff studied a photograph of Milt dressed in fancy Western clothes, thin and muscular…old trunk, old memories, old cripple ruined with vodka. The trunk would be worth a fortune to a history professor interested in cowboys and Indians and rodeos. Milt was the real thing. He was the man in the trunk, sleeping in a boxcar, shuffling on crutches, shaky drunk.

He placed each piece of paper, picture, and poster back in the trunk and closed the lid. *Buy a padlock, a good one.*

"Is it too early to have a beer?" Cliff asked. "Or champagne? This calls for a celebration. Talk about a break in our dry spell. And I've got a date tonight with the juiciest piece of fruit in the basket."

"And Pagan wants more pictures. She said I was a good shooter."

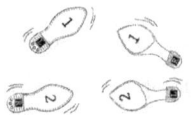

Through the gate and past the merry-go-round, Cliff saw Steve Lanning lift his hand and stopped.

"Ryersons were here today, and yesterday. Said they're checking on the calf. Something else is going on. Not about that calf. They asked me to take them to Bill."

Cliff remembered what Steve said when they drove away from the farm. Something strange, strange people on an isolated farm, twisted heads.

"What do you think they want?"

"I don't do that. Don't try to guess what people want. It don't change anything."

"Reporters can't do that. You're not a reporter."

"You want to know what happened?"

"They've already talked?"

"This afternoon, didn't want me there. Bill will tell me if I ask him. Do you want to know?"

"What's it going to cost me?"

"Now you sound like one of us. Ain't going to cost you nothing."

"I don't believe you, but yes. Yes, I want to know. You know I do."

"Find me in the morning. I know it won't be early, you romancing the Notch Broads tonight."

Cliff went into detail, telling Franklin what had happened at the Ryerson's farm, how the elephant trainer and the farmer toyed with each other over the price of the calf until they had driven away with a free, three-legged calf while the farmer was left with books of passes.

"Not like anyone I've ever met before," Cliff said. "We met a lot of different people riding around on ships, but he's not like any of them, not like anyone in Morganport. His face doesn't tell anything, no smiles, no frowns, nothing, a mask with a shrug of judgment, a little interest, a small smile at best. I watched him talk with that farmer. It was a one-sided conversation. The farmer made sounds, Steve heard them, but in the end, they were a waste of the farmer's time. He was beaten long before he knew it."

When the girls finished the last show, they hugged Franklin and Cliff and thanked them for the photographs and Pagan offered to buy drinks in the Pie Car.

Katie walked several steps behind and made sure the other dancers heard her ask Cliff, "I've written some poems. Would you read them, now? I don't feel up to the Pie Car tonight."

Pagan reached for Franklin. "You come with me." Then she told Honey and Holly to go ahead. "This tall photographer is going to take some pictures. You two ain't included." Pagan's order wasn't new to the girls. They'd been there before.

Cliff waited outside while Katie went to her room to get her poetry and change her clothes. When she returned, she was empty-handed. Cliff complimented her on her blouse and asked, "Where's your poetry?"

"I don't have any. I said that to get away from them and you're a writer, so it seemed to make sense."

"Do you like poetry? If you do, I'm in trouble. I don't understand it."

"Okay, we're even."

"Do you want to dance?"

"Always."

"No place open this time of night. Are you hungry?"

"If I can't dance, I'm hungry."

Cliff knew the Rendezvous was still open, but he didn't want to take her there. Carolyn would know before morning. No place safe. Not in Morganport, no place to go.

I can't tell her I'm afraid of being seen with her.

"I have an idea. The only place open is crummy and usually full of drunks. Let's get some hamburgers and drive to lover's lane—and eat in the car."

"Where? Did you say lovers?"

"Did I? I meant losers, no I meant livers, laughers, lifers—lovers, yes, I said lovers. Yes I did, but...but the reason is because no one will bother us there. Everyone knows why the cars are parked there and no one is interrupted."

"Interrupted from what?"

"Watching the river, eating hamburgers, reading your poetry —what else? What else would anyone do on lover's lane? We *can* dance there."

Cliff drove to Riverside Park and stopped, while keeping a distance from the other cars. The headlights threw wavy lines over the water streaming slowly past the high banks, moving to join other rivers and finally to the ocean. Clouds drifted past the moon while WGN Chicago played slow songs for lovers.

Katie turned the knob as she tried to find better music. "Dead people dance to that music."

"Try CKLW Detroit. Motown music."

"What number is it?"

Cliff put his hand on top of hers and turned the dial back and forth, back and forth. He couldn't find the station. He rubbed her arm when the music returned to the love songs.

"Maybe you didn't try hard enough." Katie leaned against his chest with her head turned away and continued to search for the dance music. He turned her face toward his and kissed her and she stopped tuning the radio and lifted her hand to rub his neck as they listened to violins playing "Midnight Music for Lovers."

She lifted her lips from his mouth. "Why are we kissing instead of dancing?"

"Everyone should do what they're good at."

Their embrace ended and Katie jumped out of the car. "Now it's my turn. Please dance with me." A repeating drum, guitar chords rolled out of the radio across the parking lot.

Cliff hesitated, embarrassed by his perceived clumsy feet. "I've got a problem here. Give me a minute."

Katie skipped and spun through the twin beams of light. Her flying hair, smiling mouth and clapping hands offered a free performance that held the attention of the couples parked in the other cars and when one driver tapped his horn in time to her steps, the other cars joined in. Cliff added to the show by grabbing her hands, willing his feet to move with her.

Cliff was amazed by his smooth steps, and amazed at her energy after eight shows.

Airwaves seemed to tremble as Chuck Berry sang "Maybelline." The other cars tuned their radios to the same station, volumes as high as they could go, and three couples joined the dance party, singing along with the guitar and drums.

When the song ended, Katie fell against Cliff. "Enough for me. Let's just watch." As Cliff opened the door for her the other couples—the men—say, "No, you can't stop, please don't."

Katie shook her head. "Have to, you keep going—please?" But they couldn't keep going without her inspiration, and in a few minutes, all of the dancers were back in their cars listening to love songs.

"How many other girls have you brought here?" Katie asked.

"You're the first…dancer." *Not Carolyn, don't have to park with her,* Cliff thought. "When we were kids, Franklin and I built a raft, launched it here and headed for New Orleans. We were going to float down the Wabash to the Ohio to the Mississippi—maybe all the way to Mexico. It fell apart about ten miles down the river and Franklin's still trying to float away. That raft's probably the reason we both joined the Navy."

Cliff described ice skating in the winter and how the raft and the necking made the river important to him. "It's what brought the Indians here, like the carnival train brought you. I wish I could write like you dance."

"Don't try so hard. Just let it happen."

"My boss won't let it happen, not with his blue pencil."

"Do what I do, dance for yourself."

"He did tell me I had a spark, but I need to work harder."

Katie pulled him toward her. "Sparks start fires."

CHAPTER 14

Like Passing a Car Wreck Trying to Ignore Broken Bodies

"It ain't all cotton candy, merry-go-rounds and money," Steve said. "What they told Bill, you need to hear. Could put you in the big time."

Horrible, a horrible story, impossible, but it wasn't.

Cliff didn't want to listen but he had to, like passing a car wreck trying to ignore broken bodies. Steve's rough words held him paralyzed. His stomach pulsed. He wanted to run. Steve's ragged words, his blank expression terrified Cliff like the day would never end, always dark and dangerous. He listened, knowing he was hearing facts that would change his life, horrible facts, why, why? He wants to scream *WHY?*

"They been hiding a freak kid on that farm. They want to let her go on the road with Bill and Ruth."

Cliff's eyes watered and he wished Steve wasn't so blunt. He had to know a better description than "freak kid."

"This is terrible, I don't want to believe it. What does she look like?"

"Hell if I know. They ain't carrying her picture in their wallets. Bill said her face is like his. This ain't 1925, Mississippi. Forty years ago, no one cared if a dirt farmer got rid of a kid born bad, just give it to a circus. All kinds of weird shit on them farms, I grew up on one, happens all the time. I knew there was something wrong when we was out there, more than a calf missing a leg."

Cliff squeezed his pencil, but couldn't make it move. That would make it real. The thoughts forced their way to the surface where he could see Bill, a little boy, tragically deformed, crying as he leaves his family's farm, never been away, hidden by stupid parents. Cliff was surprised when his pencil started to move, powered by something other than his hand.

All the circus man saw in 1925 was a valuable object, a freak boy with a grotesque face that would put money in his pocket.

Steve was aware of Cliff's distress, but kept talking. "I can help you out. Here's the deal…if you want the story, I'll tell Bill to let the kid come with us, it's her call, she's sixteen. You can sell that to *Life* magazine. If that ain't life, nothin' is. Bill will listen to me. It won't hurt the kid none, probably be the best thing for her, and you'll have a hell of a story. Put you in the big time…make you rich."

Cliff stopped his pencil. Lanning could control this terrible situation. *They have to be stopped, it can't happen. Steve can control it, one way or the other, doing me a favor. I don't want that favor, whether she stays on the farm or joins the carnival. I don't want it.*

Cliff struggled to talk. "No. It's not right. I didn't listen when you said there was something strange on that farm, too much wash on the line." Then Cliff remembered Mrs. Ryerson asking about the freaks and he knew Steve spoke the truth, as true as the fact the sun would go down and it would get dark.

"I knew something was going on when they kept checking on the calf. They been here every day. Marks don't come every day." Steve's words were lifeless, matter-of-fact.

Cliff wanted to cry—suddenly the fair wasn't a week of happy escape. It must have always been a week of torment for the Ryersons.

How long had they struggled with their decision? Have they waited for years? Waiting until she's old enough to leave home?

Life as usual on the farm, something born not right, it happened. Nothing to do about it but when the fair came, they had to decide.

Over the years, they had listened to Bill when they went to the sideshow. Heard him tell how his parents gave him away, how he'd had a good life, forty years with the carnival, better than what he would have had on the farm, money of his own.

Is that what they want for their daughter—a better life? Not a life where she can't walk in downtown Morganport or eat in a restaurant.

"Did Bill tell you they want her? Do they want to put her in a show?"

"No, they don't. He said they wouldn't do that, no more shows. They got money, got a house in Florida. Ruth always wanted to be a mother; she'll make a good one, nothing wrong inside their heads."

"When did you say it happened to Bill?"

"Nineteen-twenty-five. He don't forget."

Cliff wrote: *the carnies ignore Bill when he enters the Pie Car, they don't see his face. No control over their deformities, unjust, a terrible, terrible thing. They can't help the way they're born. None of us can.*

As he listened to Steve. he knew he was going to be involved— this was more than reporting facts. He was going to have to do more than be a recording secretary, an observer.

"Could be a big story for you."

"You're saying if you tell them to do it, they'll take the girl. I write it and sell it to the *New York Times* or *Life* magazine. Why would you do it, for some of the money?"

"No. I don't know why. Don't know how I got in the middle of this damned mess. Someone ought 'a get some good out of it. You want to be a writer."

"You're right, it could be big—Indiana farm couple gives deformed daughter to sideshow freaks, history repeats itself. That could go national."

"You want me to tell them to take her?"

"No." Cliff hesitated.

"You're blowing a sure thing."

"If I did write the story, say they do it anyway... If I did write it, I could make you the bad guy, you're part of it. How an ex-alcoholic elephant trainer with half an ear has the power to take a deformed child away from her parents and put her on a traveling carnival, living with the freaks. What if I wrote that?"

"Yeah, it could be told that way. But it ain't as good or true."

"Will Bill take your advice?"

"He will. But you need to talk to the farmer."

Cliff pleaded, "You talk to them, tell them not to do it." He didn't want to get involved. "I just report the facts. I'm not supposed to change them, against the rules." *I don't, can't, talk to the Ryersons about their daughter.*

"I ain't the reporter. It's your job." His rough words hurt Cliff's ears. How simple it seemed to Steve; no concern for the girl.

Cliff didn't know where the words came from. "Okay, I'll talk to them, but I don't want to. I don't want to, don't think I can." *This is where I cross the line.*

Turning the wheel, accelerating, following the two-lane road, not seeing the straight rows of corn, cows resting under shade trees, nothing calmed his fear.

What am I going to find?

He imagined a distorted face as it stared out of a window. Weak faith kept the car on the road, his foot locked on the gas pedal, his thoughts on the words, impossible words. Cliff felt helpless.

Will he push the typewriter keys?

The gate was closed.

Do they keep it closed to keep people out or keep someone in?

They didn't want unexpected visitors, especially reporters.

He waited, like the movies when the police sat in a squad car to catch a crook, boring business. Cliff knew he might wait a long time. Sometimes farmers didn't leave their fields for days. He could find a telephone and try to make an appointment, but he didn't think they would open the gate. And he was more afraid they would.

Probably didn't have a phone.

He turned the car around, steering away from the locked gate.

NO. No interviewing a man and his wife faced with a hideous choice. No questions about a deformed child.

He wanted to drive away from the problem, drive away from Morganport, drive to the edge of the universe, to the Grand Canyon, to the Atlantic Ocean—far, far away.

Five minutes down the road, Cliff stopped the car and turned around.

He heard Steve's voice: *if that ain't life, I don't know what is. Someone has to talk to them. Someone has to talk to them.*

It might have been ten minutes, maybe an hour, when he saw Mrs. Ryerson as she walked down the lane, approaching the car. Cliff started the motor so it looked like he had just arrived. He didn't want her to think he was stalking them.

He closed his notebook and said, "Mrs. Ryerson, I don't know if you remember me, I'm Cliff Walker with the newspaper."

"Yes, I remember." She frowned and Cliff knew his presence was going to change lives. "What are you here for?"

He was prepared for this question. "I'm doing a follow-up story on what people think of the fair and I knew you and your husband had visited several times to see your calf. Can I ask you and your husband a few questions?" *A weak answer, a lie.*

She hesitated. "I don't know if that's a good idea. I better ask him."

Cliff nodded his head and waited.

She turned back to the car. "You might as well drive to the house, save me a trip back."

Tires ground through the long driveway, thick shrubs, no sign of anyone in the house, windows covered, curtains drawn, wash hung on the line. A few days ago, he listened as Steve bargained for a load of hay and a crippled calf.

When she went inside the house, Cliff waited on the empty porch and looked over the fields of corn, the pasture where healthy cows chomped grass, their eyes unable to comprehend a distorted face, a safe place for a freak.

Silence surrounded him, like the sound of a wooden bell, empty and dead. It should have been a cold, rainy day instead of blue skies and warm sunshine.

Mrs. Ryerson opened the front door. "Wait a minute, he'll be here." She closed the door behind her.

The sound of footsteps grew louder as they descended the wooden stairs. The door banged open and Cliff stumbled backward, unprepared for the violent body.

"Walker, ain't it?" The farmer's face twitched.

"Yes, sir. Cliff Walker, Mr. Ryerson, how are you today?" He felt like an encyclopedia salesman. *How are you today? Have I got a deal for you…*

"What do you want?" Ryerson closed the door. He knew Cliff wasn't there to discuss the crops.

Hesitation no good, jump in. "I'd like to talk to you about your daughter."

Ryerson's jaw slid in and out; his hands ripped the air, his fingers opened and closed and opened, knuckles bent into a tight fist.

"Afraid of that, afraid that's what you was wanting." He twisted his jaw, chewing, grinding, his fingers clasped and unclasped. He spat over the edge of the porch.

At least he's not denying it. Afraid he'd deny it; say there isn't a daughter.

"You can handle animals born bad." Ryerson's face was desolate. "Sell an animal, give it away. Can't do that with Joan."

When he heard the name, Cliff felt his eyes fill. *Joan. No longer nameless. What will happen when he sees her?* Maybe spending time with Three-Eyed Bill had conditioned him. Joan...she shouldn't have a normal name.

Cliff wasn't sure of his voice. "I don't think letting her go with the carnival is the right thing." He wanted to be more forceful but the words had to be soft. The man was close to falling apart.

"You don't think, you..." Ryerson blinked and stuttered and pulled air through his nose, desperate. Eyes blazing, he screamed, "Goddamn it, Walker! She ain't yours to think about. You got no business thinking about her, anything about her. It's our problem, something we got to take care of. You don't know her. None, none of your business!"

Hard eyes, clenched lips. Cliff wanted to run, find protection from the fury. The shouting was a train wreck, metal ripping, and exploding, searing heat.

If Ryerson wanted to end the conversation he could have gone inside, slam the door, but he stood, searching with his hands, silent. Quiet followed his outburst.

Cliff didn't talk, the silence held them together, pulled them together after the fury. *Let it work, stay close, only thing to do, just be here, wait a minute and another, don't move, don't breathe, don't look.* Seconds passed with the men joined in wordless conversation, joined in the intensity of their shared knowledge, the empathetic, terrible fact of a deformed girl.

"How'd you find out?"

"Carnival people talk as much as town people."

"Hate that talk, people talk instead of minding their own damn business. It ain't none of their business, none of your business."

"It's my job, what I get paid to do."

"Then you got the worse damned job in the world, sticking your nose where it don't belong. You put this in the paper, it's likely to come back on you."

He's talking, listen, accept his words, quiet—invite more, connect.

"Ain't no law against letting a child of age visit friends. You say anything different and it'll come back on you, come back hard. You do your job, say how a man with three eyes and a woman with alligator skin was the first people, 'cept us, could look at our daughter without puking. Write about our choices—doctors and operations that won't never do no good, we can't afford that kinda stuff. She'll always look bad, no one wants to look at her. No one but her momma and me. We can keep her here on the farm until we die. Then what? We ain't got no money for her. Can't treat her like an animal—I know about treating animals. You think 'cause we're poor dirt farmers we don't understand. Poor, but we ain't *stupid*. Joan's ugly, not stupid. You write that and I ain't worried."

"I report the truth as best I can." Cliff knew his best would never be good enough.

Ryerson spat and opened the door and quickly stepped inside. Mrs. Ryerson took his place on the porch, her hand to her mouth, eyes red, spent. "Please listen to him. We don't know what to do." Her soft voice was a relief, a mother praying for her daughter, in despair about her future.

Cliff's heart pounded when he looked at the woman's face. "Are you going to send her with them?"

"It's not like that. Don't twist things up." Mrs. Ryerson rubbed her apron between her fingers. "Not sending, God help us, that sounds terrible. We're *letting* her go with them. Ruth's begging us and Joan wants to go. She knows they want her. No one but us ever wanted her before. Joan feels safe with someone that looks like her. She knows they look alike. We don't know what else to do. We think it's best. I pray on my knees it's the best."

"So you're going to let her go?"

"What would you do? Look at her, go on and look." The farmer was standing in the doorway, his arms wrapped around his daughter, protecting her, his face moved and jumped as he talked, wild.

Her face wasn't a face. A torn opening ran from her mouth to where her nose should have been, a wet red rip in her head, a ridged hood of bone bulged over one eye, squeezing the socket to a crumpled slit, skin folded. *A mask, let it be a mask*—but Cliff knew it wouldn't come off. She would go through life wearing this horrifying face.

Joan buried her face against her father. He kissed her hair.

"Hello, Joan, my name is Cliff." Her face blurred through his tears.

She looked at Cliff, her words muffled like Bill's. He heard her say, "I want to go. They're nice to me." Her slurred words were hard to understand.

"Do you, Joan? Do you want to go with Bill and Ruth?" She nodded her head.

Her father answered, "Maybe yes, maybe no. I got to think about it. You better go now." Ryerson pointed toward the road.

Now or never.

"Mr. Ryerson if this gets out—and it will—it won't look good for you. I think I understand, but most people won't. They'll think you've been hiding a deformed child and that you've sold her to a passing carnival and you won't be able to stay around here, they couldn't allow that to happen. Someone will help, somehow."

Empty words, promises, not worth saying.

Ryerson moved back. "If it gets out, if that happens, it will be on account of you feeding poison to the stupid bastards wantin' to read it." He stared at Cliff, then closed the door, an echo, dirt on a casket.

Away from the sad house, down the gravel lane, car windows open. Had he been breathing? Cliff hadn't expected what he'd heard. Before he talked to them, before he saw her, he'd thought in simpler terms…a dumb farm couple who were trying to get rid of a deformed daughter. But after seeing Joan, listening to her, to them, he understood the complications, no easy answers.

An awful fact of life. Not stupid—poor, desperately poor. No money for expensive surgery, private care. Small farm doesn't bring in that kind of cash.

What kind of world do we live in? Where do they find comfort?

What is clear is that she would be accepted on the carnival. Three-Eyed Bill and Ruth were accepted and they wanted to accept Joan.

Cliff was angry that it had to be this way, that his hometown was a place where they were not accepted. Cliff knew it was the way of small towns, but he had never been hurt by it before. Now he was involved and frustrated, and wondering why he'd complained about just being an observer.

There it is, Mr. Stoneman—just the facts. What are we going to do with them? Makes your questions about whores and fixed games and money seem unimportant.

CHAPTER 15

If You Ran Away with the Circus, Would We Put That in the Paper?

"You don't have all the facts, the important facts…yet." John Stoneman handed the pages back to Cliff. "When the train pulls out, you be there; and if she's on it, then we'll decide what to do."

"What will we do if she goes?" Cliff tried to keep his voice down. "I feel like we have to do something." He didn't want to admit he had thought about what it might do for his career. And the dim idea of following her didn't break the surface but lurked, a weak thought in a crowded, confused field.

Stoneman said, "If you ran away with the circus, would we put that in the paper? What do you think we should do? Come on, Cliff, act like the new editor."

Business as usual.

"If she's not important news, a sad story, maybe an editorial about Morganport rejecting ugly people. The better story is how the carnival would accept her; they accept all kinds of people, no questions. They are who they are."

"So, you think it is the right decision for her to go?"

"I do. I didn't at first, but it's better than hiding the rest of her life. She can't leave the farm. Can you imagine if she tried to walk downtown? That's the news, the sad news, the sad facts. She didn't ask for it. But she has to deal with it."

Cliff took a deep breath. "Okay, I want to run her picture on the front page, every day, until everyone gets used to seeing her and she can walk the streets without people turning away. One of our jobs, print information so shitty things can be corrected." He felt the color in his face and raised the volume, "Have you ever seen the man with three eyes?"

"I never went to the Freak Show." Stoneman looked for a pencil. "I was glad when I heard they stopped it. You'll have to be careful and not lose some of this fire. Facts have to be spelled out in the next edition and the next. Writing facts can steal their heat. If an ugly girl—or a pretty girl—leaves home, it doesn't have to be in the newspaper. If she's been kept on the farm all her life, it isn't an important fact, not in the *Pharos Tribune*. Save it for your book."

"He told me to save it for my book!" Cliff shouted over the noise of the presses. "There isn't going to be some other time…not in this town, not in this swamp of stupid people reading comic books."

Franklin asked, "Tell me again why you want me to stay here."

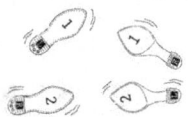

When the final curtain closed at the Broadway Review, Cliff slipped through the side flap and waited backstage for Katie to run to his arms. The other girls ignored their kiss, an embrace they'd been watching more and more often. Cliff has moved beyond Backstage Johnny to full-fledged boyfriend.

Pagan stomped past them, kicking her shoes into the air as she pulled the red patches from the ends of her breasts and rubbed the back of her neck. She shouted, "Where in the hell is a man waiting to kiss me on the neck? She finds one in Morganville...port...town, wherever we are and all I got is sore, stinking flat feet. I'm too old for this."

Katie leaned against Cliff. "I don't want this to end; is the party over?"

"You still have time to show me your room."

"I wish you could come with us."

He pulled her back against his chest and the kiss shook them. Cliff held her tight, protection from the facts moving closer and closer.

I don't want to face the reality of time, the reality that the train is going to leave town and Katie is going to be on the train. She's been here all week. I'm in love with her and I can't accept the fact that this train is going away, Katie's going away. Every day she's been here. The rides and the grab joints and the impossible-to-win games have been right here at the county fairgrounds and tomorrow they'll be gone. This big flat field will be left with empty cups and cotton candy cones and ticket stubs and empty popcorn boxes, scattered trash the only thing left to prove they were here. It seems impossible but it's true. Katie Flannigan will not be here waiting for me. Damn it, Mr. Stoneman. that's a fact. And Joan Ryerson might be with her. I have to check that fact.

"My dad's here. I can feel him right now." Katie pulled away. "I need him here, but he'll meet me in New York." Katie wiped her eyes. "I have to go. I'm getting on the train. I can't stay with you."

"I understand. It will be easier. Write me when you get to New York. We'll see each other again."

"Promise?"

"I promise. I can see you while they're loading the train."

Tears dripped from her lip. "No. That will make it harder. Write me long letters."

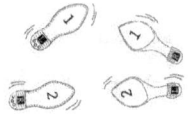

They watched as the train swallowed bits and pieces of the carnival, an iron anaconda gulping the merry-go-round, Ferris wheel, elephants, and generators. How would it all fit? A week ago it all came out, stayed one week, and now they were pushing it back in, to move to Indianapolis.

Cliff scribbled: *It's like making sausage, grinding up pieces of meat and stuffing into a long casing. Stuff and repeat. Stuff and repeat. Will Joan be part of the stuffing?*

When Steve Lanning and the elephants appeared, excitement ran through the crowd.

Cliff lifted his beer in a toast. "Captain Lanning and his animals, two-legged and four."

The elephant trainer, in control, prodded the elephants up the ramps while Milt hung over his crutches and Jack twitched and jerked. They followed the animals into the boxcar as they waited for the train to leave.

Steve asked, "You talked to that farmer?"

Cliff nodded. "I don't know what's going to happen. She might go."

Their conversation stopped when Jim Mastras arrived and marched past the flat cars, inspecting the operation. Franklin's camera flashed and pierced the dark as the tractors backed up the ramps, pushing the wagons into position. Satisfied with the work, Mastras approached the reporters.

"Good to meet both of you. Thanks for the advice and the story. Come to Indianapolis. We'll have dinner with the governor.

I hope you can join me." Without waiting for their answer, he got in his car and headed for the airport.

Cliff looked through the crowd as they watched the loading.

He thought he could see Carolyn, but she wasn't there. They hadn't seen each other since Cliff told her about Joan Ryerson. A late-night telephone conversation brought Carolyn to tears, distress, frustrated by her inability to fix Joan's problem. She pleaded with Cliff to find a way to fix it. "Please, Cliff, please," a desperate cry.

"I went to the farm. I thought her father might shoot me. There's nothing I can do. It's her decision."

Carolyn's voice caught. "Something has to be done. The editor of the newspaper can do something." Then she hadn't been able to talk anymore, but let out muffled cries until the connection went dead.

Several hours later, she called back and said she wanted to make a plan. "I can't find any information, no record of a daughter."

Cliff stayed silent as he thought about what Carolyn was doing. *Who was she talking to? What was she doing? Her questions might spread the news; alert the town.* He asked her, "I don't think it's right for us to pry into their affairs. Isn't this a private matter?"

Silence on the other end of the line and Cliff knew Carolyn was waiting for him to do something. She said they had a responsibility to help. But Stoneman had already told him what to do and he was still the editor. "John Stoneman told me it wasn't a story for the paper."

"I thought about one of the prominent ministers but there isn't anyone, no department in charge of something like this...but there should be. Please."

"We have to wait to see what happens, see if she goes."

Carolyn had said something Cliff had never heard from her, "Damn, DAMN it, Cliff! Wait? We can't wait. That's like the police waiting until after the crime is committed. Damn, that's just stupid."

And she had hung up the phone and when he called her back, she asked if he had figured out what to do and when he said "No," she told him it was their responsibility.

Cliff had looked at the telephone. He didn't know what to do. *If stopping Joan Ryerson from leaving home when she's old enough to go is my responsibility, I'd like to know who made it that way.* He knew it wasn't part of the editor's job.

Mist floated with the wind, removing the cinder dust from the train. The loading was almost finished.

Cliff sat in the car and watched while the last trailer was loaded. He checked his watch: one-fifteen. With nothing left to see, the locals drove away, and left the reporter and the photographer to witness the train slipping away to Indianapolis.

Franklin's camera winked through the dark as he photographed the engine being connected to the string of comic-book train cars, a toy under the Christmas tree waiting to be unwrapped.

Cliff stood up when he heard the sound of a motor and he squinted to see a truck with no lights as it turned the corner and rolled to a stop next to the sleeping coaches.

He recognized the truck. Joan Ryerson was catching the train— at the last minute. Ruth and Bill must have told them what time to get here. They thought no one would be left to see her take the biggest step of her life.

Cliff realized he was the only witness. The camera would ruin it. Sometimes a picture wasn't worth a thousand words. Flat photographs couldn't show what's going on, couldn't explain why two deformed people looked so happy as they stepped down from the train and wrapped a frightened girl in their arms, accepting her torn face because she was one of them. Pictures couldn't explain why a sixteen-year-old girl left an isolated farm, ready to see the world with the other damaged travelers.

Bill took the suitcase from Mr. Ryerson and they shook hands while Ruth hugged Mrs. Ryerson and offered her a handkerchief. Cliff heard her sobbing with the cloth pressed to her face; the two women held each other and cried together. Then they quickly separated and Cliff stared at the empty space between the train and the truck. The transfer happened fast with the soft rain smearing the colors of the dark watercolor, and terrible thoughts overloaded the departing truck.

Ryerson switched on the truck lights and the two small dots disappeared around the corner. Through the train window, Cliff briefly saw the new family in their small room, then they closed the blind.

As he looked at the dark frame, Cliff thought about them sorting things out, unpacking her suitcase, and he thought about Joan's parents while they drove back to the farm, the pain they must have felt and the relief they couldn't admit. They would never know if they did the right thing. Joan wasn't going on a trip that called for a happy send-off, no champagne, no pictures of her coming-out party.

Cliff's thoughts twisted in crooked waves—*it's finished, the train's ready to go.* Faces slowly appeared at windows, Katie weeping in the dining car, wiping her eyes.

Cliff Walker was staying behind, maybe alive, maybe dead, buried under council meetings, asphalt and potholes and sewer budgets and boring drivel and a relentless blue pencil.

He stared at Franklin. "She's here, Joan Ryerson's on the train, I saw her. And I want to know why." Cliff's face was hot and he pulled his lips into a tight smile, bouncing on his toes, sucking deep breaths. "No question about it. She's on the train; she's leaving."

Franklin pointed the camera toward Cliff.

The train jerked and started to move, bearings screeching in dry sockets, taking up the slack, couplings clank and slam, metal banged hard against metal. Cliff's eyes blurred as he watched the colors slide away, slipping, smearing yellow and red.

The bright hope moved, gathered speed. *I knew it would be hard but not this hard.* He paced, walked, turned, stopped and started, twisted his hands.

Cliff's eyes jumped, his body swung as his voice broke above the noise.

"I have to go!"

He locked his eyes on the train. One car passed, and with furious energy, Cliff lifted his feet, running, pumping his legs. He caught up to the dining car and saw Katie through the window.

Matching his speed with the train, Cliff lifted his arm.

Franklin followed with his camera.

Cliff shouted, "Get this for page one. Can't think about it anymore; I have to do it! Just want to ride the train, need more than facts."

So much more than facts, please tell me why.

The flash froze Cliff as he gripped the steel bar, eyes wide open, mouth clamped shut, like Milt Hinkle hanging from an airplane ready to jump. No one cheered for Cliff Walker, no wild bull to land on, maybe something wilder.

Cliff waved goodbye.

Franklin stopped running to watch as the train disappeared, glowing in the dark. Cliff swung up to the open platform.

All aboard…

Is this raft going to sink?

Part Two

CHAPTER 16

Hemingway Said
Don't Confuse Movement
with Progress

While the train gathered speed, running parallel to the river, he watched the lights of his hometown slip away. He pulled a small paperback book out of his jacket pocket.

Up that hill was the barbershop where everybody knew your name. If they could see me now, huddled on a crazy train—thrilled to be here. Hemingway said don't confuse movement with progress. I don't believe him. Franklin and I tried it with our raft. It sank a few miles from here—it was progress and fun. We laughed so hard I thought I'd drown.

A reckless move—stupid? Jump on a carnival train. For a few days, leave behind schedules and assignments and the blue pencil and ride into the mystery... I'm ready to open the door, consider the step, hesitate. Scared to turn the knob. Rush straight through the door and embrace Katie, go for it.

No one asked me to ride the train, not like Joan. Bill and Ruth invited her. Katie said she wished I could go with her. Mastras invited me to have dinner with the Governor in Indianapolis. The train is going too fast to jump off, but the door looks heavy. Will it open? Have to find out, find out why two girls are riding a painted train away from safety, into the unknown.

Not a well-planned journey with detailed schedules, reservations booked, tickets purchased, clothes packed, appointments in order. But it's a ride I have to take, have to open the door; planning would ruin this trip.

Joan Ryerson planned for this ride. What am I going to ask her, maybe nothing, none of my business? What will I ask her new parents when I put on my reporter's hat? What about her old parents?

He lifted his hand and gripped the door handle. He knew it would open. He thought about the old line—every trip started with a step, no shit—when one door closed… It was just another door, harder to open, worth the effort? Yes.

A rush of air made him tighten his grip. Jack stumbled through the door behind him.

The thin man's cloudy eyes struggled to focus on Cliff, and he swayed against the side of the passageway, bouncing on his legs, following the motion of the train. He held a paper cup in his right hand. "I seen you jump, what you doing out here? This ain't no place for editor to ride." Jack shifted his eyes to Cliff's fingers on the handle. "Open the damn door. I got to see the Captain 'bout a drink."

"Is he in there?"

"Sure he is, sure. I need a dollar."

Cliff held up the book he had pulled from his pocket. "This is for him."

Jack's face showed new interest. "He's there, with Milt. I take you. You give him the book, he gives me a drink for bringing you."

"That's worth a drink?"

"No. But I got nothin' else. You being here, editor…might help, might." Jack raised the paper cup. "You get a drink from him. Give it to me."

"I'm taking the first one." Cliff could already taste the numbing liquid.

"He'll give you a drink, *open* the door."

Cliff looked at the houses, the lights in the windows, blurring through the night.

"Wait a minute, look at those houses. How many of them want to run away with the carnival? What would happen if a magic hand shook them awake and told them they could jump on this train and beat all the games, win all the prizes?"

Jack looked at the houses, then at Cliff. He appeared befuddled; no one ever asked him questions. Steve told him what to do, but no one had sought his advice for a long time, he was not a source of reliable information.

He hesitated, gathering his thoughts and then his eyes cleared and he swallowed. "They'd jump like scalded cats, leave crappy jobs, they hate 'em, big bills, fix the fence, flat tires, punch the clock, same shit, same days. Them doors would fly open, wide, wide open, men, women, in pajamas, naked, hair wild, leap on this train and never look back, ride, ride—ride to the bright lights, win, pitch till you win, never look back."

Cliff wished he had a tape recorder. He jerked the door open and walked to Katie's booth, aware of the stares. Jack followed in a daze, staring at Steve Lanning and Milt sitting in a booth at the far end of the dining car.

A ride foreman named Smitty waved and yelled, "We got a new First of May with us. Son, you best stay with the girl, stay away from Jack, real far away."

The other diners looked up from their plates to see who it was. Some of them smiled and applauded; others stared at Cliff for a second, then returned to their food.

Cliff stood next to Katie and reached for her hand.

"What are you doing?" She grabbed both of his hands and pulled him into the seat and slid under his arm.

"If Milt Hinkle could jump out of an airplane…I can jump out of Morganport."

"What are *you* doing?" Katie's eyes were blurry with tears.

"You look like a dancer I know, real glad to know. Did you know this train was moving? Did you know Joan Ryerson is a passenger on this train?"

"What are you doing? I didn't think I'd see you this soon. Who's Joan? Oh, my God…you're really on the train." She pushed closer to him.

"I have a ticket, are you the conductor?"

"Tell me what you're doing here."

"You just asked me that."

"And?"

"And I want to ride the train, and I want to watch you dance, I need more lessons, and I want to do something besides record the minutes of boring meetings. I want to write about dancing works, not public works…all aboard. Never done anything like this before. I jumped on a carnival train! I'm not just watching—I'm here, with you."

"What are you going to wear?"

Cliff pointed with his pencil. "You can dance and you're practical. I'm only staying a few days. I'll borrow some clothes, maybe a clown suit."

"How long have you been planning this?" Her voice filled with affection. "I'm so glad you're here." She wanted to ask but didn't— *what about the librarian? Does she know about this?*

"I didn't decide until the train started moving. A mysterious force pulled me. No control over it, no stopping, too strong to fight. A mystical draw to dancers, bozos, snakes, crippled cowboys, and elephants. The air was too thick in Morganport, too close, thick fog, dense. I think I've got an allergic reaction to newsprint, couldn't stand the thought of not seeing you. I brought new notebooks, plan to fill the pages."

"Use that mouth for something." She held his face in her hands and pulled him into a long kiss that was applauded by Pagan and the other girls. They separated, embarrassed by the attention.

The waiter placed two glasses of dark liquid in front of them. "Compliments of Captain Lanning."

Looking up, Cliff raised his glass to Steve. The elephant trainer nodded his head and Milt lifted a bottle of vodka to his mouth.

Cliff tasted his drink, then offered a toast to Katie, "To the dancer." She sipped, then frowned when Cliff stood up. "Excuse me, I've got to give this to Steve, back in a minute."

Holding the book, he walked the length of the car and asked Steve, "Did Jack get his drink? He told me he had a plan. I get a drink from you and give it to him."

"Always a plan. I've heard 'em all. I sent him on a job. Told him to walk through the next four cars and there ain't but three. Maybe he'll fall off."

Cliff slid the book to Steve. "Your new friend at the library asked me to give this to you." She gave you a card, give you anything else?"

"What is it?" Steve squinted at the book. "Ain't got my glasses, read it to me." She didn't give me nothing you need to know about."

"Steinbeck's *Of Mice and Men*. Good book, reminded me of you and Milt. Did you think I'd be on the train?"

"I'm still workin' on that old fisherman. Milt said you'd be here."

Milt agreed. "I did. You ain't supposed to be dying in that town. You got to write a book about my trunk."

Steve reached for the new book. "I didn't know, but I thought you might. That one you're sitting with would make me run away, beautiful girl."

Cliff glanced back at Katie and nodded in agreement. "Carolyn said to tell you she'd write. She wants to help you with your reading."

Steve opened the book. "I got to get new cheaters. How far you going?"

"Indianapolis, couple of days. I want to write about how you helped a young girl escape the farm."

Steve said, "You might make a million dollars; someone should make something out of it."

Milt raised his head and swallowed vodka. "Trunk's yours, talk... anytime, anyyyyytime, any. You all right, kid...you jumped, not hurt—not yet. I talk, you write, make us both money. Tell you how I jumped, how we was throwed out of Mexico—he stole the pesos."

Surprised by Milt's words, Cliff waited, then he said to Steve, "I saw her, she's on the train, the girl. What did you tell Bill and Ruth?"

"Told them the press wouldn't say nothing, it ain't nobody's business. I saw her, too; they looked all right."

Cliff thought, *if it's not a newspaper story, what good are they, something to wrap garbage in? Maybe the New York Times, but not the Morganport paper. Even if I'm the editor, I couldn't print anything about what Joan was doing, nothing different than other sixteen-year-old kids leaving home.*

Cliff looked back at Katie. "Thanks for the drink, pretty girl's calling." He turned. "What's a First of May?"

"First time running away, we get some 'bout every stop."

When the food was finished, the other diners went to bed.

Cliff didn't want to sleep unless it was with Katie. "No sleep tonight, the show must go on, no business like show business. Can we continue my dance lessons?"

"Not now, I'm too tired." Katie closed her eyes.

"Not going to sleep, going to keep my eyes open, see the elephants, see Katie dance...." He dropped his head on her shoulder.

Katie asked, "Part of being a reporter, I mean, a writer?"

"I'm going for a short ride on a long, insane train."

He couldn't tell her what he was thinking. There were two dogs fighting inside, one called editor and one called something he couldn't name—maybe more—but he knew that the dog he fed the most would win. "A few days will be good experience for a new editor, feed that dog for a while."

Katie asked Cliff to let her out of the booth. "Go ahead, feed your dog. I'm going to bed."

Cliff said, "I don't have a bed."

She squeezed his hand. "You can sleep in the room next to mine."

"I jumped on the train to be with you and I have to sleep next door?"

"We'll be close, just a thin wall between us." She brushed her lips across his cheek and Cliff followed.

CHAPTER 17

Your Face Is as Beautiful as Bill's, and I've Been Kissing Him for a Long Time

er first night away from the farmhouse, Joan couldn't sleep; her first night away from her mother and father, her first time on a train. The smell of diesel smoke wasn't like the clean air on the farm. She heard the engines, the jerking *clack, clack* of couplings snapping together and she pulled the blanket over her ears. She raised her head to peer into the dim night, hoping to see her parents' truck but it was gone, long gone, left behind as the long, colored string glided through the fields carrying an assortment of sweet dreams and nightmares.

When she cried, Ruth comforted the girl and tightened the soft blankets over her shoulders. Shadows softened the jagged rip that ran from Joan's mouth to her nose, but she cringed away when Ruth moved closer to kiss her twisted face.

"It's all right, honey."

Joan whimpered and pulled back. The only other person who had ever kissed her was her mother. She lifted her hands and covered her face, shaking her head, "You can't, don't kiss me."

Ruth gently placed her hands on top of Joan's and gripped her fingers. "You don't have to hide in here, not in your own room. Your face is as beautiful as Bill's, and I been kissing him for a long time."

"This is my room?"

"It ain't much but it's yours, all yours. We'll get some nice curtains."

"I sleep here—alone?" Fear filled the room.

"You haven't been alone before?"

"Not at night. Momma sleeps with me."

"You shared a bed?"

Joan nodded.

Ruth patted and rubbed her hands. "I'm right next door."

Joan cried, "Not alone, no." Desperate, afraid, she pulled the pillow over her head.

"There ain't room for both of us. I can't get in the top bunk."

Joan climbed into the upper bunk. "I sleep up here. You'll stay down there? Say you will."

"I will. I love you."

Joan cried for a long time and Ruth sung a soft song until the girl's breathing grew steady; an even movement of air in and out of her lungs, the sound Ruth needed. Sleep didn't come to the new mother and she joined the ranks of other new mothers who laid in bed in fear when a baby came home.

They lived in two small adjoining rooms—crowded, but the new parents relished the warmth, the steady glow brought by the fragile innocence of the young girl.

Ruth immediately loved Joan, had loved her before knowing her because Ruth had always wanted a child. Her own disfigurement—alligator skin—had not prevented her from having children and Bill's twisted face had not prevented him from fathering children, but they decided not to conceive because of the danger of producing a child with defects that would force them to live hidden lives.

They looked at each other, knowing Joan's arrival was God's way of letting them be parents, a gift they had prayed for.

In the first light of morning Joan dropped to the floor and sat on the edge of Ruth's bed, the blanket tight around her shoulders, afraid of the light. Ruth rubbed her back and wrapped Joan in her arms.

Joan spread her fingers and touched Ruth's face, feeling the rough scales. Ruth looked into Joan's eyes, searching for her reaction, their eyes understood. Touching each other's faces drew them together. At first Joan shrank away, but Ruth's touch was gentle and warm, and Joan relaxed with her eyes shut and dozed, lulled by the wheels clicking over the tracks.

When Bill opened the door and saw the two women cuddled together, he silently watched. Suddenly Joan opened her eyes and when she saw Bill, she hid her face. Ruth felt caught between protecting her new daughter and honoring her husband.

"Shhh. It's Bill. It's all right, honey, it's all right." Ruth hugged the girl and gently rocked her. She looked at Bill, and he nodded his head and left the room.

When Joan heard the door shut, she looked through the window. Ruth looked with her. "Did the noise bother you last night?"

Joan couldn't talk; she was bewildered by everything she saw and heard. She cried. Ruth stayed with her, not asking her to speak or look or do anything but remain safe in her arms.

CHAPTER 18

Who Slept Here Before?
Ghosts Filled the Room

Room six was like the others on the old Pullman car—flaking paint, loose threads in the carpet, a brown stained sink, scorched cigarette burns, upper and lower bunks with thin mattresses. The blanket was old and soft.

When Cliff stretched out on the lower bed, he relaxed.

Who slept here before? Ghosts filled the room, salesmen on their way to Chicago, couples traveling to a cousin's wedding, a second-story man hiding from the Cleveland police, a doctor going to a psychiatric convention, a young reporter chasing a story, the next best seller. Am I doing the right thing? Hell, yes. I'm joining the ranks of seekers.

He knocked on the wall and listened for Katie to respond. *A thin sheet of metal separates us, where I want to be, on the other side. How does Katie know where she's supposed to be? She seems so sure. Where am I supposed to be? Tonight I'm sleeping on a carnival train instead of climbing the editor's ladder. How many doors are there?*

Had to make a choice, had to listen to the voice sitting on my shoulder, the voice that never stops, never, never stops. And there's more than one: A soprano, a bass, alto, tenor. One voice says go. Get out of town. Ride the train, write the book, dance to the music. The other voice says stay, sit, be a good boy, fetch the minutes of the meeting.

He knocked on the wall again, no response, so he got up and tapped on her door, calling her name. Katie swung the door open and Cliff started talking, rambling, as words flooded the space between them.

"And the guy on my shoulder talks louder, take the job—Editor Walker, voice of authority, man of influence, secure position—the voice always talking. Why so many choices? Why not keep it simple…like the dancing girl, just a few choices. Why all the confusion? Why not one voice so strong, one voice so loud, it makes the rest of them shut up? Joan made a choice, the kid that plays Beethoven when he's three. You have to dance, no choice, Milt had to jump. So did I."

Katie kissed him. "Come here, slow down, tell me what you're talking about. Take a breath before you explode, before you get hurt."

The brakes squealed, and pushed him against the wall. His arms absorbed the shock and he thanked Steve Lanning for the warning: *You can get hurt on this train, bad hurt, be careful, dangerous.*

When he dropped to the bed, Katie fell against him and wrapped her arm over his chest.

Cliff started talking again. "Joan Ryerson's on the train…in her new mother's arms. That's what I'm talking about." The words sent prickly sensations through his body. "Joan Ryerson jumped on the train because she wants to be where she doesn't scare people."

Katie asked, "Who's Joan?"

Her question stopped Cliff's breathing. He couldn't swallow. "How could you know? No one knows, just a few."

He closed his eyes and told Katie about his trip to the farm and his talk with the Ryersons, the parents. Their anguish and probable relief as they grasped for a solution, any solution. His words felt meaningless as he tried to describe Ryerson's rage and frustration and his own doubts.

Cliff couldn't look at Katie. His voice broke as he confided in her that his being on the train was partially to find out what was going to happen with the disfigured girl, her brave steps as she joined a new family—how brave she was.

"They were crying and smiling when they saw her get out of the truck. I wasn't close but I could see her walk from the truck to the train. I knew I was witnessing small steps that were as big as men going into space. Her courage was part of why I ran to catch the train. That, and seeing you in the dining car. I couldn't stay behind."

A deep moan, a cry came from Katie and tears rolled down her cheeks, soaking his shirt, she rubbed her hair with spread fingers. She stared at Cliff.

"Are you going to write about her? Please tell me it won't be in the newspaper." Katie pulled away from Cliff and slid into the corner of the bed. She pulled her legs up, an animal seeking protection.

The sudden tears shocked Cliff. He wanted to make them go away. He shook his head. "No. I'm not going to." Cliff drew a breath. "I can't write about her for the newspaper."

"You promise you're not going to write about her?"

"I'm not, not in the newspaper. The editor told me it's not appropriate, said it wasn't any different than a pretty girl moving away to find a better life. He's wrong; it's a lot different. A pretty girl doesn't cause fear and disgust. A pretty girl gets asked to parties, receives gifts, marries a nice boy. Joan would have rocks thrown at her in Morganport. But no one's going to read about it—not from me."

Cliff stuffed the pillow under his head and watched as the open pastures gave way to houses. He rubbed his face. *Where am I?* The voice on his shoulder assured him he was where he belonged, swaying like his ship crossing the ocean to new ports, the Indiana State Fairgrounds.

He already decided he was going to tell Stoneman he needed a couple of days off.

I'm in Indianapolis, not going to be at work Monday or the next day. Will you get along without me?

They stopped in a crowded switching yard, waiting for clearance to move through, a dozen dirty trains squeezed together like black licorice strips waiting to ooze out of the jam.

Cliff tensed when he heard a knock on door six.

Who could be looking for him? Has the word spread?

He heard Steve's rough voice. "I'm getting this train moving, thought you'd like to see how it gets done around here."

Cliff pulled on his shirt and pants and opened the door. "Why I'm here. Wait till I get my shoes."

Steve looked at the door. "Thought you was in room six. Maybe you're too busy."

"Not too busy to see how you move a train. Is Jack going to help?"

"Yeah, Jack's in charge. Truth is, Jack owns the whole show. Mastras and me are just hired guns."

"If Jack owns the show that must make you the head of the shit-shoveling detail."

"You got a smart mouth this early, must 'a had a good night."

Cliff thought it would have been better if Katie's dad hadn't been in the room.

Carrying a paper bag, Steve led the way across rows of track and navigated through the parked freight cars.

The switching yard was jammed with open gondolas filled with coal, crushed steel, tankers carrying hazardous ammonia and locked boxcars. Cliff listened to Steve explain that the yard boss considered the carnival train the same as the rest of the freight.

"Because we look different don't mean shit. We ain't no better than a load of coal. Takes some special Lanning talk to get through.

Or we could sit all week." When they got to the dispatcher's office, Steve opened the door and walked in and started talking to the surprised men in the control room. A man standing at the counter stopped writing and asked Steve what he wanted.

"Same as last year, we need your help, got to get set up for the big fair, girls ready to get naked, animals need water." Steve offered the yard boss a cigarette and lit it for him, and then handed out books of passes while he slid the paper sack across the desk.

The boss had nodded his head enthusiastically when Steve said *naked*. He pulled two quarts of bourbon out of the sack. "Here's the reason we stopped you. You're the same guy delivered last year, ain't you?"

"If he was missing half an ear, I'm the same guy. I won't see you next year, I'm buying a Cadillac, get off that rolling hell. Someone else will make the delivery."

"Tell them they better bring more than passes and whiskey."

"What more?" Steve wanted to get this deal wrapped up.

"You said something about naked?"

"Passes will get you in the girls' show." Steve flipped through a stack of the cardboard tickets. "Go early, get a front-row seat."

"Did that last year. That stripper Pagan is the real thing. You think someone might be able to get me backstage with her?"

Steve looked at Cliff and winked, then turned back to the yard boss. "Brought him with me, this guy can take care of it, fix you up. He's tight with the girls, take you where you think you want to go."

When he heard Steve's words, Cliff wanted to shake his head no, but he nodded yes.

"This young man knows his way backstage. You come out tomorrow night and he'll take you there, introduce you to the all the girls, Pagan for sure."

The yard boss looked at Cliff, waiting for an acknowledgement of the offer. Cliff's arms tightened when the man looked at him like he was an important contact that held the key to Pagan Smith.

Jumping on the train was the first step, this is the second, how many more to go? One day a small-town reporter, the next day an accomplice to a bribe, dinner with the Governor. Doors open and close so fast you can't go back through.

"I can take you backstage. I know how to get there."

"Where can I find you?"

Steve answered. "Come to the animal menagerie, the elephant tent. Ask for me, Steve Lanning. I'll find him for you."

The yard boss nodded his head, satisfied. "I'll be there." Then he pointed to the side of Steve's head and the red-stained bandage. "I thought about your ear all year, what happened to it?"

Steve adjusts his cap. "Good, good—*ear all year*—deserves an answer." Steve tilted his head sideways. "I was making it with a broad, had a metal brace on her leg. When she hit the sweet roll, she squeezed my head and clipped it off, clean."

"Bullshit, never happened. What did happen? Where did you stick your head—where it shouldn't 'a been?"

"I just told you, between her legs."

As he laughed, the Superintendent told Steve and Cliff to go back to the train. "Don't tell me what happened. I'll have you out of here in thirty minutes—and see you tomorrow night."

Following Steve back across the tracks, Cliff stared at his severed ear.

How did it happen, lion, bullet, sex? Part of his ear was gone. It told me something. He commands elephants. He doesn't drink anymore, he says. He says things that I question but hope are true: drinking with Hemingway, star of the Ringling Circus, mover of painted trains. A complex man with half an ear.

A stack of passes and a promise and a magic hand would sweep them through the crowded yard. Sometimes it didn't take much to open a stuck door. The secret was to keep pushing.

They wove across the tracks, dodging a work engine. Steve thanked Cliff for going along with the deal. "That asshole is like all of us, on the take. We always want more. Next year he'll want the key to her room and I ain't no pimp. He can get his own key and I don't want to see what happens when he tries, not with Pagan. He'll wish he'd stayed wrestling these boxcars."

"How do you know she might not like him?" Cliff asks.

"I don't. Maybe she will, and you and your dancer can go to dinner with them. I don't know. My job is to break us loose. Next year will be next year and I ain't riding the train no more."

"So I'm supposed to be the pimp?" Cliff asks.

"More like a matchmaker. Make the introduction. We get through this yard, he can find his own way to Pagan. He'll have to bring her more than whiskey."

"What about next year?"

"A long time, too long to worry about. Someone will deliver the whiskey."

"Maybe Jack."

Steve stops walking. "When the Man told me to do it, I asked him if he was testing me, giving me whiskey. He said he was. I surprised him and passed the test, delivered all the whiskey. Jack won't never pass. He might not make it the rest of the season."

CHAPTER 19

He Looked at the Outline of Her Body Under the Blanket, a Beautiful Girl, a Beautiful Dancer

When he returned to room six, Katie woke up and they curled together and stared through the window. The single bunk was narrow, forcing their legs and arms to touch, and Katie kissed Cliff, her mouth eager for his.

On the yard boss's order, the train jerked and stopped and started again and the rough ride interrupted their passion. They braced their legs and looked through the window until the train entered the fairgrounds.

"Steve told me you can get hurt on this train. He didn't say anything about frustrated."

Katie shook her head no when Cliff asked if she wanted to watch the unloading.

"You go ahead, I've seen it." She blew him a kiss. "Really, go ahead. It's all right. I want to sleep. You go. Take notes. I'll be here."

Before he closed the door, he looked at the outline of her body under the blanket, soft arms and legs, a beautiful girl, a beautiful dancer, confident, graceful, dealing with a bad situation, accepting a crap job on a grimy midway and doing her job better than the other

girls, smiling at the audience and captivating them and doing it eight times a day because she knows the work was taking her where she's supposed to be.

Where is this train taking me, taking Joan? Where are we supposed to be? There's your story, Mr. Stoneman, nothing new, three young people, toddlers, shaky on their feet, learning how to balance, small steps.

The foreman of the merry-go-round asked Cliff where the photographer was. "I thought he'd be here for sure, slobbering behind Pagan. Taking pictures of her ass."

"He didn't want to jump with me."

Cliff enjoyed being watched.

Most of the people were staring at the elephants, but some noticed the men leading them. Who were they? Where did they come from? How did someone get a job leading elephants? They'd be surprised if they knew where he was from. If they knew he was a young reporter from Morganport, they'd think he was doing his job but they'd be wrong. A job required a jump on a carnival train.

A photographer aimed his camera at the elephants and Steve stopped and posed with his arms spread wide and motioned for Cliff to join him. "Get over here, make you famous."

Milt Hinkle struggled in front of the camera, waving his crutch at the photographer. "Put me on the front page. I made the papers here—1929, I think—the 101 show."

Steve told Milt to shut up. "Get the hell out of our way. The only way you'll make the paper is if you die, and that might happen if you keep up that chin boogie. Your big days are over."

Milt moved away and lifted his crutch, pointing at Cliff. "Not over, no way. When this smart young man writes about what's in my trunk, I'll be back on the front page. Mind my word."

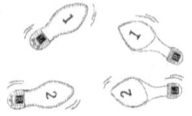

The newsroom telephone rang four times before Franklin answered. "Cliff, where are you? How was the train ride?"

"Inside the state fairgrounds, the big, big time. Come on down."

"I bet you didn't sleep. You looked like you could run all the way. Got a couple of good shots of you hanging on the side of the train. Want me to show them to Stoneman?"

"Wait till I tell you about bribing the railroad boss. Pagan asked where you were. Joan Ryerson is here with Three-Eyed Bill and his wife. I'm not the only one who left town. Show him the pictures, tell him I'm researching his questions, the money trail. Star reporter on the job."

"You did it. When are you coming back?"

"Couple of days. Can you pick me up? You ever been to the state fair?"

"Every year when we lived on the farm. I won a blue ribbon. Got my first kiss in a chicken pen. When should I be there?"

"I'll call you tomorrow or the next day. I wish you had your camera here now. The way they set up is…I know the word *amazing* stinks, but that's what it is. These guys don't look like they can add two and two, but they work together like experts—when they're sober."

"What are you going to tell Stoneman?"

"You do it for me. He might make you editor."

"Not when I tell him I'm leaving, too."

"Tell him Joan Ryerson's on the train."

The conversation with John Stoneman was brief and cold.

"No, Cliff, I don't understand, how can I? A few days? Be more specific. Listen to me. You've got a chance to do something important right here, a hell of a chance. Don't let it slip away. It's not like we've got people to cover for you. Jumped on the circus train—what were you thinking? What the *hell* were you thinking?"

"Is it all right if I stay until Wednesday? Give me a couple of days?"

"Make sure you're back then. If you're not, the job *is* gone."

Cliff was surprised by the calm tone of Stoneman's voice. "I'll be there."

Now Stoneman softened. "One more thing."

"What's that?"

"No blue pencils at the fair."

After they hung up, Stoneman smiled at what Cliff Walker was doing. He was out there, living up to his name.

Out there in the wind and rain and sunshine, temporarily free, on the edge, would he fall?

What will he write about Joan Ryerson? Whatever it is, we can't use it.

If Cliff wanted to take a few days with the carnival, John Stoneman knew it will be good for him; he'd learn that it was a community a lot like Morganport, with heroes and rats, liars and leaders, cream and scum, manipulators and nice people, dependable and irresponsible, sober and drunk, with all of the arguments, affairs and fights that humans seemed to require. Stoneman knew if Cliff learned a little of this lesson, it would be worth the inconvenience of his absence for a few days—but only a few.

If he didn't return, there would be other young reporters. But Stoneman knew most of them would not have Cliff Walker's potential, even though it only surfaced on special occasions. Then his blue pencil came out and made the page look like a storm at sea.

Stoneman saw Cliff's writing potential, but the real indication of it came from his jumping on a circus train. Stoneman understood that Cliff was the kind of writer who had to go through the experience before he would write about it, not a reporter that could stand back, detached, and report what he saw. He had to involve his senses or his words were shallow.

In his file drawer, Stoneman pulled out the copy Cliff had turned in describing the Morganport fairgrounds. The page was covered with blue lines crossing out words and sentences that didn't fit the writing style mandated by newspaper standards, a style so sterile it had almost no impact on the reader except to relay information.

When Stoneman had finished marking up the copy, he felt like he had committed a serious crime—which was why he held on to the blue-streaked pages and added them to the folder in his locked drawer. Some day they might be valuable.

Morganport Receives a Strained, Stained Train

By Cliff Walker

Yesterday elephants and smoking, groaning tractors invaded the barren fairgrounds and hundreds of cold steel-pointed stakes were pounded deep into the hard-packed black dirt, strongholds for thick ropes holding walls of rough canvas. A man with half an ear wielded a steel-tipped cane like a conductor's baton, directing the elephant orchestra in its rehearsal for the grand opening of the Capp County Fair and Exposition. In one week, the carnival train will depart with thousands of Capp County dollars, leaving behind stuffed animals and the empty taste of spun sugar and memories of senses stretched to new limits.

Stoneman had read the copy several times trying to decide what to do with it; too colorful, too wild, maybe acceptable somewhere. The comments about money leaving town were too controversial, so Stoneman had regretfully wielded his blue pencil, turning the poetry into drivel. What appeared in the paper was accurate, without excitement, leaving the editor at his worn desk thinking that the original work deserved more than a spot in a locked drawer.

Joan Ryerson's story would be added to it.

CHAPTER 20

They Wanted to Finish Fast, Hoping to Catch Sight of a Stripper

Bill and Ruth were overjoyed to have Joan with them. They knew what it was like to draw horrified stares; eyes focusing, then blinking away. They knew the stares would never stop; but, in time, they would become unnoticed facts of life, the other person's cross to bear.

In her room, Joan spent the days looking through the train window. On the farm, the view had never changed; now the scene transformed minute by minute. Mornings, when the yellow light glimmered over rides and tents, Joan watched as women dressed in faded jeans walked to the midway, to the ticket booths. They appeared and disappeared, and the reporter that came to the farmhouse hurried toward the office wagons and slowed down to knot his tie.

She said "goodbye" to Bill when he left for work; he blew her a kiss through the window.

No longer a severely damaged attraction, Bill supervised setting up the Broadway Review stage. He hired four extra hands to help bolt together the seats and lift the heavy stage into position. They soon learned that each piece had to go together on Bill's schedule.

They didn't question his method because it worked, and no one wanted to question a man that looked like he did. Besides, they wanted to finish fast so they could collect their money and stand around, hoping to catch sight of a stripper.

Bill and Ruth had spent twenty-seven years as two of the main attractions of the freak show. The two men who owned the show, Slim and Whitey, were good employers, paid their employees fair wages, operated their Ten-In-One the way Mastras wanted it run and enjoyed the benefits of being the featured sideshow on one of the biggest carnivals in the country. As the public's protests over the mistreatment of the people grew stronger, Slim and Whitey had made the decision to stop their business and they retired to Florida, along with some of the others who lived in a small community near Tampa where they could grow vegetables.

Bill and Ruth were looking forward to the end of their repeated journeys on the train and joining the others where everybody knew their names and they woke up seeing the same scenery every morning.

Joan's arrival was the last item on their To-Do list.

Today, Bill worked faster than usual. With Joan waiting, he pushed hard to finish the job.

Ruth's buying new yellow curtains, I get to put them up for...my daughter.

Daughter gave him as much pride as a young father holding a new baby in a hospital nursery.

In her room, Joan tensed when she heard a door open and bang closed. Footsteps passed in the hall and the quiet returned. She went back to the window next to Ruth, who said, "I need to stretch my legs. Will you walk with me?"

Joan wrapped her arms around her chest and clamped her mouth. "Hold my hand?"

Ruth opened the door and stepped into the hall. Joan didn't move and whispered, "You said you'd hold."

"Here's my hand." Ruth gripped Joan's fingers, pulling gently until the girl stepped into the hallway. "You hold me and I'll hold you…tight, real tight."

"Hold tight." Joan squeezed against the woman's ample side and pulled Ruth's arm around her shoulders. "Hold me tight."

They walked to the end of the hall where Ruth reached for the handle, but Joan gripped hard, jerking the woman away from the door. "Not outside, back to the room. Not outside."

"Just out to the deck for the air." Ruth hugged Joan tight as they passed through the door where the morning air was fresh and cool. Ruth ran her free hand through her hair; the breeze cleared her head.

Joan shuddered, afraid. "We sat on the porch at home looking at the birds. Me and Momma."

They saw Cliff walking toward the train.

Joan couldn't stop her cry and ducked behind Ruth. "Inside, inside. Don't want him to see me." Panic shrilled her words. She reached for the door handle and pulled Ruth back inside. As the door closed, Cliff saw the back of Joan's head.

He had heard the conversations: *How much does she look like Three-Eyed Bill? Are they going to keep her shut up in the room the rest of the season? Is this better than the farm? It will be. Will it? Better than another council meeting, better than empty words, letter by letter by letter?*

Joan ran to the room and jerked open the door, closed it and backed into the corner with her face turned to the wall. Ruth came in and pulled down the window blind and told Joan no one saw her.

"That newspaper guy didn't? He didn't?"

"No." Ruth wanted to say it didn't matter if he had.

But I know it's going to take time, a long time before she's comfortable with people looking at her, never comfortable but bearable. More the ability, when she's strong enough, to look at friends and see them smile, unaware of her face.

"No one saw you but me, and I like looking at you because you look like my Bill." They stayed in the room the rest of the day, safe under a blanket, shades pulled. Joan's muscles relaxed as Ruth rubbed her back and neck.

Later, when the sun dropped behind the train, Joan pulled the curtains closed and undressed and washed in the sink, then pulled on a clean blouse and jeans and laid down on the bed.

The room with new curtains and a picture of a lake is mine and they asked me to live with them. Mom and Dad didn't ask for me; they had to take what they got. Bill and Ruth asked for me. They said they wanted me; they meant it. And that pretty girl told me she'd teach me to dance.

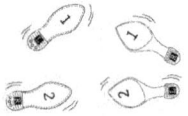

In her room, Katie worked with conviction.

Dear Mom and Dad,

He's a WRITER!

And I'm falling in love with him. And I think he loves me but he hasn't said the words. I think he's a little shy but acts like he's not, like other men I've known, but Cliff is also brave enough to jump on this crazy train.

Dad, I told him you were Irish, your love of writing and you've read Jack Kerouac. He's not sure if his writing is any good. I wish you could meet him in person. I know you'd like him; could help him be confident.

Cliff's a reporter who jumped on the train and said he did it because of me and a poor girl I'll tell you about. He jumped on the train—the most romantic thing that's ever happened to me. And he promised not to write about the poor deformed girl. I'll try to tell you about her without flooding the page.

Katie continued the long letter, writing about Joan. When she forced herself to describe Joan's face, tears stained the paper and she had to stop. Her words made it too real. So she wiped her eyes and told about Joan's courage.

She'd almost never been away from the farm, afraid to ride the train, traffic, tall buildings, cotton candy—she has a sweet tooth—but she wasn't afraid when she watched me practice.

Cliff knocked on her door. "I'm having trouble getting to sleep. A goodnight kiss will help."

"Did you say your prayers?"

"Yes."

"Okay, one kiss."

"What did you tell them about me?"

She opened the door far enough for her head to come through. "I told them you were a sex maniac. Here's your kiss. Now go close your eyes and count something."

"I love it when you talk dirty."

CHAPTER 21

Their Grief Couldn't Be Seen, but Cliff Could Feel It

The sound penetrated his sleep, a soft knocking on the metal door, a *thud, thud, thud* that echoed like a bass drum and Cliff sat up as he tried to guess who it was. His watch said nine and the *thudding* didn't stop. It wasn't Katie. She would have called out his name.

Cliff opened the door and saw Lee Savage, hand raised, ready to hit the door. "What's up?"

"The Man wants you in his plane."

Cliff wasn't surprised to see Lee. An older man who sat outside the office wagons; a doorman or bartender who mixed drinks for visitors. Somehow he knew when to be there and when to leave, according to the boss's schedule.

"Where?"

"Car's outside."

"I need a minute."

No time to wait for hot water. He let the cold shock him awake, then pulled on his pants and shirt.

Cliff Walker, reporter, command performance.

The airplane was waiting at the edge of the runway and the pilot pulled the dipstick, wiped it clean, and slipped it back and checked it again before closing the cowling. He had already checked the other engine while waiting for Mastras.

Cliff admired the plane's subdued gray and silver paint...not red and blue and yellow. The pilot shook hands with Mastras and Cliff, and stood next to the stairs while they boarded. He climbed in behind them, pulled the door shut and revved the engines.

"I just bought this plane three weeks ago," Mastras told Cliff. "I wanted twin engines and more seats. The North Carolina Commissioner likes to bring his friends when we go fishing in Canada." Mastras added, "You're only here a couple of days, I thought this would be a good way to spend some time together."

Rolling over the rough runway, Cliff felt the cracks and bumps in the pavement fade away as the plane lifted off. He felt weightless.

It took an hour to fly from Indianapolis to Columbus where Mastras told the pilot to circle the empty fairgrounds. He pointed to the wide field where his rides and shows would be set up in two weeks.

"As big as Indianapolis, growing every year. We have to bring in more independents to fill the midway." They made three turns around the Ohio Fairgrounds as they watched tractors mow the tall grass and smooth the racetrack as a crew of painters worked on the white stalls.

"I was supposed to go to breakfast this morning with the Indiana Commissioner, but I don't like bacon and cold eggs. I gave him a donation. Told him I had a meeting in Ohio."

He's skipping breakfast with the Indiana Commissioner of Agriculture and flying me to Ohio and doesn't care if I know about it, doesn't care about his small lie. A man with his own plane, private railroad car, and a lot of cash can pass on boring breakfasts if he wants to.

Looking down at the small houses and cars, Cliff fought the feeling of being above it all, part of the privileged few, and asked Mastras if it would be too far out of the way to fly over Morganport.

"Not at all. I've seen enough here."

Skimming over flat, square farms and smooth fields, Cliff was aware of his speed of passage. He stared at his small hometown and pushed his face close to the window to find the high school, a few blocks away from the pointed steeple of the Presbyterian Church and the screened front porch of his parents' house.

They banked and turned and dropped low over the downtown, the library, the limestone building built by Andrew Carnegie. He imagined Carolyn running out to see the airplane, but she didn't appear.

What is she doing? When I return, what's going to happen? What will Katie do when I leave the fairgrounds and return to Morganport? Two pretty girls, a dancer and a reader. Door number one or door number two?

High Street ran parallel with Broadway, Market, and Spear, the Elks Club, B&K root beer stand, Ford dealer, Baileys Department Store, all fronted the streets like the rides and shows and food stands fronted the midway. The Mastras Shows moved and Morganport didn't, but they were both small towns where people worked and played.

The biggest difference was Three-Eyed Bill and Joan could walk the midway, but not Broadway.

Aware of Jim Mastras watching him, Cliff felt color and heat as they filled his forehead.

"Need more time?" The engine noise made it hard to hear. Cliff asked Mastras to repeat his question. "More time?"

"No. Doesn't take long from up here." Cliff had to shout. "Every reporter should see their beat from up here. See those houses next to the river?" Mastras looked at three shabby houses separated from the business area by the railroad

"You mean where the hookers live? I heard those girls like it when the Fair's open. Locals get charged up at Pagan's show, go there for relief."

Cliff didn't know what to say. Mastras knew about the prostitutes; he probably knew about the poker game in the back of the cigar store. "How about the insane asylum? Do you know where it is?"

Mastras nodded his head. "I got a bunch of people that need to be in it."

"Morganport's known all over Indiana for hookers and nut houses. Makes us all proud."

"You ready to go back? Or is there more you want to show me?"

"Back to Indianapolis, or back to Morganport?" Cliff wanted someone to tell him where to go, what to do.

Mastras told the pilot to head back. "Indianapolis. I've got work to do. You have to decide where you're going."

They passed over the Ryerson farm. It looked peaceful from the air: Square house, a barn surrounded by open fields. The house looked deserted, but it had been like that when they picked up the calf and Joan watched from behind the curtains. He saw the crawling tractor; Ryerson trying to keep busy. Mrs. Ryerson did the washing and ironing and resigned herself to being alone, sad.

Their grief couldn't be seen, but Cliff could feel it, forcing its way through the air—he hoped it was grief, not relief. He should have gone to the house and asked them questions—what reporters were supposed to do—but that wasn't going to happen.

Stupid questions: How are you feeling, do you miss her? I don't want to know how they feel about their daughter's empty chair at the table. Stoneman doesn't care, not a story for a newspaper.

They landed and taxied next to Mastras' Mercedes. He drove them to the fairgrounds and waited at the back gate for the guard to open it.

Cliff told Mastras he was going back the next day. "I'll see you next year."

Outside of the car, Mastras hesitated. "The reason I took you up in the plane was to find out what you're doing here. I need someone with your experience—someone who can talk to the press. They ask questions, but I don't want to take the time. If you know any reporters that want to travel, tell them I have an opening."

"What do you think about the new girl living with Bill and Ruth?" *Ask the hard questions. Maybe he doesn't know about her.* "We just flew over their farm."

"I heard about her."

No surprise for Cliff. *He knows everything in his world. It is his world. Someone told him. They told him to gain favor.*

Mastras asked, "Did you know her?"

"No. I didn't know a lot of things going on in Morganport, not like you do here."

"I have to know; they have to tell me. You went there with Lanning?"

"Yes. What do you think about it?" *Do you know why I jumped on the train, about Katie?*

Mastras leaned against the car. He moved his head in a half circle.

"Understand something. I've known Bill and Ruth since I was a little boy running around the show in short pants. They're good people. They deserve her. They'll take care of her. That's what I think."

CHAPTER 22

Same as You Putting Paste on Your Face, Makes These Girls Feel Pretty

Walking with the marks, Cliff studied the ticket sellers. Hands flying, they ripped tickets, slid coins and bills and waved the marks inside the tents, loaded them onto the rides, locked tight, handed over hot dogs, spun clouds of sugar. Money poured like it was surging through sluice gates, so much it had to be hauled to the bank in a two-ton truck.

Steve lit a cigarette and shifted his attention to a man and woman standing at the counter. "Look at these two."

Dressed like they were on their way to a golf tournament, they surprised Cliff. She was wearing pale blue canvas shoes and white slacks and a green striped blouse and her gray hair was pulled back from her face, held with a silver clasp. He had on tan loafers, tan pants and a black pullover shirt.

They asked the girl behind the counter a question and when Steve saw her shake her head, he gripped his cigarette in his mouth and quickly walked to them. Cliff followed.

"What is it?" Steve kept his eyes on the attendant.

"They got some questions." The girl's lips were drawn tight, no answer.

Steve turned hard eyes to the woman, then the man, who said, "We're the producers of the *Indiana Scene* television show and our viewers like animals. You the man in charge, Steve Lanning? The office told us to talk to you."

"That's me." Steve asked if they wanted to film the red, white, and blue elephants.

Cliff thought it would be better if they asked him about meeting Ernest Hemingway or performing in Madison Square Garden.

"Why are they painted like that?" The woman underscored the question with a frown.

"Doing a benefit this week, for the Governor."

"The Governor! Isn't that paint bad for them?"

"No, it ain't bad for them." Steve mocked her question; he knew it would irritate her. "Same as you putting paste on your face, makes these girls feel pretty, too."

She lifted her hand toward her neck, but stopped before making contact. "Interesting comparison."

Cliff turned away so they didn't see his smile. He wouldn't forget the look on the woman's face when Steve compared her skin to an elephant's.

The woman looked at the man and a message moved between them. They shook Steve's hand and told him they would possibly be back.

"When does your show come on?" There was an edge to Steve's question.

"Sunday afternoon, four o'clock."

"Fair's over Saturday night. Come back next year in time to do us some good. I'll paint them again, just for you."

"What happened to your ear?"

"Lion chewed it off." Steve turned his back and walked away.

They looked at each other, surprised, and the man took the woman by the arm. When they passed Cliff, he walked with them. "I enjoy your show. If you don't interview Steve Lanning, you're missing a chance to talk to a man who lost half his ear to a lion and reads Hemingway…and met him."

They gave Cliff an irritated look and kept walking.

"Don't miss him next year. Ask Steve Lanning about performing in Madison Square Garden with the Ringling Circus."

Listen to me; don't worry about the facts.

But the man and woman ignored Cliff. He knew they were mad about Steve's lack of respect. No one had ever turned down a chance to appear on the *Indiana Scene.*

The woman said in a loud voice, "This is all crap."

Cliff guessed, *they don't want to cover the state fair, but the station president told them they had to, the annual fair was part of the Indiana Scene, a big part. Their viewers wanted to see the carnival, the prize pigs, not the new fall fashions. This was Indiana, not Manhattan, not even Chicago.*

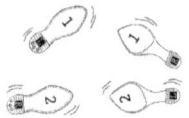

Cliff was surprised when he heard a voice. "I'm looking for the guy with half an ear. He told me he'd get me with Pagan."

"He just left." Cliff wished the tent would catch fire so the railroad yard boss would run away.

"You were with him, weren't you?" He wanted Pagan. "Yeah, I recognize you now. He said you could take me backstage."

The yard boss didn't know what to do with his hands.

Katie stayed behind the curtains and didn't step forward until Cliff reached for her hand and proudly held her close to his side.

He could tell that the railroader was overwhelmed. Their costumes covered minimal parts of their bodies, a situation the man dreamed about that blocked his ability to speak, especially when Pagan hugged him.

She thanked him for getting their "hot train away from that bad railroad place. We're so glad to meet you, Mr. Big Strong Railroad Man. What's your name? I want your name and your address so I can send you a thank-you note—or would you rather I thank you some other way?"

When strangers were backstage, Pagan danced the same routine she followed every performance and the man behind the curtains responded as the blood coursed through his erect nerves, eyes bulging. His breathing made him lightheaded. When Pagan reached the climax of her act, she ran straight to his arms and his knees buckled.

When last seen, the happy couple were enjoying twenty-five-dollar steaks in the best restaurant in Indianapolis and when the show closed, the yard boss rushed the train out of the jam, relieved that Pagan was on her way to Ohio.

His wife didn't believe he needed to work all night because the circus train was leaving.

CHAPTER 23

Pagan Welcomed Him
with a Long Kiss

They drove in heavy traffic. Franklin steered the car around Monument Circle like they were strapped in a spinning ride and headed north on Meridian Avenue.

Cliff sipped beer from a can as he slid down in the seat and talked about the party the night before.

"That was a great party. This isn't a good time to leave. It's a terrible time."

After the last show at the Broadway Review, Katie had asked the band to play longer. "This is Cliff's last night." The drummer didn't hesitate, not for Katie. He hit the bass drum, knocking out a steady beat until the guitar picked up the riff and the saxophone added mellow notes and Katie, in a sweatshirt, instead of sequins, twirled in front of Cliff. When Franklin appeared, Pagan welcomed him with a long kiss.

Even after eight shows, the other girls joined in, dancing for fun instead of working. Ride boys and game agents joined the party, drawn to the tent by the music.

Cliff and Katie held each other, knowing that it could be the end of something they didn't want to talk about. She pressed tight against his chest and Cliff looked at the stage with the faded curtains, the glaring lights and felt the floor swaying and thought about the towns ahead and the audiences that would stand and applaud the cute girl with the beautiful moves, the girl in his arms.

The audiences won't know they're participating in a once-in-a-lifetime experience as they applaud a dancer on her way to the real Broadway, to Radio City Music Hall and if they ever see her again, she'll be starring in a spectacular musical instead of a midway meat show.

She had practiced every day—hard steps, repeated, repeated until the moves were perfect. Katie told Cliff she had practiced so much her shoes fell apart. Toes blistered, legs built new muscles so she didn't get tired. She perfected every turn like the Rockette girls she'd seen on TV specials. Practice was her ticket to the Big Apple.

I'll bang the keys until they fall apart and Stoneman will complain about buying me a new typewriter.

Steve Lanning had arrived with an empty cigar box and flourished a five-spot and told Jack to pass the box. Steve had given instructions: "Dig deep, we need fuel for the party."

Steve watched Jack to make sure that none of the money slipped into his pocket and when the box was full, Steve told Jack, "Be back here in ten minutes, no more. Don't think about an open bottle until you get back."

Jack answered, "No open. I'll be back, see pretty Katie dance. I'm dancin' with her when I back, five minnas."

Jack tapped Cliff on the shoulder and asked if he could cut in. "One, jus' one?"

Katie smiled. "Thank you for asking, Jack. Can we do it some other time? I don't think I can last much longer, wouldn't be any good."

Jack tried to bend at the waist, but lost his balance and stumbled. He caught himself and stood, weaving. "Unnerstan…okay… other, other time. Other."

When they had returned to the train, Katie stopped in front of her door and lifted her arms around Cliff and rubbed the back of his head and when his lips opened, she arched against him. Their breathing increasing to desperate gasps until she stepped back and opened the door and slipped inside the room.

Cliff placed his hand in the opening, waiting to see what she would do.

Katie rubbed his fingers. "I don't want to hurt your hand." He held it in the same position until she grabbed the front of his shirt and pulled him into the room, on top of the bed and inside her body.

As her arms and legs enclosed him, Cliff knew it wasn't a dream. Her soft skin against his, a dream whenever he had watched her dance or when they moved together in time to slow music. Her breathing grew faster, her mouth and her hands in his hair as they flew in time to their private rhythm. She filled him and he knew he was receiving something more important than life itself.

"I guess your dad isn't here tonight."

"He's here. He taught me to make my own decisions."

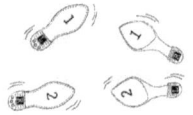

Franklin watched the traffic as he steered the car away from Indianapolis.

"Maybe you can get her to quit the strip show and move in with you. She can teach dancing at the Morganport Y."

"She likes me but not that much, not enough to miss New York." Cliff swallowed the beer. "Sure not enough to move to Morganport."

"I think it's more than like. She *really* likes you. She's a nice girl. You should save her from the carnival."

"She doesn't need saving. She knows where she's going, New York City." Cliff finished the beer and opened another. The thought of Katie in bed distorted his view of the cornfields.

The two-lane road followed the old wagon track leading north to Michigan and Cliff felt the farms squeezing in on both sides. The barns and sheds and clusters of cows threatened their passage and the remaining drive seemed impossible—an ordeal, a never-ending plod.

He emptied his can. "We have to stop. I need to pee, need more beer."

When they saw a lounge and liquor store with a blinking sign, they stopped.

"Let's just use the bathroom, buy beer and keep going," Franklin said. "I might have a date tonight."

"Might?" Cliff asked as he opened the door to the lounge. "You either have a date or you don't."

"Okay, okay, I said *might*, but it's a better chance than I've got here." Franklin walked toward the bathroom.

Cliff sat at the bar and ordered a rum and Coke. He imagined the old, narrow road back when it was a dirt track, and horses and wagons carried home the week's supplies. He tried not to think about where he was headed. He drank more rum.

Farmers planted little seeds and watched green sprouts struggle out of the ground. *Time for me to do the same thing, start a new season, plant seeds and watch them sprout. Planting words on the front page of the Pharos Tribune isn't following the rule of farming—rotate the crops. The same seeds in the same ground, season after season, kills the soil; it's time to change pastures. No crops will grow in Morganport's dead newspaper soil.*

Cliff emptied his glass and asked the man next to him if he'd ever been to Morganport.

The man nodded. "I've been there. That where you're from?"

Cliff tipped his head. He didn't want to say it out loud.

The man said, "Not a bad little town. Ohio, Indiana full of little places all alike. People around here work down in Indy, not much better, just bigger. Still a farm town."

"I just spent four days at the state fair. You ever go?"

"Wouldn't miss it, going tomorrow. What were you doing there?" the man asked.

Dancing with Katie, partying with the strippers, flying in the Man's private plane, coffee with the freaks—where do you want to start? I don't want to tell you I'm going to be the editor of the Morganport Pharos Tribune. I don't want to drive north on this narrow road, spend the rest of my life getting drunk in the Rendezvous.

He ordered another rum and Coke and when Franklin came out of the bathroom, Cliff announced, "I thought I was going to the state fair to find out what's going to happen to a girl running away with the carnival…I didn't find out so I'm going back."

"Do what?" Franklin stopped walking. "What did you say? Where are you going?"

"Will you take me back? I want to help Lanning get on that TV show and find out how much money goes in his pocket. I have to know how Milt jumped out of an airplane without a parachute." Cliff lifted his glass. "Have some of this travel fuel. Come with me, ride the train. We always wanted to go to New York. I have to go back, watch Katie dance, write the stories…stories, not news, write Joan's story. Going back to Morganport makes no sense, no sense at all. It doesn't work, no editor job for me, the wrong thing for me to do."

His words felt right, decisive. They freed him from the numbing doubt about the editor's job. He knew the rum was giving him courage, helping him see clearly, helping him understand—at least for the short-term, and the long-term was too long to worry about.

Franklin shook his head. "It's an hour, more, back to the fair-grounds. I'll miss my date." He pointed to Cliff's glass. "How many of those have you had? You can't go back, big mistake…big."

Cliff closed his eyes. "Miss your *might* date? I don't want to make you feel bad, but you have more 'might' dates than real ones. The way you and Pagan were dancing last night, I think you better go back to the fairgrounds with me."

"Are you serious? You want to go back? You're messed up. You don't mean it, do you?"

"Rum helps show the way clear." Cliff rolled the glass. "I mean it. I can't stay on this dangerous road full of potholes and violent farmers, savage hen houses, brutal machines sucking milk out of cows, exploding corn. I'm going back, now." He grabbed Franklin's arm. "You stay and work your ass off and take the best pictures you can. I'm going to find words that burn the paper. Lanning told me I didn't have the guts; he's wrong."

He knew it was the rum, but not all. *How can I go back to a slow, painful, Morganport death, choking on public works budgets? No music in Morganport, the music is on the midway. Will Joan Ryerson find love, find a home?*

"I'm not taking you, got a date." Franklin looked at Cliff, and his stare made it final. "What are you going to do about Carolyn?"

Cliff swallowed. "I can't go. If you can't take me, it's all right. I'll get there some other way. Mastras offered me a job. I don't know about Carolyn, that's a hard one. I need more time."

The man at the bar volunteered to drive. "I'll take you. I don't mind going to the fair tonight. My car's not here, but I can be back in five minutes."

"I'm ready, really going back, pay for your gas. Show you the best dancer in the world."

Outside Franklin waited with Cliff. "What are you going to tell Stoneman?"

"Don't know, *don't* care, not now. Worry tomorrow. I'll tell him I'm rotating the crops, planting new seeds. I don't know what the hell I'll tell him. Maybe like Edward R. Murrow, 'Good night and good luck' and tell Carolyn the same thing. I think she and Lanning got something started."

Franklin said, "Now you're Edward Murrow? What kind of job did Mastras offer? Carolyn and Lanning—give me a break, you know that's not true."

"Press agent, the money's good. I'll work with the *New York Times, Boston Herald*, features, and money and airplanes. Never, never, never going to happen in Morganport. John Stoneman never made any money."

When the man returned with the car, Cliff and Franklin looked at each other, both thinking about the last time they parted company, when Franklin left for the Navy. Now it was Cliff's turn and he took it, and Franklin understood but couldn't admit it.

Cliff gave the driver directions to the back gate of the fairgrounds. When the man at the gate saw Cliff, he swung the steel fence open and allowed the car to pull inside and park with the other show equipment.

"Now this is the way to do it." The driver locked his car and shook hands with Cliff.

"Thanks for the ride. Follow me, I'll get you some passes."

The driver waited outside the office wagon until Cliff returned and handed him a stack of passes. "Free passes, great, thank you."

"You're welcome, thanks again for the ride. I'd show you around but I've got to see someone and tell her I'm back. Those passes will get you a good seat so you can see her, too."

When they got to the front bally stage Cliff slipped out of the flow and stood in the back of the crowd so she couldn't see him.

Katie's moves were stopping more and more of the crowd until the midway was clogged.

I'm watching Katie dance: not talking to Franklin and Carolyn about my four days and nights at the state fair. Time to enjoy the ride; learn from new teachers, Steve Lanning, Milt Hinkle, Jim Mastras, Katie Flannigan, especially Katie, the sooner the better. And Joan Ryerson, can't leave her out of the story.

When she saw him, Katie lifted her hands to her mouth and jumped into his arms. "Don't let me go."

Cliff wiped the tears from her cheeks and kissed her mouth. It wasn't time to talk. Not caring who might be watching, they stayed together for a long time, kissing and crying. She shuddered and tightened her grip. "You came back."

"The road was closed to Morganport, couldn't get through."

"Closed? Really closed?"

"It kept getting narrower and narrower, corn fields squeezing on both sides, farm houses, barns, chickens, pig pens, until I couldn't go any further, had to turn back. I have to see you dance with the Rockettes."

"You're going to stay until New York? What about your job?"

"I'm rotating crops."

"I'll write that to Dad. He'll like it."

He came back—partially for me. Cliff was supposed to go back to his hometown to become the editor of the newspaper but he got partway there and turned around. I told him I loved him.

Dad, he said it was time for him to rotate crops, time for him to see more of the world. Who does that sound like? A young Irish priest in love with a pretty American girl?

I feel like this is a blessing. We have two months before we get to New York and I was getting to the place where I wasn't sure I could keep doing eight shows a day but Cliff's being here is wonderful. As you can tell, he's different than anyone else on the show. I'm lucky to find him.

CHAPTER 24

Too Soon.
Too Soon to Leave the Train,
It's Too Soon

Joan rolled on her side and looked down, and when she saw the empty lower bed, she couldn't breathe. She was alone, far away from the farm—in another state, Ohio. Joan lifted the blind and saw Ruth, sitting outside on a folding chair reading a newspaper. In the early sunlight, tiny shadows played across Ruth's scaly skin.

Joan dressed and held her breath and stepped down to the ground and leaned against Ruth, as she flicked her eyes up and down the line of sleeping cars, alert for danger.

Ruth put her arm around the girl's waist. "Did you sleep all right, honey?"

"I dreamed about the calf, dreamed it grew its leg back. Can I see it?"

Ruth thought, *too soon. Too soon to leave the train, it's too soon.*

Ruth had wished for a daughter, but never allowed herself to think it could happen and it did. A girl to take care of, to buy dresses for, to comb her hair, to show her the world. She awakened during the night, got up to look at Joan, felt the warmth of her presence.

"How about later, when Dad's done working. We can see the calf later."

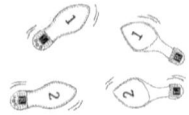

Steve Lanning saw them coming.

The three people looked like hooded peasants as they made their way through a medieval village of tents. Steve noticed a few marks as they glanced at the faces under the hoods and made hard turns away, but for the most part, Joan and Ruth and Bill blended because they walked erect, like they had a purpose.

When Bill saw Steve sitting behind the banners, he raised his hand in greeting and then pointed to the new banner of the calf with three legs. Ruth and Joan followed his finger. The calf's eyes were painted sky blue and the curls surrounding its light brown face were creamy yellow. Kicking up one rear leg, emphasizing the missing limb, the calf was drawn as a cute young animal romping in a field of red, purple, and yellow flowers.

Bill led his wife and new daughter to the menagerie entrance and Steve stood up to welcome them. Joan slid behind Ruth to hide from the elephant trainer.

Inside the dim tent, Bill slipped the hood away from his face. "When did you get the new banner? It looks good. Duke does a nice job, don't he?"

"You like it?"

"I do. Cute little calf," Bill said, and looked back at Joan. "She wants to see it."

Bill and Ruth had talked privately about allowing Joan to see the calf. They were afraid it might make her want to spend more time with it. Ruth had said they should just ask her instead of guessing for her and when they did, Joan had answered in a flat voice, "I used to feed her. I kind of want to see if she's all right."

Steve led them to where the calf was standing inside a small roped-off area just inside the entrance. Bill nodded his head, "Good place, give 'em a free look. Is it bringing them in?"

"I'm doing about the same as always, maybe a little better. Can't tell yet."

They watched the calf and Joan moved closer to pet it, but the frightened animal backed away with its head lowered. Joan also backed away with her arms behind her, searching for Ruth. "She don't remember me, scared like me."

Ruth placed her hands on Joan's shoulders. "What does she like to eat? If we bring something she likes, she'll be all right. What does she like?"

"Apples, sugar cubes."

Ruth turned Joan around and grabbed her hand and led her toward the midway. She told Bill to wait. "We'll be right back."

When they returned, Joan held white cubes in her hand. "I just called her Little Three. She was the littlest one we ever had, smaller without a leg."

Steve held his arms up to stop the marks from moving too close to the pen. Joan leaned over the rope, but the calf cowered in the corner.

Steve lifted the rope. "Walk slow, honey, don't move too fast. Talk to her."

Joan looked to Ruth for permission. "Go ahead, Joanie, like Mr. Steve says, slow, let her smell you."

As Joan moved closer, the calf bolted to the other corner and the girl dropped the cubes and cried and ran back to Ruth. They stood rigidly, watching the calf. It sniffed the air, looking at the white cubes, then cautiously took two steps forward. Finally, it hopped straight to the sugar and extended its wet tongue and lifted one cube and stood still, savoring the sweet flavor.

Ruth bent over, placing her face near Joan's. "Little Three likes that sugar, no need to cry. Let's leave her alone, come back tomorrow. She'll get better, like you."

With their faces hidden behind scarves, they mixed with the crowds, watching the wooden horses on the merry-go-round.

Joan asked Ruth to see the kiddie rides, so they moved near the squealing four year olds and watched as they twisted steering wheels and waved to their beaming parents while the small cars rolled gently over the narrow track. Joan smiled behind her scarf as she watched the children, but she held back, afraid to get too close.

Bill bought a cone of cotton candy and they found a quiet spot where Joan could pull small clumps of the spun sugar from the cone. She dropped her scarf and pushed the sweet candy into her mouth.

Two small boys ran past, taunting each other over which one would win the race to the miniature race cars. Before Joan could pull the scarf back over her face, the boy in the lead suddenly stopped running as he stared and forced his eyes away. He quickly turned back, unable to not look at Joan's face, his own face twisted in fear, afraid of what he saw. Anguish froze him into disbelief and he asked if she was wearing a mask.

Ruth dropped her scarf and motioned for Bill to lift his hat from his face. "We're all wearing masks, honey. Go on and catch your cars so we can see you. You look like real good race drivers. You've got on your good racing masks."

The boys beamed at each other. "Okay, watch us, hope I win."

CHAPTER 25

Thought You Should Know —There's a Dead Elephant Blocking Traffic

Twirling the cane around his wrist, baseball cap pulled low over the side of his face, Steve signaled Jack to stay close. "We'll make the call today." They walked in front of the elephants, with the usual spectators watching from the side of the street.

Jack stumbled, surprised. "Make call—here?" He pulled his lips together, making his thin face thinner.

Steve kept walking. "We never done it here, have we?"

"Can't remember, don't think so. Where we at, Ohio?"

"We make the call today. Let them know the show's in town."

Before leaving the rail siding to walk the elephants to the fairgrounds, Steve had invited Cliff to go with them. "When the press shows up, you talk to them. They will show up. Stay to the side so it don't look like you're with us."

When they reached a business center, Steve spotted a pay phone and signaled the elephants to stop and they obeyed, because the swinging cane reminded them who was in charge. Steve prodded them into a semi-circle, then dropped to one knee to inspect the lead animal's foot. On the sidewalk, Cliff watched excitement spread from face to face. They glanced at each other, thrilled to see the elephants up close.

"Foot. Queenie, foot." The animal lifted its leg, allowing Steve's fingers to grope between the thick toes. A tense ripple ran through the spectators. "Look, he's under a giant animal."

Cliff watched Steve from the sidelines. *What's he up to?* His posture told Cliff he knew what he was doing, always seemed to know.

Following a silent command, Queenie dropped forward on both knees, then lowered her bulk, a tumble of wrinkled skin covering the pavement. Cars stopped in both directions and the crowd pushed closer to look at the elephant.

A brave boy cautiously slid near enough to touch the animal's back, then leaped away as the adults yelled for him to *move, be careful.* They would long remember where they were standing the day the elephant collapsed on the busy street.

Cliff clamped a hand over his smile and understood why the press would rush to cover this special event. He imagined what was about to happen in the newsroom, *shrill telephones, presses stopped, layouts changed.*

Queenie's sides lifted and fell as she snorted through her trunk, blowing an odor of dead grass over the crowd. Steve looked at Jack and nodded his head toward the telephone. "Go on."

Jack put on a pair of dirty glasses and searched through the directory, then dug in his pocket and came up empty-handed. He looked at Steve and extended his empty hand and mouthed, "No change."

Aware of the eager faces, waiting for the next step, Steve twisted his head to keep from shouting and motioned Jack back. "Dumb ass, take the dimes." Steve held his hand low against his leg and passed Jack several coins. "Hurry up!"

Jack clenched his shoulders and wove back to the pay phone. He dropped the coin into the slot and turned the dial. He heard a voice answer, *"Herald, may I help you?"*

Pointing to the elephant, Jack gathered energy from somewhere in his past and his voice became crisp. "Thought you should know there's a dead elephant blocking traffic, Main and Ninth Street. Yes, yes, I'm looking at the poor beast right now, near a bank, First National. Yes, that's right, an elephant. You're welcome, just doing my duty."

He nodded to Steve and hung up the telephone. He slipped two dimes in his pocket and returned to hold Queenie's foot.

"Can I get your name?" The reporter gripped his pencil. "I'm with the newspaper."

"Lanning, Steve Lanning. That's L-a-n-n-i-n-g."

On his knees, Steve turned away and continued probing the padded foot, searching in the cracks and crevices. The two men had done it before. They held and lifted and shook their heads, moving the play through act one.

Jack struggled with the heavy foot. "Got anything?"

"No, can't feel anything." Steve lifted his chin while a cameraman centered the rough face in the viewfinder.

Steve talked to the camera. "Shot of a lifetime. I've been running elephants for thirty years, never seen this before—down in the middle of town."

Cliff looked at the reporter to see if he was smiling at the rhyme—*down in the middle of town*—but what he saw was Steve frowning, peering at the huge foot, his face tight in worried concentration.

A TV camera kept rolling and Cliff imagined the evening news filling screens with tight shots of the pile of wrinkled skin and the man with half an ear. He saw the faces in the crowd, but they didn't see him; their eyes were fixed on the animal lying on the pavement.

Milt Hinkle stood behind Steve and Jack, and watched them go through the motions of examining the animal's foot. Milt was familiar with the charade, the one-act play of a giant animal incapacitated with a bad foot, putting it prostrate on the pavement with a line of cars stopped in the busy thoroughfare, always one of the busiest streets in town.

Milt positioned himself so he was included in the photographs and smiled and hoped the reporters would ask him a question, but they didn't—so when the final scene closed and the elephant rose to its feet, Milt moved in front of the reporter with his crutches spread to block his way. "Maybe you heard of me, Milt Hinkle?"

Steve shouted, "No! Milt, he ain't heard of you. Shut your mouth!"

Jack stood up and agreed with Steve. "Never heard. Never!"

Milt shuffled on his crutches and faced Jack. "Might. He might have heard."

The two men repeated this routine almost every day.

"Never did."

"He ain't old enough."

"Never heard."

"Might."

"Never."

"Might."

Cliff wouldn't forget the scene, the image of Jack and Milt as they argued, unaware of anyone else. They didn't stop until they ran out of energy, tired of throwing *might* and *never* back and forth, content to play catch until one of them dropped the ball and they quit.

Milt said, "Done it again, blew my interview. He knew me. I could tell he knew me."

"Never."

Just when Cliff had convinced himself he either had to become a used-car salesman or stick his head in a gas oven—a carnival train had arrived in town. Now he watched a trainer as he poked his fingers between an elephant's toes, looking for…what could he possibly be looking for? Didn't matter as long as the camera rolled.

A police car arrived, siren blowing, blue lights flashing. The officer jumped out, flustered by the blocked cars honking their horns. The standing elephants dropped large piles of manure on the street.

"I know it's a dumb question, but what the hell's going on? We heard there was a dead elephant." The officer stared at Steve.

"Not dead. Foot's hurt, can't walk."

"You got five minutes to get it to walk, or you and the owner of this outfit are going to jail. This is a state road. Look at the mess they're making. Someone might fall in that crap. Traffic has to move."

Steve offered the cane to the policeman and talked to the camera. "I'll be glad to go with you, officer, if you want to take charge of these animals." Steve pointed to Milt and Jack. "You want to arrest somebody, arrest them. Public intoxication. Take them to the jailhouse before they hurt someone. That skinny one's escaped from the funny farm over in Indiana."

The policeman looked at the elephants and shook his head.

"You've got to do something. I don't care about those two. You got the traffic stopped both ways. This is a main street, can't be blocked. Get them out of here, *now*." He returned to his patrol car and talked on the radio.

Steve motioned Cliff closer. "Help that reporter get what he wants, might make the national news."

The cameraman framed the shot so Steve's head was in the foreground, the jagged half ear, the weathered face, the small bandage blending with the elephant's wrinkled skin. In the background, red lettered on the side of a wagon, *Mastras Shows—America's Finest Midway*.

Tension built as the flashing lights on the patrol car seemed to grow brighter. Struggling with the heavy foot, Steve's voice cut through the air.

"Feel something." His arm tightened. He nodded his head, and when he lifted his hand, he held a small piece of metal between his fingers. "Got it. No wonder she couldn't walk. All right now, all right. *All right!* Get a picture of this, big enough to bring down a two-ton elephant, like David and Goliath." He handed the scrap of metal to the reporter. "Keep it, a souvenir."

The crowd cheered as Queenie rolled to her side and lifted her heavy body to a standing position. The reporter held the piece of metal. "That probably did hurt. Has it ever happened before? We'll get a close-up."

"Forty years, played every town in America, Ringling Show, center ring. Never anything like this." Steve moved closer to the camera. "Come and see us, tell you all about it."

Steve ordered the elephants into position. Trapped in the drama, the crowd moved with them and Cliff stood beside Steve, as Milt and Jack continued their exchange of threats. Milt waved a crutch, telling Jack to shut up while the skinny man explained how he saved the day with his telephone call.

The policeman slapped his hat against his leg. "What about this mess? Who's going to clean up this crap?" The cameraman moved in to record the fresh piles of dung.

Cliff wrote: *Ragged voice, determined, smiling defiant, small piece of jagged metal, giant toes, streets full of crap, at least two chapters.* "That was pretty small, wasn't it?"

"Their feet are tender. Don't take much."

"Never would have guessed—never, not that little thing."

"You saw it."

"And so did that photographer. Do you always give them a souvenir?" Cliff could hear the editor, *who, what, where, when.* "How many times have you pulled that trick? Have you done it in a big city, Chicago? You could stop traffic on Lake Shore Drive. Maybe you have?"

"You ask a lot of questions."

"Listen to every answer—believe half of yours."

Steve led the parade, smoking a cigarette. He was already counting the extra money in his cigar box.

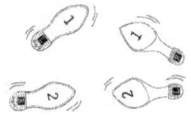

Cliff and Jim Mastras sat in leather chairs, drinking rum. The elephant "incident" was scheduled for the evening news, a report that would guarantee more customers pushing through the gates. On the television screen, they saw Queenie sprawled on the pavement and Steve on his knees, holding her foot. Cliff told Mastras that the camera crew arrived within a few minutes of the phone call.

"They probably guessed it was a stunt, but they couldn't be sure; the traffic was a mess, so they sent the reporter to be safe."

The reporter explained the situation to the viewers. "A carnival train, the Mastras Shows, arrived in town early this morning to set up for next week's fair. What you see behind me is one of the elephants, Queenie, collapsed on Main Street, in front of the First National Bank. It seems Queenie had a serious problem with her foot and was unable to continue walking to the fairgrounds." The reporter moved next to Steve and squatted beside him. Steve probed between the thick toes, his fingers moving over the soft pads. The cameraman zoomed in to fill the screen with a close-up of the big foot.

"Steve Lanning, the elephant trainer, told me earlier that elephants' feet are very sensitive." When the reporter looked straight at the camera, Cliff felt like their eyes connected on the screen.

Steve slowly shifted position as he pushed his fingers deep into the furrows. He scowled while he searched for the cause of the problem and when the cameraman moved to a better angle, Steve shifted sideways to block his view.

The camera switched back to the reporter who needed to say something to fill the time. "As you can see, the trainer is missing part of his ear. He told me it was chewed off by a lion and that's the reason he switched to elephants."

Steve jerked his shoulders and looked up. "I got something." The camera zoomed for a close-up. Again, Steve blocked the view, hesitated, and then turned to face the camera holding a small piece of jagged metal between his fingers.

Cliff explained to Mastras, "He told me he was tired of rocks, the jagged metal looks better, more convincing."

The segment closed with Steve leading the elephants away while the reporter gave the details of the Fair. "Opens tomorrow and runs through Saturday. You can see Queenie and the elephants at the menagerie just inside the front gate. They tell me there are several exciting new rides, and you don't want to miss the wonderful, home-cooked food and homemade ice cream in the local church tents."

Mastras turned off the TV and shook hands with Cliff. "Good work, that's what it's all about."

"I didn't do anything except watch." When Cliff started laughing, he knew he needed to explain. "I'm laughing how Jack got Steve going today, told him he didn't have a dime to make the call."

Mastras said, "Wish I'd seen that. What did he do?"

"He was pretty cool, but I could tell he was mad. Slipped Jack the money and acted like everything was routine."

"No one pulls his chain very often. Lanning's usually giving it to someone else, like Hinkle." Jim Mastras thought for a minute, then asked, "Was Hinkle drunk today? Did he try to get in the act? I know he was."

"Keeps talking about starting a new show. He talked to me about it. What do you think?"

"I never get involved with anything new. Let someone else take the gamble, put up the money, see if it works. He might make some money. Should get good press."

"One thing I'd like to know, the truth—what really happened to Lanning's ear? Do you know?"

"No. What'd he tell you?"

"One time he says a lion chewed it off, other times he says it got shot off by a German in the war. The story changes."

"He might not know himself. Could have happened when he was drinking. You missed that excitement. I never thought he would quit, but I guess he has." Mastras finished his drink, then opened his billfold and handed Cliff a one-hundred-dollar bill. "I appreciate what you're doing."

Cliff folded the one-hundred-dollar bill into a small square, and put it in his front pocket.

"Thank you. I might still be in Morganport if the newspaper handed out bonuses. I hate to think what I would have missed."

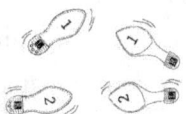

Franklin picked up the telephone.

"Cliff, before you say I told you so, let me say something. Indianapolis is a much better place to live than Morganport. I really like it, but you were right about the newspaper. The only difference between the *Star* and *Pharos Tribune* is the *Star* is thicker. More photographs, longer stories, but it's the same superficial crap. And I brought that damn trunk with me."

Franklin didn't wait to hear Cliff's response. "You called me. How's it going? Are you getting them on page one? What's going on with the dancer? Are you sorry?"

"Sorry? No." Cliff thought about what he was saying. Franklin was the one person he could talk to about what he was doing, how he was learning to deceive the press, taught by a master.

"Embarrassed…a little. Elated with page one and the hundred dollar bonuses Mastras gives me. I rationalize by remembering the facts: An elephant was lying in the middle of the street and a couple of hundred people were witnesses. It's no different than the mall hiring Santa Claus to listen to kids describing the presents they want. There is no Santa Claus and there's nothing in the elephant's foot. And it's giving me time to write about Joan and Steve Lanning's ear and Milt Hinkle jumping out of an airplane. I do more of that because I don't have to write about street sweepers."

"What are you talking about?" Franklin asked. "What foot?"

"Lanning has this stunt when he's parading through town. Queenie's trained to lie down in the street and he pretends there's something wrong with her foot. I call the newspaper and the TV stations and tell them an elephant's blocking traffic. They send reporters. Lanning works them, then finds a stone or a piece of metal stuck in the foot. They get names, pictures, I answer questions, he takes out the metal, page one, no remorse on my part. They know it's a trick, no one hurt."

"They do?"

"Probably. But there was an elephant in the street, and piles of shit." Cliff hesitated. "You said you have Milt's trunk with you?"

"Yes."

"I need a favor, a big one. Will you send it to me?"

"How?"

"Railway Express to Harrisburg. We'll be near there next week."

"What are you going to do with it?"

"I need some clippings to show reporters. Put some braces on it so it doesn't fall apart."

"This is a big favor."

"Thank you. I'll put you in my book."

"What about Katie?"

"She's the main character, counting the days to New York. The more I'm with her, the more I'm amazed by someone who can put up with this to get where she wants to go. I hope some of it rubs off on me. She's teaching me to dance lying down. How's your love life?"

"I have to tell you something."

"Okay."

"Carolyn's coming down this weekend. I've got an assignment to shoot an art exhibit. She's going with me." Franklin waited.

"Art exhibit?"

"She likes art."

"Sounds to me like she likes Franklin."

"And because of that, she's forgetting you."

"Franklin to the rescue."

"Just looking out for a friend."

"And her boobs."

"Now that you mention it, she is a member of the opposite sex."

"Enjoy the exhibit. I'm glad you're learning to dance."

No surprise about Franklin and Carolyn. Maybe he can save her from Morganport.

Katie my love,

A writer, your first? The only thing better would be if he's Irish. I think Walker is an English name. I'll meet him in Boston—yes, Boston! I'm getting things arranged so I can come east early—can I still stay on the train? It sounds like you might not have room in your room. I hope there's some-place for me. This will be my first time away from the church in years and being with you is all the reason I need. In my mind, I see you dancing across America, dancing from town to town like you are meant to do; it's definitely what you bring to the party—a blessing to each audience.

Our members are taking on more and more new projects. They're eager to get involved and some of the AA members are joining in, and that pleases me as much as anything. When the recovering addicts work with the church members helping others, they share a joy that is contagious. It's spreading on its own.

We love you,
Dad

CHAPTER 26

Joan Was Brave Enough to Ride in the Van

After breakfast, Bill and Ruth put on their work clothes. Joan dressed quickly, faded jeans and a work shirt, a scarf for her face and waited patiently on the edge of the bunk while Ruth finished her preparations.

Joan bounced to the ground, then turned to watch Ruth as she struggled down the train steps. She had to turn backward and gripped Bill's hand to lower her heavy body. They waited for the van to the fairgrounds and made a stop near the middle of the train to pick up more workers, then continued through the back streets and were waved through the gate where the driver parked near the office wagons. Bill kissed them goodbye and walked to the Broadway Review to repair a broken spotlight.

The early air was cool and clear. The wide-open midway was serene, with the rides standing still and majestic and the loudspeakers quiet. Ruth and Joan walked, unnoticed, to the menagerie.

Ruth stopped in front and told Joan to go on inside. The girl then walked through the entrance, and briefly looked back at Ruth with a small wave of her hand. When Joan appeared, Little Three hopped to the edge of the pen. Joan rubbed the calf's neck, pleased that the animal had started expecting to be fed when she appeared.

Hearing noise, Jack raised his head and reached for the bottle of wine, drank a mouthful and rolled onto his knees and squinted through the door of the trailer. He blinked and strained his eyes to watch the girl as she carried the hay, then he fell back on the dirty mattress.

Before he could get back to sleep, he remembered his instructions from Steve and swallowed another mouthful. He threw the door open, looked at the steps and sat and slowly scooted down, one step at a time. On the ground, he stood upright and grabbed a stick to steady his steps.

"That little darlin' likes you." Jack's words were slurred. "Sugar, hay, sugar and hay. She got enough?"

Joan patted Little Three on the head. "Enough for now."

"You want to feed the elephants?" Jack's knees felt limp, and he had to sit down.

"Yes."

Joan walked out of the tent, returning with her arms filled with hay. She scattered it in front of Queenie, then walked back and forth until the three elephants had been fed. Jack stayed on the stool, considering his options of how to get back to the bottle of wine.

When the animals were all fed, Jack pulled five one-dollar bills out of his pocket, keeping them concealed in the palm of his hand. Steve's instructions played in his mind and Jack fought the impulse to put the bills back in his pocket. Five dollars would keep him supplied with wine for the rest of the week.

He heard Steve in his head: *Don't tell her it's from me, don't tell her where it comes from, just make damned sure she gets it. If I ever find out you didn't give it to her, I'll break your fingers.* Jack flexed his fingers around the bills and extended his arm so Joan could see the money.

"Work around here, you get paid." Jack motioned for her to take the money.

Joan grabbed the bills and backed away. She knew he was drunk, but she'd gotten used to showing her face in front of him. Five dollars helped, and her father was slightly drunk on Saturday night on the farm. She turned and ran to the cook tent to find Ruth.

"How was the calf?" Ruth asked, as she put her arm around Joan.

"Hungry. They give me five dollars." Joan handed the money to Ruth, who handed it back.

"You keep it, honey."

Joan kept one dollar. By the end of the day, she knew she would have three dollars in her suitcase. "I want to pay some."

Mornings and afternoons, Joan left the train to help in the menagerie. Ruth no longer had to go with her; Joan was brave enough to ride the van.

Inside the gate, she made her way behind the tents, out of sight, away from the midway traffic, until she got to the back of the menagerie, then carried clumps of hay to the animals.

After Little Three, she moved to the chimp's cage and laughed at its grinning face when the monkey stuck its hands through the bars. The hippo was the only animal in the menagerie that didn't respond to her. Most of the time the huge animal stood motionless, staring at nothing, and Joan imagined it dimly thinking about Africa. The elephants rocked back and forth and swung their trunks, searching for food. They made noise deep in their chests.

Engrossed with her work, Joan didn't notice the marks staring at her. She had a reason for being there and if she started to feel their eyes, she moved into the shadows and used a shovel to pick up piles of manure, then sat on a stool and brushed Little Three until the calf's coat was clean and shiny. The menagerie tent was like the farm buildings, only the animals were different.

"What are you doing with your money?" Steve already knew. It was a small town and the buzz had spread. Joan was a sucker for shiny rings and bracelets and cotton candy.

"Give most of it to Ruth, keep a little." Joan held her face away from Steve's eyes.

"You like feeding them, don't you? Taking care of the calf." Steve knew when the marks saw her, they were shocked, like they were with Bill. When they realized it was a young girl, they forced their eyes away.

Joan didn't look at him. She nodded her head.

Steve had no trouble looking at her face, and watched her pull clumps of cotton candy with her twisted lips. He asked if she would like to make more money.

"I guess."

Steve told Jack to move the calf closer to the entrance. "The marks see her, they stop."

CHAPTER 27

How to Beat
the Fixed Games

Cliff held the door for Katie and the reporter, then led them to a booth, the same booth where Katie had been sitting the night Cliff jumped on the train. It was their favorite place, good atmosphere for a reporter.

He knew how this reporter felt about interviewing a man who jumped out of an airplane without a parachute. Compared it to covering public works meetings; it was jalapeno peppers instead of onion soup. Cliff had also promised a conversation with the wild animal trainer and maybe a stripper...maybe.

Reporters arrived on the midway with different instructions; some told to listen, others want to expose the abuse of freaks, or the bad working conditions. Some want close-up footage showing how to beat the fixed games.

Cliff was learning to control them by taking them to the right people. Steve Lanning was one of the right people; he could talk and lead a reporter where he wanted him to go. At first, his rough voice and menacing eyes were intimidating—until he talked about the power of the press and then reporters felt lucky to be part of something bigger than what they had expected.

Cliff had explained to Katie how he felt like he was doing them a favor. "My service to journalism, give them a thrill. I can see it

in their eyes when they find out I'm one of them, on a different assignment."

Steve and Milt, on his crutches, entered the dining car and Cliff saw the reporter staring. They should be stared at—two characters with scars and marks to prove their years in a violent setting.

While Bruce Malvern checked the spelling of their names, he looked around the Pie Car, then at Katie, and struggled to keep his attention on the men. He told himself it was obvious what Katie added; a soft touch, as she smiled and listened. Her presence buffed the rough edges. Malvern heard Steve's words, but he wanted to switch the interview to Katie.

When Steve stopped talking, Milt lifted a copy of *True* magazine and told the reporter, "First and last time anyone tried this stunt. Dumb—made the front cover. And I ain't been able to walk since. I'm getting ready to open a new show about it, lining up my backers now."

Malvern flipped through the magazine, scanning the story and the drawings. "No photographs?"

"There was some in the Laredo paper, Spanish. Got a few copies in my trunk, but they're faded bad. Never been back to see if I could get the originals."

"Too bad. I can write the story, but pictures would make it better. I'd like to see that newspaper."

Milt traced the drawings with his finger. "We'll use these in my new show. People like true stories. I'll tell them all about it."

Cliff had listened to Milt. He wondered, *will the marks crowd around to hear him talk? In their minds is the old West still magic, cattle rustlers and bank robbers? Will they buy tickets? Maybe they will, maybe they won't, worth a try.*

Cliff understood Malvern's reluctance. Even with the *True* magazine in his hands, the reporter was following his training— question everything, get three sources, check the facts, don't accept them from just one person—especially when the person talking wanted his name in the paper and would say anything to get it there. "I'll get you the Laredo paper. I've seen it."

"What year was this?" Malvern asked Milt. "Were you in Mexico or Texas?"

"Nineteen thirty-seven in old Mexico, Nuevo Laredo, across the Rio Grande."

Malvern turned to Steve. "You were there, too?"

Steve exhaled cigarette smoke and nodded his head.

"Did you see him jump?"

"No, but I heard the crowd and I saw them carry him on a stretcher and I saw the dead cow and I spent a week in the Laredo jail, a hellhole. You can believe it. Just like it says in that magazine. What it don't say is how we crawled away from there flat broke, no pesos."

"That's right, wasn't nothin' else I could do, I had to jump." Milt's forehead shone with sweat. "You need to understand—we was close to the biggest jackpot ever, for us. But none of it was coming our way 'less someone jumped outta that airplane. Ended up it was me. Fifty thousand Mexicans had come to the rodeo, come to see the show. We had the best cowboys, meanest bulls in Mexico. And they'd done their job, put on a good show, but them people wanted what we'd promised, what they'd paid for, some had walked three days to see. They wanted to see a brave cowboy bulldog a steer from an airplane. And Chupalto, the promoter, held all the cards...all the cards. Steve here was in his office, eyes on the prize—pesos—but it didn't matter, Chupalto was the *man*, held the pesos, and we wasn't never getting any, none, unless someone jumped. Airplane circled, I was hanging from the wing, watching the cow run like it was drunk. When the plane got low, right over, I let go and flew and smashed the cow and the crowd was on their feet, waiting for the dust to clear. When the wind blew, they saw a dead cow and a paralyzed cowboy. But they got what they paid for."

Milt turned to Steve and waited for the elephant trainer to say something.

Steve nodded his head. "It was the biggest deal we ever tried." He stopped talking and waited until the reporter stared, waiting.

"Something always went wrong. We never hit the jackpot. If it wasn't broken legs and dead cows, it was something else. Milt Hinkle always had a reason. He's always had a reason why no one ever got any money. As long as I been around him, it's been the same bad deal. This next one might be the same, might not. We keep trying. Don't ask me why."

Cliff sank in his seat, hoping Milt would ignore Steve's remarks, but the old cowboy unclenched his jaw and said, "Hard words, hard, hard. Fact is, you got out of Mexico with a wad of pesos stuck down your pants. You know you did. I got out with a busted-up body. Don't be telling this young man lies."

Steve raised his voice, shouting, "Damn, Milt, you don't know a lie from the shit on your shoes. It ain't no lie. You cried broke after every rodeo we ever played. If you ain't the biggest thief in the world, I don't know who is."

Milt shook his head. "No! The truth is, you was always too drunk to know anything. If there was any money left, it didn't make no sense to give it to a drunk. That ain't no lie." Milt looked at the reporter, then said to Steve, "We ain't doing ourselves no favors talking like this."

Cliff saw a swift agreement pass between the two old actors and he understood they had completed act two of their rehearsed performance. The tension between them struck the reporter and he tightened his grip on his pencil.

Katie unfolded her hands, lifting them with palms up, and asked Milt to talk more, then she softly clapped them back together and leaned against Cliff, ready to let the old man's high tenor voice carry her to Mexico.

Cliff shifted in the seat and tried to read what Malvern had written. Then he thought about the notebooks in a canvas bag under his bunk. He had already filled five of them with descriptions and scribbles, but he was starting to think that bags full of money might be better than flimsy words.

Steve offered cigarettes and lit them for Bruce Malvern and Cliff. Katie stretched her arms across the table, and reached for Milt's hands. She didn't say anything and the gesture as she gripped his huge hands was like a mother telling her child it's a good thing for him to do. Milt was uncomfortable feeling her small, soft fingers, but he was locked in her grip and slowly relaxed his arms. They sat quietly for a few minutes while the reporter scanned his notes.

Bruce Malvern tapped his pencil on the table and nodded his head, then smiled and said to Milt, "I don't think you got those stiff legs from being run over by a train. Your being in town deserves space in the paper. I'll write it."

Cliff broke his silence and added what he had learned about Nuevo Laredo. "I had the Spanish newspapers translated. It's more than a story about a young cowboy doing something dumb, it's about a man keeping a promise." He raised his voice. "It's a great feature. You'll never meet men like these two again. Milt's father *was* the sheriff of Dodge City, Kansas. When he was a little boy, Milt heard about Bat Masterson, Jesse James. He's got a trunk full of pictures of himself with Jack Dempsey, Johnny Weissmuller, Tarzan. And now he's dying on a carnival train. Steve here is in the Hall of Fame, former star of the Ringling Brothers Circus. Trust me...you won't regret writing about these two."

The reporter was laughing as he listened. Cliff joined him and continued with a laughing chant.

"Meet Milt Hinkle, meet Milt Hinkle, last of the real cowboys, see the man shake his hand, see the man and shake his hand. The man without a parachute, alive on the inside."

Steve rubbed his ear and looked at Cliff, thinking, *we got the college boy now. He's convinced himself. He won't turn down partner in a sideshow starring the only man in the world to wrestle a steer from an airplane; hell, it's starting to sound good to me. Maybe we can win some serious green.*

Bruce Malvern finished writing and closed his notebook. Milt took a breath, then pushed up on his crutches and thanked the reporter for listening, and he and Steve left the dining car.

Katie leaned against Cliff. "I love that old man."

Staring because he just finished a strange interview, Bruce Malvern looked at Cliff. "Not a bad human-interest piece. You're doing a good job promoting him. It has to be more fun than arrest reports."

Cliff looked at the empty side of the booth where Milt and Steve had been sitting. "It's too early to tell if it was a good decision. You will do something?"

"I will. Thanks for setting it up." Malvern looked at Katie. "Will you tell me about your life under the big top?"

"I'd rather not."

"Why?"

"Milt. Milt's story is better. I don't want to interfere."

"Don't you want your name in the paper? Cliff tells me you're headed for New York."

Katie changed the subject. "You should help him." Her body tensed when she talked. "He wants to have a show on the midway. I wish you would help him."

"I might be able to get him some coverage, but I'd like to know more about you."

Her silence surprised Malvern. Cliff understood. "If you want to know about her, watch her dance."

"I did, last night."

Malvern checked his watch, "Got to go, deadlines, always deadlines." He stopped. "Tell me again, you really were going to be the editor?"

"Yes."

"You didn't want it?"

"I like reporting, but not on sewers and budgets. The biggest story I had was the purchase of a new street sweeper."

Malvern thanked him for the tip and shook hands with Katie. "I wish you'd consider talking to me. I'm intrigued. I've never met anyone…like either one of you."

The booths in the Pie Car filled and the beds in the coaches filled, gifts from the rain clouds.

Katie wished she could feel the car swaying, she wanted to keep moving to New York, but there were still six fairs to go, six weeks, eight shows a day. Over three hundred more Broadway Review shows that she would scratch off her list—a day at a time. When the last one was finished, she would pack her suitcase and catch a ride to Radio City Music Hall.

Katie asked, "Do you think I was rude not talking to him?"

"If he knew you were teaching Joan to dance, it would be a very big story for him."

"No. *No.* And he won't find out. Please tell me he won't find out." She squeezed her hands together. "It would be terrible. She's afraid of so many things. You said it wasn't news. I want her to learn to dance but not for the newspapers. It's my gift to her. She forgets her face when she dances, like I forget the midway. Everyone forgets when they dance."

"No, he won't find out. It isn't news." Cliff reached for Katie and she leaned against him. He said, "Six weeks is a long time, too many train rides. Mastras wants me to drive the station wagon to Boston. Will you ride with me, get off the train?"

Katie nodded her head.

Cliff held her hands. "We can go through Lowell, see Jack Kerouac's house. I want to show it to you. See the home of a real writer. Would you like to do that?"

"I want to be with you."

"Do you care if Steve goes?"

Katie didn't answer.

Cliff held her cheeks in his hands.

She moved away. "Don't make me say anything." Katie dropped her head. "I don't want to say anything." When she saw the look on Cliff's face, she spoke in a whisper. "He isn't a nice man and I'm not looking forward to spending time with him. And I'm already sorry I said it."

"He isn't that bad. Thank you for going."

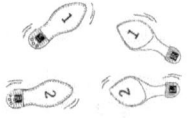

Dad –

A newspaper reporter wanted to interview me today—Cliff invited him to the show but I don't want to be in the paper—not as a dancer in the strip show. I agreed to be there to help Cliff do his job. He's good at getting them to do interviews. They all want a chance to hear and see the inside of a

carnival. I don't want to be interviewed because I'm not part
of the story—not like Steve and Milt and Pagan and Jack and
Mr. Mastras. They're the good story. Cliff knows it and makes
sure the reporters talk to them, but this one was determined
to talk to me. I hope I didn't hurt Cliff's chance of getting in
the paper. I don't think I did. And if I did it would be all right
with Cliff. He's starting to be on the same schedule as I am—
the journey will end in New York City.

I'm riding to Massachusetts with Cliff this week so we can
go through Lowell to see Jack Kerouac's house. Cliff thinks he
visits his mother there, but spends most of his time away—on
the road. The bad part of the trip is Steve Lanning's going
with us. He's crude and foul-mouthed, but Cliff likes him be-
cause he's an elephant trainer and was a star with the Ring-
ling Brothers Circus. You can add him to the list of characters
you've been able to spend time with—I don't think you'll get
too far convincing him to help the church.

Thinking about you being here lifts my spirits – I love you!

"She's going with us." Cliff and Steve were drinking coffee in
the cook tent.

"I better wash my ass."

"She was right, said you weren't a nice man, she's right."

"I clean up, she'll change her mind."

Cliff finished his coffee. "I'm getting some more. You want any?
Going to be a long night." He returns to the table with full cups.

"Maybe I shouldn't go?" Steve questioned.

"You can go." Cliff considered his words. "This is important,
listen." He waited. Steve put down the cup. "You can go. But don't

say anything about Joan. I was afraid you were going to say something to that reporter, Malvern."

"No. Hell, no. Save her for something better."

CHAPTER 28

The Difference Is,
on the Midway, You Pay First

t midnight, the lights on the rides went off. The teardown crews emerged from the shadows, wielding hammers and wrenches, and the steel garden wilted like dead leaves after a hard frost. The heavy canvas drifted flat over the flattened dirt. As the trapped air escaped, the gray fabric heaved and relaxed in a thin blanket. Jack directed the extra help through the steps of rolling the canvas, coiling the ropes, lifting crates, and loading the wagons that were moved to the train and rolled onto the flat railroad cars.

"Queenie, Alice." Steve called the elephants into formation. They walked trunk to tail, with a few marks following, caught in the animals' grip. The giants followed Steve until he led them up the ramps and they disappeared into the boxcar.

Jack and Milt arranged their beds of straw, and twisted the cap on a fresh bottle of vodka. In his room, Steve washed his arms and legs and dried with a stale towel and fell asleep in his clothes, knowing that in a few hours he would jump when the train started to move.

The jerking and screeching metal snapped Steve's eyes open. He grabbed his coat and slammed the door and jumped to the ground, matching his steps to the speed of the departing train. He stood on the solid cinders. *Not this time, no train for this old man. Jack and Milt can ease their way with vodka, but not me.*

Cliff stopped the car and waited for Steve to open the door and take the front seat.

Fresh air blew through the windows and Cliff wished Katie was next to him, but she insisted that Steve take the spot so she could stretch out in the back seat, legs up. Cliff realized he was nervous about anything Steve might do or say to ruin the trip.

The sun pushed through the clouds, warming the breeze, throwing long shadows over the low hills of western Massachusetts. The car was painted bright yellow with *Mastras Shows* lettered on the doors, and it drew stares as they took their time along the main streets, enjoying the storefronts and window displays.

Cliff stared at Dan's Pawn Shop and compared it to a banner on the midway. Next door was the Quality Clothing Store, done in red and gold and there were flags streaming over the Ford parking lot. He compared the midway with the main street. Bright signs and banners tempted you to come in the door. *The difference is, on the midway, you pay first.*

The train wouldn't get to the fairgrounds until late in the day; that gave them time to linger in Lowell and act like tourists. Cliff's reasons were vague. He couldn't allow himself to believe the reason was because he saw himself as an author and not a reporter. He needed to see the house where Kerouac lived when he wasn't on the road.

Looking at the house won't turn me into an author but it might help. The Hemingway house in Key West helped me understand the financial benefits of being a good writer.

Steve asked again, "Who is this guy? Never heard of him. What'd he write?"

"*On The Road*. I'll give it to you."

"As good as Hemingway? He use big words?"

"Different..." Cliff opened his window. "Not better, different, like this fast, furious, frenzied air." He tilted his head through the window, letting the wind whip his hair. "Hemingway is all control. Kerouac's out of control." He looked at his watch. "His house isn't too far."

"What are we going to see?"

"Just a house. I think his mother lives there. Did you see the Hemingway house in Key West?"

"Just a house." Steve looked at his package of cigarettes. "I'm out. Stop someplace."

Katie leaned over the seat. "Yes, please stop. I need to use the bathroom."

Her voice surprised Cliff. She was being very quiet, curious about looking at a writer's house. *She's reading* On The Road *because I talked about it and she heard the urgency in my voice.*

Cliff drove while Steve read the newspaper article by Bruce Malvern. "Damned good." Steve complimented Cliff. "You got the touch with reporters."

Former rodeo star Milt Hinkle, best known as the only cowboy to bulldog a steer from an airplane, a stunt that left him crippled, has announced a new show featuring memorabilia from his thirty years as the star of Wild West productions when he performed with Buffalo Bill and Geronimo. The beautiful Katie Flannigan is dancing in the midway musical show to support herself on her journey to the Radio City Music Hall. Ex-reporter Cliff Walker is exploring his options as a press agent with a traveling carnival. He said a book is in his future.

"He got it pretty good about Milt. We'll use it, turn it into some serious money."

"How did he find out my name?" Katie asked. "Did you tell him?"

"I didn't tell him. I promised you I wouldn't."

"I didn't want my name in the paper."

"That's what made him dig for it—good reporter."

Cliff stopped the car and spent several minutes reading the story, the descriptions of Milt's broken legs, his daredevil leap from the airplane, and Katie's journey to New York City.

He handed the paper back to Steve. "You—and Milt, if he's sober—make it easy. When you talk, they know they're hearing the real thing. I can tell them all kinds of crap, but when it comes from you, it sounds right. We can keep this up for the rest of the season. Kick it up if Milt's show opens. You really think a sideshow with Milt will be a winner?"

Cliff laughed at his question.

"You ain't going to make me to say it. I think it will do all right. Better than him taking money off me."

"You really don't care about anything but money?"

"Nothing. Nothing else. Not no more."

"What about making Milt famous? Money or not?"

"He's been famous, I been famous and broke, money's better. You'd take famous over money?" Steve asked the question like there could only be one answer.

"I'd like both."

"If you want to be famous, write about your girlfriend teaching the freak to dance. That could do it."

Cliff couldn't breathe and he jerked the car in gear. He hoped the squealing tires would erase what Steve just said; maybe Katie didn't hear it. Quiet in the backseat. He looked in the rearview mirror, but couldn't see her. He knew she heard. She had heard Steve's ragged words *"teach the freak."*

What will she do? Maybe nothing. Maybe she'll get out of the car the next time we stop. Maybe she'll ask me to push Steve out of the car.

They drove in silence, weaving through traffic, and Katie said, "You're disgusting. You make me sick." Her soft voice ripped through the car and Cliff listened as if she were a stranger. "Please stop, I need a bathroom." He couldn't see her in the mirror. She had both hands over her mouth, heaving. When the car stopped, she ran to the gas station.

Steve rolled down his window and Cliff sat rigid behind the wheel.

"You dumb bastard, you apologize! You tell her you're sorry. Do you ever think before you open your stupid mouth?"

Steve dropped his shoulders. When he saw Katie come out of the station, he went to her and pulled on his cigarette and said, "I forgot you were back there. I'm sorry."

"Thank you." Then she laid down in the back seat with her arms across her eyes.

Cliff held the steering wheel as if he were gripping a hammer, fingers clenched around the rim. What he feared had happened. Steve's mouth, didn't think, didn't guard his words, and now he ruined the trip. *He doesn't give a damn about a young girl learning to dance, to live, forgetting how she looks, about the friendship between the two girls, the trust.*

Cliff knew Joan's story would be told, someday. Not on a sheet of newspaper to be read and thrown away. A book—pages for readers to hold where they shared the hopes and loves and fears, faith...someday.

Someday they would read about Katie Flannigan, the dancer, stretched out on the backseat of a yellow car, sobbing because she couldn't make Joan Ryerson look normal.

Entering Lowell, they passed deserted textile factories with weeds growing through the parking lots, a sagging slum. He drove slowly past a row of two-story frame houses built close to the sidewalk. The wooden balconies leaned over the street.

Cliff glanced at a piece of paper, then looked for the numbers.

"There it is, Nine Lupine Road, about what I expected, just another house, duplex. In a few years, this house will have a plaque on the front door, recognition of Jack Kerouac, a local boy made good."

"Listen to me, listen. You don't need to see his house. You don't need no one else. Write about Milt yourself. I watch you with the press, tellin' them about Milt's jump. You do it better than he does, like you was there." Steve blew a stream of smoke through the window. "I am going to put together a new show with him. Make some money out of those stiff legs. You write the pitch, work the press. Help me make it work."

"How much money?"

As he waited for an answer, Cliff looked in the mirror and saw Katie looking at him. A thin smile, then she tapped Steve on the shoulder. "I apologize for calling you disgusting. I wish you wouldn't call Joan that, but I'm just as bad for calling you disgusting."

Steve turned in the seat so he could look in her eyes. "Truth is, I've been called that before, but not since I quit drinking. You're a nice girl."

"Thank you. It's nice that you want to help Milt. I know you've been friends a long time."

Steve didn't offer an amount. Instead, he surprised Cliff with a question. "What are you doing here?"

Cliff didn't know how to answer. He took his time before he said, "What do you mean? I want to know how much money."

"What are you doing here? Did you really graduate from college?"

Cliff nodded. "Really, I did. I'd show you my diploma, but my mother framed it to hang in the living room."

"And you passed up the editor's job?"

"I really did. You want to know why a young man with a college degree, an officer in the Navy, good family, promising newspaper career would be riding around the country with a beat-up elephant trainer? Like Katie said, not a nice man."

"It don't add up."

"Do you believe I'm a college graduate?"

"Maybe. But it don't matter if you are or not. You know how to con the press, the rest don't matter."

Cliff opened his wallet and pulled out an identification card. "Here's my Navy ID. Proves I was an officer in the United States Navy."

Steve squinted at the small type, the picture. "Guys around here can get you one of those. Get one for the FBI if you want it."

"This one's real. Believe it or not."

"Like I said, it don't matter—not to me. I can see why you'd want to get away from Indiana. Don't need college to figure that out. I still want to know what you're doin' here."

Cliff talked with a rhythm. "You know—what I'm doing—here. Same reason—you slid down—the drainpipe. That's what they should do for graduation. Instead of caps and gowns, we should slide down drainpipes. They asked me what I was going to do; I said I didn't know because I've never done enough to know. How do you know you want to be a lawyer if you've never tried it? When you slide down the drainpipe, you don't know where you're going to land. I'm sliding down drainpipes."

Katie said, "I think I know where you're going to land."

"Tell me. No, don't tell me." Cliff asked Steve, "How many kids, people, have you seen run away with the circus in forty years? I'll turn it back to you—why did you ask that stupid question?"

"What'd you learn in college?"

"I read a lot, Thoreau. You know who he was?"

"No. am I about to?"

"A smart man, turned his back on normal, lived in a cabin, wrote what he thought was important, not what everyone else thought was important."

"Did it make him any money?" Steve asked. "You know money's God to me."

"Thoreau said it's vain to write when you haven't lived. Best thing I got out of college. You're helping me live so I can write… someday. Big part of why I'm riding around with you is so I won't end up telling my son how much I hated my job, like my dad and the post office. I'm a lot like you. You don't hate your job, do you? Are you sorry you didn't stay on the farm?"

"No, worse than death. Sliding down the drainpipe about killed me, but the farm would have for sure." He asked Cliff to let him out in front of a restaurant across from where the train would be parked.

"Thanks for the ride. Maybe I'll try your buddy there, Karack. Feel like I know him, visiting his house and all. His mother makes some good coffee, don't she?"

"Where do you get that stuff? I wish he could meet you. He'd probably listen to what you have to say."

Cliff started to pull away, then stopped and rolled down the window. "I'll buy you a steak if you read *On The Road*, then we'd have something to talk about."

Cliff and Katie drove to an empty field where they could see the tracks and waited for the train. Like teenagers in a drive-in movie, they rested in each other's arms and Cliff talked in a low voice about seeing the house.

"Just an old house, but a celebrity writer grew up there."

"I'll write Dad, tell him about seeing his house. He wants to ride the train so he can be on the road—for a little while." Katie paused. "Do you know how the Irish worship writers? I can't wait until you meet him; you'll find out. I just want to hear the two of you talk."

"I don't have anything to show him. Some of the wild stuff Stoneman rejected, all blue lines. I couldn't show him that stuff. I can talk about writing, just not do it…yet. I want to tell you something else."

"All right."

"I told Steve." He hesitated. "Maybe your dad."

Katie kissed his cheek. "I'm ready."

Cliff told her how much he admired her commitment to dance in New York. "I went to college hoping to find that kind of goal, but it didn't happen. I think it will, sometime, but it hasn't yet, maybe in Spain."

"You want to write. Isn't that enough?"

"Yes. That's my goal, but it isn't as clear to me as dancing is to you. I don't have your confidence. I'm afraid I can't do it. I know I can write newspaper stuff, but that's not what I want to do. In college, I knew I didn't want to work for the post office. I knew I didn't want to work for a big company. I thought about being a lawyer because my uncle is, but that didn't last too long. I've never told anyone else how I feel. Hard for me to admit."

"Is that all?"

"No."

"What else?" She added, "You've got a lot of confidence or you wouldn't be here."

"You got me here." He sat up straight. "When I graduated from high school, I got arrested for stealing beer and spent a week in jail, and the judge told me I could go to college or reform school. I decided college was the best choice. No one on the show knows about it…but it wouldn't matter, half of them have long arrest records."

"Why did you steal beer?"

"Too young to buy it. I wanted to be a big shot with my friends. The week in jail didn't bother me. I was pretty sure I'd be able to go to college. It worked out. I'm not sure I should say this, but part of me looks at jail like something I'm a little bit proud of, part of my trip. Like I'm looking at this job with the carnival. We—me—we found out how good beer made us feel. Did you feel that the first time you had a drink?"

"I know what you're talking about. I thought it was sweeter than I'd imagined."

"You thought it was sweet? Is that all you remember, not how it made you feel?"

"Not really. I don't remember how it made me feel."

"That's amazing."

"Because I remember exactly where I was, how I reacted and exactly how it made me feel…like I was floating outside my body and everything was beautiful and I was beautiful."

"Does it still make you feel that way?"

"Yes."

"No wonder you like to drink."

"Steve warned me about drinking too much."

"I guess he should know."

"Before I even joined the Navy, I knew I didn't want any part of making it a career. All I wanted was the travel and avoiding the Army draft so I listened to an older officer who'd become a good friend and when we had to request duty assignments, he told me about a ship on the list that spent its time in the Indian Ocean and had a reputation as bad duty because it was painted white to deal with the heat and all you saw were camels and women wearing black masks. But he explained that the ship was really on a diplomatic mission to remote parts of the world and spent most of the time in exotic ports entertaining local dignitaries. I made it my first choice and asked him to not tell anyone else about it and, in fact, he helped me add to the rumors that it was a terrible ship and when our assignments were announced, I got it as my first choice.

"It turned out to be one of the best naval tours anyone could imagine. It convinced me that conventional paths aren't good for me. Now I'm thinking my conventional path is the unconventional one for most people. Does that make sense?"

"Yes. And please tell my dad what you just told me."

"He'll understand?"

"Remember I told you he's a defrocked priest who sometimes drinks a little too much…not exactly Father Convention. What else do you want to tell me?"

"So, when I was discharged from the Navy, I decided to go to journalism school to pursue writing. Again, the conventional route didn't resonate with me. I could tell from the professors that journalism was all about following rigid rules: punctuation, sentence structure, story guides and following the formats dictated by the newspaper you'd be working for. After one year of journalism school, I went back to Morganport to a job at the daily newspaper and after one year of that, I ran away with you."

Katie sat up straight as she listened. "You're going to tell me something about Spain?"

"One way or another, I want to go to Spain and write, and learn to write like you dance."

"I understand. Will you tell my dad?"

"If you want me to."

"I think you should tell as many people as possible, especially yourself."

"Why?"

"Makes it more real. And he'll want to go with you."

CHAPTER 29

Let Her Go!
You Want to Kiss Someone,
Kiss Me!

Katie slipped through the back entrance of the animal menagerie, holding her breath against the stench of the ripe cages. She surprised Joan by wrapping her in a tight hug.

"Guess who," Katie whispered.

"I guess Katie." Joan turned; she knew she was right. "No one else would do that...except Momma or Ruth." When the girls looked at each other, they shared their brief past, cotton candy, dancing, crying, laughing.

"Let's get a Coke."

Joan's eyes brightened, then faded. She shook her head, "Can you bring 'em here?"

"Sure can." She was still afraid to show her face on the midway, but she had grown confident enough to learn new dance steps.

"Take my money," Joan said. "I can pay now."

Katie looked at the folded bill and understood the significance of the offer, so she accepted the money. "I'll bring back the change. I'll buy hot dogs. You want a hot dog?"

Sitting on bales of hay behind the tent, they ate while Katie talked about the day. "It's nice you can feed your calf."

"I gave it a bottle when it was a baby."

"I have a dog in California. He's with my parents. I miss him." Katie rubbed her eyes and looked away. "I'm sorry we're not going to have time to dance now. My call's in a few minutes, I'll come back later, we'll have more time."

When Joan smiled, Katie could tell what she was doing. It wasn't a smile like one might expect, but mostly it was the movement of the muscles around her mouth and the light in her eyes.

"That's okay. I'll work on what you showed me yesterday, make it better, you'll see later, I'll be ready."

When Katie walked back inside the tent, the dim light blocked her view. No marks were peering in the cages. One man wearing a hat stepped cautiously in front of the elephants, long strings of hair curled over the back of his neck, his shoulders moved up and down like he was trying to protect his head.

Katie approached him and asked, "Excuse me, do you have the time?" As soon as she realized what she had asked, and the way the man looked at her, Katie shook her head. "I mean what time is it; do you know what time it is?" Her lungs caught in a short gasp.

He hid his watch behind his back. "I sure have the time for you, you sweet thing."

Katie realized no one else was in the menagerie. Smelling the liquor on his breath, she backed away, "I have to be at work. Can you tell me the time?"

"Where do you work?" He moved his hand to his side. "You a stripper? We have time."

"Dancer, not a stripper."

He grabbed her and pulled her into his arms. "Will you dance for me? I bet you're a real good dancer. Dance for me."

Katie tried to pull away. "Let me go!" He tightened his grip and pressed his face against her neck. Katie screamed for help and kicked the man's legs. "Please! Let go of me. Jack!"

"Dance first. I want a dance. I want more than a dance, dance in your pants."

From the shadows, Joan ran toward them, screaming. "Let her go!" Her contorted face was bright red, jagged lips, swollen, glistening with saliva, eyes burning. She planted her feet and pushed her face close to the man. "Let her go! You want to kiss someone, kiss me!"

Joan lunged toward the man and he stumbled back, shuffling his feet to get away from the horrible face. Joan yelled, "Jack, Jack, help! Help us!"

The man released Katie's arm. "What the hell is that?" He couldn't look at Joan and covered his mouth with his hands and turned his head away. "What the hell is that?"

Swinging a cane, Jack ran through the back of the tent and pushed the steel point against the man's chest. "Get out or I'll bury this hook in your stupid head. Move your ass…*now!*"

Joan's face—and the pressure of the steel point—forced the wind out of the man's lungs. "What in God's name is that? I'm going, I'm going." When he turned toward the entrance, Jack pushed the point into his back, prodding him faster. He kept pushing and shoved the point into the back of the man's neck as he ordered him to get off the fairgrounds.

"If I see you back here, I'll cut you up for the lion. You'll get more than your money's worth."

They watched the entrance to make sure the man was gone and Joan shook all over, crying. Katie put her hand on Joan's neck. "I'm sorry, so sorry." She rubbed Joan's back. "I'm sorry that had to happen."

The girls hugged each other. "It's all right. He's gone. We're all right."

Katie held Joan tight. "You saved me. I don't know what would have happened." She kissed Joan on the cheek and wiped the tears from her eyes. "Thank you. Thank you."

Joan tightened her arms around Katie, shaking from the encounter. She thought, *Will a man ever want me? Maybe, if he looks like Bill.*

When Katie left to go back to work, Joan couldn't stay inside the menagerie and followed Jack behind the tent. She sat on a folding chair and he offered her a can of beer. "Steady you down. Beer will help, always helps. You was pretty brave."

Joan looked at the can, and wondered what it tasted like. Her father drank beer on Saturday night and her mother didn't like it, saying it wasted money and made him change, made him act bad.

Joan wanted to know how a can of beer could make anyone change. Her father didn't look any different. The only thing he did was stare at the stars, swear at the corn and sleep, but her mother insisted he changed.

She held the can and smelled it and raised it to her lips and slurped the fizzy liquid through her twisted lips. Some of the beer escaped down her chin and she grimaced and spit the rest of it out of her mouth. "Terrible, tastes terrible. You like that?"

Jack nodded his head. "Don't waste it."

Beer ran down the front of Joan's blouse, soaking through the thin material, shiny foam spread over her chin. Jack grabbed the can out of her hand.

"Damn, girl, give it to me." Jack's eyes rolled as he strained to focus on two cans, one in each hand.

Joan took back the beer. "Try again." She drank a mouthful and swirled it in her mouth and choked as it burned down her throat. "Bad, bad. Tastes bad, Jack. Why do you drink bad stuff?"

"Take another drink, you'll see." He watched her swallow again, this time without gagging, and she looked at the can and drank again.

"Now you see why? Fly up to the pink clouds is why."

Steve had heard the commotion from inside the cab of his truck where he'd been reading and when he walked inside the tent, he knew he was looking at one of the strangest things he'd ever seen. He looked to make sure, to confirm he really saw Jack sitting with the deformed girl, who was finishing the first alcoholic drink of her life.

Watch her turn silly. She'll toss her cookies in his lap.

Steve told Jack, "Make some coffee. She can't go to the train like that." He looked at Joan's thin arms; he knew how fast the beer would affect her. She leaned sideways in the chair and Steve had to hold her shoulder to keep her from falling. "Easy. Put the can down. You're feeling it pretty good, ain't you?"

Joan giggled, then dropped her head between her knees and vomited a shooting stream of beer and cotton candy until her stomach was empty. Steve moved his feet.

He helped her lie down in the wagon and told Jack to cover her up and watch her. "When she wakes up, give her coffee. Tell her I said to drink it. Be sure and tell her. Don't mess this up…you hear me? You stay with her until she's okay to go back to the train. You hear me? You hear me good."

In the morning, Cliff walked through the empty midway, taking his time to make notes. The contrast with the times when people filled the spaces between the tents and rides and food trailers was like seeing an aquarium with no fish.

Katie had told him she'd be at the Broadway Review tent and through the quiet he heard music playing inside the tent. And when he got closer, he knew what was going on: Katie was teaching Joan more dance steps.

He stood where they couldn't see him, but he had a clear view of the stage. The girls were already shiny with sweat as they moved to the driving beat of the music. Joan was laughing and smiling with her twisted lips mouthing the words.

Joan could dance.

Her disfigured face had made Cliff think she couldn't do anything except feed the calf, but there she was, keeping time to the drums. She concentrated on Katie's steps and mimicked them. She kept time to the music and had improved from the first time he watched her. She didn't have Katie's style, her flowing motion, but no one had that, only Katie. Cliff had watched them practice before, watching their relationship form and grow, and he felt like he was part of an experiment.

Joan's feet moved in unison with Katie's, her body flowing, and Cliff was frozen where he stood. When Katie saw him in the shadows she pursed her lips and shook her head telling him to stay put and smiled to let him know she was glad he was watching, to see the progress her pupil was making. The girls held hands and twirled, lifted by the lush background music, violins and saxophones and the singers' harmony.

"Bounce on the balls of your feet, back and forth, left right, left right and turn a half turn and one two, one two. Rest a minute and listen to the music. When you hear the change in the beat, add some moves with your shoulders, like this."

Cliff moved his feet when he saw how natural Katie blended with the music. He asked himself, *who loves Joan? Katie's always there to make it right.*

He knew he loved Katie, but would anyone, besides Three-Eyed Bill and Ruth, ever love Joan? The happiness on her face was startling. It was in her eyes. Happiness poured out, and overpowered the twisted, contorted cheeks and lips—nothing detracted from her eyes.

Katie turned the record player off, and ended the morning lesson. She and Joan pulled on sweatshirts and exited through the back of the tent, leaving Cliff, still unseen by Joan, standing alone as he stared at the empty stage.

He had been a one-man audience watching an inspired performance. He knew he had witnessed something beyond written description, an event that couldn't be explained with thin lines on flat paper. Katie's dancing had to be seen; the music had to be heard and felt. Anything else was a feeble approximation.

Katie love,

The thing making me the proudest is your courage and passion about the people you're meeting. I'm sure it will eventually influence your dancing. One of the older members of the church told the group that getting to know different people in the community who share similar talents is the best part of what we're doing. It sounds to me like your dancing with this poor girl is the same thing. Will I be able to spend time with the two of you?

Our project is growing. Some of the AA members are eagerly digging into their memories and getting past the guilt of their addictions and realizing they have skills they can use to help others instead of just remembering their mistakes and the way they drank their way into despair.

We might both be able to make the trip but probably just me—Mom wants to wait until you're in New York.

God grant me the serenity
To accept the things I cannot change;
Courage to change the things I can;
And wisdom to know the difference.

told himself that when he had time he'd turn the thin words into intricate sentences that would carry the readers straight into the lives of Steve Lanning, Milt Hinkle, Jack, Katie and even Joan's journey from the Indiana farm to...*where, where was she going to end up?*

"Why don't you use your notes for my dad?"

"I might. Are you trying to tell me something?"

"He told me to use my gifts and not worry about getting paid. That's why they're called gifts."

"Makes me nervous to meet him."

CHAPTER 31

I'm the Reason
They're Buying Tickets;
See Milt Hinkle

The coffee pot, balanced on the smoking coals, was bubbling and Steve told them it was time to make some decisions.

"We got to get a few things straight." He stopped. "No, just one—how we cut up the money."

The three of them sat on folding chairs in a triangle, with Cliff's young features in radical contrast to the wrecked faces of Steve and Milt.

Holding the coffee pot, Jack made a slight bow in front of each of the three men while he poured black liquid into their chipped cups. He asked Steve, "You want me to make notes? I used to do that." Jack put the pot back on the fire and walked unsteadily to the tent, not waiting for an answer.

"Is that when you was president of the bank?" Steve lit a cigarette. "Go on, shovel out that chimp's cage and don't let no one back here. Leave us alone."

Jack turned away and continued stumbled toward the tent as he nodded his head, acknowledging the orders.

The three men stared at the opening where Jack disappeared, until Milt broke the silence and asked Cliff if he would pull up another chair. "Leg's bothering me this morning. If I can keep it up, it ain't too bad. I'm going to have to set in that tent all day; I'll need a good chair. Jack's gonna have to help me, too, figure out some way to go to the can."

"You go in your pants. Don't start talking about taking a shit; we're talking about the money. Cliff's gonna hold it and he gets half. He's putting up the money. You and me split the other half."

"Ain't fair. I should get half. I'm the reason they're buying tickets; see Milt Hinkle, world champion!"

"You shouldn't get nothing until I get back what you stole from me." Steve turned his hat. "But I ain't gonna do that. You and me split half, that's the way it's going down. I don't want to hear no more about it."

Milt opened his mouth, but Steve cut him off. "Shut it, not one word. This young man is stepping up for you. Keep your mouth shut. He's telling the press about you. He's putting up his money, so he holds it till the end of the week and takes half. We pay the man and cut up the rest on Saturday night."

Cliff opened the notebook. *This isn't me, Cliff Walker, newspaperman, this is an imposter, someone dressed like me. I'm taking a big step with two thieves, two men wrestling for the gold ring and I'm grabbing with them, not an outsider taking notes, part of the deal, a partner with Milt Hinkle and Steve Lanning…Cliff Walker, show owner. They want me for my money, for my ability to snag free press, but they want me and I want in. No more watching other people…it's my turn.*

"I think we make the front look like an old-time sheriff's jail, bars on the window. Milt can sit behind a roll top desk with a swivel chair. Make posters out of the stuff in the trunk." They exchanged brief nods of agreement.

"With a foot rest, I got to have a foot rest. What about food?" Milt rubbed his stomach. "I'm hungry now. Sheriff's jail sounds good to me. What do you think, Steve?"

Steve leaned forward on his forearms. "All right, whatever it takes. Jail front won't look like none of the other shows. Make people notice. But different don't always work. Whatever we do, it's got to sell tickets. Don't matter what's inside, we don't give refunds."

"I hope we sell enough to worry about refunds," Cliff said. "If we do this right, it could be one of those shows that people talk about, and that talk sells more tickets. If they talk about it enough, it could lead to a lot of things for Milt. I see a TV documentary. He could end up famous."

He thought about the nights on the midway when the ticket sellers worked non-stop, when marks were standing in line at every attraction, when the parking lots were full. He imagined the new show starring Milt Hinkle with long lines of paying customers waiting to buy a ticket to see the famous cowboy. They wanted to talk to the man that was the National Rodeo Champion, who knew Bat Masterson, who jumped out of an airplane.

Steve told Cliff to stop. "Don't start on that shit, he'll be hard enough to put up with as it is. You think we got enough to frame a good show? Most people look in that trunk and think it's nothin' but trash. You look at that stuff and think we can make money with it. You got the right idea." Steve dropped his cigarette and covered it with his boot. "He could also end up like he is now, a poor drunk, living with the animals. I give it a fifty-fifty chance of going either way…and that's generous."

"The odds are better than that, a lot better. Like you just said, the stuff in that trunk is worth something. We do it right, good pictures, right words, Milt might become one of those one-man shows that tour theaters, real theaters for real money. I'm willing to put up the money." He asked Steve, "Where's your trunk full of stuff? Make both of you famous."

"Can you afford to lose it?" Steve ignored Cliff's question.

"If it's gone, it's gone. Don't you have anything about yourself? Star of the Ringling Brothers Circus."

"Never kept any of it."

Milt banged his crutch. "I told him, keep it, told him it would be worth something someday; posters from Buffalo Bill, pictures of me and Tom Mix; big names; the biggest. Steve in the center ring, thirty-five elephants. He ain't got nothin' to show for it."

Cliff looked at the worn men: forty years, wins and losses and bad breaks and triumphs, experiences faded and dead in their memories. He stood up. "Here's what I think—getting there's half the fun—more. I'm tired of watching, I'm going for it."

It's time to start adding to my own trunk. I've got to try. I'm going to do something that may or may not work, but at least I will have tried.

"You got a lot going, you're young. If it don't make money, it ain't the end of the world for you."

"We might make a fortune, and a Hollywood producer might ask me to write a screenplay about Steve Lanning and Milt Hinkle, members of the Hall of Shame…I mean Fame. Who knows what might happen?"

"We should have a drink." Milt poured his coffee on the ground. "As soon as we get open, we'll have a drink. I'll buy."

"Let's shake on it."

When he gripped Steve's hand, the coarse skin and the broken nails told who he was—a man who spent his time picking rocks out of elephants' toes.

Cliff knew his hand was soft compared to theirs.

The ends of my fingers might be a little callused from typing: time to rough them up.

CHAPTER 32

Milt's Got the Goods.
You Can Sell Tickets
If You Do It Right

The rum worked, and he told himself the show would be a success, a moneymaker and a testimony to a man who did something to keep his word: Milt Hinkle—the last of the cowboys. More rum, and it didn't matter if the show was successful. Just putting it together was the real trip.

He wrote in his notebook: *The journey is more important than arriving.* He looked at the note and unscrewed the cap and drank and shook his head: *Do I mean it?* According to Steve Lanning, the only thing that mattered was the money.

The next day, Cliff and Katie wove their way through the empty wagons and trailers. Large sheets of canvas were stretched tight on wooden frames and the sign painter, Duke, sat in a canvas director's chair and held a sketchpad.

The artist listened to Cliff and said, "Milt's got the goods, the real goods. You can sell tickets if you do it right. You frame the right show with Milt Hinkle, you'll be a big-time impresario, the new Barnum."

"What's right? How do I do it right?"

"Naked broads wearing tin badges. Call them the sheriff's pretty posse. Let Milt stay inside with the rest of the animals. You'll sell a million tickets a day."

Embarrassed by the artist's suggestion, Cliff looked sideways at Katie so he could see her reaction. She frowned, her eyes on the ground. Then she looked up and squeezed Cliff's hand and told the sign painter that his idea was wrong. "You know it's wrong. That doesn't have anything to do with Milt Hinkle."

"No, I don't know it's wrong. You wear a bikini and stand out front, and they'll buy a lot of tickets. Like you do on the Broadway Review." Duke held up his sketchpad. "I don't know what works and what doesn't. I just paint what people tell me to. Why I'm living in a van on the back lot of a carnival midway. I never made it like my old friend, Norman Rockwell, doing *Saturday Post* covers. He could paint Milt and make it work, but you can't afford him."

Cliff said, "Come on Duke, help us out. You're the artist, you dream up banners for strippers, freaks, midgets, snakes. I think we should make it look like a sheriff's office, a jail, Wanted Posters. How does that sound?"

Duke swung his pencil over the notepad, sketching smooth lines. Cliff had always envied someone who could draw. The pencil soared over the paper, leaving thin trails of windows and doors and steel bars. The pencil tilted sideways and smudged in shadows and clouds and weathered wood and, with a stabbing motion, Duke dotted the front door with scattered bullet holes delivered by the James boys when they broke their brother Jesse out of the slammer.

Cliff pointed. "Make it look like a real window with a mannequin hanging by his neck."

"Better yet, make it a real window with a nude hanging inside." Duke added strokes to the words *Sheriff of Dodge City* across the top of an arched banner. The sign was outlined with flourishes in red.

"Who's writing the pitch?"

"I'm working on it, writing for Lanning. His voice works, doesn't it?"

"Yeah, good, real good. Stands out, strong. He and I worked out the one he's using now, Lanning came up with *see old George, the blood-sweating river hog, big as a truck, long as a whale.*"

Duke continued drawing. "Your idea for the jail front?"

"Hinkle's dad was the sheriff of Dodge City, wasn't he?"

"Who knows? Don't matter. He convinced some reporter it was true and they wrote the story and it was in the newspaper so you can use it, makes it true."

"Do you think this is a good idea?"

"It is a good idea. And so is the window with real bars. I still think a naked broad inside would be the best thing, but then you got to pay her." Duke let his eyes drift over Katie. "Unless you want to work for free, help your boyfriend." She ignored him as he continued. "Get a mannequin and have it hanging by the neck with blood running out of its eyeballs, blue tongue about a foot long. What else you putting inside?"

"Blowups of the posters, newspaper stories, photographs… what do you think?"

"Okay, maybe too much like a museum. Put up something to scare the shit out of them. They want thrills, not education. Naked broads."

Katie was quiet as they left. She put her arm around Cliff's waist and rested her head on his shoulder. Cliff turned his head to kiss her and said, "I'm not sure this will work, but I know Duke can paint a good front.

Katie stopped and hugged him tight. "Maybe you shouldn't do it. Can't you keep getting newspapers, TV, to do something for him? You know what I think about his ideas."

Cliff didn't respond for a few seconds, then he said, "I love listening to Milt talk about his past, real facts. It will take some work, practice to get him to tell it the right way, but I think he can do it. His experiences speak for themselves and, like Duke said, he's the real deal."

Cliff released Katie. "That's what I should do with you. Write about the facts of your life."

"Which ones?" She laughed when she asked the question. "Not much so far."

"You can be pretty sarcastic when you work at it."

Katie smiled, then turned serious. "You know my dream. It hasn't changed and it won't. The only thing different is the idea of teaching. Joan is helping me understand that gift. Maybe you can bring the Milt Hinkle show to New York City."

"That's a great idea. I can book him on all of the talk shows, set up performances in the small theaters." Cliff wrapped his arms around Katie. "No, he's just an old cowboy. We'll be lucky if this show works. Have to figure out some other way I can get to New York."

Katie love –

Thank you for the news. You and Cliff involved with a new sideshow is tantalizing! And I'm supposed to be the one bucking convention. You're making my work—changing the way church is done seem tame next to new sideshows and dancing on a carnival midway. Do you think I could add a church tent to the line-up?

New members are joining us. They are responding to the idea of serving others as much as listening to sermons. This is rewarding for me, especially when I see the joy on their faces, the feeling they get when they know they are using their skills and helping—what God wants us to do.

I hear what you're saying about the money issue. Too much and it might ruin the project.

May the road rise up to meet you.
May the wind be always at your back.
May the sun shine warm upon your face;
The rains fall soft upon your fields
And until we meet again,
May God hold you in the palm of His hand.

Love, Dad

Cliff sifted through the stacks of posters, flyers, and photographs, deciding what to use inside the tent. *It's important they understand that what's inside is the real thing, not a phony woman with a penis and a vagina.* The newspaper clippings and the *True* Magazine told the story.

Cliff's chest tightened. It would be his entry into the world of entertainment. Not a big event but a start, a small show on the midway. Not Broadway or Hollywood, but Cliff Walker's show would be open for business.

The sign painter had told him, "As long as Milt can keep talking, you might do okay. Keep him drunk enough to never stop, but be careful he don't pass out on you. Lanning knows how to keep him juiced just right. They practiced together a long time."

Cliff admired the jail front Duke painted. He worried that the Sheriff of Dodge City was nothing but an old man sitting inside a tent with posters and pictures hanging on the walls.

He was caught in the dream that the front would support a twenty-five-cent ticket. They paid that to see a woman sitting in a snake pit, to see a hippopotamus in a cage, to see a man with three eyes. Milt Hinkle would give them more for their money. They could ask him questions and hear the answers. They could hear the details from the man that shook the hand of Bat Masterson. They could ask Milt where he got the courage to jump out of an airplane without a parachute. He could keep it up all day as long as they bought tickets. *There's no business like show business.*

Duke swept the paintbrush, adding even more highlights to the words *Sheriff of Dodge City*. It looked finished to Cliff, but the painter continued to add small splashes of red and yellow, which made the words shimmer on the canvas. The painting looked authentic. Duke had brushed the weathered boards, so the wood looked like you could feel the grain.

As Cliff started to walk away, Duke said, "Don't ignore the idea of using broads. That dancer you're playing house with would be perfect. And don't forget my money. I need half before you can use this."

"I'll bring it tomorrow. I'm waiting for the mail." Cliff had over five thousand dollars in his checking account, but he had listened to Steve Lanning's advice. *"Don't pay Duke no more than half until it's finished and we're open. He can wait for the rest like everyone else."*

Cliff planned that the five thousand would be more than enough to cover the new show. Five hundred to Duke. Two fifty for enlargements of posters and photographs, five hundred for the used tent, and another two or three hundred for loudspeakers and a tape recorder. All in, Cliff thought the show could open for about two thousand and it could make that back in less than a month. He had heard the snake show sometimes grossed over five hundred a day and Steve's animal menagerie could do three hundred on the ding donations.

It was a good investment. Milt Hinkle was going to be Cliff's answer to the first draft of a novel.

When he returned to the office wagons, Cliff threaded a reel of tape into a recorder while Steve smoked a cigarette and looked at a sheet of notebook paper.

"Can you read it? I made the words big so you could see them without your glasses."

Steve read the words, moving his lips, chanting. Cliff knew his rough voice would overpower the other spiels.

"Meet Milt Hinkle, member of the Cowboy Hall of Fame." Steve shook his head. "No damned good. No punch. Won't sell ticket one."

"Don't hold back, tell me how you feel."

"We ain't teaching history here. We got to stop 'em out front."

"Keep going, it gets better."

"Bulldogged a bull from an airplane—without a parachute. Still no good, won't get it."

Cliff pulled the paper out of Steve's hands. "You're worse than John Stoneman. I should get you a blue pencil. I don't know what to write. What should it be?"

He knew he was writing like a reporter, dull. *Stoneman isn't here. I'm selling tickets to a sideshow, not reporting on the budget meeting.*

When he squeezed the pencil, he wanted to break the point, rip the paper with brutal words.

Steve blew smoke at the microphone. "Don't ask me, you're the writer. I know what ain't gonna work. I don't know what will."

"Duke told me you did your tape. *See Old George the blood-sweating river hog, big as a truck, long as a whale . . .*"

"I stole it from a guy on the Ringling show."

"A poet. It's poetry; I don't write poetry."

"You better learn or you're gonna lose your ass."

Cliff spent the rest of the day standing in front of sideshows, listening to the grind tapes.

You can't get out of the glass house, silly old, goofy old, crazy glass house. The midget horse, so tiny, so small a silver dollar makes a perfect shoe. Old George the river hog, big as a truck, long as a whale. Takes a boxcar to tug him, a freight train to lug him. You can't get out, you can't get out, you can't get out of the glass house.

His favorite was the snake show: *Big snakes, little snakes, snakes big enough to break every bone in the body of a cow or a horse...a quivering mass of reptilian flesh, the crazy old, goofy old Okefenokee Swamp Girl.*

He wrote every word of the spiel and memorized it and then spent the rest of the night in his room, writing.

The next afternoon Steve looked over the copy while Cliff waited to start the tape recorder.

While Steve read, the recording light blinked. "*Meet the man, shake his hand. Milt Hinkle—friend of Billy the Kid. Meet the man, shake his hand. Hear the amazing, astounding, Aston...ish. Astonis...*what's that word?"

"*Astonishing! Asssstonishing.* Hit the first part, hard, AS-SSSSSSSSTONishhhhhhing!" Cliff shouted.

"Big words. Didn't learn them in the fourth grade." The words rasped as Steve drew them out of his throat. Rough, guttural sounds and when they played the tape back, the small speakers rattled.

"Stick with me, you might get literate." Cliff was pleased with the spiel. He could see the marks stopping to listen—but would they buy a ticket?

"*Assstonishing, hear his true story—bulldogged a steer from an airplane, friend of Billy the Kid. Teddy Roosevelt's bodyguard. Twenty-five cents, one small coin, a quarter of a dollar, takes you all the way through and the show never stops. Meet the man, shake his hand. THE TRUE story.*"

Cliff smiled. "You've got it. I think he's got it. Like *My Fair Lady*... by jove, I think he's got it. That tape will sell tickets. I saw the front today, it's almost finished. Duke's good. He painted the canvas to look just like an old jail front, bullet holes around the doorframe. There's a blow-up of the *True* cover and a life-sized drawing of Milt riding next to Teddy Roosevelt. We get this sound track right and we're ready to go. There's no business like show business..."

As Cliff listened to Steve practice the spiel, he felt the same doubts.

Will it get them inside the tent? Will they be disappointed? Don't care if they pay.

Milt could tell it like it happened, make them feel the wind ripping his hands loose from the struts, hear the wild screaming, smell his fear. And he could show them his stiff legs, proof of the foolish stunt.

And if that doesn't work, bring on the nude women.

CHAPTER 33

You Talked to
My Young Associate.
Now You Talk to Me, Please

Everything was ready, except for the posters and the tent; *maybe we don't need a tent.* He asked Steve if it would be all right if the marks just saw the posters, the painted jail front and heard the tape grinding out the spiel.

"If they buy tickets and walk into an open lot with Milt sitting in a swivel chair, I don't need a tent. If all we have to do is get them to buy a ticket…why have a tent?"

"You make that work, you'll change the business. Won't work."

"You ought to be able to help me with a tent, you're a circus man."

"Try one of those places, rent tents for weddings. They usually got some old ones they'll sell cheap."

"Go with me. I don't know what I'm looking for."

"I'll send Jack. I can't leave the lot."

"Jack! He won't be any help. Are you trying to blow this deal before we get started? Why can't you leave? Taking Jack would be like buying shoes at the city dump."

"Can't leave." Steve didn't elaborate. "Jack knows tents. Take him. You take care of Sparky yet?"

"No. What's he get?"

"If you don't take care of him, you won't get any power. You won't do much with no tent and no power. Sparky's got to get paid."

"He owns the electricity?"

"No, he don't own it. The Man owns it. Sparky just decides when you get it and if you get it. How he gets paid."

"I pay the Man for my location. Why do I have to pay Sparky?"

"How it works and it works pretty good. Everyone's got some action. You pick up a little green for giving Bozo words. What makes the show work. Look at it this way—you do business with these guys, get to know them. Some of them are worth knowing."

"Everyone? What about Jack?"

"Bottom of the barrel. He gets a dollar for shoveling shit."

"I'm supposed to give him something for finding me a tent?"

"If he does the job, up to you. He does know how to get a tent."

Cliff walked away. He didn't want Jack's help finding a tent, but he didn't have a choice.

Jack thinks he owns a chain of restaurants. He drinks vodka and makes imaginary telephone calls and now Lanning wants him to help me buy a tent. Can't believe he might help. What's happening to me? Like inviting a ghetto man with a gun to help count the cash in a bank.

As they left the fairgrounds in the yellow station wagon, Jack said they should be driving one of the old trucks. "They see us in this car, the price will double, they think we got more money than Fort Knox."

Cliff was relieved to hear Jack speaking coherently. "Should I go back?"

"No. I can handle it."

"I have to say, I've never heard you talk like this before."

"Won't last long. We get the tent—you get me a bottle—the elocution's over."

"Elocution? You know what that means?"

"Maybe, yes."

"Maybe's not an answer. Do you or don't you?"

"Yes. Let's get the tent. I'm thirsty. My head's broken."

"The guy I talked to said they had a few."

"Let me do the talking, elocution."

They parked on a side street to keep the *Mastras Shows* car out of view. The showroom was filled with party props, sound systems, record players, bubble machines, confetti blowers, silver paper hats, blue streamers, ice dispensers. Jack had brushed his hair and was wearing a clean white shirt and pants.

"Can I help you fellows?"

Cliff started to answer, but Jack returned the man's smile and shook his hand. "We telephoned earlier asking about used tents."

"Yes, yes. I talked to you."

"You talked to my young associate here. Now you talk to me, please." Cliff was speechless. He knew he was witnessing a miracle.

Where is it coming from? How can this disgusting, stumbling drunk suddenly be poised and eloquent? Cliff reached in his pocket for a pencil.

"You need a twenty by twenty?"

"Bigger."

"We got a thirty by thirty, not bad shape."

"Too wide. How about a twenty by thirty?"

"Yep. Got one. Costs more, special size."

"That might be of interest."

Cliff had to smile. Now he was negotiating for a tent, hammering out terms for a million-dollar merger. *Might be of interest.*

"Have these tents been used much? We have a busy season ahead of us."

"Different condition. You have to check them out."

"What is the price of the twenty by thirty?"

"How long do you want it?"

"Three weeks. If things go right, we want to buy it. How much of the rent applies to purchase?"

Cliff nodded his head. Jack had done this before.

The salesman wrote numbers on his notepad and added columns. Then he consulted a price list and added more numbers. "Rent for the twenty by thirty will be a hundred a week. Fifty percent applied to purchase, no more than three weeks. Purchase price is five hundred."

Jack turned his right palm up, then walked away from the salesman with his head lowered. He stood alone, moving his forefinger back and forth in the air, and pushed it into the palm of his hand. In a few minutes, he returned to the salesman. "Who am I talking to? Am I talking to the right man? How much is the twenty by twenty? You said the twenty by thirty was a special size?"

The salesman shook his head and consulted his price list and added numbers. "Fifty a week, same percent applies to purchase."

"What is the purchase price?"

"We got two. Three hundred for one, three fifty for the other one."

"Will you do the twenty by thirty for sixty a week, seventy-five percent to purchase at three fifty?"

The salesman looked at Jack, then turned to Cliff. "Don't he hear good? I told you the prices."

Cliff spoke softly. "I think he hears fine."

Jack extended both hands, gripping the salesman's right hand like he was holding a rope. "That's the right question. You must think I'm deaf. I'm just trying to find out how bad you want to sell a tent. Didn't you say fifty per week? Am I talking to the right man?"

The salesman said, "For the twenty by twenty, not the twenty by thirty. You're talking to the right man."

Jack released the salesman's hand. "How can there be that much difference for ten feet of canvas that might not be in good condition? Seventy-five dollars versus fifty dollars for ten feet of used canvas seems excessive." Jack grabbed the salesman's hand again and pulled him close, uncomfortably close. "I don't think you're a stupid man. You look like a smart man interested in making a sale. Isn't that the way you see it?"

"What are you talking about? I sell tents, Coke machines, balloons."

"Why?"

The salesman pulled his hand out of Jack's grip. "Why? Because someone wants to have a party."

"Bingo. We want to have a party and you're invited." Jack folded his hands together, then reached into his hip pocket and pulled out a stack of passes. "Get you into the party on the fairgrounds. Gorgeous girls, Pagan Smith, you ever heard of Pagan Smith?" Jack kept talking. "Doesn't matter, these passes will make it possible for you to get to know her, know her really well, if you know what I mean."

Cliff looked at the drops of sweat forming on Jack's face as he swallowed air in short bursts.

Jack pushed one of the passes into the salesman's hand. "Like you said, you sell tents to people who want to have a party—that's us. We need a better deal, we want to invite you to a party, a good party."

"Okay. You can have the twenty by thirty for seventy-five a week."

"What about the percent applied to purchase?"

"Has to stay the same."

"We're making a little progress, aren't we?" Jack flipped the rest of the passes, fanning them in front of the salesman. "Do you sell lawn mowers?"

The salesman slid the pass into his shirt pocket and swung his eyes around the showroom. "Do you want a lawn mower?"

"No, but you have a better chance of selling us a tent than you do a lawn mower. We don't need a lawn mower. No one has a party with a lawn mower, especially Pagan Smith. It doesn't seem like I'm talking to the right man." Jack's words ended softly in a low moan that only Cliff heard.

"I'm not trying to sell you a lawn mower. We don't sell lawn mowers."

"Bingo. And I don't think you're really trying to sell us a tent." Jack pushed two passes into the man's hand. "Make it seventy-five percent to purchase and we'll forget about the lawn mower. You don't want to insult Pagan by suggesting you mow her lawn. But there are other areas of her landscape that need attending. Try and see your way clear to these terms. Take a chance. You won't lose and you might have a wonderful party."

"I think you're a little crazy, but okay. I need fifty bucks down to hold the tent. When do you want it?"

"We want it delivered to the fairgrounds as soon as possible. The show opens next week. Pagan opens daily—you have a pass to her garden."

Jack hurried to the door and waited for Cliff, who was giving directions. "Tell your delivery man to ask for me, Cliff Walker. I'll get him in."

Inside the car, Jack held his head with both hands. "I could have done better if I had a drink, best I could do under the circumstances. God, I need a drink. If you have any feelings at all, you'll buy me a bottle in the next five minutes or drive me to a funeral home."

Cliff slowed down in front of a liquor store, but he didn't stop. Jack clawed at the window. "What are you doing? Stop, God, please make him stop."

"I'll stop and buy you an all-day bottle if you tell me something." Cliff let the car roll slowly past the liquor store.

"Anything, just *stop!*"

"How are the games fixed? Steve told me you know the gaff on all of them."

Jack nodded his head, his eyes fixed on the liquor store. "I do but I'm not talking without vodka. I'll tell you the innermost secrets of the games: secrets that must not be revealed on threat of a hideous, painful death. Vodka will unlock the secrets."

When Cliff returned to the car, Jack reached for the bottle, a desperate grab, but Cliff pulled it out of his reach. "You can have it when you tell me how that game is fixed where you have to drop the round discs to cover the red spot."

Jack surprised Cliff. "I know what you're doing, but you want to know for the wrong reasons. We got the tent, give me the bottle."

"What are my reasons?"

"Give me the bottle."

"One drink, then I get it back."

Cliff had to pull the vodka away from Jack's mouth, letting some spill down the front of his shirt. Jack rubbed the stains, trying to catch some of it in his hand.

"Why do I want to know, what wrong reasons?"

"So you can tempt the press."

Cliff screwed the cap back on the bottle. "It will work. They always want to know secrets."

"Yes, it will, but you'd only do it once. Wouldn't be worth it."

"Why not?"

Jack licked his hand. "When the reporter pursues the crooked games, and tries to make a name for himself, it could force the DA to press charges, so you'd have to stop the reporter by fixing him up with Pagan and getting pictures of them in bed, and that might tempt you to blackmail the reporter and then it just never stops."

Jack reached for the bottle. Cliff blocked his hand. "Not until you tell me how the games are fixed. I'm not going to tell a reporter. It's just part of my research, no blackmail. Where do you get those ideas? You should be the writer. Someday I'll write about you and the games."

"I need another drink. I'll tell you about the good ones, creative."

Cliff let him swallow two gulps. "Okay, what makes a good one?"

"Best one is the bottle tip. Where the mark has to hold a short pole with a ring hanging from a string and slip the ring over the neck of a bottle lying on its side on an angled board." Jack swallowed two more gulps. "The trick is for the mark to raise the bottle on the angled board and try to ease it up so the bottle stands up on the board, upright, not falling over like it always does, always."

"Always?" Cliff kept the bottle.

"Always unless the agent does…does." Jack's eyes searched for the bottle.

"You mean when the agent tips it up, it stands?" Cliff knew Jack only had a few minutes left. "What's the gaff? Can he change the angle of the board?"

"Another drink…'nother."

"Tell me first." Cliff moved the bottle closer to Jack's mouth.

"Genius of the criminal mind, smart carnie figured it out, no one ever caught it. Smart."

"What?"

"One more."

Cliff held the bottle while Jack drank. "What did he figure out?"

"Bottles made in Chicago are heavier on one side. They turn the weight up, bottle stands. Weight down, bottle falls over, always falls over. Call 'em flat stores 'cause you flat can't win."

Later in the day, Cliff stood close to the game and watched the agent coax a mark to pay a quarter to lift the bottle into a standing position.

The mark hesitated, so the agent placed the bottle in position and slipped the wooden ring over the neck and lifted and the bottle rocked back and forth, but stood upright on the angled board. He offered the mark a free practice turn, and the bottle remained upright. But when the mark parted with his money, the agent placed the bottle in position, the mark lifted the ring and the bottle fell over and rolled off of the board.

"Close, very close. Next time you'll get it and take the prize, any prize on the shelf." The agent waited while the mark considered his next move.

"I'll tell you what. You're a nice guy. I'll give you another practice turn. Then you pay me fifty cents, stand it up and you can pick two prizes from the shelf. The best deal I can give you and you can't lose."

CHAPTER 34

I'll Tell You What I Do See,
a Beautiful, Sweet Girl

Cliff and Katie went through Milt's pictures and chose the best ones for the show front. The rejects went back in the trunk. "Guess where the tent guy told me to get the posters made?"

"Where?"

"Right here in Boston. Place supplies a lot of the theaters in Manhattan."

Ordering the posters was more complicated than Cliff expected. The manager of the shop was old, thin-faced, and blunt. "Are they going to be inside or outside? I'm not supposed to copy magazine covers, but this one's so old it won't matter. *True* magazine's outta business."

"Outside. They're going on the front of a sideshow on a carnival midway."

"You'll want them weatherproof, won't you?"

"I guess. The other sideshows use painted canvas banners. What's the price difference?"

"Depends on other things. If you want this *True* in color, waterproof, thirty-six inch, it's going to cost seventy-five dollars; black and white, thirty-five."

The sign maker picked up the glossy photograph of Milt comparing the size of his fists to Jack Dempsey's. "This is a good shot, probably taken with a speed graphic, big negative, it will blow up good. Some of these are too blurry to enlarge much. I did some things for one of Dempsey's fights."

They decided on seven pictures to be enlarged and weatherproofed, and mounted in frames.

"Okay, they'll be ready day after tomorrow. The total will be two hundred and ten dollars. I need fifty percent to start. Rest when you pick them up."

Cliff slid the money over the counter. "You do any carnivals?"

"A few."

"What do you think of our stuff?"

"Fifty years making signs, I don't think anything. I don't see it, don't want to see it." The old man looked at Katie. "I'll tell you what I do see is a beautiful, sweet girl."

Katie Love –

How can I tell you? I can't make Boston—it's devastating. Our lead director with the day care program in the Spanish neighborhood has left her husband. He's coming apart and I can understand why and it could threaten our bigger effort. Thank God there are two assistants who are stepping up to keep things going.

I think the program will be all right. The plans to expand will have to be put on hold but it won't destroy what's been started. What hurts is this breakup of a marriage. It's one of the big problems we know might happen and does happen from time to time; but when it does, it throws a cloud over everything. We know people are people. And we know their best intentions can go down the drain. Apparently she's gotten involved with another man. I wouldn't have guessed in a thousand years.

She loves the program, the kids. She's so gifted with them. She has organizational skills like I've never seen. She has charisma that draws the kids to do the best they can. I could go on and on but I won't. I have to stay here through this crisis to hold things together, to insure everyone keeps in mind that there are no guarantees and that we have to trust God and keep our hearts on the bigger picture on the faith we have in loving each other and focused on continuing our drive to hold our groups together to serve and spread the gospel of Jesus.

Lord, make me an instrument of your peace;
where there is hatred, let me sow love;
where there is injury, pardon;
where there is doubt, faith;
where there is despair, hope;
where there is darkness, light;
and where there is sadness, joy.

Pray that I can still make it to NYC to be with you.

I love you –

Dad

Cliff paced back and forth, watching Jack as he climbed the ladder and tied the canvas to the metal poles. Before the canvas got pulled tight, wrinkles made the front look like a distorted cartoon instead of an old-time jail. Jack got down from the ladder and pulled the material smooth, then he attached the blowup of the *True* magazine cover next to the jail door. The enlargement was big enough to be seen across the midway.

"Looks like the real thing, don't it. Milt's the real thing." Jack stumbled to one knee and waited for a dollar bill.

Cliff was worried. "It looks different than the rest of the sideshows, maybe too different, too real."

No comment from Jack. Real or unreal didn't register with him. He knew a dollar would buy a bottle of real Thunderbird.

The Tilt-A-Whirl was being assembled on one side of Milt's tent and the glass house on the other. Curiosity drew the crews to see how the new sheriff show was coming together.

Katie arrived, wearing a raincoat over her costume. She hugged Cliff and stepped back to view the front. It was a big day when something new appeared on the midway and it had to be inspected.

"We get the pony tied to the hitching rail, give it a real touch. What do you think?" Cliff asked.

"It looks great from the outside." Katie paused. "So authentic, Duke is good. I wonder if he does something besides these banners. I bet he's a famous painter hiding on the back lot of a carnival and his best pictures are hanging in New York galleries, Europe."

Cliff hugged her. "That would be one for the front page. Probably not true, but you're wonderful for thinking it."

Inside the tent, they looked at the enlargements of Milt's rodeo posters and photographs and newspaper clippings. Cliff knew it would be hard for the customers to compare the young cowboy in the photographs with the blob of an old man sitting in a big chair talking, talking, talking.

A saddle and bridle were draped over a sawhorse and quilted blankets hung on the walls. A grotesque mannequin dressed in black swung by the neck from the ceiling. Painted blood seeped from her eyes and mouth. The dim light hid the fact that there wasn't much inside the tent except the posters and faded news clippings and a fat cowboy.

It could make a little money, enough to keep Milt out of Steve Lanning's pocket and maybe enough for the winter. Cliff knew it wasn't the best show on the midway, but he had high hopes for Milt's ability to talk, to bullshit the marks.

Katie didn't say anything. Her silence was concerning.

When Cliff looked at her, he realized he hadn't seen her for two days. He knew he saw her every day, but he hadn't seen her. She did her job and spent time with Joan.

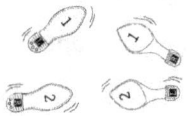

The phone rang three, four, five times before Franklin answered.

"I wondered what happened to you the other night."

"Sorry, I had to hang up fast. Mastras came in. He probably wouldn't have minded if I told him I was talking to a newspaper photographer."

"Has your show opened?"

"A couple more days. We're putting the last pieces together. I think it's going to be a winner, a little winner. I wish you could be here, take pictures."

"You know I'd like to see what you're doing, have to see it to believe it because I sure can't believe it. But it sounds great, a Morganport guy with a carnival sideshow. Doesn't get much better than that."

Cliff moved the telephone away from his mouth as he shouted, "Believe! You've got to believe, believe in the power of the word, believe in the last link to the old West—Milt Hinkle, alive on the inside, and the show never stops, not even if he has to piss his pants, and twenty-five cents, one quarter of a dollar, takes you all the way through, BELIEVE that!"

"Are you drunk again?"

"It helps me not think about what happens if this show doesn't work and I'm stuck with an old crippled cowboy that smells bad."

"You can always go back to Morganport."

"Never, never, never! If this doesn't work, I'll stay in New York with Katie, collect tin cans if I have to." Cliff had swallowed enough rum that he wasn't worried about what might happen.

Franklin asked Cliff why he was so intrigued by Milt Hinkle and Steve Lanning. "I sure didn't see it."

"That's it! I might be wrong, but I see it. The last of the cowboys, friend of Billy the Kid. Meet the man; shake his hand, alive on the inside, meet the man; shake the hand of the daredevil, bulldogged a bull from an airplane. That's what I see. You would, too, if you were here for a while. I get a thrill every time I listen to him."

"Did you write that?"

"I'm creating a new art form. You should hear some of the stuff I've written for Bozo. He's doing good business with it, gets the marks so mad they blow serious money trying to get him wet. Drown the clown, dunk Bozo, do something useful—throw your balls at the clown."

Franklin said, "Your art form might have a big audience, you never know. The shots I got of Pagan taking off her clothes—talk about an art form."

Cliff ignored Franklin. "Lanning recorded it. His voice works better than any on the midway. It will get their attention." Feeling the rum, Cliff's words flew around his head. "It really, really does look good, good enough to get them to stop and buy a ticket and that's all we care about. It's what's out front that counts, all that counts."

"I have to tell you, Cliff, Carolyn's front is just fine. Didn't think she'd ever leave Morganport, but she did, and she likes Indianapolis. And she likes me. I hope you don't mind."

"You're right, I didn't think she'd leave. I'm glad she likes you. She's a good girl."

"Good luck, Mr. Barnum, let me know how it goes."

"If you're still in Nap-town next year, you can take pictures of the Spectacular Milt Hinkle Sideshow and Western Extravaganza."

Dad –

You will be in New York! You have to be in New York! I pray you'll be there. Cliff is almost ready to open the new sideshow. He needs your help. He's unsure of his talent; that's where you have to help. Like you do with your members. Help them see their gifts. You were my cheerleader. You know how to do it. You could always see the best in people, especially when they couldn't.

CHAPTER 35

Maybe I Can Justify Naked Women, If They Get the Marks in the Tent

S*uccess, money-winner* and *smash hit* were not the words to describe the grand opening of the Sheriff of Dodge City sideshow. The midway was almost empty. Opening on Monday afternoon was always slow, but Mastras gave the orders.

Cliff understood: Milt wasn't shocking, outrageous, thrilling or scary—maybe not right for the midway crowd. They didn't want to be educated. They wanted to be terrified.

They wanted to be horrified, nauseated.

Cliff couldn't watch as marks walked past without buying tickets. He had been expecting to see long lines at the ticket box, but instead, he saw the marks glance at the posters and then keep walking until they stopped to listen to Bozo's verbal attacks and waited for him to take a swim.

Duke was right, naked girls with tin stars covering their crotches would sell tickets. It might not be too late. Cliff couldn't believe what he was considering. *Maybe I can justify naked women if they get the marks in the tent. Is the old man worth hearing? Or is it an idea that isn't as good as I thought it was? The price is right: twenty-five cents, but it isn't working. They get what they pay for.*

He thought about Joan's twisted face looking through the barred window. She would stop them, but would she sell tickets? He turned away—not Joan, never.

Looking for distraction, he wasn't surprised that no one was throwing balls at Bozo.

"I need a ball player, real ball players. High and dry, high and dry. I need a ball player."

Cliff picked up three balls and loosened his arm and flung a ball toward the bulls-eye, sending it hard against the canvas backstop. The force of his throw took his mind to a different place as his muscles burned. He grabbed three more balls and threw, and then three more. He didn't care if he hit the bull's-eye, but imagined Milt's face and flung the balls as hard as he could until his breath came in gasps, and he threw again.

From behind the bars, Bozo screamed, *"What have we got here, a ball player? Looks more like a fish to me—after a few throws, he stinks! He's a real inspiration to all of you other village idiots standing out there. Pitch to me, pitch to me, you pea-brained waste of good oxygen, drown the clown, drown the clown."*

A sense of satisfaction filled Cliff as he heard the insulting words he wrote for Bozo. It wasn't literature, but it wasn't reporting on police calls, either.

Marks got in line for a chance to dunk Bozo, as they laughed at his remarks.

"If stupid was water, this guy would be Niagara Falls, pitch to me, pitch to me! Is that your nose or did you run into a banana?"

Cliff laughed with them. *Maybe my calling is a writer and a shill for a loud-mouthed clown. Now Mom and Dad will really have something to brag about.*

Cliff listened as Bozo shouted out the sarcastic patter, put-down poetry. *At least Bozo's making money with my writing.*

After the last pitch, when the show closed, they met behind the water tank and Bozo handed Cliff fifty dollars. "A couple of those big shots dropped serious money tonight. Keep the good words coming."

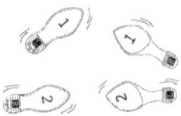

Cliff stood in front of the office wagons waiting for the reporter, a rum and Coke in his hand. As the sun closed behind the tents, the edges of the shows and rides softened in the weakening light, their scars and scratches melting away in the dusk, colored lights blinking against the black night. Cool air blew through the hot machinery, lifting the spirits of the ride jocks and the game agents.

Cliff liked the daily shift from light to dark. The shadows and the rum prepared him for his appointment. The reporter had been promised the inside scoop on the mysteries of the midway, and she sounded enthusiastic on the telephone. Cliff knew the interview would take his mind away from the empty money box.

Carol Fraley was older than Cliff, dressed in solid shoes and pants, and all business. While they walked, she wrote in her notebook and listened intently as Cliff pointed out the dangerous tricks of the motorcycle riders, the grace of the dancers, especially the young girl with the short hair, and the weird career of the Okefenokee Swamp Girl.

Cliff was feeling the rum. He stumbled, then caught himself. The reporter didn't notice because of the people crowding around them. Like someone threw open the floodgates, the oval path was jammed with marks and the music, the lights, and the smell of the deep-fat fryers clogged the air.

Cliff and the reporter stopped in front of the Sheriff of Dodge City tent and listened to Steve's voice on the grind tape.

Meet the man. Meet the man, shake his hand...The Sheriff of Dodge City, the rodeo champion of the world.

"You're in for an interview like you've never done before—Milt Hinkle."

"Want to bet?"

"No. You've been doing this for a while, probably interviewed genius professors from Harvard, world-class actors."

"You're right."

Cliff felt like he was looking at the mock jail front for the first time; the rum changed his perspective. He felt proud of the front, but the inside, the content was weak. Milt Hinkle was boring.

Cliff couldn't express it, but he dimly understood that the real reward was simply putting it together. If he tried to explain, he would tell himself to shut up. He knew it was a failure before it opened. So bad, he made an excuse to not be on the midway on opening day.

When they walked to the stage, Milt sat straight and tipped his hat. A few people were looking at the posters. Milt looked uncomfortable, with his stiff legs stuck out in front of him. "Pull them chairs up here so we can talk."

Cliff slid two folding chairs to the front of the stage, leaning on one for support.

Milt shook his head, "Not there. Put 'em up here—next to me."

"On stage?"

"Yeah. They'll think you're part of the show."

Cliff emptied his cup and helped the reporter step up on the stage. They sat and faced Milt. "This is Carol Fraley, *Boston Herald*. She's letting me show her the midway."

"Mighty pleased to meet you, Mrs. Fraley." Milt shook her hand.

"Thank you. It's Miss."

"Have you ever met a real cowboy? Not many make it to Boston. I was here with the 101 Wild West Combined Shows, long time ago."

Cliff closed his eyes; he dreaded what he was about to hear.

Milt looked ready to be taken away in an ambulance. The brim of his soiled hat was torn; his boots were worn through at the toes, shirt buttons missing. It was like he dressed as shabbily as possible to appeal to the charity of the marks, not entertain them.

Carol Fraley said, "I interviewed Gene Autry a few years ago, does he count?"

"You did? He ain't no real cowboy but he counts, sure does."

Milt patted Cliff on the leg. "She's the real thing. And a looker. Thank you."

"Milt was the USA Champion Bull Rider." Cliff's words drifted, his mouth was dry.

"My daddy, George Hinkle, was High Sheriff of Dodge City, the real Dodge City, whipped Bat Masterson for the job. When I was eight…"

Cliff signaled Milt to stop talking and leaned back in his chair and almost fell, but Carol Fraley didn't notice.

"How much of that is true?" Waiting for Milt's answer, Carol turned to a clean page.

"Young lady… all of it, every word."

In a soft voice, Cliff said, "Let her do her job, Milt, she has to ask."

"Look at these posters, show her the trunk, the *True* magazine, pictures. Read them posters, it's all true."

Cliff agreed. "I've read all of it, checked references as best I could. You can believe what he says." He looked at Milt—*maybe*.

"When I'm dead, it's going to the Cowboy Hall of Fame, in Austin, Texas."

Cliff handed Carol a photograph of Milt standing next to a man dressed in boxing shorts. They were comparing the sizes of their fists.

Milt eagerly pointed to the picture. "That's Jack Dempsey when he was heavyweight champion of the world. My fist was bigger than his." Cliff imagined the press agent got paid a bonus for getting the shot in the paper.

"This is the best thing he's got." Cliff handed her the original *True* Magazine. "You need to hear Milt tell how he bulldogged a steer from an airplane. Go ahead, tell what happened."

"Truth is I hadn't never planned to jump. I was too old, too smart—I thought. Them Mexicans was screaming, shaking the bullring. The cowboy supposed to jump was puking his guts out. Wasn't no choice but for me to do it. If we wanted our cut of the jackpot, I had to, it was in the contract. I let go, but I didn't fly like no bird. I dropped like a big bomb. Killed the cow and damn near killed me."

A few customers had been listening and they moved closer to see Milt. Cliff looked up and saw people entering the tent, pushing to look at the posters. A crowd filled the space in front of Milt, their eyes darting from the pictures to the man, while families and couples holding hands walked around the sides of the tent.

Cliff stood up, trying to see what was happening; where were they coming from? Steve Lanning appeared in the entrance to the tent and raised his hand in the victory sign and, when Cliff nodded his head, the elephant trainer turned and disappeared.

Milt sat up straight in his chair. "And miss, I'll show you how true that story is." He turned his chair toward her and pulled up his pant legs to show his scarred, twisted knees, permanently locked like the limbs of a tree. "My hips is the same, but I'd have to know you better, a lot better, to show you that part of my body."

Carol scanned down the page of the *True* magazine. "No pictures?"

"They was some in the Nuevo Laredo newspaper. I never went back to get 'em, don't know if I could. Fifty thousand Mexicans seen it happen. So did Steve Lanning—you met him yet?"

"Not yet. Then you two go way back?"

"Way, way back. We been chasing dollars for a long time. When we was together in Mexico, he was the drunk. He dried out and I took it up. They say I'm an addict."

"Why have you been together so long?"

"Truth is, he thinks I cheated him and he wants it, and I ain't had no place else to go."

"Did you?" Cliff nodded. He wanted to know the answer, was glad the reporter asked the question.

"No. No I didn't cheat. Just wasn't enough to go around. Business is like that; sometimes, most of the time for me."

"How is this show doing?"

"Brand new. A little press wouldn't hurt none, let the folks know we're here." Milt looked at the nearly full tent. "You can write we're filling the tent."

Carol Fraley closed her notebook. "We can help. I'll check the facts, but I think we can help. Thank you for talking to me. You've had an interesting life. And you're right, not many real cowboys in Boston."

"I ain't trying to win a big jackpot, just like to share some stories, tell folks what happened. I'm the last one, the very last of a bunch of good old boys."

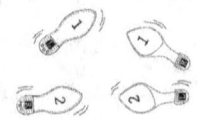

They threaded their way through the crowded tent and Cliff felt the lift of the rum. *Serious money in the cigar box, what was Lanning doing to get them inside?*

Carol Fraley said, "He's not Tom Mix. Sounds like the real thing. Can I get copies of the magazine article?"

"Tomorrow morning, anything else?"

She pointed to Cliff's hand. "Some of whatever you're drinking."

"Good reporter, you noticed. Is it obvious?"

"No. Not too obvious. Enough to make me thirsty."

Cliff led the way to the office wagons and was relieved that Mastras wasn't there.

"Do you want rum and Coke?"

"Ginger ale if you have it."

"Seven-Up?"

"All right."

Carol swallowed half of her drink. "How long have you been doing this?"

He told her the truth. "A few months. Or did you mean drinking?"

"How much longer? Not the drinking."

"I'm not sure. Until something better comes along." He didn't want to say anything about owning part of the Sheriff of Dodge City sideshow. "Would you like to meet a former star of the Ringling Brothers Circus?"

"I would. What's his name?"

"Steve Lanning. He was with Milt in Mexico; they work hard to steal from each other."

Cliff escorted the reporter behind the menagerie tent. She looked concerned, as they stepped over the coiled electrical cables and Cliff held her arm to guide her through the frayed ropes and stakes.

Steve was sitting in his chair, reading by the fire. He stood up when Cliff introduced Carol and shook her hand and insisted that she take his chair.

One listened while the other talked, an act they'd rehearsed for several weeks. Cliff provided a quick introduction. He told Carol about Steve directing thirty-five elephants in the center ring of the greatest show on earth, the Ringling Show.

On cue, Steve raised his voice and walked around the fire and stopped in front of Carol. "This ear—" He leaned at the waist and turned his head so she could see the scarred skin rippling over the top of his ear. "This ear was torn away by a lion."

It was a good act and it usually worked. They had made the six o'clock news. Sometimes it was a German bullet, sometimes a lion, never sex with a woman in braces.

Steve didn't talk about growing up in Wisconsin, working on the family farm, sunup to sundown, no school except in the winter, his Black Irish father as mean as an infected mule, a summer break when the circus came to town and he slid down the drainpipe and ran away with the bright lights. Steve didn't tell the reporters that story. "What for? Kids run away all the time."

Carol Fraley finished her drink. "That's your voice on Milt Hinkle's show, isn't it?"

"Yeah. How'd you like Milt?"

"You were in Mexico when he jumped?"

"That's right, I didn't see it because I was guarding the money but I heard the yelling. Put that in the paper."

"No. I'll be lucky to get Milt's show in, but I think I can."

Before Steve said any more, Cliff interrupted, offering one more interview. "I want you to meet Jim Mastras." He moved to block her view into the menagerie tent.

"Can I see the elephants?"

Inside the tent, Joan was brushing the calf. Cliff didn't want the reporter to see the deformed girl.

He knew Carol Fraley was the kind of reporter that would have to talk to someone that looked like Joan. She might not do anything about Milt, but she wouldn't ignore a chance to talk to a deformed girl brushing a calf with three legs. He thought about his promise to Katie; *nothing about Joan, not a story for a newspaper.*

"We can see the elephants later. Let's get more ice and see if Mr. Mastras is available."

"What are you trying to keep me from seeing? I want to see the elephants."

Cliff asked her if she would like to see the motorcycle daredevils before the elephants. "Come on, they're about to start the next show. Let me get you another drink and we'll go. The trick rider is fearless, a real talented guy. The elephants won't go away."

Cliff walked behind Carol and signaled Steve to get Joan out of the tent.

They stood on top of the wooden barrel, The Wall of Death, and looked down over the edge where the riders balanced their motorcycles on the vertical wall. On their way past the ticket takers, Clipper, the lead rider, had given Cliff a nod and raised his hand with a thumb up.

A heavy wooden door in the bottom of the barrel opened and three riders dressed in tight pants and high-topped leather boots entered the motordrome. They kick-started their machines and executed a series of increasingly difficult tricks: racing on the straight up and down vertical walls, riding no-handed, standing on the bottom foot plate while circling and looking up at the audience.

After two turns backward Clipper spun back to his normal position, twisted the accelerator and raced to the top of the barrel where he brushed the thick cable directly in front of Carol and Cliff, forcing them back to safety, then dove to the bottom of the barrel and repeated this climbing and diving routine for three more rounds.

Outside the motordrome, Clipper was waiting for them. "I hope you had a good view. Thank you for coming. Let me know if you need anything else. If you want, I'll take you for a ride."

Carol said, "No way, maybe someone else but not this reporter."

Cliff led the way toward the menagerie. "How about three Indian elephants and a nightcap?"

"Thank you for the tour, but I'm done for the night. You said the elephants aren't leaving. I just have time to get something ready for tomorrow's edition. That motorcycle rider surprised me, very poised."

"Just one more of the Pulitzer Prize-winning stories on the midway. Clipper is a great performer. A lot of the people out here are low on the food chain, but there are a few who make it worth being here. He's one of them."

"I'm envious you're getting to know them. We'll keep in touch."

Cliff motioned to a man waiting with a golf cart. "He'll take you to your car. Thank you very, very much for coming out. I enjoyed meeting you and I'm looking forward to talking more."

"I hope we can. I'd like to."

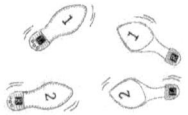

Cliff and Katie entered the Pie Car and opened the newspaper, spreading it on top of the table. Cliff stopped reading and drank his beer and looked through the window, relieved that most of the booths were empty.

Katie read aloud. "Cliff Walker is a young ex-reporter who is trying his hand at public relations with the Mastras Shows."

"Not that part, read about Milt. There's a half page on him." Cliff reached for the paper but Katie pulled it away.

"I like this part better." She scanned the page and continued reading. "The annual Brockton fair is an old-fashioned event celebrating the fall harvest. Things to see at the fairgrounds include quilts and chickens and cows and Milt Hinkle, a former national champion cowboy out of the Old West. A feature story in this issue covers Hinkle in greater detail."

Katie stopped reading and rubbed Cliff's neck, then returned to the paper. "One of the young people working on the midway, Cliff Walker, merits extra comment. He's doing something many would like to do, run away with the circus. Walker spends his time showing the press the ins and outs of the carnival and with his help, I was able to go behind the scenes. Walker introduced me to Milt Hinkle and Steve Lanning, the elephant trainer, and bought me a drink from Georgia Boy. I'm sure there's a lot more going on that I didn't see, but that's what keeps us coming back."

Cliff reached for the newspaper but Katie wouldn't let him have it, and continued reading. "Walker is an ex-reporter from Indiana and he says the carnival job will be useful—someday. He wants to write a book about the midway, stunts with the elephant trainer, freaks, strippers, and old cowboys and beautiful dancers, and games almost impossible to win."

Cliff slid closer to Katie. "I didn't see that coming, not from what we talked about last night. I did have too much to drink. I think she knew it. What do you think about the part where I might write a book?"

"A picture of you would have been nice. I love what she wrote because you will write a book."

Cliff folded the newspaper, avoiding Katie's eyes. "I'm glad she didn't find out I was owner of Milt's show. She might not have written the story. Read what she said about Milt, maybe it will help business, something needs to."

"What does she mean about more going on?"

"Not sure. When we left Steve behind the menagerie, I had to keep her out of the tent because Joan was there. She asked me what I didn't want her to see."

Fear crossed Katie's face. "Thank you for protecting her. I know she won't, but I wish Joan would stay away from the midway. Something's going to happen and she's not ready for it. How did you keep the reporter out of the tent?"

"I took her to see Clipper. He charmed her."

Steve already had a copy of the newspaper. He pointed to the paragraph about Cliff. "Now I get it, you write a book, make a million. What you been talking about."

Cliff shook his head. "I talk about a lot of things."

"Can you do it?"

"When I'm drinking, I know I can."

"I know how that works." Steve scanned the newspaper. "You might make more money as a promoter. I heard Milt had a good crowd last night."

"Real good crowd, at the right time. How did you do it?"

"Put an elephant down on the midway." Steve didn't blink.

"Tell me."

"Put Pagan topless in the ticket box."

"Are you serious?"

"She wasn't topless."

"Okay, don't tell me. It doesn't matter, we made the front page. The cigar box was overflowing."

"You got Milt on the front page."

"Your name's there, too. Half ears make the news."

Katie love,

Our prayers have been answered. My reservations for New York are set. The crisis here has been resolved. Like many of these incidents, this one is turning out to make us stronger. The couple are not going to reconcile and he's moving back to Ohio, but the two assistants have pulled together with some creativity allowing us to expand the day care program.

Obviously we regret the initial problem but it isn't one we can control. We accept it and keep moving, like a wonderful young girl I know riding a train across the country.

Several new volunteers have joined our project and some of them have said they want to join the church. They said they were joining because of the purpose, the chance to serve.

Thank you for the news and details of the new show. Milt Hinkle and Steve Lanning sound like characters this old Irishman should not be allowed to mix with. I might embarrass you but we've been there before.

I'm filled with the joy of knowing I'm going to be with you in a few days.

I LOVE YOU!!!

CHAPTER 36

Kid Smart Enough to Get a Story in the Newspaper

The story worked. Milt played to a full tent. And he complained his throat was drying out, but he smiled while complaining, happy to have people to talk to.

Cliff had the newspaper story enlarged, big enough to make a large poster on the front of the jail; the headline could be seen across the midway.

No Parachute for Veteran Cowboy

Two hundred and fifty thousand readers had seen the story by Carol Fraley, and Cliff wondered how many would buy a ticket to see Milt, maybe talk to him. There was money in the cigar box and Cliff emptied it once an hour.

He thought, *they're reading about the reporter from Indiana, the young man running away with the circus. She covered who, what, where, and when, and made an attempt at why but that's the hard one, someone's opinion, usually scratched out with a blue pencil.*

Cliff knew why he ran away from the boring editor's job, but he wasn't clear where he was going. *For now the midway was enough*: the lines at the Sheriff's show, the money in the cigar box, and two stories in the *Boston Herald* and Katie Flannigan more than anything else.

He called Carol Fraley and thanked her for writing about him. "It isn't that I want the publicity. You've made me think about why I'm here." They confirmed they wanted to talk more about writing and would get together in the next few days.

Mastras showed his appreciation for the story by handing Cliff another C-note, and told him again it didn't matter whose name got in the paper as long as it was someone from the show. Cliff heard from people he didn't think could read, people on the midway who pointed to the story and congratulated him for pulling marks through the front gate. It elevated him to the "Kid Smart Enough to Get a Story in the Newspaper," and the ones who said the sheriff show was a dumb idea, a mistake, had forgotten they said it and were quick to bitch about Cliff getting a show of his own. And sure, it hit the jackpot. The Man gave it one of the best spots on the midway and spent money advertising, so the paper printed a story on Milt Hinkle. How could it lose?

Some of the praise soon changed to jealousy; *he ain't nothing but a smart-assed college kid who knows how to spell.* Others were happy for Cliff and Katie.

The ticket seller told Cliff that Milt had been asking for him. "He hobbled outa here a little while ago, wanted to see how much was in the box, but I wouldn't let him look. Told him I didn't know where you were."

In his room, he dropped on the bed and let the money roll beside him. Now he knew what Ace King felt like after eight Broadway Review shows, Bozo after a wet day with good pitchers, the Okefenokee Swamp Girl after licking the heads of black snakes, when the ding donation bucket was full. He thought about all of the bags of bills and coins piled up in the office wagons, weighing so much they had to be hauled in a truck and deposited in accounts scattered across the country. The carnival roamed east and west, north and south, collecting money.

He pulled the cardboard box out from under his bunk, aware of how heavy it was. The side of the cardboard was ripping down one seam and he thought, *I need a stronger, bigger box, a safe.* The room was filled with money, no room to sleep—a lot of money, freedom in Spain. The hassle of building the show was paying off and it was just getting started.

Cliff separated the bills into stacks of ones, fives, tens and twenties, and counted the numerous piles of coins, entering the total into the ledger. One hundred fifty-three brought the total to four hundred seventy five dollars and fifty cents. Not bad, and three days to go, three days with 250,000 newspapers bringing them through the gate.

Finished with the money, Cliff re-read the story about Milt, then turned to the short item about the young press agent running away with the circus. The reporter said he was doing something a lot of people dreamed about, and Cliff thought Carol Fraley was doing what he dreamed about. She had a job with a good newspaper, writing about people like Milt Hinkle and young press agents. But she never got to lie in a bed of money.

He laughed at the differences in what they did. Her work reached thousands of people who read the daily newspaper. His work reached thousands of people who listened to Bozo the Clown and Milt's spiel. One job paid more than the other.

"Now, I need it now." Milt's voice wavered. "You got to give me something now. I been sitting in the tent for four days, long days, pissing in a bucket, half the time no one brings me no food. Now, not the end of the week. I need money now."

"We agreed to divide up the end of the week." Cliff's fingers squeezed the money in his pocket.

"Can't wait."

Cliff gave him five, while he thought about what would happen if he bought vodka. "If you get drunk, you'll ruin things. I'm taking money out for your new clothes."

"Five? What am I going to do with five? Give me ten."

"Take it or leave it. I told Georgia Boy not to sell you anything. Get something to eat. Five will hold you till the end of the week."

Milt was still protesting when Cliff walked out of the tent. *The old man can't chase me. Steve told me what would happen. He was right. Have to treat him like Steve treats Jack, a dollar at a time, five would kill Jack. Might be too much for Milt. He can get a fifth somewhere. Georgia Boy isn't the only place to buy vodka. Jack will get it for him if he thinks Milt will share.*

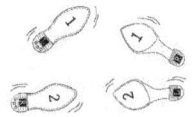

He slid the lockbox from under his bed and lifted a bound stack of bills marked one hundred. The wrapper snapped free and he slid the roll into his front pocket.

Should be more than enough.

While Cliff was dressing for the party, Lee Savage knocked on the door and told him Mastras wanted him to come to the office wagons. Cliff was torn. He desperately didn't want to get trapped in one of the mandatory dinners with the "big shots" of the night.

Cliff was going to be the big shot of the night. He had made arrangements for a bar to stay open after hours for a private party, a celebration hosted by Cliff Walker.

"Who's there? Do you know what he wants?"

Cliff knew he wouldn't get an answer from Lee. The old man heard and saw everything around the office wagons, but he didn't tell anything. Mastras was the only one who received information from Lee Savage. If Cliff didn't show up and Mastras asked Lee where he was, the old man would say he did what he was told to do, he gave Cliff Walker the message.

"Wait a minute." Lee watched while Cliff pulled the roll out of his pocket and extended his hand with a five pinched between his fingers. "Tell the Man you couldn't find me, okay?"

"Double that an' you invisible."

Cliff handed the old man two fives and watched them get folded over by the thick fingers. "You haven't seen me. For ten dollars, you don't even know my name."

"He'll think I'm stupid if'n I don't know your name. I knows who you are, just not where you is." With no more words, Lee walked away.

Cliff used his key to open the supply room and picked up a case of Canadian Club, stepped to the ground and put the box in the trunk of the car. He lifted one bottle out of the case, twisted the cap and swallowed straight whiskey. *The party will be a good one, music, food and dancing brought to you by Cliff Walker, your genial host, the man with the money.*

He sat in the car and kissed Katie. Her perfume drifted over the railroad tracks. Cliff pulled his arm away from her shoulders and turned the steering wheel to maneuver through the traffic leaving the fairgrounds.

"They're going home, pockets lighter, some of it in my cigar box. I was worried for a while, but now it's working."

Katie didn't respond and Cliff knew she didn't like to talk about money. He told her Milt was benefitting from the show. "It's his money. For the first time in a long time, he's earning something instead of begging. And no one knew what the publicity could do for him. Two hundred and fifty thousand people saw the story in the paper. He could get asked to appear on TV. That was where he should be, where people could see and hear him, like in the tent, but a bigger audience. He could end up famous after all."

They drove through the dark streets and parked in front of a closed nightclub, tapped on the door and waited for the owner to let them in.

"Just in time—thirsty people inside."

Cliff opened the trunk and handed the case of whiskey to the man. "This will take care of them. Thanks again for letting us use the club."

"You bringing free booze opened the door."

They walked inside and Nick locked the door and carried the case to the bar and surveyed the Mastras employees seated at the tables. People who had been spending money with him during the week, some of them he knew for a long time, once-a-year regulars, others—Cliff Walker, Katie—were new, and Nick thought a nice addition to the group, class.

A case of Canadian Club, cash for the set-ups, Katie dancing and, my God, that Pagan...he didn't know how to describe Pagan, a force of nature. Tonight she would dance with him and let him blow in her ear. She was wearing one of her leisure outfits, tight wherever it touched her skin, a pair of yellow pants and a bright blue blouse unbuttoned from her neck to her waist.

The saxophone played a melody; carrying the party to the dancers' dreams, love songs. Remembering the words, Cliff held Katie, blind to anything except the music and the warmth of each other. Cliff graciously accepted their thanks for the party and matched them drink for drink. The whiskey and the praise lifted him to an invincible place, king of the night, a dancer with wings on his feet, money in his pocket, moving to the music with Katie. Smoke blanketed the air, drums talked, perfume and soft skin and full glasses.

Katie danced with invisible links joining her hips and shoulders, her movements clean and smooth.

I don't know how she does it. When she moves that way, all my pain is gone. Cliff knew the rum was talking but he also knew the rum was helping him see. No one could dance like the girl he was watching and he knew she was dancing for him.

"Drink up." Cliff filled Nick's glass. "You enjoying yourself?"

Nick's face was thick and red, and he thanked Cliff again. "You're the man, the man with the Canadian Club. You know, you look a little like Mr. Mastras, act like him, too."

Cliff opened another bottle and drank. *Not sure if I want to be compared to Mastras but why not? Better than being compared to Bozo. Not like any of them. Not Mastras, Steve Lanning, none of them. I'm Cliff Walker, writer…someday this night will be captured…someday.*

He felt the urgency. *It will happen. I will write this, all of it. If I don't, I won't be able to live with myself, tell what it's like to jump out of the comfort zone, to laugh with the clowns, to drink with the animals, to fly with the boss. Words are all I have, why don't I use them, the big, big why?*

"If Milt keeps bringing in the marks, I'm going to stay until the end of the season. Not just for the money…" Cliff paused. "It is for the money, but not for the money's sake. I want to do what you're doing. I want to write like I don't need the money. I need money to do that."

"I understand." Katie pulled him closer.

"Do you? Or are you just saying that?"

"I understand. I do."

Her answer left him feeling empty. Relieved that she didn't ask the hard question: *If you want to write, why don't you? Do the work instead of producing sarcasm for Bozo and meaningless drivel for Milt—and drinking to avoid it.*

He held her tight, happy she didn't ask. He wished someone or something could force him to do the work.

"I understand how good it feels to hold you." Cliff kissed her cheek and she turned her face to him, offering her lips.

"Wonderful." Katie pulled him closer. "Kissing is wonderful, can't be put in words."

"One more. One more and one more." Cliff didn't want to waste time finding a glass but he knew drinking straight from the bottle wasn't the way to do it, not in front of Katie.

No clean glasses; cigarette butts and pieces of food littered the tables. He found a glass behind the bar and filled it with rum and added Coke and swallowed and thought about the words he would use to describe this scene. Reporters knew all about drinking scenes, all writers did, it was part of the apprenticeship, part of making it right and true, the way to see clearly.

He picked up another bottle and circulated through the tables, filling glasses and kissing necks and stumbling to the shifting rhythm of the drums, wondering why the music sounded so erratic, *maybe they're tired, maybe they're as drunk as the rest of us.*

At four in the morning, the saxophone player announced the last dance and Katie and Cliff sat together in the same chair singing with the band, *make it one for my baby and one more for the road.*

As they put away the instruments, Katie thanked the band members for the music and the saxophone player thanked her for staying until the end and said, "You are a great dancer. You should try it professionally."

When Cliff started to tell him she was a professional, Katie squeezed his hand and shook her head and led him out of the club.

"I didn't want to tell him I'm dancing in a strip show."

"What about Radio City Music Hall? That would impress him."

"It's all right, he paid me a nice compliment."

Cliff didn't argue when Katie sat behind the wheel. She drove slowly with the window open and he leaned against her, resting his head on her shoulder. There were few cars on the roads and he didn't want to get to the train.

"You better stop." Cliff opened the door and jumped away from the car. In his blurred view, the stars and the moon were spinning and he dropped to his knees and vomited until he thought his intestines would come up. It didn't stop and he stumbled further away, hoping Katie wasn't aware of the quantity, wishing she would put the car in gear and leave him alone in the ditch.

When he returned to the car he fell into the seat and slid against the door with his face toward the open window, away from her, and passed out. When they got to the train, she couldn't wake him up and left him asleep in the car.

The pain woke him up, pain in his head and shoulders from the cramped position against the car door. Cliff walked slowly, shaking, unbalanced in the dark, and quietly knocked on the door. She opened it and pulled together her robe, "I don't want you to sleep in the car but not sure why." She reached for his hand. "Let's walk. You need some fresh air."

"I need some toothpaste."

The warmth of her hand surprised Cliff. No stars showed in the black sky. A breeze promised rain, cool air covered them and moistened the cinders. They walked the length of the train, silent rooms except for the radio playing in the Pie Car where a few people were playing cards. Cliff moved his arm to her shoulders and they leaned against the car and he hugged her, wishing the toothpaste had been available.

"What does your dad think about you staying out all night?"

"He's okay with it…"

"Let's go back to bed."

"Not tonight."

"I really want to."

"I know."

"You don't want to?"

"Of course I do. I'm normal, but not tonight."

He hesitated, trying to control the tension. "Why not tonight?"

"Please don't." Katie squeezed her eyes shut as tears spilled down her cheeks. She put her arms around Cliff. He pulled her closer, smelling her hair, feeling the softness of her body against his.

"I don't want to leave you tonight."

"I don't want you to, either." Katie took a breath. "I need to explain something."

She leaned against his chest and brought her lips to his and kissed him. The passion started to build and she pulled away. "You could come with me, write in New York."

"You don't have to explain. It's really all right. It frustrates me, especially when you're so close, when I can feel you and smell you—it's frustrating as hell but it's who you are."

"I don't know how to take that."

"Don't take it the wrong way. I mean it in a nice way."

"I'm not sleeping with you because…"

"Because?"

"I'm afraid it will hurt you."

"Making love will hurt me? What are you going to do?"

"Not that. I'm afraid if I tell you the reason, it will hurt you."

"Tell me. I can take it."

Katie stepped back and took both of his hands in hers. "It's the way you acted tonight, when you're drinking and throwing money around. I don't like you like that. It isn't who you are. I'm not Pagan. I'm not one of them."

He heard what she was saying, but the words couldn't be real. *Didn't she understand?* The work, building a sideshow that made money, was worth celebrating. He didn't want to admit that she had seen through it, seen through him. It was too much for him to admit it was a shallow success, meaningless victory.

"I don't understand. Was I that bad? I just wanted to share with some of the others. Aren't you happy that Milt is doing well?"

"Yes, I am."

"What's wrong with a little celebration?" When she didn't say anything, Cliff felt his irritation getting stronger. "I think we better stop this."

"If that's what you want."

"It's not what I want. I want you. But I don't want your dad, too. That's what this is about isn't it—your dad."

"Yes, partly. He started it but now it's me, mostly me. You're the same way, aren't you? Doesn't your dad influence you?"

"Not like yours. I don't want to meet your dad."

"He'll be in New York."

His head was starting to clear, but he still felt the rum. "I can't do it this way. You ask too much."

Katie's voice broke as she cried. "I'm going to bed, alone. Please don't say anymore. We'll talk tomorrow."

Cliff shook his head and the night squeezed down around him. His eyes focused enough to see her as she climbed the steps. He hoped that she would turn and motion for him to join her, but she disappeared inside the train. He sagged with frustration.

For balance, he slid his hands along the sides of the hallway and slumped against the wall, staring at the closed door, wanting to be able to twist the knob and walk into her arms. From where he was standing, the door looked like a bank vault.

His body ached for her and he imagined her undressing on the other side of the thin metal.

Punching his fists together, Cliff turned away. When he got to the end of the car, Pagan opened her door, smiling, a bottle of wine in her hand. Her blue blouse had been replaced with a soft white robe, red hair like frosting on a cake.

"Can you help me with this cork?"

"Your dad isn't in there, is he?" Cliff asked.

"I want you to be my daddy for a while."

Cliff's legs shook as he stepped toward her, then he stopped and turned away. "Not happening. Don't get me wrong, not about you...wrong thing to do tonight."

Outside, he walked to his car and slid into the back seat and slumped, with his eyes crimped shut.

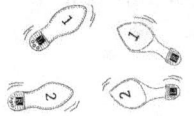

In the morning when Steve saw him, he didn't question why Cliff was sleeping in the car. The news of the party had spread up and down the train. Steve tapped him on the arm and waited for him to wake up.

Cliff blinked in the light. "What?"

Steve said, "I know what. You was the king of the hop last night, that's what. You want some breakfast?"

"Coffee, hot coffee. Who told you?"

"The Man. He said you were trying to be the big man."

"I guess he's not mad, then." Cliff's head burned. He didn't care what Mastras knew about the party.

"Didn't act like he was mad. If he is, it's because he wasn't invited." They drove away from the train to a diner squeezed between a shoe factory and a grim apartment house. Across the street, the neon signs on a beer joint were dark, sunlight reflected from the glass tubes. Cans and paper and cigarette butts shifted in the wind, back and forth against the curb like filthy surf.

Cliff took the first booth, his stomach thumping, the smell of grease and bacon sticking in his throat. "What else did he say?"

"Said you passed the test."

"Test? What test?"

"Young man on his way."

"Where?"

"Sixty-four-dollar question—where?" Steve lit a cigarette and offered one to Cliff. "Where do you think?"

"You tell me, I passed the test." Cliff leaned his head against the booth, holding the hot cup against his forehead. "If I passed a test, it was rigged."

"There are all kinds of tests. Don't pass the one I did, you might better watch out for it."

"Which one you talking about?"

"Major league drunk, not a test you want to pass."

"Big leagues with Jack?"

"Like I say, it ain't a test you want to pass."

"You trying to tell me something?"

"No. I learned at the AA meetings you can't tell anyone nothing, no one could tell me. I knew I was a drunk, but I didn't want to stop until I believed I would die."

"So what test did I pass?" Before he heard Steve's answer, Cliff dropped his head to the table. "I know I didn't pass a good test with Katie, just hope I didn't fail completely. It was a good party— what I can remember. Failed the test with Katie, never drink again. Not until tonight."

Three blocks away they stopped at a convenience store. "Get me a pack of Camels."

Cliff looked at his face in the rearview mirror. "How about you getting the cigarettes and me some beer."

"What kind of beer?" Steve opened the car door.

"Any kind of dark beer—and aspirin."

Steve came out of the store carrying a paper bag. He pulled out his cigarettes and handed the bag to Cliff and said he was going to a used bookstore across the street.

Cliff asked, "Why?"

"Buy a book. What you do at a bookstore, ain't it?"

"You want a book?"

"Book or a bottle."

Cliff opened the bag and pulled out the six-pack. "Budweiser?"

"All they had."

"Did you look for dark beer? You didn't look, did you? You got your Camels, but no Beck's."

"I don't like German beer. Gave half my ear to a German. Buy American."

"At least you got the aspirin." He shook out three tablets and swallowed them with a long drink of beer and wondered what Steve would buy in the bookstore.

He finished the second beer and walked across the street to the bookstore. He found a worn paperback copy of *The Great Gatsby* and paid for it and handed it to Steve.

"Read this instead of those cowboys and Indians."

"What is it?"

"Fitzgerald."

"I've heard of him."

"One of the best. You read that and Kerouac, you'll be a real know-it-all literary giant."

The clerk listened to Steve's rough voice, stared at his rough clothes, his rough hands thinking they didn't go together. The young guy looked like a college boy and the old guy looked like a truck mechanic and they were discussing F. Scott Fitzgerald.

They returned to the train, grateful for the few hours before the show opened. Cliff closed the door to an empty room, laid down, and lowered the blind. The beer and three more aspirin and he slept and dreamed about holding Katie's hand in New York City. He dreamed about being stuck with Milt Hinkle forever, terrible dreams with Mastras and board members and a ruined relationship with a girl that knew where she was going and no one would give him directions.

In his dream, he heard soft knocking on the door and Katie's voice and it pulled him awake. He raised his head, listening, then he rolled out of bed and opened the door and saw her leaning against the wall.

"Come back, please." Her eyes were red.

"How did you find me?"

She raised her hands to his cheeks. "You were shouting in your sleep. You look sick. How bad do you feel?" He held her in his arms lifting his head above hers so she couldn't smell the beer on his breath. He wanted to hold her close as long as she would stay.

"I'm so glad you're here." Cliff whispered. "More than you know."

Katie pulled away and nodded her head. "Do you want to tell me what happened last night?"

"I drank too much. I'm drinking too much, too much of the time."

Her eyes accepted the answer and Cliff knew there would be no more questions.

"Come back to the room. I can't stay out here."

They didn't know what to do in her small room. He turned away and slid down to the floor with his back against the wall.

Katie sat on the bed. "That isn't comfortable. Come up here."

"I'd better stay here." Cliff held her hand. "I'm sorry about last night."

"Thank you. I worry about you." Katie slid off the bed and leaned against him on the floor. "What is it, what's bothering you?"

"I drink too much."

"Why?"

"Jumping up and down every time Mastras clears his throat. I wish I was a dancer. You get to dance. I don't. Maybe I wouldn't drink if I could dance. I do the boogie whenever Mastras tells me to."

They sat on the floor and Cliff felt his eyes begin to close and he wanted another beer. He didn't want her to leave. He wanted to ask her questions about her dad's church, about dancing. He wanted to talk about his plan, about writing but she had already heard it. *Not the kind of man you saw last night. Not really someone who does whatever it takes to make money. Don't always drink, act like a big shot.*

"We said doing a show for Milt Hinkle would be a good thing, something to help the old man, tell people about his life. But people don't care about an old man's colorful life. They don't come to the fairgrounds to be educated. They want to be thrilled, scared, aroused, nauseated, titillated—but not educated."

Katie said, "You look like you're not long for this world. Why don't you get some sleep? I have some things to take care of before the call. Will I see you later?"

He kissed her goodbye. "Sorry about the beer breath. I'll be there when you close. Mastras has a dinner set for tonight, but I won't be going. No puppet act for me tonight."

He Would Be Able to Fill a Canvas Bag with Coins and Bills, but He Knew It Was the Gin Doing the Talking

Milt's show stumbled and faded and fell, the cigar box almost empty.

The competition—stuffed animals, foulmouthed clowns, snakes, naked women and thrill rides—drew the marks away and Milt didn't sell many tickets. Cliff couldn't hustle newspaper coverage in every town.

They walked past the painted jail front, listened to the grind tape, and continued walking. Cliff walked past the painted jail several times a day, checking the cigar box, then his visits became fewer and fewer until he found it impossible to go to that part of the midway—impossible until his curiosity overpowered him and he forced himself to look again, hoping the box would at least have the bottom covered with coins and bills. The pony tied to the hitching post in front of the jail was the only thing which drew much attention and the kids could pet it for free.

Mastras told Cliff they would be entertaining the Fair Board that night at the best restaurant in town, and Cliff was relieved to know he would be someplace where he couldn't check the till. As

much as he grew to dislike spending time with the local officials, it was better than spending the night where he could watch as the customers passed up a chance to talk to a legend.

Best thing was to go to dinner with the Man, drink too much, act busy and important, and avoid the situation.

At the restaurant, Cliff ordered gin and tonic and imagined the cigar box filling up so he would be able to fill a canvas bag with coins and bills, but he knew it was the gin doing the talking.

He found it hard to talk about the good weather and how much would be added to the Fair Board's bank account. They wanted to build a new grandstand and the Mastras money would make it happen faster. Cliff thought how the Broadway Review was grossing serious money. Steve Lanning's menagerie was crowded most of the day and the Okefenokee Swamp Girl was breaking records. Everyone was carrying heavy bags to the office except Cliff.

After dinner, Cliff escorted the board members around the midway, smiling past his depression. He understood it was part of the business.

When they approached the Broadway Review, the front stage was empty, and Cliff could tell from the music that Pagan was starting her act. He told the men that they could catch her last performance if they hurried, but he wasn't going to join them because he felt sick and they agreed to go in without him. They didn't care if he was dying—as long as they could watch Pagan.

Cliff waved them through the entrance and told the ticket taker to find them front row seats. "This is the last show of the night. Thanks for coming out tonight. I hope to see you again before we leave." He dropped his forced smile when they entered the tent, wishing he could go backstage and wrap Katie in his arms, but he couldn't make himself sit in the audience.

He returned to the office. Mastras handed him a hundred and told him, "It never changes, never. I don't like it any more than you do, but it's what we do. They build a new grandstand, bring in big names and we make more money."

Cliff slid low in the chair. "Thank you. I need more money. Milt isn't doing worth a damn. Like the guys selling watermelons, Milt thinks he needs a bigger stage."

Mastras said, "I checked the numbers."

Cliff shook his head. "Nothing to get excited about."

He didn't want to admit it had been a mistake. He chalked it up to experience, inexperience, to greed. "Not many marks want to pay a quarter to listen to a lecture on western history, not when they can watch the swamp girl slip a snake in her mouth."

"We're like any other business, if we don't give them what they want, they keep their money in their pockets." Mastras told Cliff his strategy. "I wait to see what works, let someone else try it out first. If I see it's a winner, then I buy one."

"I thought I did that with Milt." Cliff said. "All the history he's got in his trunk, the reporters love him, story in the *Boston Herald*. It worked, we did pretty good...for a few days."

Mastras nodded his head. "Good press doesn't always work. Something else is wrong."

"Real wrong. I put two thousand in the tent, the front. Milt's always begging for money. The way it's going, I won't ever get my money back and it keeps costing me more."

Mastras told Cliff to shut it down. "Walk away before you lose any more. If you want, tell him I'm shutting you down, put it on me."

CHAPTER 38

You Better Watch, That Booze Will Get You— It's Got You Real Good Tonight

N o good alone in bed. In the dark, the empty cigar box seemed to fill the room.

Cliff imagined the jail front faded and peeling, a savaged ghost town, weeds winding through the broken boardwalk, paper, litter, stacked against the door, splintered, jagged glass hanging in the window frames, rusty tin cans left by bums and drunks. His imagination turned it into the jail of terror where the ghost of Milt Hinkle would show you his broken hips and frozen legs, and tell you long, boring stories about the good old days in the good old Wild West.

He opened the door to the liquor storage room and picked up a fifth of whiskey, unscrewed the cap and chugged deeply, not gagging anymore. Then he plowed into the Pie Car and sat next to Steve and teased Milt with the open bottle.

When Milt reached for it, Cliff pulled it away.

"Get a glass."

Milt looked pathetic as drool spilled from his lips, his wild eyes searching for a glass. He heaved his chest over the tabletop and pushed with both hands, trying to stand, and Cliff told him to sit down.

"I'll get you a glass, but tell me: Is it Springfield? Maybe they don't like cowboys and Indians. What is it? What's wrong? We haven't made enough to feed the pony. They like naked women in Springfield. They like snakes. They don't like the Sheriff of Dodge City." Cliff tapped the fifth. "I hope we catch up in Providence. Drink up, partner."

Looking at the level of whiskey, Cliff swallowed again and offered the bottle to Steve Lanning. "Want to break your dry spell? Let's drink to cigar boxes full of money."

Steve shook his head and lit a cigarette and moved his eyes from Cliff to Milt. "If you're trying to keep Milt from asking for more money, you picked a good way to do it."

"Would I do that? Not that devious." Cliff refilled Milt's glass and said to Steve, "Sorry I asked you to drink—not right."

"You better watch, that damned stuff will get you—it's got you real good tonight."

Cliff lifted the bottle and poured the whiskey on the floor, a pool of clear alcohol lifting dirt as it puddled over the matted carpet. One cigarette butt dissolved in shreds. He poured until it was empty.

Steve laughed when he saw the look on Milt's face. "Look at that, Milt. Good liquor on the dirty floor. Get down there and lick it up. If you could, you would. You damned sure would." Steve offered Cliff a cigarette. "I don't guess it's got a hold of you yet, not if you can do that."

"No, not the booze, just the money. I'm not sure which is worse." Cliff could see the full cigar box, feel the sun in Spain. "Will we catch up in Providence?"

"If you get his picture on the front page. If you don't, it ain't gonna work. I should have known better, bad idea. He's always been a bad idea, nothing changed. Only good thing, you might be the last one getting hurt by his bad deals. No glory in that except you can say you're the last of the last."

Maybe one more story would do it. Cliff was tired. Maybe they wouldn't care the story already ran in Boston. Maybe a new angle? *Meet the man—shake his hand, meet the man.* Were there any new angles? The last of the last. That's something for a book.

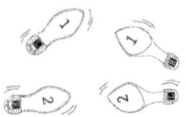

During the set-up, Cliff entered the name of the town, Providence, in his notebook and added that it wasn't going to be provident for Milt. *It isn't prudent management. Prudent management says shut it down, cut my losses.*

Jack stumbled and tore a poster, and when he taped it back together, the paper was wrinkled, the headline hard to read. Cliff tried to straighten it, but the damage was done and when he looked around, the crappy posters and small pictures embarrassed him; not what it was supposed to look like. But the kids liked to pet the pony. He told Jack to leave, before he broke something else.

Milt Hinkle's last stand, a sagging tent, faded posters, cheap loudspeakers, empty words, Jack imitating an airplane to attract customers.

They call this show business?

Lesson learned. Listening to Milt, digging through his trunk, the newspaper articles, the posters, photographs, excited crowds paying money to see the rodeo champ jump out of an airplane. Small pieces of his life were visible on the walls of the tent, but not enough to fill the moneybox, not enough to attract the crowds, not enough to do justice to Milt Hinkle's life.

Cliff wondered if Milt's life was interesting to anyone else. *Just because I think it's fascinating doesn't mean anyone else thinks so and apparently, they don't. What's it say about me? Doesn't matter what they think.*

Jack opened his hand. He expected money, fingers bending and unbending.

"See Steve if you want money, you work for him."

Cliff knew he would be better off setting up without Jack. *Hiring one of the kids looking for free passes would be better than putting up with the smelly drunk. I will get hooked on booze if I have to keep this up. One more week, if the cigar box isn't full this week, the Sheriff of Dodge City will end up in a history book no one will ever read.*

Around him, the tents and rides grew like spring crops, metal stalks pushed into the air, leaves and buds, flowering girders that turned and swayed in the breeze, mushroom tents ballooned between the spindly iron blossoms, a garden offering spoiled fruit to the marks.

Cliff walked away from the sheriff show. He watched the rides and shows, the ones that would have full cigar boxes. It should be depressing, but Cliff still saw opportunities. He understood the sheriff show wasn't one of the big winners, but he believed there were ways to get a piece of the action. He was surprised by his optimism, thinking Milt was just a warm-up, a lesson learned. Mastras told him the secret—get something that was a proven winner. Don't be creative.

He heard himself saying, "don't be creative." *What else is there?"*

What am I doing? The same old, same, same problem. Got to have the money. Do I? Is it easier to chase the money than do the hard work? Writing isn't hard if I believe in it. The question is do I believe? Katie sure believes. Kerouac believes. Hemingway believed so much he won the Nobel Peace Prize, that's some serious belief.

A TV crew was taping the activity, focusing on the merry-go-round. Cliff introduced himself. "I'm Cliff Walker, Public Relations

Manager. What can I do to help? Can I give you some information on this merry-go-round? It's one of the finest and oldest in the business, hand-carved by Italian craftsmen."

The reporter shook hands with Cliff, telling him they didn't have much time and all they needed were general shots of the carnival. "We have enough for now, but we'll be back later. Can you show us around?"

"Anytime. Here's my card, you can find me at the office wagons, by the front gate. If I'm not there, they'll send someone to find me. What was your name?"

"Jason Parker, channel six. Thanks for your help."

Cliff thanked Parker.

It's a win-win situation, Parker will get an exclusive interview with Milt Hinkle, a scoop on the rich piece of western history hidden in a tent on a carnival midway. I'll get something in the cigar box, long green for a creative winter in Spain.

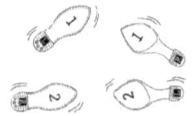

The next day Cliff found the TV camera already set up, aimed at a milk bottle game and Jason Parker was watching two young men throw hardballs.

Cliff was angry. He had spent the morning prepping Milt, cleaning him up, ready to give the TV reporter an interview, but Parker returned to the midway and hadn't asked for him.

Parker told the cameraman to zoom in on the wooden milk bottles. "We can fill the screen with a bottle, get the balls flying past without knocking them all down." He asked Cliff if anyone ever won. "I tried to find you, got distracted."

"Okay, I found you. Winners every day. It's not impossible. Sure they win. No one would play if they didn't. Do your viewers want to see men throwing baseballs at milk bottles? What about the rides, the shows, the Okefenokee Swamp Girl, the Sheriff of Dodge City?" Cliff stopped talking when he realized how he sounded. *A hired flack trying to sell a story, not what a real reporter wanted to hear.*

"I've never seen anyone win." Parker watched the young men throw and miss, throw and hit the bottles, but one remained on the stool, throw and miss until they shook their heads and told the agent they were through and walked away as they looked back at the bottles which seemed to taunt them as they sat anchored to the stool. "We want to find out if anyone ever wins."

Cliff followed them when they moved the camera to the balloon toss. He watched as the darts missed the inflated targets. He listened when Parker asked the player if he had ever won. "Do you think it's possible to win?"

"I did last year. I seen a few girls carrying big bears."

"Not many, though?"

"Not too many. I don't care much about them cheap bears, rather drop that loud mouth clown in the water, never done it, not yet. I'll get him tonight."

They moved the camera to the cat rack where players threw at the fuzzy animals. The cats tipped over but they didn't fall down, their smiling faces begging to be hit.

Cliff made eye contact with the game agent and pointed to the camera, message sent and received.

The agent understood, nodded his head, and handed the boy three balls. "Knock them off, knock three off, three for a quarter, and take your choice, any prize on the top rack. You got the arms, big arms, who's the winner, who's gonna grab the big prize, the top shelf prize? Do it, do it for your girlfriend."

Two balls hit the cats and knocked them off the rack, but the third ball grazed the fringe, sending the stuffed animal backward but it didn't fall clear, lying on its back, mocking the pitcher. The cameraman focused on the player's disappointed face.

"Almost, almost a winner." The agent handed the pitcher three more balls. "You'll get it this time. Tell you what I'm going to do. Pay me fifty cents, knock off two—not three, two—and take your choice—top shelf."

The pitcher handed over two quarters and picked up the ball and stepped back from the counter. He shook his arms loose, rubbing the ball with his fingers. Calmly he wound up and threw, not hard. The ball hit the cat squarely in the face, sending it off the rack.

"One down, one to go. Here goes one, here goes a winner."

As the mark prepared for his second throw, the agent leaned against the counter and used his knee to shift a lever sideways so when the ball hit the stuffed cat, it fell back, back and off the rack.

"There goes one, there goes a winner, a big winner!" The camera zoomed on the mark as he picked out the biggest stuffed bear on the top shelf. "Another winner, another prize. Who's next, who's the next winner, where are the ball players? Where are the winners? There goes another one!" His knee shifted the lever back.

Cliff could already see the mark's big grin filling the screen on the eleven o'clock news. If the editor knew what he was doing, he'd realize he had more than a short clip on midway games, he had a tight story about winning and losing, an upbeat tale of a town boy overcoming impossible odds, a happy winner carrying a big, worthless prize.

Too bad the camera couldn't record the agent's knee as it moved the lever. Now that would be a great story. That story would have layers, how the agent controlled the game, deciding who wins and when, estimating how much money the mark was willing to lose to win the cheap prize, layers of manipulation of the press, not-so-subtle tricks played on unsuspecting journalists, subtler than a stone in an elephant's foot…but not much.

Too much for TV, not right for the newspaper.

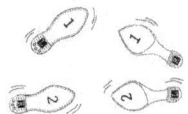

Jason Parker's attention was drawn to intense conversations moving from game to game, small clusters of agents sharing serious words, shock showing in their eyes, and when Cliff saw Canadian Red stop hustling the marks, letting several players stand with money in their hands, he knew something had happened, something out of the ordinary.

Jason Parker sensed a story and motioned the cameraman into position.

Canadian Red saw the camera and moved closer to Cliff, then passed a message in a quiet voice. "They just found Jack dead behind the menagerie, elephant smashed his head."

Dead. Cliff imagined Jack dead. *How could they tell? Dead or dead drunk. What does his head look like, smashed, broken, blood and brains oozing between the elephant's toes? He was just begging money from me. No more. Dead? Jack can't be dead. I just saw him. Now the reporter will get a story, real news, a great big head-crushing story.*

The camera crew was waiting. Jason Parker knew something had happened, the tension on the creased faces wasn't because of casual conversation. Cliff wanted the reporter to leave, but he knew it wouldn't happen.

Don't want him to find out what's happened, don't want thousands of viewers to hear about an elephant killing a carnival worker. What will happen to the elephant? Then again, it doesn't make any difference whether it's good news or bad news, as long as we make the news? What am I saying? But I did. I did think it. What's happening to me?

"What's going on?" Jason Parker asked. "Something's going on."

"I'll tell you in a minute, wait here."

Running to the office wagons, Cliff knew Parker and the cameraman were following. Turning into the office compound, he realized his mistake. He had delivered the TV crew to the middle of the problem. Mastras and several superintendents were standing in a tight knot, as they listened to Steve tell what he knew about the death.

"An accident." When Steve made the statement, he spoke slowly and clearly. His words were not to be doubted.

Mastras was the only member of the group permitted to ask questions. "Are you sure?"

"I'm sure."

"Why?"

"I know them animals. If it wasn't an accident, he'd be in worse shape, tore up."

When Mastras saw the camera, he whipped his finger across his lips. "Dummy up." The silence drew more attention than if they had continued talking.

"What's happened?" Jason Parker asked Cliff. "You know we'll find out."

"Not sure how it happened, but one of our employees has been found dead."

"People die every day. What's special about this one?"

It was the right question, but not the one Cliff wanted to answer.

Parker was a good reporter and he knew there was more going on, more than what he'd been told. If a man was dead, it was more than a heart attack. It had to be an unusual death, what a reporter was trained to find out.

Cliff looked at Steve Lanning, silently asking for help, but the trainer shrugged his shoulders and turned back to Mastras.

Before Cliff stumbled with an answer, two policemen entered the compound. Without hesitation, they saw who was in charge and asked Jim Mastras where the body was. "We got the call from dispatch, someone killed by an elephant?"

No stopping the camera, the scene was being recorded and Jason Parker could already see the evening news. He knew the dialogue between Steve and the policemen would tell the story and the twisted faces of the listeners underscored the words.

The policeman listened to Steve. "A long time. He's been with me a long time."

Steve's voice was rough, but Cliff heard a vulnerable note that surprised him. "Never know. Could 'a been he scored a big bottle. He should 'a been dead a dozen times. Didn't think it would happen, not after all them other times. Tractor run over him one night but missed his head, hardly got hurt." Steve shook his head and lit a cigarette.

The policeman told Steve they needed to inspect the scene. Before they went behind the tent, the cop in charge told Jason Parker the TV crew couldn't follow, and they stretched yellow tape across the opening. The TV crew waited.

A flash blinked as the police photographer took pictures of the body and the elephant's foot.

"Why?" the officer asked Steve. "If he made it this long, why now? Did he do something to provoke the elephant?"

"He might of, hard to say." Steve inhaled. "You're a cop, you get your share of drunks? None of 'em make sense, neither did Jack. Didn't make no sense most of the time. You want to try and figure out how his head got smashed, okay. If you do, it won't make no difference. He run out of luck and now I got to find someone else to shovel shit."

"What was his last name?"

"Lawrence."

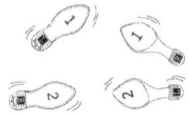

Backstage at the Broadway Review, Pagan told the rest of the dancers what she had heard. Katie listened and shook her head; tears fell, and she wiped her eyes.

Seeing Katie cry softened the older girls, and one by one, they joined her. None of them had ever paid much attention to Jack and they wondered why Katie was so upset. She was quietly crying and it affected them in a way they didn't understand. Her shaking shoulders and sobbing brought tears to their eyes. Pagan was the only one that wasn't crying, but as she watched, she knew the next show would be delayed.

Marks stood in lines and waited for the rides to start turning, but the operators didn't pull the levers. They stood still and listened to the message being passed around the midway. Wisps of cotton candy drifted out of the spinning machines as the vendors leaned on the counter, while the vendors ignored customers' requests. Bozo dropped his platform and climbed out of the water tank to find out what was going on.

For a short time, the midway slowed down. It didn't come to a complete stop. Music still blared from the loudspeakers, but the ticket sellers, the ride boys, the game agents left their stations and traded what they had heard about the accident. They looked at each other and nodded their heads, sharing the death, until the presence of outsiders brought them back to the business at hand and they pushed the levers and the merry-go-round spun again.

Cliff decided to call Carol Fraley. Her Boston newspaper might cover Jack's death. If it did, he hoped she would write more than easy facts. Jason Parker's video would appear on the six o'clock news, without footage of the elephant or Jack's head, but the *Boston Herald* could print something that would do justice to Jack, the man who thought he owned a chain of restaurants—maybe he had at one time—a man who had an education, maybe he had graduated from college—a man who was an expert at hustling enough money to buy booze every day, who lived and slept with the animals on a pile of straw—who counted as his best friend the legendary Milt Hinkle, star of the Sheriff of Dodge City show, appearing on the Mastras midway from Florida to Maine. Jack deserved more than a thirty-second shot on television.

When he got Carol Fraley on the phone, he told her what had happened. "You can see it on channel six." She wanted to know more details and agreed to come to the memorial service scheduled in the Broadway Review tent. She wasn't under the same time pressure as the TV crews. She could take a few days to dig up background on Jack and weave it into a feature and, if the editor liked it, the story might make the Sunday edition.

Television sets in the house trailers and midway offices and the Pie Car told the story. Accidental or intentional, death by elephant foot was big news and Cliff morbidly knew if one of the sideshow owners had been in charge of the broadcast, there would be multiple close-ups of Jack's flattened head filling the TV screens. Fortunately, the cameraman wasn't able to record any footage of Jack's body except when it was carried away, zipped tight inside a body bag.

He wished he didn't understand it, but he did. The marks would want to see for themselves, see the head-smashing elephant, alive on the inside.

The next day, the lines at the front gate extended into the parking lot and there were loud complaints when the marks found out the elephants were not on view.

What is it about these people? What makes them want to see the foot that killed Jack Lawrence? The same thing when they see an accident on the highway, the drivers slow down hoping to see brains between the toes.

"How's Milt doing?" Steve pulled the string tight on a canvas bag.

Cliff felt the folded bills in his pocket. "Everyone's doing good business…I'm sorry to say. Tells us a lot about people, doesn't it?"

"All we got to do is kill someone in every town. Do your job for you."

CHAPTER 39

You Know You Can't Use Common Sense with a Drunk

The police didn't know what to do about Jack's death.

They questioned Steve again. How could the elephant accidentally step on his head? The walls of the interrogation room were covered with photographs of the scene and a black outline has been painted on the ground, showing the position of Jack's body.

"How could he sleep so close to the huge animals?"

"With a quart of vodka in him, he passed out under the train one time, across the railroad tracks."

"The elephants were chained?"

"Yeah, always."

"So he had to go to them, they couldn't move to where he was?"

"I just told you he slept around. He could 'a been filing their toenails. God knows what was going on, you never know with a drunk. I know what I'm talking about, I drank with him for a long time…a long, long time. Look what happened to my ear. You *know* you can't use common sense with a drunk."

"What happened to your ear?"

Steve shook his head. "I woke up and it was gone." Steve looked at the photograph which showed the outline of Jack's body. "He got run over by a tractor one time, broke his leg, should have killed him then."

"We're getting pressure from some of the animal activists. They think you're mistreating the animals. They want the elephants removed from the show and this death gives them a reason."

"It happens. They come around, we show them how the animals are treated; they go away. It's worse on the big circuses." When Steve told them about his career with the Ringling Brothers and Barnum & Bailey Circus, the police were impressed.

In the end, the chief investigator decided it must have been an accident and submitted his report to the county coroner, who accepted the decision without further question, largely because the police and the commissioners and the mayor had too many conversations about what they would do with the elephant. The only option was to put it to death, and that possibility was considered very briefly and only once. They wanted the Fair to complete its run and the carnival train to leave town. In a year, the incident would be forgotten and the show would go on.

No witnesses, and therefore impossible for the police to know how Jack had died. It was like Steve said. He was drunk, drunker than usual, blind drunk, dazed and numb.

He had crawled under their thick, powerful legs, falling down three times, finally sliding on his stomach where he pulled himself upright by leaning on bales of hay and a wheelbarrow and stumbling in circles in front of the elephants.

And he had ranted, talking to the air, announcing how he was going to lead Queenie to a headstand, a dance, a performance never to be forgotten. "Watch me now, watch me…Joan, Katie, watch… watch…watch…"

When Jack's eyes closed, his hands clawed for support, his legs buckled, stumbling against the elephant's trunk and he wrapped his arms around it, embracing something steady and the animal innocently waved the muscle back and forth, trying to dislodge the irritating man, swinging back and forth while Jack told the air to watch.

"Watch me now, Joan…watch, Katie…here we go, where we stop…we stop." Like a leaf, his body somersaulted and flipped over, landing under the big front foot, and when Queenie stepped down, Jack's head exploded and he died instantly.

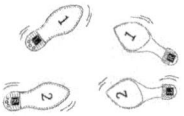

Milt hobbled into the Broadway Review tent and sat next to Steve.

The stage was empty, daylight seeped through the canvas, shining an awkward glow over the people seated in the tent, a gathering of mourners where there were usually noisy men waiting for the strippers. In the daylight, the stage appeared worn, in need of repair.

Cliff thought how at night the yellow spots created a glamorous illusion, but in the thin morning light, the tent was appropriate for a memorial service. He suggested to Carol Fraley that she write about the Broadway Review tent becoming a temporary church. No suits and ties, no proper dresses, instead, an assortment of tattoos, twisted faces, missing limbs, greasy pants—friends who lived on a rainbow train. She sat quietly next to Cliff, sporadically moving her pencil.

Somewhere in the crowd, they heard voices crying. Cliff wasn't surprised at the number of people and he wondered who was shedding tears over Jack. Joan and Katie walked down the aisle hugging each other, holding tissues to their eyes. Cliff's eyes watered when he looked at Katie. She stopped next to his seat and he stood and felt his legs weaken when she wrapped her arms around him. Cliff didn't want to let her go, but he understood she was helping Joan. They took their seats next to Bill and Ruth.

Carol Fraley wrote a question. "What is that about?"

Cliff shook his head and whispered, "How much time do you have?"

The tent was filled to capacity; Jack had been one of them.

Seamus Flannigan walked to the front and faced the crowd. He looked like Steve Lanning's taller brother: black hair with small traces of grey over his ears—both intact—average height, thinner than Steve, wearing a black coat and a white collar around his neck. He spoke with a distinctive Irish accent.

"I'm Seamus Flannigan, so sorry to be meeting all of you on this sad day. God is with us."

Flannigan? The connection—Katie's father—passed from mouth to mouth, from row to row. *Katie's Dad. He's a priest; brought God with him.*

"This is not the way I planned my arrival. But here I am to help with this service honoring Jack Lawrence, a man I so wanted to meet among the living, but we have no control over death so I'm going to have to meet Jack through all of you. My daughter Katie and I have been corresponding over the time she's been with you. Her letters have helped me learn a little about your family of travelers. She's a faithful writer because she and I have shared our lives and all of you have been included. We will have time to continue this sharing after the service because I hope to stay for a few weeks and make new friends."

Seamus was aware of the reaction to this announcement. Concerned looks pass among the crowd: *Just what we don't need, a priest.*

"At his request, Jack Lawrence has been cremated and his ashes spread around the midway and packed into place by the footsteps of customers—marks, as you call them. It was what he requested and what has been done. So today we're here to say goodbye to a man who started life like we all do and ended life like we all will. And between these two events, there were the usual highs and lows like we all experience. Obviously I can't tell you any of his details other than the fact that Jack had found a home, a place where everyone knew his name."

He paused and reached to the back of his neck. He unbuttoned the collar, pulled it off and folded it and slid it in his pocket.

"I don't wear a collar anymore except when I want to make it understood that I'm a Christian, without all the rules. When the Catholics told me I couldn't get married, I took the collar off and replaced it with a wedding ring, so I could follow the rules of marriage and the other rules we try to follow to live together peacefully. Did Jack live by rules? Maybe. Maybe not. I think he did, his rules. He had a drinking problem—so do I. And my rules tell me not to drink, hard to follow. Most rules are hard to follow. When I ask my AA friends what they value in life, they usually say the expected things: family, money, work—but they never say they value alcohol or drugs or whatever they're addicted to. But in reality, what we're addicted to is what we hold in the highest value. Jack lived seventy years away from the values of society. This is the last time he will be remembered by this many people gathered in one place, so let's share some memories of Jack Lawrence."

Cliff listened to the pastor's words. *Now they know who he is. They know he's Katie's dad, a preacher. They like Katie, a pretty girl who can dance and that helps Ace sell tickets. Nothing else matters. Her dancing doesn't mean anything, except it sells tickets. He's here to see where his daughter has been living and dancing and to ride the train. The carnies understand that about him. But they question—what kind of a father would let his pretty daughter spend time with us; what is he thinking, doesn't he know we're bad news?*

"Let us pray." Seamus raised the Bible. "God, we ask you to comfort these people and support them through their grief and let them accept Jack's death and place their faith in your love for all of us. We ask this in the name of Jesus. Amen."

Seamus lowered the Bible. "I didn't know Jack, but like many men who fall victim to alcohol, Jack lived a life hidden from most of society, a strange life but one where he was accepted. It's apparent, from the number of you seated here, that he will be missed. Jesus taught us to love and accept each other. He taught us, 'When you see a sick man, a starving child, a poor widow, you see me.' I'm afraid Jack would not have been tolerated by most of our local citizens and they certainly would not attend a memorial service for him, a service where we acknowledge we are all in this together. I know your community isn't perfect, none are. You have your share of problems, likes and dislikes, arguments, disagreements, but you do it, you live together. Jack wasn't one of your outstanding citizens but he wasn't shunned or put in jail or any of the other terrible things that are done to unacceptable citizens—and you can be proud of that. You can be comforted that your tolerance and acceptance of each other follows God's will for all of us."

Seamus stopped talking and nodded to the saxophone player, who lifted his instrument and gently played "Amazing Grace." In the stillness of the morning, the music was soft and mellow, a perfect use of the tarnished horn.

Cliff glanced at Carol's notebook and saw her words "hymn from a dented horn," he thought she was on the right track, *a strange service in a strippers' tent.*

At first, the preacher's words had sounded wrong. But when they looked around, they saw the man they argued with about extra help, the woman who stole a husband, the mechanic who loaned his socket wrenches, the couple that brewed fresh coffee in the afternoon, the old-timer that delivered the mail. They saw each other and, at first, they didn't understand what the preacher was saying, but his words planted the seed and they felt something shared and they settled against each other, remembering Jack.

"Now if anyone would like to share something about Jack, please come forward." Seamus smiled at the audience, calmly waiting for a brave person to start.

Milt pushed his hands against the chair seat, and slowly rose to a standing position, balanced by his crutch. "Jack and me rode together a long time, don't know how long, lot of time lost in the bottle. Like you said, Reverend, lost. But we was lost together. Jack helped me and I helped him…lost. When I got a little green in my pocket, I shared it with him. We shared what we had. He did what he could to help with my show. I'm gonna miss him." Milt ended his words with his head bowed, and slowly sat back down.

Joan stood and pulled Katie's hand, asking her to come to the front. Katie whispered "No" and closed her eyes, but Joan pulled harder until Katie rose and they walked together to the front of the tent and faced the audience.

Cliff didn't need to look to know that Carol Fraley's page was almost empty. *Couldn't be put into words, a priceless picture, no way to describe the two girls, the differences between them, their faces, one beautiful the other unbearable, hideous.* They twisted their feet, uncomfortable with the eyes staring at them.

Joan turned her face away from the audience and nodded her head up and down, telling Katie to speak for her.

"Joan wants me to tell you how Jack made her feel, made her welcome. He bought her ice cream and told her he was glad she was here because she was the daughter Bill and Ruth had always wanted. He made her laugh. He told her it might be the vodka, but whatever it was, he didn't see anything different about her, nothing that mattered. He helped me teach Joan to dance and after that, she wasn't afraid to leave her room. He promised to let her ride an elephant."

Carol Fraley handed Cliff her notebook and pen. "Help me. I don't know what to write."

Cliff moved the pen, "Ugly is in the eye of the beholder." He looked at Carol.

She whispered, "And it's only skin-deep, and a picture's worth a thousand words. What am I going to do? Can I interview her? I have to."

Cliff stared at the notebook, "I'll set it up." Then he bore down on the pen, tearing through the paper while underlining his last sentence.

The girls sat down and Joan buried her face in Ruth's arms, and Katie wiped her eyes. Cliff knew her tears were from the relief she felt, relief that Joan had taken another step, another step in accepting who she was and forgetting it long enough to pay tribute to Jack, unaware of her face.

Seamus waited patiently to see if anyone else wanted to talk. When Steve Lanning walked to the front, Cliff knew the rough voice would close the service properly.

"I knew him a long time, knew more about him than most and that ain't much. He always told me he come from good people, money people. Claimed he graduated from college, had good jobs. Said he owned a chain of restaurants. Get on the pay phone, talk forever. I don't know what was true, what ain't. I don't think he put any money in the phone. He just wanted me to think he did. He knew how to use a pay phone. We got it down pretty good, stopping cars with the elephants and Jack talking to the newspaper, talk like he had a brain, get the reporters to come out, put us on the front page."

People smiled as they remembered seeing the thin man holding the telephone to his ear, gesturing with his forefinger.

Carol Fraley shook her head at Cliff, whispering, "Not nice to fool the press."

Steve lit a cigarette, waiting for quiet. "His old man showed up once. We was drunk, as usual, and the old man told Jack as long as he kept living like a dog, he wasn't getting any money from him. So I guess the money part was true. Pissed the old man off when Jack asked him what he had against dogs, man's best friend. Did one piss on his leg? I doubt they ever saw each other again. We was Jack's family."

Pagan laughed out loud, showing her preference for dogs. The rest of the congregation picked up her laughter as the smiles passed from face to face.

Steve continued, "Try this one. He liked ice cream with his vodka, said the ice cream cooled his throat, helped get it down, he didn't need no help getting it down. When I was still drinking with him, I tried it, give me the trots. Probably done the same for him. He never did smell too good."

The laughter came quickly and Steve dropped his cigarette to the ground, crushing it with his boot heel. "I tried to run him off… after I dried out, but he wouldn't go, said as long as I was on the show he would be, too. He'd stay away for a few days, then bring me a cup of coffee. We worked together a long time, long time, made some money, lost more."

Steve hesitated, then spoke slowly. "Now we got to come up with some money to buy a stone. We need to dig deep; none of that change, come with the long green so we can honor Jack the right way."

Money passed down the rows and Eddie the bookkeeper collected it and Steve finished talking. "He wasn't much, I ain't either.

Most of the time he didn't do what I wanted, but no one does. I liked him—he liked me."

Cliff looked at Carol Fraley, sharing what they just heard. With his rough words, Steve said it all: *I liked him; he liked me.*

Cliff thought, *what's left to say? Jack bought a deformed girl ice cream, talked to her. He liked people. He made up telephone conversations, ice cream and vodka, lost.*

No one else spoke and Seamus offered a short, closing prayer.

"God likes us; God loves us. We must remember Jack Lawrence as a man who liked people, a man who helped a frightened girl feel welcome. We can rest assured Jack has been welcomed into God's heaven."

Jim Mastras shook hands with Seamus, then turned to his employees. "Like Steve said, we were Jack's family. We're all in it together."

The tent emptied as the carnies dispersed to their trailers and tents and the cookhouse where they waited for the fair to open.

Carol Fraley said, "I want to talk to Mr. Mastras. Where can I find you later?"

"I'll be in the cook tent." Cliff looked at Katie who was sitting alone, looking at him, her eyes filled with tears.

When he put his arms around her, she struggled to control her breathing. "I didn't think she'd do it."

Cliff agreed. "Says a lot."

Katie strained to control her voice. "Standing up in front of everyone, it's unbelievable. She's been crying all day. Why I'm crying."

"For Jack."

"What he did for her. She could never have gotten up there." Katie stood and hugged Seamus. "He helped her more than anyone will ever know. I'm sorry you missed him."

She realized Seamus and Cliff hadn't met, and she reached for both of them. Seamus knew Cliff. He could tell by his daughter's eyes this was the young man she loved, the young man in line to be his son-in-law.

"Cliff, I didn't think this would be the way we'd meet. I imagined dinner in a quiet New York restaurant where we could exchange superficial information: names, jobs, hobbies, parents, simple stuff before we'd get into the deep stuff; but meeting here after an emotional memorial service held in a tent on a midway puts it in a different light. I want you to know how much I've been looking forward to this."

"Dad, do you want to rest before dinner? Let's put your things in my room. I bet you're tired. I know you're not too tired to talk about writing, but what about you, Cliff?"

"Never, but I do need to see if the reporter needs anything. It is my job."

The men shook hands. "Mr. Flannigan, we'll get to it later. I'm glad you're finally here."

"Seamus, please. Thank you for the welcome. I haven't slept right for weeks thinking about this trip."

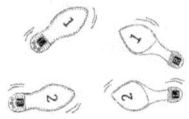

The tables in the cook tent were filled with mourners, friends needing to be together, finding comfort with each other.

Carol Fraley found Cliff alone at the rear of the tent. He had to tell several people that he was expecting someone. He helped her with her chair and asked, "Something to drink? I'm having coffee."

"Nothing for me. Do you appreciate where you are?"

"Sitting in a tent on a carnival midway with a formidable feature writer from the *Boston Herald*?"

"You know what I mean. A dream assignment, every reporter in the business wants a foreign assignment."

"I don't have a passport."

She moved her pencil. "What are you going to do with it? You're in business with an elephant trainer with half an ear and a voice like crushed stone, a crippled cowboy, dancers, daredevil motorcycle riders, snake charmers, freaks."

"I take notes, pages of notes." He flipped through his notebook. "They'll make sense to me, someday. Jack's in here." He ran his finger over a page. "I made notes about him shoveling crap and begging money and pushing the elephants out of his way. He acted like they were annoying children. We'll never know what happened. Notes about him—and Milt—about them being roommates with elephants and a hippopotamus and llamas and a chimpanzee…plenty of facts, but they don't tell the story, don't tell *why*, the hard part."

As he finished his coffee, she listened to Cliff gloss over the life he was living, avoiding the deep issues as he told her about writing sarcasm for Bozo. "I can think up words that make the marks mad so they spend a fortune trying to drown the clown and I get part of the take. I like the direct response. I write, he talks, and I get paid. It's all about the money out here."

"I wondered about that. Nothing wrong with money, none of us have enough of it." Carol tapped her pencil on the cover of Cliff's notebook. "Who else's in there?"

Cliff's breathing increased when he talked about Katie and how she was lied to, deceived about the job. "She thought she was going to be dancing on state fair stages, not strip show tents. Katie knows where she's going. She didn't quit when she found out she was going to be dancing in a strip show. She just knew the train was headed for New York City and she knows she's going to get a job at Radio City Music Hall. She'll dance there for free if she has to. Her dad supports her decisions. I don't understand it. I won't write Bozo's lines for free."

"Are you going to New York with her? You know she wants you to."

"I should. Starve in the big city and write the big novel. I went to Kerouac's house a couple of weeks ago, with Steve Lanning. You like him? He wrote a big novel."

"I interviewed him last year." Carol Fraley made the statement without giving away what she thought about his writing. "Are you avoiding the question about going to New York with Katie?"

"No, I might go. What's he like?" He avoided her question.

She answered in a flat voice. "Hard to tell. I think he has a serious drug problem, didn't make much sense, but I got enough to satisfy the editor. He talked like he writes, rambling, on and on, overblown, sometimes like poetry, music. I guess I don't know how he does it. Maybe it's all booze, drugs. *On The Road* has sold well. I'm staying with newspapers."

"Are you going to write about Joan Ryerson?" *I have to talk about the elephant in the room. A feature writer for the Boston Herald, she can't skip at least talking about Joan Ryerson.*

"Katie asked me not to but…but I think I have to—no pictures."

"Will your editor run it?"

"No. It's not right for our paper. TV news would love it if they had the video. Like you say, crap TV."

"Why write it if it won't run?"

"I turn in some stuff that I know will get killed. It gets me points."

"Does it work?"

"Once in a while. This new editor's catching on pretty fast, but if he cuts Joan, and he will, then Milt will make it."

"What should be done with Joan?"

"Put her in your book."

Cliff nodded his head.

"What about Katie? Are you going to write about her?"

"Maybe. She doesn't want me to."

"I can fix it."

"How?"

"I'll tell her you're going to interview Joan, but you won't if she lets you write about her."

"You're devious."

"Learning. Steve Lanning's a great teacher. Or I'll tell you how the games are fixed. What about that?"

"Not interested."

"Why?"

"Already common knowledge. Everyone knows they're fixed, but they play anyway, but only men, stubborn pride, stupid."

Carol asked Cliff if he would fill in some of Katie's background. "I would like to know more before I talk to her."

"I don't know much. You've met her father. A so-called talent scout told her that she was going to be dancing at state fairs. She went for it because she needed more experience."

Carol Fraley let out a long breath. "That's enough for the front page of the entertainment section. Add that she's teaching an unfortunate girl to dance and she's putting up with the carnival because the train is taking her to Radio City Music Hall and the story's guaranteed."

She held Cliff's arm. "And your problem is better, or just as good a story."

"My problem?"

"You can't deal with it if you don't admit you've got it."

"Tell me, please."

"Fear—you do question your ability, I give you that, but you don't own what's blocking you. You're afraid, so afraid you can't do the work. You take a lot of notes but that's not the work you need to be doing. You need to be writing. Faulkner said it. Don't say you're a writer, say you're writing."

CHAPTER 40

I Want You to Know
How Much I Love You.
You Know Katie Loves You,
Bill and Ruth Love You,
and God Loves You

eamus and Katie caught the van to the train so they could talk in private. The room was small. There was space for his clothes in one drawer and he hung a few shirts on a piece of wire, strung from one end of the top bunk to the wall.

"We sleep here. There's a shower and a toilet in the bathroom at the end of the car, cramped but cozy. Cliff is in the room next door. You can put your suitcase on his top bunk."

"It's serious, isn't it?"

"Yes."

"Marriage?"

"I don't know when. He wants to write a book first."

"Lovely."

Katie took his hand in hers. "Yes, it is. Before we do anything, I want you to meet Joan—Bill and Ruth. They need you."

"Need me?" He dropped his suitcase and removed his suit coat.

"Need you. They've never had anyone like you. Not anyone I've seen. The people on the show have been with them many years. Not in love. They need your love."

Ruth had grown up in a country church. Bill had not. Joan had not been inside a church, not since she was born. Her parents had attended infrequently, so when she was born, they stopped and no one said anything. No one had visited the farm for sixteen years.

"I saw all of you at the service." Seamus hugged Ruth.

"And, course, we seen you. Katie told us you was coming. She's happy as a pig in mud."

"As am I. To see her, to see you, to be here long enough to meet everyone I can."

Seamus moved in front of Joan. She slid back. He took her face in his hands; smiled at her. She twisted her head, but he gently held her. "Joan, I love you. I want you to know how much I love you. You know Katie loves you, Bill and Ruth love you, and God loves you. I've loved you since Katie told me about her new friend."

He loosened his grip on her face and reached for her hand, then held Ruth's hand. Bill and Katie completed the circle. "We learn from our children; please, Katie, the prayer from the old country."

"May the blessings of each day be the blessings we need most."

"Thank you, love." Seamus put both arms around Joan. "Joan, you're the blessing I need the most today. Your remarks at the service were a profound blessing for everyone."

Ruth's eyes filled with tears. "A blessing, blessing to us."

She put her arms around Seamus, the only man beside Bill she had ever touched with emotion. Bill stepped closer and reached for Seamus's hand, and was surprised when the pastor grabbed him by the shoulders in an embrace.

"Now listen to me. In my time as a pastor, I've married people and baptized babies, buried them, but this time—right now—we are in the presence of God. I'm deeply humbled to be a part of it."

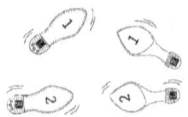

Steve and Cliff were faced with the problem. Milt's show was failing, but neither one of them wanted to make a decision.

"What did it cost you?" Jim Mastras was leaning against the front of his desk, smoking a cigar. Cliff was sitting in one of the leather chairs.

"I haven't added it up." Cliff held the ledger in his hand. "It's all in here. The bleeding stops when I shut it down tonight."

"About how much?"

"Over two grand, when I pay Duke." Cliff closed the ledger and forced a weak smile. "Spent two grand, took in three hundred and four dollars, gave you half, bought a steak and lobster dinner. Only answer is to build more shows, make it up in volume."

"Good lesson. You can take over the Snake Show for me, makes good money, not serious money, but does all right. I want you to get your money back. Don't worry about paying Duke, I'll take care of him."

The Okefenokee Swamp Girl, won't Mom and Dad be proud; something to brag about at the class reunion. When I get my money back, I'll quit. Just do it long enough to get even, enough for Spain. I'm not going to get trapped in a snake show.

Cliff knew why Mastras was offering him the show. Steve Lanning told him. "The Man wants to keep you around. You're better than the other bums he keeps and he knows money is the best way to do it."

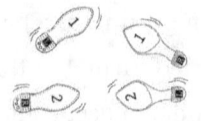

When Cliff and Steve entered the tent, they saw Milt sleeping in the chair, head dropped to his chest. The empty tent saddened Cliff. He wanted to turn and run, not face the failure. Steve cleared his throat, then called Milt's name to wake him up.

The old man looked feeble as he tried to see who was there. "You fellows paid customers? Not a lot of 'em…today. But look out for tomorrow."

"You ain't sellin' tickets, we're shuttin' it down." Steve didn't waste time making the announcement. "Airplane jumpers are not in style."

"What?" Milt was wide awake. "You want to do that?"

Cliff crossed his arms. "I'm out two grand. It isn't working. Apparently the name 'Milt Hinkle' doesn't mean as much as we thought it did. I can't afford to keep you open."

"If I had any money…" Milt's voice trailed off.

Steve snorted. "You ain't got nothing but a big appetite. Cliff here wants some help with what he's lost. He still owes Duke. You can't help."

Milt lifted his hands. "What am I gonna do? Don't have no money."

Cliff knew this would happen. Milt asked for money. Every day he wanted money, more if attendance had been up. "Can I use the posters? I might make a little with 'em. You ought to give me something. Don't just kick me out."

Cliff felt the burn and raised his voice. "All that shit in the trunk is yours. I don't want it. Don't want to look at it again, ever again." His shouting filled the tent. "I don't want to see you ever again." Then he turned on Steve. "You told me he would make money, a lot of money. Where's your share? You didn't put anything in."

Steve answered; Cliff was giving a good performance. "I said it might. I also told you I never made a dime with Milt Hinkle. He's my forty-year mistake. Truth is, I'm out a damn sight more than you, get in line."

"I'm out the money this time. There isn't a line to stand in. Don't you think you should have put up something?"

"You didn't ask, you wanted the biggest share. No, I don't think I should have put up anything. I warned you. You're a big boy."

"Take the posters, pictures, that worthless trunk. I don't give a damn what you do." Then he looked at Steve and nodded his head, as he let him know the performance was over. And it was real.

Milt rubbed his stiff legs, and suppressed a smile. He didn't say anything, just waited, looking at the pictures like he was deciding what to do with them. "I've seen lots of twists, never one like this one. Ain't no need for you two to act like this. I know an act when I see one."

"Look out. When he starts talking about twists, look out." Steve's words were serious. He pushed his face close to Milt's. "What the hell are you talking about?"

"You won't believe this one." Milt spoke with confidence.

"I don't want to hear it." Steve walked away, slapping his hat against his leg.

Milt called after him. "You're part of it. You do want to hear this one."

Steve threw his cigarette on the ground, shook his head and kept walking, disappearing through the opening in the tent. His departure forced Cliff to listen to the old man.

Milt's face flushed as he took a breath. "I'll tell him later. He'll want to know."

Cliff didn't know why he was still listening. "Is there money involved? If there's money involved, count me out."

"You're all right, kid, you're learning." Milt sat up straight. Something had changed. He spoke clearly. "Don't get too blinded by the money. Closes too many doors, makes you march to the man paying you. I always had to do it, never liked it."

"Damned easy for you to say, not your money." Cliff thought about Bozo paying him for writing insults.

"You're right. Dead right. I don't know if there's any real money with this deal, but maybe, just maybe."

"What's left of mine stays in my pocket."

"When Steve hears about this, he'll shit. Can't hardly believe it myself. A professor from Boston come to see me—read the story in the newspaper, wants me to come to Boston College and let them go through the trunk and talk to some of the classes. Boston College! I got you to thank for the story."

"You couldn't make that up. Are you serious? A college?"

"As I ever been, on my father's grave. Serious as the gold in Fort Knox. He come in here, looked at the pictures, posters, listened to me ramble for an hour, 'til my voice give out. Asked me to come to Boston College, said he'd send a car."

"Did he offer an honorarium?"

"A what?"

"A fee—an honorarium, money."

"There you go again. I did say I needed a little walking-around money. He said he'd be back, go over the details. Wants Steve to come, too. He wants to talk to both of us."

"Did he show you any credentials?"

"No."

"Did he have a business card? How do you know he's really a college professor?"

Milt looked at Cliff, then let his gaze drift around the tent. "I think he was serious, talked good, couldn't hardly understand him, said big words, something about Western ethos, didn't understand. Ethnog…I don't know what he was saying."

Cliff asked if he said ethnography or anthropology.

"Yeah, that's it—what is it?"

"Like Western history, culture."

"He did say history, understood that. Said he was surprised to see me here, knew who I was. Can you believe that? A Boston College professor knew my name. A college man knows Milt Hinkle."

Cliff thought only an Ivy League college would have a professor so deep into American history he would know Milt Hinkle.

Did he know about the airplane stunt? Probably. What else does he know? How Milt was the last promoter of the dregs, the dismal remains, of the Buffalo Bill Cody Rodeo and Western show, how he had hustled enough money from naïve investors to pull together a bunch of has-beens and drunks and cowboy misfits and played five towns before the money ran out and Milt left town in the middle of the night. Steve Lanning would be more than happy to tell the professor that story.

Milt said, "He could be some nut, read the story in the paper and gets off jerking my chain. Don't think so, we'll see if he comes back. If there is any money in this I'll see that you get some of yours back."

No. Cliff thought, *no. I've learned one thing out here. There are always strings attached. I don't want even a tiny thin thread connecting me to Milt Hinkle.*

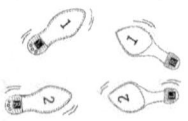

"No. I said no, plain and clear. No!" Steve paused. "That professor wants Milt, not me. He's the one that jumped, got the stiff legs to prove it. I'm staying with my elephant money. I say no because there ain't no money I can see. Boston College's a waste of my time. Milt can have the glory. I'm still not caught up with what we lost in Nuevo Laredo, even with the pesos I stuffed down my pants. Them students won't be no better off listening to Milt, but you never know. Marks won't pay for it on the midway but I guess Boston College's different. I don't know, never been to one."

Cliff said, "I can get this in the *New York Times*, listen to this: *Boston College copies carnival sideshows on the campus. Big books, little books, books big enough to scare a genius or choke a jock, see the crazy old, goofy old, boring old professor, takes a wise man to hear him, a Harvard man to fear him—alive, alive, alive on the inside, on the Boston College Campus, all alive in the classroom and fifty thousand dollars takes you all the way through and the lectures never stop. Step right up, step right up, get 'em while they're hot. Big books, little books ...*" Cliff shouted. "Tell me that isn't the best spiel you've ever heard."

Steve's face was expressionless, but his eyes smiled and he nodded his head. "Some paper ought 'a go for that shit. You got a lot of it, don't you?"

Cliff folded the paper he had been reading from. "We should both go listen to him. It might be his finest performance...it might be his last." Cliff continued, "You have to go. You have to be there. You were there when he jumped. You've been through too much to miss this one. Just imagine Milt bullshitting the students. At least it will be a good laugh."

"I'd have to be drunk to go and I don't drink. You're the reporter. You go and write it up, use small words so I can read 'em. I ain't goin'. He won't do nothin' but tell the same lies he believes."

"Don't you want to be there when this professor calls him out, makes him tell the truth? The reporter from the *Herald*'s going to be there. She wants to listen and she wants to talk to you some more—free press."

"You got something going with that reporter broad?"

"No. She wants to see what happens. It was her story that got him there. Katie's dad, Seamus, is going."

"I might go too, if he's going. I like him."

CHAPTER 41

Professor Lost in History, Hiding on Campus Like I'm Hiding on the Midway. We Have Something in Common

Cliff drove, with Katie next to him. She turned to the back seat and asked Steve why he changed his mind. Seamus nodded and listened for the answer.

"Your boyfriend said I had to see what goes down. Me and Milt been down a lot of roads, no time to miss this turn. I heard this place costs ten grand a year. Tell me, preacher, what do they get for that kind of money?"

"A fine education, almost as good as the one Cliff's getting from you. Right, Cliff?"

"I think someone should give me a big certificate 'Master's of the Midway,' signed by Captain Steve Lanning."

As he drove, Cliff thought about the impression the orange and red car would make on the campus. It wasn't as shocking as the train rolling through the center of the campus, but the *Mastras Shows* car with its ornate script and bright colors would announce their arrival as loudly as a train wreck, let them know something different was happening on campus.

Milt Hinkle in the Ivy League,

He parked the car and they walked through the campus and he held Katie's hand, glad to be away from the garish car so they could blend with the students, but he realized no matter how they were dressed, they stood out because of Steve's worn work clothes, his faded cap, scuffed boots and his half ear. At least Milt wasn't with them. The professor had sent a car. A few miles between the midway and the campus put Boston College in outer space.

Milt was sitting at a table in front of the classroom with his cowboy hat on the back of his head. Sitting next to him was the history professor. The rodeo posters and the *True* magazine cover had been mounted on the walls. Cliff thought the posters looked okay in the classroom, better than the tent. He and Katie and Seamus and Carol Fraley sat together. Cliff opened a new notebook. Steve had moved away from them to the back of the classroom with his baseball cap pulled low over his forehead, over his ear.

Cliff wrote: *Professor lost in history, hiding on campus like I'm hiding on the midway. We have something in common.*

Professor Cameron beamed as he spoke. "Many times we become too isolated in our universities, listening to academics speaking in lofty academic terms. Today, we're fortunate to have a man with us who is not an academic but the genuine article, as you say—the real deal, a link to the old West, a former National Rodeo Champion, a brave but—I think he'd agree, foolish—man who jumped out of an airplane in Mexico, without a parachute, to bulldog a steer. I know it sounds unbelievable, but when I first heard the story, I researched the article in *True* magazine." He pointed to the copy on the wall. "So when Milt talks about it, you can believe what he says is true."

Katie whispered to Seamus and Cliff, "Now you know for sure."

"It didn't help us make any money, but it is good to know, I think."

Seamus sat on the front of his seat, and listened intently to the facts about this new friend, from another niche in life.

The professor continued. "An associate of Buffalo Bill Cody and the son of George Hinkle who was elected the Sheriff of Dodge City, Kansas, and arrested Billy the Kid. Milt Hinkle is touring with the Mastras Shows, and delighting the public with tales of his past. He has agreed to spend some time with us and share his collection of memorabilia, some of which you can see on the walls. Please welcome Mr. Milt Hinkle."

Milt used a crutch to draw attention to the illustration of the airplane. "Like them warnings on the TV, don't try this at home— these stunts are done by professionals."

Milt stood taller and straighter than he had in a long time. His stiff legs supported him, the crutches balanced against the podium. From the seats, they couldn't see the rip in his coat. His high-pitched voice was uncharacteristic for a man his size, but the students soon forgot the sound as they listened to his words.

"Like the man said, it was foolish, worse, stupid. People die from stupid, I was lucky. Ask my friend, Steve Lanning. He's settin' there in the back of the room. Tell 'em, Steve, ain't I lucky? Tell 'em, Steve." Milt waited, coaxing his old friend. "Steve Lanning, the only man I know can talk starving dogs away from a meat wagon."

When the students' turned to see who Milt was referring to, they saw a man wearing a baseball cap with his right hand raised in the air, middle finger extended.

The students laughed when they heard Steve growl, "You ought to get more than his bullshit for ten grand a year."

Instead of raising her hand, a girl stood and walked to the aisle and looked at Professor Cameron. He asked her if she had a question. "Yes, Kiersten, do you want to ask Mr. Hinkle something?"

"I want to ask *you* why you put us through this boring presentation. I understand you get off on cowboys and Indians, but this is a useless waste of my time and I doubt if Milt Hinkle thinks the Indians were mistreated at all."

The girl accepted the students' applause and walked out of the room.

Later, Carol Fraley asked Steve if he was glad he'd changed his mind and attended the lecture.

"Hell, yes. He give 'em a pretty good show till that little broad got going. She's a piece of work. He'll talk, long as they give him a little green; at least he's out of my pocket. Now I shovel shit again. Back where I started. Milt gets to be a phony professor."

Carol Fraley laughed. "You should be up there with him." She didn't want to stop the conversation. "How about a cup of coffee?" She turned to Katie for support. "Don't you want something to drink?"

Katie agreed. "It's nice being here. I like the students, the beautiful buildings."

"You look like one of them." Cliff held Katie's hand. "We could be another couple on campus except we've got a real strange-looking man walking with us. Seamus, I don't mean you."

They sat in a booth and Steve said the young people didn't look like college students. "Why do they all dress alike? Those colored shirts?"

"Cliff looked at the students and agreed—most of them seemed to be in uniform, wide legged jeans, tie-dyed shirts, scarves. "What's the deal with the uniforms? It comes from San Francisco, the hippies. They are making a lot of noise about Vietnam."

They heard a group of students singing, "Where Have All the Flowers Gone?" and waving posters to stop the fighting, their shirts adorned with the peace sign.

Steve touched his ear. "I'll tell them about the Germans shooting it off. War *is* dangerous."

"Is that how it happened?" Carol and Seamus ask at the same time.

"Are you ever going to tell the truth? No, don't tell me. It's better not knowing." Cliff nodded to Carol.

They listened to Steve's version of the Nuevo Laredo jump, the way the Mexican promoter had it wired from the beginning. "We thought we was smarter than a bunch of dumb wetbacks, we'd win the serious money, didn't happen. And I'm still a dumbass tryin' to do something with Milt and one more time, it don't work."

Steve spoke to Cliff. "You lost money, you get anything for it?"

"I'll get my money back, someway. Maybe I'll be like Katie and dance for free." Cliff hugged her. "Isn't that what you said? You'd dance at Radio City Music Hall for free?"

"Money isn't why I dance." She asked Carol Fraley if she did her job for the money. "I bet it's not the reason you're a reporter. Dad doesn't work for the money."

"No, I don't." Seamus winked at Katie.

Carol Fraley considered the question. "Not the money. That's like being a school teacher for the money, it doesn't work. I keep doing this for the same reason as when I started." She changed the subject. "I'm going to close my piece on Milt by reporting that he's lecturing at Boston College and I don't think it's the end of his career." She paused. "Then I *have* to interview Joan. That's why I'm doing it."

Cliff closed his eyes; he didn't want to see Katie's reaction. He and Carol had planned it this way, but Cliff was uncomfortable with the deception. He knew how much it hurt Katie for her to think about Joan being used like a piece in a game. Her face wasn't something to be displayed in a newspaper, TV or a sideshow.

"Please, please, no." Katie reached for Carol's hands and tears ran down her cheeks. "Write about me, but not Joan, please."

"All right. If that's what you want. Seamus, will you let me interview you too, with Katie?"

"Why?"

"How you can be away from your church for so long. What you think about your daughter's travels. I know you weren't planning on this visit to Boston College. You two are a better story than Joan."

CHAPTER 42

I Eat Too Much of It
and It Makes Me Pass Gas—
Aggressively

arol Fraley didn't want to delay interviewing Katie and Seamus. She asked them where would be a good place to talk, a quiet Boston restaurant, maybe Faneuil Hall—no, too noisy unless it was mid-afternoon.

"I prefer the train or the cook tent," Seamus said. "Right, Katie?"

"Right."

"Are you okay with it?"

"Now that you're here, it's all right. Never did want to be asked too many questions."

On the ride back to the midway, they couldn't seem to stop talking. Seamus, in particular, had a lot to say about Milt, about the fact that he was getting a chance to know him. "I guess I'm like anyone else, I think about carnival people in a derogatory way. And I'm a pastor. I'm not supposed to pre-judge. But Milt Hinkle—no way to be prepared for him, but I don't think I pre-judged him."

Cliff said, "The Pie car might not be suitable. In the afternoon, it's empty, no one on the train, but if anyone did come in, they'd be too disruptive. I think we'll be all right in the cook tent. Steve Lanning's the only one who would do anything, but I think he's perceptive enough to leave us alone."

"I've been doing this for a few years." Carol Fraley was in control. "Let's start with my usual question. What's your favorite food? And for how long?"

"Unusual question." Seamus looked at Katie, knowing how she was going to react. "You're suppressing a loud laugh."

"I am your only living child."

"Cabbage casserole soaked with Jameson whiskey and honey. And it isn't funny."

"Oh no? Why do waiters laugh when you request it?"

Seamus tried to stop a laugh, but couldn't. "I eat too much of it and it makes me pass gas—aggressively."

"My dad, I love him! Next question?"

"Let's get the basics out of the way. How long were you a priest, where?"

"Nine years. Galway and Dingle."

"You quit to get married, where did you meet your wife?"

"A blessed spring day on the Dingle peninsula, a flat tire blessed us like glitter dust from a leprechaun."

Carol Fraley lifted her pencil like a baton, moving it in circles through the air. "You know Fraley is Irish?"

"Married name?"

"No, my dad is Connor Fraley. His dad was Sean, born south of Belfast. I grew up listening to stories with glitter dust."

"Good, we won't need a translator."

They spent an hour with Seamus while he spread Irish charm, describing how he changed a tire for a pretty American girl and her two friends on a summer's camping trip around Ireland. How he found himself throwing away his priest's costume and the church's ridiculous rule of celibacy and hitching a ride with the girls, bringing his backpack and mountain tent and cook stove and rain gear.

"By the end of the summer we were engaged and by October, married in a Presbyterian church in central Illinois."

Seamus had many other reasons for leaving the church, but decided to save them for a later conversation.

"Katie's older brother, Michael, was born the next July, Katie the next May, and they wanted me to remain a virgin."

Carol Fraley captured every important word and added some of her own: *handsome, comfortable with himself, loves his daughter, seems to love everyone.*

"Where is Michael?"

"He was killed on his bicycle when he was eight."

Carol Fraley closed her notebook. "I'm sorry. I have to go. Can we continue later?"

Katie said, "Not until midnight. Too late then, but Dad might be able to. He can't watch every show. Right, Dad?"

Seamus agreed to meet back at the cook tent. "Seven okay? I'll buy you dinner. I know reporters don't make a lot of money."

"I'm on an expense account. It will be fun to turn in a receipt for dinner with an Irish pastor in a carnival food tent. My boss will expect a Pulitzer."

Shortly before six, Cliff climbed the steps to the back stage to watch Katie. Seamus was already there and Cliff sat beside him. "How many writers would like to be here?"

Cliff answered, "All of them."

"Good answer. Writers, painters, photographers…they all would love this seat, best seat in the house. And speaking of seats, I'm supposed to be seated at a table in the cook tent with Carol Fraley in an hour. Why don't you join me?"

"All right, part of my job. Good, I like to be seen as the expert. I shouldn't admit it to you, but I'm being honest. I can be honest with you, can't I? You are the father confessor, aren't you?"

"I get that a lot. People around here are already after me to listen to them. Everyone needs a good listener."

"Who listens to you?"

"Katie, my wife, and God, and this newspaper reporter. I'm going to confess to her."

They watched the opening act where all the girls, a juggler on a unicycle, the singer Bobby Tempo, the comedian appeared with flashing lights and an upbeat drum to warm things up.

Then the lights dimmed and Ace announced the first act. "The beautiful girl from the movies, please welcome the one and only Holly Wood!"

When she skipped between Seamus and Cliff she kissed them both while the applause increased. A seasoned dancer, Holly paused and spread her arms wide like she was embracing everyone in the audience and they cheered for more and she kicked her leg and whirled to the front of the stage.

Seamus watched until Holly started to remove her clothes then turned away. Katie knew that would happen. He wanted to see it all, up to a point. Holly just passed that point.

Katie had asked Cliff to take Seamus around the midway. Outside the tent, Seamus asked Cliff if he wanted to stay to watch the rest of Katie's show.

"No. I've seen it so many times, from all directions, with dignitaries and politicians, I'm glad to have something else to do."

"If you don't mind, walk with me before I meet Carol Fraley." Seamus made the request and smiled. "When I conduct a memorial service or a wedding, afterward they want to talk, or call me over and they want to talk about God. They have questions about the church, about religion, about heaven, is there a hell? And it goes beyond questions, they want to tell me about their experience with religion, the church they grew up in, the church camp they attended in the summer. It always happens. The church has made a big impact on everyone. God has created a situation where he is controversial, he is doubted, he is adored, he is hated, he is loved, but he's not ignored."

"Anyone talked to you recently?"

"The sign painter, Duke? He told me about doing a painting of the manger where Jesus was born."

Cliff thought, *the word is spreading that he's okay. He makes people want to be with him.*

When the motorcycle rider balanced on the vertical wall, Seamus said he would like to meet the daredevil. "His performance is one of the best things I've seen."

They followed Clipper to the back of the motordrome where he poured them mugs of beer. "I'm drinking water, at least five more shows. Need a clear head for all of them."

"It's obvious you have a gift for riding motorcycles. Where do you think it came from?"

"My old man's sperm mixed with Mom's eggs. Pretty basic stuff."

Seamus waited to hear if Clipper offered any more. The three of them looked at each other as the noise of the rides and shows filled the air. Cliff knew Seamus wanted the question to lead to more discussion.

"It is pretty basic biology. In school when we heard about sperm and eggs, we laughed at the girls who were embarrassed; they weren't the girls we asked for dates."

Seamus smiled at the remark. "Did you just think that up?"

"Just now. You can use it if you want."

"Not sure if it would ever fit in a sermon, but it was pretty clever. You're a clever young man, aren't you? How did you get started with the motorcycles?"

"I'm an adrenalin junky. If I don't get my fix every day, I'm out of balance."

"Were you hooked the first time you saw it?"

"Sure was. I was just out of the Army, already hooked on adrenalin; I was in charge of a bomb disposal team. We defused live bombs. Talk about a rush. I got the shakes after I left the Army, saw the motorcycles, and had to try."

"Do you think it's a gift or a problem?"

"If the man upstairs gave me that desire and the skill, it must be a gift. That's what you're getting at, isn't it?"

"Yes it is."

"Okay with me."

"What?"

"Okay, if that's the way you want to look at it. All I know is it's something I have to do. 'Course I also drink too much, another addiction. Does that go along with it? God gives me that desire? Don't take any skill, just swallow."

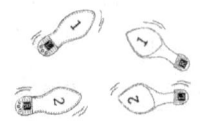

"I've been wondering how you stay in your pastor's role while traveling with your daughter," Carol Fraley asked. "And I already have the answer."

"I'm always a pastor, just like you are always faithful."

"Good answer, Seamus. I get it."

"Good."

"Problem is, it cuts our interview very short. We don't have anything else to talk about. Do we?"

"No...I mean, yes. We can talk about the differences I see here compared to California."

"Where in California?"

"Near Monterey. And I don't see any differences. People in both places have questions about God, the church, heaven or hell. Always the same."

"Do you have answers?"

"Sure."

"Do they work?"

"For some yes, some no."

"More yes or no?"

"I'm like an athlete. I keep trying and sometimes, not often, I hit a home run. It works if you just keep trying. I'm never going to stop trying, like you're never going to stop being a faithful writer."

"Is being faithful the same as believing in God."

"No different, to me. We get up in the morning, faithful that the sun will come up and faithful that the sun will set. If we believe that, we believe in God."

"We don't have any control over sunrise and sundown."

"Do we have any control over the rest of our lives?"

"How does a reporter answer that? We do, but not to the extent we think we do. Is that the way you feel?"

"Yes. When I became a priest, I thought I was in control. Now I know I'm not. Do you mind if we walk? I would like to control how we continue this interview."

"Yes, we can. One more question first."

"All right."

"I don't believe in God. Am I going to hell?"

"You believe."

"I just said I didn't."

"I don't believe you meant it."

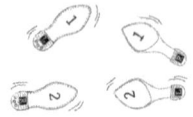

They passed the Dunk Bozo stand. No one was playing.

"*I need a ball player, need a ball player, drown the clown.*"

Seamus waved to Bozo.

"*How about you, preacher man. Can you dunk the dummy? Think about it like the Baptists, full immersion, none of that sprinkling crap. I need a ball player, need a ball player, baptize me. Step right up, step right up, three balls for a quarter, for you, it's four for a quarter, religious discount. Drown the clown.*"

Seamus handed the girl a quarter and picked up a ball and threw it and scored a bull's-eye and Bozo dropped into the water.

"*Wait a minute, preacher man, wait a minute. I didn't mean it. I've been baptized once. Ain't that enough?*" Bozo climbed back on his seat, wiping the water from his face.

Seamus threw again and dropped Bozo back into the water.

"*I said I didn't mean it! Don't you hear good? When I said I didn't mean it, I meant it. You must be a Baptist.*"

Seamus missed the bull's eye with the third ball, but the fourth scored again, causing Bozo to protest loudly because he had a crowd watching the preacher put the clown in the tank.

And Seamus wished he was wearing his white collar so they would know he was a man of God.

Seamus lingered for a few minutes, watching the men in the crowd step forward to try their luck. When he and Carol Fraley continued walking, he explained how he mastered his skill of throwing baseballs. "Practice, hours of practice, while Katie danced. Have you seen the motorcycle rider?"

"Yes. He's a good show. He practiced, didn't he?"

"My point. We all have skills. I just asked the motorcycle rider where it came from, the skill. He said it was from his father's sperm and his mother's eggs."

"I know why you asked it, too."

"Why?"

"You're a pastor. You've practiced that a long time. You know if you ask certain questions it will bring out the real story, the story behind the story. Am I right?"

"Yes."

"What's the answer to my question? Heaven or hell?"

"Didn't work this time. I don't know the answer."

"Is there a hell? A heaven?"

"I don't have an answer for you. Just for myself."

"A hint? Where do our skills come from?"

"Ask the motorcycle guy. He said they come from God. I don't know the answer to that either. All I know is that we have skills, talents, abilities and we have a desire to use them for a good purpose and our faith is what supports us."

CHAPTER 43

And You Might Ask What an Ambitious Young Writer Is Doing with a Snake Show

Cliff knew he had to decide: take over the snake show and get back the money he lost with Milt, or take a chance—a big chance—and stay with Katie. See what New York had to offer. Instead of making the decision, Cliff shoved it out of his mind. He told himself he could decide later, wait until the last minute, wait until the show closed in Jersey City, wait until the train was ready to leave and then, at the last minute, hope the answer would be loud and clear like a billboard on the highway.

"What is it?" Katie asked. "What's wrong?"

"Three months ago, I was working in Morganport, bored. Can't say *bored* now. I've lost two thousand dollars, had my name in the paper with yours, sat in a college class with Milt Hinkle and now I'm sitting with the girl I love and her father. She's about to start a new chapter dancing in New York City. If you're bored with that, you're dead. And I *almost* stayed in Indiana."

"Do you care about losing the money?"

"No, like I told Carol Fraley, putting it together was the best part. And I'll do it better next time."

Cliff stopped talking and drew in a breath and reached for her hands. Katie listened.

"Mastras wants to help me get the money back. He gave me the snake show. It's easy to run, the star of the show does everything, makes a good profit."

"Oh."

"Yeah, *oh*. Says it all. What the hell am I thinking? *Oh?* Oh yes, I'm the owner of the Okefenokee Snake Show, one of the feature attractions on the Mastras Midway. And you might ask what an ambitious young writer is doing with a snake show, and I have to say it's not *just* about the money. Snakes are good material, one of the main characters of the Bible. Maybe that's why they bring in so much money."

Cliff said he wanted to change the subject. "You told Carol Fraley you'd dance for free. Tell me, Miss Flannigan, would you really dance for free?"

"Yes, I would. I will. But not in the Broadway Review. No more midway for me."

"I won't run the snake show for free. Why will you dance for free?"

"Stay with me now, dance with me…in New York. Help me get the job at the Music Hall. You write. I'll dance, no snakes."

"I can't. I need the snake money so I can write…in Barcelona."

"And I need you…I love you."

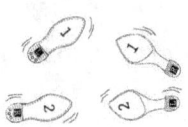

Steve watched Joan spread hay for the elephants, then filled the hippo's cage and watered the chimp and groomed Little Three. While she was working, she didn't notice the marks staring at her.

The work satisfied her. She didn't see their terrified eyes. But Steve saw them, their blinking stares. He saw the marks as they gravitated to the elephants, always attracted by their massive heads and weaving serpent trunks.

Then when they saw Joan's face, their senses erupted, caught in an impossible place. A bent nose forced to grow to the side of the uneven split pushing from her mouth up between her crooked eyes. They forgot the animals and the foul air. Fear smacked them—what could it be, what could it possibly be? It couldn't be human, but she was.

Steve wanted to make money with Joan. He didn't talk to anyone about what he wanted to do, because it was none of their business. He knew an opportunity when he saw it. Joan was the best chance he'd had in a long time to make serious money.

Milt's show didn't do it. Should have known, did know...bad idea. The kid talked me into it after I talked him into it. I started believing my own bullshit. The kid told that broad from the Boston Herald that Milt was a genuine...called him a folk hero or some shit like that, and I know he ain't nothin' but a busted-up cowboy drunk and anybody spends a quarter to see him is a walking dumbass. Only good part was the kid putting up all the money. It just wasted my time. Anyone that can make her impact, shock the wind out of their lungs, draw hot tears, rip howls from their throats—anything with that power is worth a lot of money.

Steve had traveled from town to town, coast to coast on trains and trucks exhibiting, performing for thirty years and Joan's face exceeded the best of them... Steve thought *superstar, a guaranteed magnet for the folding stuff and she's working in my tent and if I play it right, she can put me where I want to be.*

He told Duke what he wanted. The painter lowered his brush.

"You want me to make her look uglier? You can't take it that far. They won't pay for ugly. Bill didn't pitch ugly. He pitched three eyes. Ugly wasn't his main draw. And it don't matter anyway; I won't do it. Bill and Ruth don't want her in a show and you know it. What the hell are you thinking? You can probably get someone else to paint you a banner, but you can't get away with it, not on this show. I won't have anything to do with it or you."

Steve said, "They'll change their minds when I give them their cut."

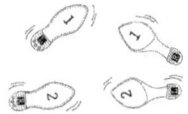

Daphne settled on her stool, gently moving her feet between the snakes, and settled her straw hat.

She was surrounded by wide-eyed marks who stared at the small green garter snakes draped around the brim of her hat and in the pockets and folds of her red gingham dress. The faces jerked away when she picked up a four foot black snake and coiled it around her shoulders where it twisted and flicked its tongue, a thick dark tube of muscle sliding and curving around her throat.

She scooped up a handful of squirming black and blue snakes, and dropped them between her legs in the fold of her skirt. Every move and gesture was done to thrill the spectators. They looked and turned away, unable to stop staring at the intertwined web of creatures that moved and crawled through the folds of clothing like glistening worms.

Cliff watched from behind the pit as he waited for her to turn the tip, waited for her to empty the tent to make room for more paying customers. Tickets sold faster when the marks were moving in and out, and Daphne knew how to make them move.

She had explained it to Cliff. "No training, nothing. I walked on the lot one day and heard the swamp girl was dead, car wreck, and I decided to give it a shot. How hard could it be, sit in the shade all day with snakes that ain't got no poison?"

Cliff had listened to her talk about twenty-seven years as the Okefenokee Swamp Girl and how she made enough money to spend the winters in Florida in her own house and he thought how different than Morganport, different than anything he learned in college, different enough for a winter in Spain.

Daphne rang a cowbell and lifted a cardboard sign and swung it back and forth, making sure the marks read the copy:

Toss a Silver Coin in the Pot
See What I Can Do.

She rang the bell and waved the sign until coins began to clink in the bottom of the tin bucket, and the ringing continued until Daphne was satisfied that the rain of silver had stopped.

She removed the straw hat, stood up with the long black snake in her hands and offered it for all to see, moving close to the edge of the pit, extending her hands until the marks stepped away, afraid of the writhing animal. Tense, ready to run, they covered their eyes as they saw Daphne slip the head of the snake in her mouth and swing it freely, her lips clamped softly over the squirming animal. The tension was too much for some of the marks and they panicked and forced their way, shouting, out of the tent. More followed, making room for the next audience and the tent filled quickly and the money poured in, money filled the bucket, money that was missing from the Sheriff of Dodge City.

At closing, Daphne handed Cliff half the take from the tin bucket and he added it to the stash under his bunk; canvas bags filled with coins and bills. When he added the numbers to the ledger, he underlined the total and thought: *It's not dirty money, is it?* Coins and bills weren't dirty, not like drug money or hookers, but it sure wasn't anything to be proud of.

Will it ruin the winter in Spain, don't think so, getting there will make it okay, I think.

Jim Mastras was helping him with the snakes, but he knew Mastras was doing it for other reasons. He wanted Cliff to stay.

It was tempting, so much money. Marks paid to see a woman hold a snake in her mouth and he got half of the bucket and he had been getting fifty big ones a night from Bozo.

My God, how the money pours in, pours in. Time to book a reservation, New York to Barcelona.

CHAPTER 44

She's a Good Dancer. Sitting in a Tent with Snakes Would Destroy Her

The cook tent conversations were about Jack's death and Cliff's big score with the snake show and when Milt would be back from Boston College.

After Jack's funeral, the gossip revolved around his high-class family and his maybe-money; everyone had pockets full of maybe-money.

Steve knew about Jack's past, his family, the time his father showed up and told Jack he wouldn't inherit a dime if he didn't sober up and act like a normal person.

After Jack's death, Milt found an address for the Lawrence family and sent them a note, telling them what had happened to Jack. Milt thought they might send something to pay for a stone, but nothing came.

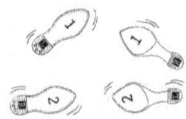

Joan liked the candy and the money and wanted more, so when Steve suggested to Cliff that she would make a good Okefenokee Swamp Girl, he was ready for the response.

"No! Don't say that, no!" Cliff felt the muscles in his neck tighten. "What are you talking about? No, not ever. The poor girl's got enough to deal with. She's starting to make a little progress. She's a good dancer. Sitting in a tent with snakes would destroy her, people staring at her."

The image of Joan with snakes draped around her neck startled Cliff and made him cringe when he realized the appeal she would have for the people who bought tickets to freak shows. He had learned to recognize their expressions; the wet lips, sideways glances, tense steps to the edge of the snake pit where they stared in a trance, mesmerized by the serpents slithering over a woman in a gingham dress, snakes coiled on her bare shoulders.

Joan's crumpled face and neck adorned with black and green snakes would be a game-changer, a quantum leap in sideshow attractions, and he felt the nausea choking higher in the back of his throat.

No change appeared on Steve's face. "She likes the money I give her. You could give her a lot more. She ain't got many choices. You add her to the show and your gross will go way up, double or more. That old lady that sits there now don't bring marks in like Joan would. You want to sit on the beach in Spain, don't you? She can sit in Florida with Bill and Ruth and have her own money."

Cliff felt the conflict. "You're not thinking about her best interests. What are you trying to get out of this?"

"If you don't do it, I am. Be better if you use her. But either way, she's going to make a lot of money."

"I'll do whatever it takes to not let that happen." Cliff twisted his head to breathe. "And so will Bill."

"If she wants to work, ain't it her choice? You'd look like an asshole stopping someone from earning their own money instead of begging all her life."

"And you want part of it," Cliff shouts. He clenches his teeth. "You don't care how it would hurt her?"

"Way I see it, she's hurt worse by being broke. A roll of green in her pocket makes up for a lot of staring people. Bill did it. He took the money and bought a house in Florida. I say let her work with what she has. What would your buddy Karack tell her?"

Steve's question shook Cliff. In the heat of the argument, the mention of the novelist made Cliff aware of the strange place he was in. *This isn't fiction. This is the real dark side; the harm people do to each other.*

"Who knows what Kerouac would say? Whatever, it wouldn't be good advice, about like yours. Keep out of it. Keep the newspapers, TV stations, out of it. This isn't about news, or money, this is about the rotten deal handed to a girl, who now has a chance for a normal life. Putting her in a sideshow is wrong and you know it."

"I don't know shit about that. You think it's wrong. You better ask her what she thinks. Remember, you ain't God."

When the sun faded, Ruth closed the shades and waited for Bill and Joan to return to the room in time for the chopped hamburger and mashed potatoes warming on the hot plate. Hearing their voices in the hall, Ruth moved to the edge of the narrow bed to make room for Joan and picked up the laundry covering Bill's folding chair. They hadn't eaten together for a week, and Ruth was worried about Joan changing the routine and staying in the menagerie with a hot dog or a hamburger that she bought with her own money.

Ruth told herself that it was only right that Joan was learning to be self-reliant, but was she ready for it? Would she ever be ready?

After leaving the family farm, Bill had learned to live by himself and he had done it for fifteen years until Ruth, the alligator-skinned lady, joined the show and after two years of gradually building a relationship, a Justice of the Peace married them.

Ruth's dream was to help Joan adjust to a routine without the agony of doing it alone, and definitely not in a sideshow. When Bill asked Ruth to marry him, it was a question he uttered in a series of choking gasps and mumbles. She had to close her eyes to hear what he was saying and even then, it was unclear what he was asking, so she had put her hand on his twisted mouth and repeated what she thought she heard.

"Do you want me to marry you?"

Bill squeezed his ripped eyes shut and nodded *yes*, and wrapped his arms around her. It was the first time anyone had hugged Ruth since her mother died, and Bill was the only man that had ever hugged her. His proposal and his embrace changed their lives like nothing they had ever dared dream about, and Ruth prayed the same blessing could come to Joan.

The hamburger and potatoes were cleaned from Joan's plate and she thanked Ruth for the meal. "Will you show me how to cook?"

Ruth relaxed and squeezed the girl's hand. "When we get to Florida, you can have a real kitchen to learn in."

"I want to buy the groceries sometimes." Joan dropped her eyes. "I want to earn my own money."

Bill and Ruth faced each other. They knew what she was saying. They knew Joan had been paid by Steve Lanning, and she was buying hot dogs and slum jewelry and learning what it was like to have money in her pocket, the comfort of heavy coins and folded bills.

"We'll give you money."

"You don't have to. I can make my own. Mr. Lanning told me I could."

Bill finished chewing his hamburger, taking his time before speaking. "I know Steve gives you money, I know it. But we're almost finished here, going to stay in Florida, don't make no sense to start that business now."

"I like feeding the elephants, Little Three, and the chimp likes me."

Bill pushed the hair away from his eyes. "We'll get you some animals in Florida, we got room. Maybe you'd like a horse." They painted a picture of what life was going to be like in Florida in their three-bedroom house, one for Joan where she could paint the walls any color she wanted and Ruth would help her make curtains and plant flowers outside the window.

"Gibsonton's all show people like here, no one stares. We can eat in the diner, shop at the grocery store, buy clothes, and no one stares."

Joan said she wanted yellow walls and blue curtains. She wanted the bedroom, but she knew she would also miss seeing new towns, lying in bed on the train feeling the room sway, buying cotton candy and shiny rings.

"I can keep feeding the animals, can't I?"

They talked about the remainder of the season, the fairs in Philadelphia, Washington, Richmond and Atlanta and Albany and Tallahassee. Bill said, "When the train is parked in winter quarters, we'll pack our clothes and the hot plate and drive to Gibsonton."

Joan heard the names of the cities, her eyes glistening, then she dropped her chin, understanding that when they moved to the three-bedroom house, they wouldn't be returning to the train.

When they went to bed, Bill whispered to Ruth, "Steve asked Duke to paint a new banner of her."

"Is he going to?"

"No. He told Steve he wouldn't. But Duke ain't the only place to get one."

"What are we gonna do?"

"It won't happen. I won't never let it happen. You know it."

When she heard the conviction in Bill's voice, Ruth let her shoulders drop onto the soft pillow. She realized she been holding herself rigid for several days and spending most of her time searching through the window for a glimpse of her daughter.

Bill didn't usually make strong statements, but that night, his words worked like sleeping pills.

CHAPTER 45

Her Eyes Flooded with Tears, She Moaned Like a Fatally Wounded Animal

The menagerie was closed, with a rope tied across the entrance. It was early morning, time for Joan to be alone with the animals. No marks stared at her from the midway. On her knees, she brushed her calf, hugging the animal as she gently massaged the stump where the leg didn't form.

As the calf licked Joan's twisted cheeks, Katie stood behind the chimp's cage where she could let the tears flow and drip onto her blouse. She lifted her hands to her face, then folded her arms across her chest, and stared and blinked as she focused on the picture of the girl embracing the calf, a loving contact between two creatures, both born defective.

"Little Three loves your brushing."

Joan stiffened and muffled a shout. "Scared me. Oh, Katie, I didn't hear you. She does like brushing."

Katie didn't know what to do or say. Her thoughts collided, torn between leaving the tedious, awful Broadway Review and moving to Radio City Music Hall. What could she say to Joan, a sweet girl trapped behind curtains and scarves?

"Would you like to go on a picnic with me…and Cliff and my dad?" Katie didn't know where the idea came from. She just suddenly heard the words, as if they originated from some other mouth.

Joan dropped the brush and jumped to her feet. "I want to! I'll tell Momma Ruth. Can we? Never been on a picnic."

"Yes, ask her if it's all right, if they can go. We'll meet you at the train."

She walked to the office wagons where Lee told her Cliff had left the fairgrounds with the Man. He shook his head when she asked when they might be back. As usual, there were other men sitting under the awning outside the office. Wood chips covered the ground. The potted plants, the steps to the office doors were wet and clean and the men stopped talking when Katie appeared. They tried not to stare at the pretty dancer.

"If they come back soon, would you mind telling Cliff I'm looking for him?"

"I'll tell him." Lee smiled at Katie. Lee didn't smile at anyone, but he smiled at Katie.

She started to leave when Cliff turned the corner and she could tell from his expression that something was wrong.

Cliff knew Joan was a good dancer. But sitting in a tent with snakes would destroy her. People would stare at her and he would reap financial gains. He would never do such a cruel thing."

"Katie, are you all right?"

"Yes. No."

"Can I do anything? I need to tell you something."

"I don't think so—I don't know."

He took her hand and led her behind the wagon. "Steve Lanning wants me to use Joan in the snake show, make her the Okefenokee Swamp Girl."

Katie clamped both hands over her mouth, her eyes flooded with tears, and she moaned like a fatally wounded animal.

"I told him no. You know I told him no."

Katie's eyes were blank. She nodded in a trance.

"But if I don't do it, he's going to use her in the menagerie. He told me she wants to, she wants the money."

Katie folded her arms around Cliff and held him until she could talk, then asked him to go with her and take Joan away from the train.

Her embrace soothed his pain. Cliff closed his eyes as Katie pressed against him. Her lips were soft on his neck and he never wanted to leave this private place, never wanted to leave this sweet girl who was asking him to help. He pulled her closer, gathering her strength.

He parked the car under a stand of sycamore trees. Broad green leaves fluttered on thin stems and white limbs, trees like Cliff used to climb in Morganport.

Joan picked a leaf. "We have these trees at home. I used to help my dad rake them in the fall. I liked the smoke from the fires."

The park was surrounded by the city, a grassy island in the middle of tall buildings and parking lots and factories—far away from the midway. A small river flowed through, cooling the borders of the shallow valley, a narrow path of moist air feeding the daffodils and dandelions reaching for the sun. The park's smell was rich with gurgling water, sweet green grass, and fried chicken—a relief from the hot electric motors and grinding diesel generators.

They had stopped at a Kentucky Fried Chicken and Cliff bought a bucket of breasts and legs and thighs, rolls, slaw, and green beans and Cokes. The girls had waited in the car and when Joan pulled the scarf over her face, Katie had to bite her lips to keep from crying. In the park, Joan let the scarf fall to her shoulders while she swung from a low branch and walked through the tall grass.

"Aren't you hungry?" Cliff asked Joan. "I can't resist this chicken. Come on and eat," he said. "In the spring, my mom used to make fried chicken and we'd go to the Indianapolis 500 time trials. Did you ever go?"

He wished he could pull back his question. *No, she didn't go to the races, what am I thinking?*

Joan dropped to the blanket and picked up a piece of chicken. "We listened on the radio. Dad wasn't much on leaving the farm."

"I want to bless this food." Seamus reached for Joan's hand. "Lord, we ask your blessing on this food and your blessing on this family. We know you're with us right now and in our faith, we turn to you. In Christ's name, we ask it, amen."

After finishing the food, Seamus invited Ruth and Bill to join him on a walk along the lake—under the spell of the wooded park, so different from the spinning midway.

Ruth said, "We don't know what to do about Joan. She's pulling away from us. Steve Lanning's giving her money. We never had no kids around."

"You've talked to her?"

"Yes. We want her to feel safe. Learn to not be scared. I bet you never had anything like this with Katie."

"Yes, we did. But it was different. We raised her from a baby. You're just getting started. Joan's not a baby. She's a teenager with not much experience, except she's away from her parents, away from the farm, and this is all new. I'm sorry but I don't know what to say. I could advise you to pray…and I do, but that's not what you want to hear."

"We thought about talkin' to Katie."

"Good idea. Can I do it with you?"

"Please do."

Cliff and Katie and Joan were stretched out on a blanket, watching clouds drift overhead. A light breeze bent the trees and leaves fell from the force of the wind. Joan felt safe between Cliff and Katie.

She sat up. "Let's try those new steps."

"Yes. I like watching you dance. You're getting very good."

Katie was pleased she could offer this compliment with complete sincerity. She looked at Joan's legs and arms, her full breasts, her graceful hands and thought how normal and pretty she was below her neck. And she could move in time to the music, inventing her own steps as well as any other dancers, better.

"Do you think I am?"

"You know I do." Katie held Joan's hand. "You know you've learned a lot, almost everything I know."

"I can't never be as good as you."

"Yes, you can."

Cliff listened to the girls. He wanted to say it didn't matter. *What can she do with it? She can dance by herself behind the wagons on the midway but that's all, not in the Broadway Review, not in Radio City Music Hall. I'm watching a beautiful dancer and a deformed girl. Not long ago I couldn't have done it. Now I can. I don't see her face anymore. I see her feeding the elephants, brushing her calf, and dancing like she's free.*

Joan stopped. "I want to use what I got, my face. You got dancin', I got my face."

Her words exploded in the quiet space, a loud blast that no other sounds could penetrate. Katie slumped over, with her hands over her ears.

Cliff turned to the clouds, hoping to see a solution. Instead, he saw Joan's crumpled face. *What is she saying? Who has she been talking to? Steve Lanning, Milt? She wants to use her face to make money?*

When Katie turned to Joan, she was shaking her head. She couldn't speak. Back and forth, she twisted her head and forced a silent *No.*

Joan rubbed Katie's arm. "It will be good. Don't worry. I can work and earn enough money to spend the winter in Florida with the other people that look like me. God give me this face for a reason. Like he give you dancing."

Katie held up her hand, her eyes closed. She kept her hand open, and took deep breaths as she struggled to talk. "You'll… break their hearts. You'll break them."

Joan said, "I don't think so."

Her short answer didn't allow a response. Cliff vowed to not be a part of it. He wouldn't let her work in the Snake Show, but if she did something with Steve Lanning, it would be her decision.

Katie put her arms around Joan and couldn't stop crying.

They returned to the train where nothing had changed, the picnic slipped from their memories. The fried chicken, the sycamore leaves, the rain on the car was gone, but Joan's wishes remained. She didn't talk about her plans with Bill and Ruth.

When she woke up in the morning, she pulled on her clothes and left the train before Ruth could talk to her and she stayed in the menagerie all day into the evening, until the midway closed at midnight. Then she returned to the train, and when Ruth tried to question her, she pulled the blanket over her head.

In the morning, Seamus and Katie walked through the Pullman cars and knocked on the door. Ruth and Bill looked upset, their faces and eyes pulled tight.

"She leaves first thing." Ruth felt like she had to explain. "What a change. When she first got here she couldn't look out the window, now she's okay going from the train to the lot."

"Scares the hell out of me." Bill wouldn't add much more to the discussion.

"I feel like I'm watching a toddler learn to walk," Katie said.

"We thank God for you every night and I do all day long." Ruth held Katie's hand. "She loves you."

"I love her. I can't think about leaving."

"What do you think about Steve Lanning giving her money?"

Katie looked at Seamus and he nodded his head. "I think with Jack gone, Steve is paying her to help take care of the animals and that's good."

"But she stays there all day and part of the night. Don't come home until time for bed. You never did nothing like that, did you?"

"Sure I did. Sixteen years old, you want to do your own thing. They let me—to some extent," Katie continued. "What do you think happened when I announced I was going to take a bus to join a carnival so I could get to New York City?"

They looked at Seamus, who shook his head. "You weren't sixteen."

He knew there were big differences between Joan and Katie, besides their age. "And you knew how long you had to stay with the carnival and you were determined to audition with the Rockettes. We knew you were good enough, and that had been part of your plan for years. We weren't thrilled with what you had to do, but we knew you could take care of yourself. Joan's a different matter, completely different."

Bill and Ruth agreed with Seamus. "She doesn't want to listen to what we say." Ruth asked Katie if she would talk to Joan. "I know she respects you."

"Of course I will." Katie didn't want to tell them that she had already talked to Joan. "And I'll spend more time with her practicing our steps. That's probably the best thing to do. I think Ace would put her in the show if she was going to stay."

Seamus prayed. "Lord, we thank you for your blessings on this couple who have had their prayers answered with the arrival of their daughter, Joan. Their faith brought her to them, and it will be their faith that continues to support them and answer their questions about how to be the parents you want them to be. Give Joan the assurance that she has skills that she can share with others. I ask this in Jesus's name, amen."

That night Ruth fell asleep as soon as Joan returned to the room.

Most Come to the Fair But Not the Midway; Might See an Ankle or a Tit

After Jersey City, the train moved west to Lancaster, the last stop before the biggest fair of the fall in Philadelphia. Lancaster wasn't a bad date. The Pennsylvania Dutch farmers came to the midway, but their Amish rules locked most of their money in their leather billfolds.

"Parking lot will have horses and black buggies." Steve explained to Cliff how the Amish families traveled. "They don't have electricity, most come to the fair but not the midway; might see an ankle or a tit. They got milk cans full of cash."

"Do they like the elephants?"

"We do all right, but no one does great. The women look at quilts, the men check the bulls and pigs, chickens."

The run from Jersey City to Lancaster took six hours because the switching yards were congested with freight trains. Joan rode with the animals in the boxcar. Katie had invited her to ride in the station wagon, and was worried when Joan declined. "I want to ride the train."

"Do you mind my asking why?" Katie didn't want it to sound judgmental, but it did.

"Too many people around. I like the boxcar…with the animals."

The train was parked late in the day. The siding was across the road from the fairgrounds, so they could sleep late in the morning. It wasn't much time, but they could make the opening by working all night.

John Mastras was proud of the fact that, if necessary, his crews could tear down and set up in less than twenty-four hours. And the Lancaster contract called for it. He didn't like working in the dark, but they had to a few times each season. At least it wasn't raining.

Seamus was up before dawn, intrigued by the efficiency of the teardown and the set-up. His real interest, however, was in the black horse-drawn buggies. He put on his priest's collar and approached one of the drivers, who was wearing a plain blue work shirt, a flat black hat and a neat beard outlining the lower portion of his face.

"Hello. I'm Seamus Flannigan." He extended his hand.

The farmer returned the gesture. "A pleasure to meet you, Mr. Flannigan. I'm Caleb Miller. I see you're a man of faith. Are you visiting?"

"I'm traveling with this carnival, taking a break from my church, and traveling with my daughter. She performs in one of the shows."

"Which one?"

"The show where girls take off their clothes. My daughter is one of the dancers; she doesn't take off her clothes. I'm not that open-minded."

The farmer had trouble deciding what to say. The annual fair put a strain on his conservative faith and this priest was more than he could take. "You're calm about it?"

"I imagine what I've just said is hard to understand. I get that." Seamus unbuttoned his white collar and took it off, then unbuttoned the top buttons of his shirt and pulled it open. "Since I left the Catholic Church, most of my beliefs are similar to yours."

"Enjoy your stay in Lancaster. God is protecting your daughter."

The farmer turned around and walked away with his wife but then he stopped and turned back.

"Our Meeting has a food tent near the main entrance. Please join us for a meal. Bring your daughter."

The food tent was easy to see with its white canvas, pots of blue and yellow flowers around the entrance, and wooden stands holding large clay containers of cold buttermilk.

Seamus discovered the buttermilk the first day the fair was open. He accepted a glass from Caleb Miller and confirmed that he and his daughter and her boyfriend would have dinner with them before the Fair closed. The ice-cold buttermilk jolted his mouth and throat, like it did on the farm in Ireland.

"Would you like fried chicken or pork chops?"

"I'd like a salad; hard to dance on pork chops." Katie answered.

Seamus and Cliff both ordered fried chicken. "Is Caleb Miller here today?"

"He just went to the Fair office."

"If he gets back before we leave, I'd like to talk to him. We met earlier. I'm Seamus Flannigan."

"Thank you for eating with us."

The tent was filled with diners, and a line had formed at the entrance, waiting for tables. Cliff and Katie told Seamus that the Amish food tents had been talked about by the carnies for weeks prior to the Lancaster Fair. Large platters of chicken, pole beans, fresh corn, and sliced tomatoes were brought to each table. There was no doubt the food had been growing nearby in the past few days, fresh from the vine. And the carnies didn't shy away from eating it—they felt the acceptance of the peaceful Amish and Mennonite people.

"Mr. Flannigan. They told me you were here. And this is your daughter?"

"Mr. Miller, meet Katie and her friend, Cliff. We've just about finished a fine meal. Can you sit with us?"

Cliff wrote: *Plain Amish farmer, who plows with a team of horses sitting with ex-Irish priest, girl who doesn't take her clothes off and a reporter.* Not a bad opening.

"The wife and I watched you dance last night. We guessed it was you, especially in contrast with the other girls."

Seamus slapped the table. "You're *not* Amish, are you?"

"Mennonite, we are. We decide what's acceptable. Watching the dancers is acceptable if I close my eyes to the nudity. I'm the only one that knows if I did or not."

Seamus and Caleb laughed together. Two men of faith, secure in their faith, understanding each other's rebellion.

"Mr. Flannigan, I'm glad you're here. Maybe you and Cliff can help me."

"If you call me Seamus and I call you Caleb."

Katie excused herself. "The next show is in ten minutes. I have to change into the costume that doesn't come off." When she stood up, she stepped in front of Caleb. "Can I hug you? And thank you for the good food?"

"If I close my eyes."

The three men watched her walk away. Seamus and Cliff waited for Caleb's comments, but the farmer remained silent. Finally, he broke the quiet. "If you two can help me, I'm buying a new tractor and need help with the transaction."

"How can we help?"

"Carry the money."

Seamus and Cliff looked at each other. Later, they determined they were both thinking the same thing: a strange request from a strange farmer. And the carnival was supposed to have the strange people.

"I can help. What about you, Cliff?"

"Tell me what to do."

Caleb led them behind the tent and opened the back of a pickup truck. Inside they saw boxes of supplies: knives, forks, paper plates, napkins, and two large metal cans. Cliff recognized the cans as ones used to carry milk, a common sight along the roads running past the farms where farmers milked their cows, filled the cans, and placed them on the side of the road for the processing dairy to pick up.

Caleb gripped one of the handles and directed Cliff to grip the other, and they lifted the heavy can out of the truck and placed it on the ground. Then Caleb and Seamus lifted the other one. "This one's lighter. Us old guys can handle it."

"What's in them?" Cliff thought he knew, but it couldn't be.

"Money for the new tractor. The one is heavier with coins."

Caleb lowered a two-wheeled cart from the back of the truck, placed the milk cans on the platform and started pushing them around the back of the midway. Seamus and Cliff followed, not knowing what they were going to do, but they followed because the strange farmer asked them to.

Cliff whispered to Seamus, "You think he's going to pay cash for a tractor?"

"I'd say that's a good guess."

It took almost an hour for Seamus and Cliff to pull stacks of paper bills and coins out of the milk cans and hand them to Caleb so he could sort the bills, count the money, and place it into stacks of one hundred dollars each. The tractor salesman watched Caleb's hands and verified each stack. He wound a rubber band around the stacks until there was seven thousand dollars on the table.

"Eight hundred and forty more, and you'll own a new tractor, Mr. Miller."

"Three hundred and forty, isn't it?"

"Mr. Miller, we went through this last time you bought a tractor. Let's don't do it again."

"I don't remember that."

"I do."

Cliff smiled to himself. *How hard is he going to push this? He should take lessons from Steve Lanning. Offer the salesman free chicken dinners.*

Caleb looked in the milk cans. "Not but three hundred left."

"Make it six hundred and we have a deal."

Caleb counted out five hundred and handed it to the salesman. They shook hands, deal closed.

When they returned to the food tent, Caleb and Seamus asked for coffee, and Cliff said he needed to return to the office.

"Mr. Mastras might need me. Thanks for letting me count your money. That's what we do around here—as much as possible."

Caleb said, "He seems like a nice young man. Is he going to marry your daughter?"

"He hasn't asked me yet."

"And when he does?"

"In our way of life, the decision is Katie's. Asking me is an old custom, doesn't mean much. What would you do?" Seamus wanted to know Caleb's position.

"I'll have to decide that when the time comes. Our daughter is twelve."

Seamus sat quietly, waiting to see how the conversation proceeded.

"What do you think about my buying that tractor?"

"Odd question. I think you probably needed a new tractor for your farming work."

"That's right, but I'm the only farmer in these parts that uses a tractor. The rest still use mules to plow. They think I'm breaking some of God's rules."

"You don't?"

"Show me in the Bible where it says thou shall not use thy tractor."

"Like me. I couldn't find a rule in the Bible *thou shall not marry*. So I did and they kicked me out. They won't kick you out for driving a tractor?"

"No, they won't. Times are changing."

Seamus wished he and Caleb were closer friends. Men that had shared experiences over several years so they understood how far they could go with each other.

He's pretty open about breaking some of his rules. Uses a tractor. "Why not drive a car, just the tractor?"

Cliff had returned to their table. "I'd like to know that, too."

"I don't need to get anywhere faster than horses can take me. The tractor lets me grow more food so I can give more of it away." Caleb folded his hands. "All right—your turn, Mr. Seamus Flannigan. I know you broke your vows so you could get married. But there's more than that—isn't there? Spill it."

"I sense we might be dangerous together."

"We've had a good teacher."

"And look what happened to him."

"Don't say it."

"I won't." But Seamus was thinking—*he got nailed to a cross.* "I've taken to heart what a Catholic teacher has written and preaches on a wide scale. He makes the point, Jesus didn't say *worship me,* he said *follow me,* feed the hungry, clothe the poor, cure the sick, love our neighbors, have mercy. When I understood that, I realized the church is a big set of rules, especially the Catholics, Irish Catholics. Special prayers, certain chants, bells, specific times, certain days in special buildings—wear the right hat and on and on, eat fish, don't eat pork, candles, incense. I don't think that's following, that's worshipping. And it gets in the way of what he said, *follow me.* And he broke a lot of rules during his ministry."

Caleb put his arms around Seamus and kissed him on the cheek. "A Catholic teaches this?"

"Yes, A Franciscan, and his following is growing. Follow is the key. Do something, take action, the desperate needs are right in front of us but they're ignored because we're too busy worshipping."

Caleb said, "Wait a minute."

"Yes?"

"I want to say we don't have that issue. But you sure said it clearly."

"No?"

"No. The core of our belief is our mission to follow. We grow food. We share it with others. We do what we can for the sick. We teach our children the way to live, every day, give more than an hour. But many of our children are pulling away. And I'm afraid the time we're spending with them still isn't enough or what we're teaching them can't compete with what they hear and see from society. We're also guilty of silly rules—mule or tractor, beards or no beards."

"Unfortunately, that's hurting most of us."

"I know. I do know that. And that's what I'm dealing with. Seamus, you know I understand. I do. That's why I use a tractor. I understand you're a pastor that wants to lead your flock to do the work of the Lord, not what society tells them to do. I pray for your success because I can't do what you do and God knows how much we need it."

After the cook tent closed, they started their service and Caleb opened with an explanation of why he invited Seamus.

"He's doing some things—with his daughter and their church— that we can learn from. I've been in a position where I don't always hear what God is telling me. And I feel like Seamus might have been sent here for me to learn something."

Elizabeth Smith asked, "Like how to let our daughters wiggle their bodies? Not what he's telling me."

"I guess our square dancing doesn't include body wiggling because we keep our clothes on? At least until we get home?"

"Caleb Miller, if I didn't love you…"

"Elizabeth, I thank God you do. And I love you, too. Now we're all tired, been a long day. Let's let our guest talk."

Seamus sang, "*Dance, dance wherever you may be. I am the Lord of the dance, said he.* If I remember right, dance is an acceptable part of worship. And that song comes from the Quakers. I know you're not Quakers, but similar. Now, Caleb and I have been sharing our faith—just the two of us."

Seamus stopped talking and waited. The silence became a strong comment. They looked at Seamus, expecting more, but he sat quietly.

They looked at Caleb.

"Is that the summary of your comparison?" Caleb asked. "If it is, you're not very articulate—all of a sudden."

Seamus lifted his hands and shrugged his shoulders.

Caleb said, "She doesn't take off her clothes. And she's a good dancer. She considers it a gift from God. Seamus taught her we all receive gifts. We can't keep them for ourselves. We have to share them."

Elizabeth said, "Another reason to wonder about you. How did you get to be a judge of dancing—good or bad?"

"I'm not blind and we've been to Radio City."

"We all know you have; everyone knows you've seen the Rockettes."

"The reason I invited Seamus is because he's had to deal with the same thing we have to deal with, and it looks like he hasn't lost his relationship with his daughter. I want to know how he's managed to do that. A lot of us have not figured it out. No matter what we think or do or believe, the fact is some of our children are not buying into our old ways. They want to leave home. They want to pursue different careers. They don't want to farm with mules. Either we accept this and learn how to accommodate them, or we're in danger of losing our relationships with the children we love. I won't let that happen. I hope Seamus can help me."

Cliff looked up from his notes. Seamus was staring at the notebook. "Getting some good stuff?"

"Yes. I hadn't thought this through."

Caleb asked, "What? What are you thinking about?"

Cliff was reluctant to speak to the group. He ran his finger under the pencil marks. Talking quietly but clearly, he said, "I'm young. I haven't seen the world like Seamus has or you have. I'm thinking about your way of life; Seamus' way of life when he was a priest. You're not that much different; both live by rules set down by your churches."

He stopped talking, unsure of what he was saying.

Seamus encouraged him to continue. "Go ahead, Cliff, we're among friends."

"Are you sure?"

Both men encouraged him to continue.

"Seamus broke away and has found a way to live that he believes suits God. Most haven't figured it out and I'm not sure they want to." Cliff asked, "You want to, don't you?"

"I do and I hope you write about it, about us." Caleb looked at Elizabeth. She shook her head.

"I will." Cliff realized he'd made a commitment.

"I'll help," Seamus offered. "What about you, Caleb, will you help?"

"Probably. I want to hear what you have to tell us first. But I think it will make a good story."

Seamus felt the animosity from Elizabeth Smith, but she sat patiently and listened with the rest of the group.

"Seamus, please tell us what took place that put your daughter in this position." Caleb's question was the right one.

"Katie has danced since she could walk. Of course, my wife, Rose, encouraged her. My favorite memories include Rose and Katie rolling back the rug in the living room, picking out their costumes: sometimes tights, sometimes full, flowered skirts, scarves, hats, feathers. They played loud music and sweat on their faces and love in their eyes and high steps, glide steps, stomping and singing until the record was over and they'd do it again. I'd beg them to keep dancing.

"Those sessions put Katie in the position of saying yes when the agent offered her a dancing job traveling the state fair circuit. She was ready to grow. He didn't tell her it was in the midway strip show; he made it sound like it was with the stage shows in the grandstands with big bands and Broadway stars. When she arrived to start work, she learned the truth. She asked if she had to take off her clothes and how long was it going to take to get to New York City. When she had the answers, she called me and asked for my opinion and I told her it was her decision and here we are—two weeks away from Radio City Music Hall."

Caleb asked Cliff if he got it all.

"I've already heard it, and yes, I've got it all."

Seamus asked Caleb, "What else can I tell you?"

"You had no doubt about Katie's actions? About her conduct?"

"None."

"All right. Now tell us about your church."

"Do we have time?"

Caleb looked at the other members and they nodded their heads. Caleb motioned for Seamus to continue.

"Another pastor we follow encourages his members to use the gifts God gave them. Like we've just discussed, we're born with skills and talents and when someone does something naturally, it comes easily. And that's when we're in the best position to serve—when we do what we're good at. Then it's easier to share. We usually feel joy when we're using our gifts and others can feel that joy. It's contagious.

"My daughter, Katie, is a good example. It's a long story, but a few weeks ago a deformed girl arrived on the carnival to live with a couple who are also deformed and had worked in the freak show for many years. The details of how this came about are not important, except for the issue that the deformed girl was facing problems in life because her severe deformities kept her isolated on a remote farm. The deformed couple took her in, like a daughter. They can provide a life for her that is almost normal because the carnival people are accepting of these conditions.

"When Katie got to know the girl, her first thought was to just be friends because the girl was afraid and having trouble adjusting. As their friendship strengthened, the young girl, Joan, let Katie know that she would like to learn some dance steps. Katie has been happy to teach her and be friends with her and this has created a situation where Joan is now able to mix with the carnival people and earn money by taking care of some of the show animals and not feel like she has to hide for the rest of her life.

"God-given gifts come in each one of our packages, but most of us don't know what they are. The trick is to become aware and use them to help someone else. That's why they're called gifts—gifts to us and we serve God by giving them to someone else. I think about our gifts like a machine, a tractor, maybe an airplane. People are designed to do things, to dance, to use our motors, to use our wheels, pull plows. That's what we're here for. We have the basic skills to stay alive—as long as we're fed but we also have skills to invent things, to serve others, to fix problems. Our purpose is to use what we've got the best way possible. Albert Camus said we have a moral obligation to use our gifts."

Caleb put his arms around Seamus. "A blessing, Seamus. Thank you, God bless you. You've given me ideas how to keep close to my children. I've been praying for help."

"Did I talk too long? It felt like it."

Caleb asked the other people to respond. "I was enthralled, what about you?" He directed the question to Elizabeth. She hesitated. A few seconds later, she took a breath, "I'm not sure I could mix with a group of carnival people, but maybe."

No one had a response to her comment.

Seamus motioned with his hand to stop Caleb from saying anything.

"Elizabeth, I have a suggestion for you." Seamus waited.

She looked at him. "All right."

"I enjoyed my meal here in your cook tent and I'd like to invite you to join me for a meal on the midway. Say lunch tomorrow?"

She closed her eyes; her mouth clamped shut.

Caleb answered for her. "I'll come. Can we bring a group?"

"I'll reserve tables in the cook tent; bring as many as you can."

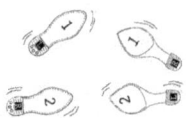

Seamus and Katie were resting in their room, sharing events of the midway, and especially the time spent with the Mennonites.

"There was a controversial time over a hundred years ago in England when Quakers were taking members away from the traditional churches. They claimed they were the true followers of Jesus and it caused an uproar with the Catholics and the Church of England, Episcopalians, so when I saw the black buggies parked at the fairgrounds, I was intrigued."

"You're always intrigued, aren't you?"

"God works in many ways. I think I'm obligated to try and understand His ways, as much as I can. And my interest has been made stronger with our recent contacts."

A knock on the door surprised them.

When Seamus saw Caleb and Sarah standing outside, he made a soft sound, a forceful sigh and grasped the other man's hand and pulled him inside. "I just said to Katie that God works in many ways and here you two are."

Caleb kissed Katie on the cheek. "I'm so glad to catch both of you. We want to apologize for our rude behavior last night. And it's getting worse."

Sarah hugged Katie and Seamus.

Katie asked, "How did you find us? I'm glad you did."

"We got directions every step of the way. Rest assured, your carnival friends know where you live. To tell you the truth, we wanted to see the train."

"What's getting worse?"

Caleb's posture sagged. "I can't convince Elizabeth to come to lunch with us. She refuses to accept your invitation. I'm mad as hell!"

"Caleb!" Sarah forced her words.

"And the others?"

"They're embarrassed by her stubborn attitude, but don't want to come, either. We're letting one stubborn member make a decision that makes all of us look bad. What kind of people are we? It makes us look like people who take the money, but shun the people who bring it. That's as bad as the rest of the world, worse. I don't know what to do about it. It's this attitude that many of our children rebel against. What should we do? Help us."

Sarah agreed. "We're so upset. Help us if you can."

Seamus didn't know what to say. He sympathized with Caleb and Sarah, who were caught in the middle of a conflict that had been running for a long time. The difference between beliefs created real damage, but it didn't go away.

"I don't have any suggestions for you." Seamus looked at Katie. "What do you think, my love?"

Katie answered, "I don't know, either. Maybe we just agree to not agree."

"Would it be asking too much for a tour of the back part of the midway, the part the rest of us never see?"

Katie smiled. "Yes. I'm about to work on a dance routine with Joan. Join us?"

"Will Cliff be there?"

"I can find him. We'll meet you in the tent."

Caleb gripped Seamus' hand. "God's here. We all feel his presence. We've heard true words because of it. We share the same vision and problems. Is it too late for us?"

"Not if we all agree to listen to our kids. They will lead us if we let them. Katie's dancing has brought me here."

"Wait until Elizabeth hears this."

Later that day, the tables in the Mennonite food tent were filled with diners. Caleb and Sarah welcomed new customers, seating them as soon as space was available and they exchanged glances and smiled, expecting something special. Trays of food were carried from the kitchen and tables were cleared when the customers left.

Caleb checked his watch, and signaled one of the other men to set up a new table in the middle of the tent. And on a preset schedule, a group of new customers appeared at the entrance and Caleb and Sarah greeted them with hugs and embraces. The new group followed them to the middle table, aware that the other diners were staring at the scarves and hats pulled over their faces. When they were seated, they removed the coverings.

Joan and Ruth and Bill kept their eyes aimed at each other, gathering strength from being together for the first time in a place they had never been brave enough to enter until now.

Their strength came from the welcome they received when they arrived, that, and from the joyous time Caleb and Sarah spent while Katie and Joan practiced the new dance routine.

When their food was served, the waiters thanked them for being there and for traveling to Lancaster and bringing the rides and games and shows that they looked forward to seeing every year.

Cliff whispered to Seamus that Elizabeth was standing behind the counter, watching.

"She's a tough one."

Seamus agreed. "That she is. Reminds me of old Sister Elizabeth in Ireland, beat my hands bloody with a ruler because God told her to."

Cliff held up his notebook. "The image of a mean nun in a white uniform beating your hands bloody, red drops oozing from your fingertips, is powerful."

Exploding Rage and Fury Transformed Bill into an Overpowering Threat

On Saturday, the last day of the Lancaster Fair, the midway communication network raged like a hot fire in a drought. The news moved from tent to tent, ride to ride, grab joint to grab joint, and even jumped the divide to the free exhibits.

Bill was late to hear what had happened because he was napping, getting ready to work all night loading the train.

When he approached the front of the menagerie, Bill's sickening nightmare came alive.

Over the entrance, Steve Lanning had installed a new banner, a large canvas showing Joan's face in bright colors and exaggerated lines. The rip where a mouth should be was outlined in red and yellow, and her crooked nose was bright blue. She was sitting on the ground holding her three-legged calf, with the stub of its leg drawn as an exaggerated stump, an ugly picture that stopped traffic.

Bill dropped to his knees with his face in his hands, unaware of the marks moving around him. They watched the sobbing man as he pulled his eyes away from the banner and searched for Steve Lanning, who was standing behind a truck where he could see Bill, but Bill couldn't see him. Steve had been warned that Bill was on his way.

Bill lost control, remembering the pain of leaving his parents' farm—the pain of them wanting him gone. He had been sixteen, same as Joan, when the stranger came to the farm and shook hands with his father. When Bill was in the back seat of the car, the stranger closed the door, turned the ignition, and steered the sedan away from Mississippi. He drove through the night until they parked behind the midway, and Bill went on exhibit as the boy with three eyes.

The anger generated by the gruesome banner drove Bill to the edge and brought him to his feet, determined to kill Steve Lanning.

He ran to the banner pole and jerked at the ropes holding the canvas in place. The ropes were as thick as a finger and they were threaded through metal grommets sewn into the corners of the large canvas banner. Bill knew how the ropes and pulleys operated.

"Let go, Bill. Not your property." Steve grabbed Bill's arm. "That's my banner, let go of the rope."

"No. No, you ain't doin' it, no! Not with my Joan, NO!" Bill continued to jerk the rope but Steve's grip stopped him and Bill let go.

He ran away and returned, carrying a club. "Take it down." His voice trembled with anger and fear. "You want your head beat? *TAKE IT DOWN—NOW!*" His violent anger could be heard and felt by those watching, shock waves of energy overcoming the noise of the midway, a force of exploding rage and fury transformed Bill into an overpowering threat.

Steve loosened the ropes and dropped the banner.

"It goes back up in Philly. You bring that club back and see what happens." Steve rolled the banner, turned his back on Bill, and disappeared into the menagerie.

Bill pounded on the door of the office wagons, but it didn't open, so Bill paced and waited, and wrung his hands and waited. When the tractor arrived to pull the office wagons to the train,

Bill was still wringing his hands and waiting, but he didn't know Jim Mastras was already in Philadelphia, asleep in a suite in the Marriott Hotel.

He had no choice but to hitch a ride to the train, where he cried and sobbed with Ruth. They laid awake in bed, their anguish intensified because Joan wasn't in her room. They didn't know where she was, but if they had to guess, it would be in the boxcar with the animals. They rolled into the siding near Philadelphia's Lighthouse Field and Bill returned to the midway to wait for the Man.

Cliff arrived before Jim Mastras. He asked Bill, "Are you waiting for the boss?"

"I got to see him, GOT to. It's important."

Cliff didn't want to ask why. Now he could look at Bill's face, but he started to panic when he thought he might have to do something else.

"Can you help me?" Cliff wanted to walk away, but something in Bill's voice stopped him. Something in the pain kept Cliff from leaving.

"I don't know. What do you need?"

As Bill explained about the new banner, Cliff looked away. He didn't want to hear anymore because he had already heard Steve's suggestion to make Joan the new Swamp Girl, as well as his conviction that Joan was going to make someone a lot of money—serious money—and if it wasn't Cliff with the Snake Show, it may as well be Steve's menagerie.

Tractors chugged up and down the midway, delivering wagons and rides and set-up crews pushed their adrenalin buttons for energy to make up for a lack of sleep. Cliff had arranged interviews for a TV crew and a feature writer from the *Philadelphia Enquirer,* and he didn't want to miss them.

"What can I do?"

"Help me talk to the Man. He's the only one can stop him. If someone don't stop him, I'll kill him, tell the Man. I *will* kill Steve Lanning. I'll kill him so fast he'll be dead standing up."

Cliff knew he had to make a decision. He returned to the room on the train and sat on the bed and rubbed Katie's back until she opened her eyes and smiled.

Cliff felt his temples pulse because he knew his decision would crush her smile. He told her about the new banner. "Please don't fall apart. We need to… I think we can…"

Katie pulled on her jeans and a blouse. "What? Do what? Oh my God, my God. Tell me, please tell me."

Cliff asked her to go to the office wagons and help the reporters with their interviews. "If you do that, I can go to the Marriott and we can see the boss. Bill wants him to stop Steve, or Bill says he'll kill him…and I know he will."

The risk was the interviews might not proceed as planned. Katie had walked with Cliff and reporters during several fairs but she had never escorted them alone.

At first, he wanted to ask her to wear something other than a blouse and jeans, something that showed off her body, something that would keep them from staring at her red eyes. Then he realized she could handle the job, no matter what she was wearing.

Katie couldn't stop her tears. "Yes, yes. Don't worry, I won't cry when they get here, I won't if I can do it now. Please, God. Please don't let this happen. I'm going to find Dad. I need him."

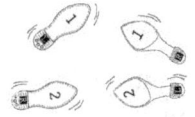

On their way to the hotel, Bill repeated, "I will kill him. I never been in a fancy hotel. I'm scared, but I'm going, I don't want to kill him. I will if he don't stop."

They entered the lobby of the Marriott Hotel. It was mid-morning and business executives were involved with breakfast meetings. The lobby was filled with comfortable chairs clustered around low tables. Something forced the men and women to look; their senses were drawn to the two rough men violating their space.

Cliff wasn't worried about being seen with the man with three eyes. Bill was wearing a denim work coat, denim pants and a brown flannel shirt and his usual cap, pulled low on his face, almost to his nose. Cliff looked at Bill, wearing the same thing for thirty or forty years and walking through the lobby where he'd never been. If someone stared and reacted, it was their problem—not Bill's. He didn't see them. He walked with his head down, focused on one thing, talking to the boss.

When Cliff had hung up the telephone and told Bill they could see Mastras at the hotel, the man seemed to smile, but it was only a slight twist of his lips and nothing else. Cliff guessed it was all he was capable of. On the drive to the hotel, Cliff had asked Bill what he was going to say to the Man. Staring straight ahead, Bill said, "Make him stop or I will kill him."

It was all he said during the thirty-minute drive. It was a short answer and Cliff didn't ask any more questions. It wasn't time to act like a feature writer.

In the elevator, the two men looked up to watch the lights flash. A third man had entered with them and he got off on three and jerked his eyes at Cliff as he hurried away. Cliff wondered what the man might have done if Bill had offered to shake his hand.

Mastras answered the door and invited them to take two chairs by a coffee table. "I ordered coffee and pastry. It will be here in a minute." Bill declined, and Mastras and Cliff poured theirs. Mastras asked Bill, "What's on your mind? It's important enough for you to leave the lot. What can I do?"

"It's Lanning. He put up a banner of Joan. I made him take it down, swung a club at his head, but I knew I wouldn't hit him. He said he's putting it back up. If you don't stop him, I'll kill him." Bill's words were slurred like he'd been drinking, but he didn't drink alcohol and Mastras understood his muffled speech because they'd been around each other for many years.

"A banner, I heard about it," Mastras said. "What about it?"

Bill cried, "What about it? It's about you taking mine down 'cause we didn't want no more freak shows. Lanning's trying to start it up again, with my daughter. He's been giving her money, a little more, a little more, and he's moved her calf to the entrance where the marks can see her and the calf, and now he's put up the banner. It's been hard for Ruth and me. Joan's sixteen, she likes the money, and I bet he's promised her a big week in Philadelphia. We try to tell her not to do it but you can stop him, shut him down. I got to stop him."

Bill kept talking. "Boss, you know me a long time, know me good. I ain't sure you know where we're going. You probably think we ain't gonna quit, but we are. This is the last season for us. We're taking Joan home." He choked. "All these years being stared at, every day, me and Ruth. No more. We got each other, I would 'a killed myself if I didn't have Ruth, she brought me through. Now we got Joan. We got a family. We never thought we'd have a daughter. We can't lose her."

Mastras nodded. "All right, I'll do it."

Bill sighed and dropped his head between his knees, then looked up with tears shining on his twisted cheeks. "Thank you. God bless you. I'll give you whatever you're gonna lose with him shut down. Just tell me how much you think it will be, we can cover it. Thank you, thank you."

"I think I get how you feel. I thought when he quit drinking he was through pulling this shit. I guess not. He's like the rest of us. Money."

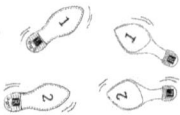

The menagerie tent and the loudspeakers and floodlights and tent poles and all of the banners had been unloaded from the wagon and spread over the matted grass.

Steve was shouting at Jack's replacement, while the extra hands shifted from one foot to the other, waiting for them to finish arguing so they could get on with setting up the tent. They'd been promised a bonus if they finished by five and they'd also been promised the honor of walking with the elephants from the train to the midway, an event that always drew the TV crews and the newspaper photographers, while there was still plenty of light. There was a good chance their pictures would be in the paper, or they'd be on TV—or both.

Steve offered the same promise in every town. He stopped the argument by telling the new man, Gary, that he should shut his mouth. "Before I'll shove this elephant hook down your throat and rip out your voice box. I guarantee it will stop your bullshit."

The work stopped on the rides and tents when the crews saw the shiny Mercedes weaving through the tractors and wagons and stopping next to the menagerie. John Mastras stepped out of the back seat and motioned for Steve.

"You have to move. I've given this spot to Bill Bronsey; his new ride just came in from Italy."

Steve stared at Mastras and then looked away. Steve knew not to open his mouth. Years earlier, when he was drinking, he would already have been out of his mind, shouting, blood vessels popping on the sides of his neck and forehead, but now he knew to wait. He stood silently, and waited on the next step.

"Put everything back in the wagon. I'll tell you where to go when we find another location."

"You gonna pay these extra guys?" Steve worked to hold down the volume, but the edge was still there.

"I'll pay them."

Steve watched the Mercedes as it angled past a tractor and weaved toward the office wagons.

The new man, Gary, took a step toward the wagon, and Steve raised his hand in a signal to stop. "Don't move anything, not 'til I know where we're going."

He thought the new man wasn't Jack, who—even drunk— would have understood what was happening, and who would have had the good sense to stay away.

The change in the set-up for the Philadelphia Fair was a problem and added to the new man's confusion. The extra hands looked at each other, trying to find their instructions but none appeared, so they stopped and waited.

Jack would have calmed them down. He would have told them what to do, a voice of authority.

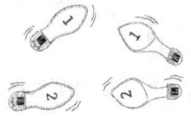

Cliff was watching from the other side of the midway. Mastras had told him to be out of sight, but close enough to hear.

"What am I going to hear?"

"Never know with Lanning, never know, probably nothing much. When I leave, you go to him, play dumb. See what he says."

Cliff waited five minutes, then walked to the wagon where Steve was sitting, blowing long plumes of smoke. The elephant trainer tipped his head. "If you're looking for him, the Man just left. He's making some changes. You probably know about it."

"What changes?"

"Moving me, make room for a new ride. I don't think there's any place to go. I'm sitting tight until he tells me where." Steve ground out his cigarette, then lit another. "Do your job and tell him what I said."

"What's that mean?"

"You know damn well what it means. Go tell him."

The office wagon was surrounded with men asking questions. Philadelphia was a big fair where everyone did well, the marks streamed through the front gates and crowded the ticket boxes and filled the canvas bags and late at night, the trucks hauled full loads of money to the bank. The big city produced big crowds.

The men stepped back, and made room for Cliff to open the office door. He no longer needed to knock. Cliff had a key to the Man's office and entered at any time. Having a key made an impact on how he was perceived around the midway. They made way for him.

"Lanning told me to do my job and tell you what he's doing."

Mastras was sitting in one of the leather chairs smoking a cigar, his legs stretched out and his tie loosened. "He better be loading the wagon. What's he doing?"

"Said he wasn't going to load until you told him where he was going."

"Good. Now I can shut him down." Mastras abruptly stood up, opened the door and looked over the men standing under the awning. "Come with me." He picked three trusted employees and told them to follow him. Mastras pulled on a baseball cap, and he and Cliff led the group to the empty menagerie wagon.

When they got there, Steve was still sitting in the back of the wagon, finishing another cigarette. "Where am I going?"

"I told you to get this stuff loaded. What are you doing sitting on your ass?"

"Waiting on you. Where am I going?"

"Nowhere. Not this week." Mastras gave instructions to the men. "Show the extras what to do. Load this equipment and send the wagon to the train." He turned back to Steve. "I can't make room for the menagerie this week, not with the new rides coming in. You take the week off, go down to Atlantic City. Win big at the tables."

Steve flipped his cigarette into a puddle and watched the last of the smoke as it drifted over the ground. "This is because I put up that new banner, ain't it? You got to have the elephants, it's in the contract."

Mastras laughed. "I'm sure glad you're worried about *my* contract." His voice could have cut steel. "If I were you, I'd be damned worried if I still had a contract."

Mastras didn't wait for a response and he motioned for Cliff to walk with him.

"You think he'll go to Atlantic City?" Cliff asked.

"No. I just hope he doesn't start drinking again. If that happens, I've screwed up."

"He knows why?"

"Sure he does. He also knows who owns the menagerie, the elephants, the train and it isn't Steve Lanning."

CHAPTER 48

You're Going to Get a Command Performance

Steve wasn't seen for the rest of the week. No elephants, no animals, news of the new roller coaster spread through TV spots and newspaper ads, and attendance grew every day.

Cliff thought it wasn't likely that Steve was drinking, but it was strange that he wasn't on the midway. What was he doing? What was he thinking? He must know he wouldn't be able to use Joan, but what if she wanted to do it? Katie might be the only one who could change her mind.

Joan's reasons for being on the midway—the animals and Little Three—were absent, so Joan spent the mornings backstage at the Broadway Review, learning new dance steps with Katie. During the afternoon she wrapped the scarf, her security, around her face and walked the midway and stopped in front of the new roller coaster where the animals were supposed to be.

She watched the faces of the people screaming down the first big drop and smiled behind her scarf. After watching for several minutes, she walked up the ramp, past the ticket taker who motioned her through, and sat in the front seat of the next car with the safety bar tight across her waist.

She leaned back as the car was pulled to the top and just before it pitched forward, in the heart-stopping dive, she pulled the scarf away and when her body floated over the seat, she raised her hands in the air and screamed all the way down until the car jerked back up, climbing out of the death dive.

Joan continued riding in the front seat, arms raised, her face generating long stares from the marks waiting their turn. More stopped to stare, then bought a ticket and rode and then got back in line for another ticket.

As she returned to the train, Joan covered her face, but she let the scarf slide away when the wind blew.

Ruth opened the door and pulled Joan into the room, hugging her tight for several minutes. "Are you all right? We missed you, we love you."

"I rode the new roller coaster! They let me on without a ticket."

Ruth kissed Joan's twisted mouth. "Of course they did."

"I heard why the animals are gone. Daddy Bill did it, didn't he?"

"Daddy Bill will do *anything* for you."

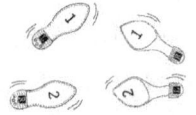

Closing night in Philadelphia, and the word on the midway was the last show in the Broadway Review would be special, because it was Katie's last night. In one week, she would start her new career at Radio City Music Hall. She was climbing out of the bottom of the barrel.

Clear skies coated with moonlight and a cool breeze and newspaper and TV ads and the new roller coaster brought thousands of marks through the front gates and they spent their money like a brother giving blood to his dying sister. Ace King filled all the seats in the Broadway Review with two turns on the bally stage and he signaled the ticket sellers to close. They were finishing the week with standing room only.

Ace had heard the girls planned to do something special for the grand finale, but he didn't care what it was. They could strip naked or appear in nun's habits, whatever, it didn't matter to him. It had been the best week of the season and they wouldn't burn the lot with one show, not the last show of the week. He wished they weren't doing anything special so he didn't have to go, but he couldn't miss Katie's last dance.

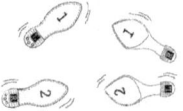

"I've been working on a new routine."

Cliff said. "I'll be in the front row."

"You're going to get a command performance." She squeezed Cliff's hand. "Are you ready?"

His eyes shone with approval, with pride in being with her. "My pencil is sharp and ready."

She skipped into the spotlight, moving in time to the beat of the guitars and drums and Cliff realized that workers from the midway were also sitting in the front rows. They followed her, knowing they were about to experience something special. They chanted, "Katie, dance, Katie, dance," and they moved with her. A wave of satisfaction swept through the crowd as they clapped their hands and tapped their feet to the driving guitars and the deep thud of the drums, the sound waves rolled over the audience, jerking them into motion.

Cliff wrote: *They know her. They think they know what to expect.*

One by one, the other dancers joined her in a strutting step that slowly built and built and Katie led the audience into a hand-clapping, foot-stomping sweaty party.

The drummer kept up a medium pattern with the bass drum, a steady syncopated beat backing the guitar chords and the melody from the sax. Three girls appeared from behind the curtains wearing masks, pastel colors wrapped their faces. Katie put on a mask and joined them and the four bodies with blank faces moved in unison; the fixed faces enhanced their turns. Motionless eyes contrasted with twisting arms and legs.

Cliff looked at the crowd and saw them questioning. But in a few seconds, the masks didn't matter as the dancers spun intricate steps and captivated the crowd until the audience was moving— energy ran through the tent, a force sucking people into the magic. Like an infection spreading and jumping from nervous system to nervous system where the symptoms were furious applause, footsteps, knee bends, shoulder flexing and escalating laughter and smiles, fast breathing.

Everyone joined in. They followed the masks, mixing together, each in harmony with the other, moving in response to what they saw and felt. Like a flock of birds dramatically darting, soaring, and shifting together, following the silent leader.

Cliff had watched Katie and Joan practice so much it was easy to tell them apart, but the rest of the audience only saw dancers performing in tight movement; executing intricate steps with wild enthusiasm, turning together, point and counterpoint that brought the audience to their feet.

The dance and the music affected everyone who was loved. Cliff looked at the audience and saw people who were grateful for someone to help them through the night.

They doubled the tempo and each dancer ran and jumped and landed with their arms locked together and they bowed with their masks turned to the ground. The applause built and the crowd called for more.

When they stood, the dancers touched their masks with their fingers, then took a final bow and walked backstage. The faces weren't important.

Cliff was the only one in the crowd who knew Joan's dancing was as good as Katie's. Cliff had watched them practice behind the tents. He had seen her improve, but it had been hard to accept because of her face. Now, behind the mask, Joan was as good as the others, as good as the best.

Cliff found them backstage. He wrapped Katie in his arms. "I love you...I love you."

She let the air out of her lungs and smiled and kissed him. "I love you, too."

"Where does it come from?" Cliff had asked her the question many times. He knew she couldn't give him an answer, but he asked again, hoping to find out more about his own dance, the secret to writing like she danced—joyful, engaging, inspiring, stimulating, all the dreamed-of results.

Katie brushed away his question and squeezed his hand. "Wasn't Joan wonderful?"

Joan removed her mask and pulled a scarf across most of her face. Cliff was glad that she was comfortable with him. She slid closer to Katie and tilted her head and whispered, "Will you tell him for me?"

"She wants me to explain why we wore masks and didn't take them off. I wanted to, I wanted to take them off and make a statement that looks don't count in dancing. But Joan said no. In fact, she told me, *hell no!*" Joan giggled. "She told me the dance was the most important thing and if she took off her mask, it would ruin it."

Cliff's eyes watered and he turned away, unable to say anything and he didn't know what to do with his hands. He was locked to the ground, waiting for someone or something to lead him out of his paralysis.

Katie thought she understood his helplessness. She watched him for a few seconds, then said, "You can cry if it's from happiness, and I think it is."

He nodded his head and was relieved to be able to take a small breath. "That made the music hall look like..." He stopped talking, then took another breath. "Can't find words."

He couldn't tell her what he really thought, and he was angry with himself for thinking it; the *New York Times*, the *CBS news*, picked up by the wire services—if she had danced for them and took off her mask. But even Joan knew it would have been a cheap shot to make the news for the wrong reason.

He waited until his heart slowed down and asked Katie, "Ready for Radio City?"

Katie locked her fingers around his hands. "It's going to be great. But I'm still going to help Joan. If I couldn't, I wouldn't go."

Cliff rubbed his eyes. "You just got the job. I thought the music hall was your dream."

"It's one of my dreams."

Leaving the tent with the rest of the audience, Bill and Ruth walked with their arms around each other, unable to speak. Because it was her last show, Katie had asked them to be there, but she hadn't told them that Joan was going to be a big part of the performance.

They had never seen Joan dance. They had heard her talk about the lessons and how Katie was so patient with her, but they had no knowledge of her ability. When they saw her performance, they were left speechless. It was beyond their imagination to believe a girl with Joan's deformity could possibly be so gifted, so graceful. Surely this would stop her wanting to use her face to make money.

"She can dance in Florida."

When the train got to New York, Joan and Katie cried. Joan thought that Katie was saying goodbye, maybe forever and she had to sit down. "Not today, not now."

Katie explained, "It isn't far, I'll see you this week. I'm just moving into an apartment but I'll have time to come back to see you."

Katie kept her promise. Joan asked if they could plan a picnic like they did before. "You and I plan it, and get the food. I'll ask Ruth to help. We can make potato salad and baked beans and get fried chicken from the cook tent."

"Let's ask Cliff to bring the drinks," Katie said. "He'll want to do something."

Katie was happy that Joan was planning the picnic and that she hadn't said anything about what was going to happen at the end of the week—when the train moved south to North Carolina, when Katie started her new job with the Rockettes.

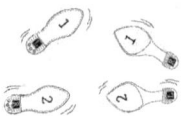

When the meal was finished, Ruth and Bill and Seamus and Cliff relaxed in the folding chairs.

Joan laid on a blanket with her head in Katie's lap. "I'm sad."

Katie didn't want the conversation to go this way, not yet. When she didn't respond, Joan continued. "Want to know what I'm sad about?"

"I think I know."

"Bet you don't." Joan looked up and smiled. "You think I'm sad because you're not going with us, don't you?"

"Yes."

"I'm sad about that, but that isn't what I'm really sad about today." She sat up so she could see the others. "I'm sad because Jack got killed and didn't get to see us dance. He would have cheered the loudest and he would have liked this picnic."

Joan pulled a folded envelope from her pocket. "Another reason I miss him is because of this letter."

When she started to read, Cliff looked at her eyes and realized it was the first time her face disappeared while he listened.

"Mr. Lanning gave me this letter yesterday. He had to help me read it because of some of the words."

Law Offices of Joseph Thomson
400 Grange St.
Boston, Mass.

SPECIAL DELIVERY
TO: Mr. Steve Lanning
C/O Mastras Shows, Jersey City, N.J.

Dear Mr. Lanning:

I hope this letter catches up with you on your travels with the Mastras Shows. We have you listed as the contact for Jack Lawrence.

Our law firm has the assignment of settling the estate of Mr. Jack Lawrence, Jr. In his last will and testament, he made the following provisions:

A sum of $20,000 (twenty thousand dollars) to be given to Joan Ryerson, in care of her adoptive parents Bill and Ruth Smithson. Mr. and Mrs. Smithson will be responsible for this money, as long as Joan resides with them and until she reaches the age of twenty-one. Until she reaches this age, the Smithsons may provide her a weekly allowance, as they see fit.

A sum of $20,000 (twenty thousand dollars) to be given to Katie Flannigan and it is the hope of Mr. Lawrence that Miss Flannigan use some or all of this money to help other young, unfortunate children learn to dance.

A sum of $10,000 (ten thousand dollars) to be given to Mr. Steve Lanning and Mr. Milt Hinkle, with the provision that they make a mutual decision as to how this money is to be used. My office is required to review their plans and make a determination if the plan is acceptable.

Please notify me as soon as possible where to send the checks to Joan Ryerson and Katie Flannigan, and when you and Mr. Hinkle have developed a plan, please provide it for my review.

Sincerely,
Joseph Thomson
cc: Mr. Jack Lawrence, Sr., Executor

CHAPTER 49

We All Have Gifts from God. Our Responsibility Is to Use Them

They could see the Statue of Liberty from where the train was parked, the lifted arm of hope anchored near the entrance to the land of free enterprise. It was party time in the Pie Car, a celebration of the good business in Jersey City.

Pagan and the other strippers made their exaggerated entrances dressed for the train ride, in jogging sweats, slippers and scarves. The mood in the dining car was upbeat because of the short run to Long Island. The community of carnies was on the move. They relished the break sharing each other's wins and losses.

"Drinks on me, ladies, anything you want." Cliff spread bills over the table.

Pagan ruffled his hair. "I heard the snakes was winning good money, serious money."

Katie and Seamus and Cliff had spent the day before in Manhattan, not running out of things to say as one comment led to another and another. Cliff was thankful for the time. The conversation had moved through different subjects, like flitting bright bugs on a dark night.

Seamus had asked hard questions about Cliff's writing and how important it was to him. "Do you feel blessed by it? Is it a gift from God? Please understand my feelings: We all have gifts from God. Our responsibility is to use them. It isn't a game. Albert Camus said it's our moral responsibility to do the best we can with the gifts we have to work with. To me it's a simple fact of life but one of the hardest facts we have to deal with."

"I don't know. I haven't thought about it. A gift with strings attached?"

"The gardener at our church says he's blessed to work with the flowers, no strings attached. James Joyce said writing was a blessing and a curse. Tell me, Cliff, are your carnival people blessed? I know some of them are, which ones?"

"Katie for sure, but she isn't one of the carnival people, but blessed more than anyone. You know that, don't you? I think the motorcycle rider, Clipper, is blessed, but he sure doesn't feel that way. He doesn't think in those terms. And Milt Hinkle, a long time ago, was aware of it, aware of his ego driving him on and on. There are others."

Seamus waited for Cliff, who looked to Katie for help. "How about this?" Seamus said and put one arm around Katie and one around Cliff.

"Do you feel blessed when you look at each other?" His white hair framed a soft haze around his head. Cliff imagined him as a young man changing a tire for a pretty girl.

They both answered, "Yes" at the same time.

"That's the right answer."

Katie asked if they would like something to drink.

Her father nodded his head. "We need to offer a toast. Now what do you say, Katie love?"

Katie smiled at her father. "Yes, a wee celebration with hot tea."

Seamus kissed Katie and turned to Cliff. "In the past, I would have taken too much whiskey, but no more." He folded his hands. "I would like the tea. Now, Mr. Cliff Walker, I'm asking you to give me your words. Please tell me, in your voice, some of the things that you will never forget about this time you've spent with the traveling show. It has to fill you with lush words and sights and smells and sounds of people laughing and loving and fighting. I know you have the words, God has given you the words."

"Heart, from your heart." To make her point, Katie gripped her father's hand with both of hers. "Dad always told me the heart is the most important part of the body. It's how he taught me to dance. What did you always tell me?"

Seamus' voice was a lullaby. "You've got to dance like there's nobody watching." His eyes drifted across the ocean. "Cliff, *please* give me your words, settle them on me."

Cliff flipped through his notebook. "I've filled a bunch of these with things I've heard and seen and smelled and felt." Cliff wasn't put off by the questions because of the gentle way Seamus had asked.

"Guard them with your life. Guard them. They're valuable, priceless." He faced Katie. "Help him, my love. You two help each other...please. I pray that you do. Can you tell me one thing you'll never forget?"

"It's hard to pick one. I'll try. It will help me sort it out. The obvious thing is Joan Ryerson, but I don't think Katie wants me to talk about her."

Katie said, "You can talk about her with us, just not to the newspapers."

"Will you start?" Cliff whispered the question.

"No."

They sat in silence.

Seamus wanted to say something but he knew it wouldn't be appropriate. When Katie had talked about Joan, she had to wipe tears from her eyes.

Cliff brushed through the notebook and stopped and ran his finger under the words and read them out loud, his weak voice gathered strength as he talked.

"*I drove Bill to the hotel so he could talk to the boss, Mr. Mastras, about saving his daughter, his deformed daughter who he loves with a power as great, greater than any force in the world. I drove him because he said if I didn't, he was going to kill Lanning and I didn't doubt him. I knew he would and not regret it, ever. The force of his words knocked over my doubt. I knew if I didn't drive him downtown and walk with him through the hotel lobby, this man with a cap pulled down to hide his deformed face, would commit murder. The people in the Marriott Hotel lobby were shocked when they saw us, but their stares didn't matter. Bill didn't care. Two women sitting on a sofa muffled their voices and buried their faces in their hands. I think my being able to walk with him is the bravest thing I've ever done. Bill could have been walking into machine-gun fire when he marched into that hotel lobby. He walked with strength that anyone seeing him could feel. It would have pulled me through the fires of hell. My heart was pounding. A father protecting his child. A girl, a miracle gift, placed in his custody by her grieving parents, a new member of the carnival family, a nomadic family of misfits. One greedy member was not going to exploit Bill's daughter and no one was going to stop him from protecting her.*"

Cliff had to breathe. "Empty words. I feel like writing them diminishes their truth."

Katie pushed against her father's shoulder. "Not empty. They're true, powerful. And they'll be true in your book and true when you write how Joan uses her money, and mine, to teach other girls to dance. Then you can write her story, her true story...and include how you helped stop Steve Lanning. You told me he was not a nice man. You were right. But I'll say this, he's stubborn after money."

"And there's the elephant in the room," Cliff said, "Jack's money. Joan's money, your money. You asked me what I'd never forget: the money from Jack. Seamus, you didn't know him—unfortunate. He was a mystery. Total mystery. Completely addicted to vodka. With Jack, you got to the point where all you expected was a stupid, confused man. Once, I saw something different, briefly. He pulled a part of his past life out of somewhere and negotiated the purchase of a tent for Milt's show. He lasted about twenty minutes, then fell apart. And he begged me for a drink that I gave him. He was pathetic. But he was brilliant while it lasted. And somehow he did what had to be done to give you and Joan a nice sum of money."

"I want to share mine with you." Katie stared at Cliff. "Is that all right?"

"The snakes are making good money. You keep it."

"Let's get married and move to Spain so you can write."

Seamus drew a breath, held it. "Over there." He exhaled, pointed across the ocean. "In the green valleys and the clouded mountains, they write from their hearts. They bleed on the paper. We defer to them, the great writers and the not-so-great, more than doctors, solicitors, priests. Those men are important, but the writers, the writers. You get into the guts of the people. You have an obligation to work hard at it. That bit about going to the hotel was sound. There are no empty words if they come from your deepest feelings. I heard your heart pounding on every page."

"I want to tell you something else."

"I thought so. Please, go ahead."

"Never told anyone before."

"I'm honored."

Cliff sees the surprise on Katie's face. He isn't sure about what he's going to say. "Admitting things from the past is hard to do."

"Why? Is it embarrassing?"

"Maybe, for me. I don't know why it's so hard. It might be because your dad's a pastor."

Seamus closed his eyes. "Think of me as Jack's brother, not the Pope."

"That makes it much easier. Extreme, but easier. When I was twelve, my friend Johnny and I were allowed to go to the fair at night, our curfew was eleven. We could leave the fairgrounds at fifteen 'til and make it home on time. We were leaving when a man and a woman selling salt water taffy stopped us and asked us if we were Christians. Johnny was a Baptist and I was a Presbyterian. We both went to Sunday school and church with our parents, and I answered, 'Yes, I guess so.'

"The man handed us a few pieces of wrapped taffy. 'Have you accepted Jesus as your savior?'

"Neither one of us knew what to say. Baptists and Presbyterians don't act like that.

'You know, boys, it's real important that you ask for forgiveness from your sins and promise to follow Jesus. Will you pray for this with me?'

"I was getting real nervous. We were running out of time to make our curfew."

Seamus asked, "What did you do?"

"We looked at each other. We couldn't answer. He asked again and again and, finally, I said we would."

"What was his prayer?"

"He asked us to repeat it after him. *Dear Lord Jesus, I know I am a sinner, and I ask for your forgiveness. I believe you died for my sins and rose from the dead. I trust and follow you as my Lord and Savior. Guide my life and help me to do your will. In your name, Amen.* The man and the woman hugged us and told us we were now real followers of Jesus. We said we had to leave or we'd be in trouble with our parents. They told us to go and remember Jesus was with us. We ran as fast as we could and made it five minutes late, but didn't get in trouble."

"Is that all?"

"The next morning, I woke up with a sense of belonging and when I asked Johnny how he felt, he said, 'About what?' I was surprised and said, 'about Jesus?'"

"Nothing."

"A few days later, I didn't, either. But I've remembered that night for twenty years. I've never asked Johnny about it again. I'd like to. But I don't see him much anymore. His answer was upsetting, but not enough for me to do anything about it, not then."

"Do you think that prayer has had an impact on you?"

"It did that night, when I was in bed. I thought about what the taffy man had said, how we were safe in the arms of Jesus, safe with millions of other believers. Now I don't go to church. Don't do what I want to do, should do."

"Give it time. The thing I heard in your story is the way the taffy people found you in a strange place. That's real faith."

Seamus shifted in the chair. Katie noticed and asked, "What are you thinking about?"

"Salt water taffy. I'd like to find that couple, probably impossible. What do you think, Cliff?"

"Impossible. That was twenty years ago. They might be dead."

"I'll ask Steve and Milt. They might know them. At least it will give me a good reason to talk to them."

"You're after them, aren't you?"

"Who, Steve and Milt or the taffy people?"

"Steve and Milt."

Seamus said, "You know me well. Of course I am, why I'm here."

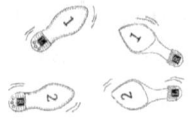

The train jerked and the wheels broke free and rolled on the smooth rails, the couplings smacking together, taking up the slack as the long sections of rainbow cars moved slowly in one string, faster, then even faster.

Cliff raised his glass silently, toasting no one in particular. *At least Katie isn't here. She has resigned from this community, and I'm not here for long.*

Cliff kissed Pagan on the cheek and lifted a suitcase and his small canvas bag and told them goodbye. "Mr. Seamus Flannigan got my attention. I've got to see what I can do, time for me to leave."

With no hesitation, Cliff walked toward the end of the car and Pagan directed Steve out of his seat. He caught Cliff and they stood outside on the open platform.

Cliff shifted his eyes to the ground and back to the train, and shook hands with Steve. "Maybe I'll see you next season, somewhere..."

"You can't jump now, we're moving—too fast."

"Not too fast. Just about right."

"Right for what?"

"Like Professor Hinkle. I want to jump out of the airplane, meet the man, shake his hand."

"How much have you had to drink? Look at his legs, he almost killed himself."

"Nothing to drink, it's time for me to leave. My show business career is over. I'm jumping into something new."

Cliff pulled a copy of *On The Road* out of the small bag and handed the book to Steve.

"What's this?"

"You finished Fitzgerald, this is your next assignment, time for you to take on something different."

"This that guy from Lowell, Karak?"

"Kerouac. *On The Road*, like you."

The train gathered speed and Cliff stepped down and pulled an envelope out of his coat pocket.

Steve shouted over the noise of the train. "Milt messed himself up real good. Don't do it, don't jump."

"It isn't an airplane, not far to the ground. Thanks for everything." Cliff pushed the envelope toward Steve. "Snake money, two thousand large. It's all yours if you tell me the truth about your ear. The real truth."

Steve looked at the envelope. "Keep your money. It was a German bullet. Buzzed around inside my helmet like a chain saw. Lucky it didn't kill me."

Cliff grabbed Steve's belt, pulled it forward and shoved the envelope down the front of his pants. "You be sure and give Milt some of it." Cliff laughed. "I know you will."

He dropped the suitcase, and it flew and bounced and rolled through the tall grass. Cliff swung on the grab rail, looked down at the suitcase, then jumped clear and stumbled when he hit the ground, but didn't fall. Cinder dust swirled around his face. He held the small bag with his notebooks close to his chest, ran beside the train, and stared at Steve.

Steve leaned down, shook his head and shouted, "Nothing for Milt, not a dime, he still owes me." Then he rubbed his ear and shouted, "That lion hit me fast, didn't see him, ripped my ear off before I saw him move. You take your pick."

The train pulled away and the two men laughed at each other. Cliff danced and turned and sat on his suitcase and waved goodbye.

The look on Steve's face, in his eyes, a glimpse of a personality unlike any Cliff would ever meet again, the only one in the world, like the rest of us.

Cliff walked to a pay phone outside a convenience store and waited for his call to be answered.

"Franklin, I jumped off the train. You should have been there with your camera. The picture would have made a great opening shot for the *Life* story."

"You left all that money? Where are you going?"

"Can't tell you right now, not for a while. I'll let you know where I end up. You'll be invited."

CHAPTER 50

The Broadway Review Tent
Is Now a Sanctuary,
Ready to Host This
Sacred Ceremony

There was no question, no doubt, where they'd get married. When Cliff had proposed to Katie, she said *yes—in the Broadway Review tent*.

Cliff agreed. "The only place, no question. Invite the whole show."

The show train was in Portsmouth, Virginia to play the Tidewater Marine Exposition. That gave them enough time to prepare for the wedding with seating in the big tent for everyone, including out-of-town guests. Even the sailors from Cliff's former ship, the *USS Duxbury Bay* docked in Little Creek, Virginia, having just returned from a long cruise, would be invited.

John Mastras provided his airplane to fly to New York to transport Katie, Seamus, and Rose back to Portsmouth to help with the arrangements. They took two days to decorate, including the installation of a small altar in front of the main stage, so the wedding party could stand at ground level instead of being elevated like the usual naked strippers.

Rose Flannigan had arrived in New York a week early so she and Katie could shop for a dress.

"When we got married in Ireland we were on the run." She repeated the story how she and Seamus had decided to get married with their traveling friends standing up with them. The priest knew Seamus was an ex-priest and didn't want to perform the ceremony, but Seamus was so convincing that after the wedding, the other priest also quit his job to marry a girl in his village.

Joan was the maid of honor; Franklin the best man, Carolyn and Pagan and the other girls were bridesmaids, Steve Lanning and Milt Hinkle groomsmen; like a wedding scene in a silent comedy.

Carol Fraley made the trip from Boston as part of her new job—feature writer, with the *New York Times*.

The saxophone player had rehearsed "Here Comes the Bride," and played the soft song slowly with a guitar strumming chords in the background, timing it so that the bride and her parents walked together down the center aisle.

Seamus welcomed everyone to the wedding. "The Broadway Review tent is now a sanctuary, with canvas walls and an altar ready to host this sacred ceremony."

Seamus spread his arms. "Weddings happen in many different places. Rose and I got married standing on an Irish cliff overlooking the ocean. Now my daughter is getting married in a tent on a carnival midway. And I have to say, this tent looks as nice as many of the churches where I've officiated. Just because a different event takes place in here at night doesn't make any difference to the sanctity of this service today."

Pagan stood up. "I just hope this event don't have a bad effect on my show. No bad vibes. Why don't we get Ace to sell some tickets to this really, really big show? Katie can dance through her vows."

Seamus face was bright red. "Laughter, it's an Irish thing, particularly when your only daughter is getting married and I get to do it. You may or may not know that I am both an ex-Catholic priest as well as an ordained Presbyterian pastor—the official credentials. I'm sure it's not going to have a negative impact on your pristine performance."

Pagan repeated, "Pristine performer! Can I use that? Maybe this reporter will put it in her article. See pretty Pagan the pristine performer!"

Carol Fraley had asked Seamus for a few remarks before the service started.

"When Katie and Cliff decided to get married, this was only place they would consider for the event. I've married people in churches, hotels, parks, private homes, even boats; but, as you might guess, this is the first time in a tent on a midway."

Seamus prayed, asking God to bless the couple and to bless Cliff's parents, who had driven from Indiana to attend, and to bless all of the guests. They repeated their brief vows and exchanged rings and Seamus held their hands and turned them toward the audience.

"Friends, guests, it is my pleasure to introduce you to Mr. and Mrs. Cliff Walker." The applause supported them along the center aisle where Franklin organized the wedding party for the official pictures.

One of the sailors took charge of the camera. Looking through the viewfinder, he directed them into the right order: Katie and Cliff in the middle, Franklin and Joan on either side, bridesmaids and groomsmen flanking them. One, two, three, four shots and the incredible event was captured forever.

Later, when eight-by-ten color prints were distributed, the faces exploded out of the paper. Milt Hinkle's fat face looked like a wad of loose clay melting in the heat. Seamus and Rose expressed their Irish pride, similar to the parents seen in hundreds of Irish weddings. Cliff and Katie could have been featured in the society section of the *Times*, and Joan and Katie's faces reflected two delighted friends sharing a new benchmark in their lives. If you looked past the exterior of their faces, looked into their eyes, the image was of two girls who loved each other. The glow filtered Joan's torn features.

Her disfigured face might be a Halloween mask. Underneath the mask was a person who liked to dance and eat cotton candy and feed the animals, just one member of a joyful wedding party.

Steve Lanning had turned his head slightly to the right to make sure his half ear was visible.

As a new reporter with the *New York Times*, Carol Fraley needed the picture of Katie and Joan. Her professional standards pulled at her. It could be the story and the picture to kick-start her new career.

She had honored Katie's request to not write about Joan and she respected people's desire for privacy, but when someone like Joan overcame a horrendous problem, it could serve as inspiration to other disadvantaged people—bolster their hope. Maybe Cliff could help.

She decided it was worth a try and asked him if he could help. "I'd like your advice."

"You want my advice, a *New York Times* feature writer? I can't imagine." But he could imagine the obvious, and he couldn't stop the thought that it might help with his own writing career.

"Tell me if I should ask Joan if I can use her picture."

"Don't put that on me."

"Will you help?"

"I don't know. I do know she's changed—a lot since she got here. She's learned to dance. Katie's an inspiring teacher. She's inherited a lot of money and she's comfortable with her new parents. They love her more than you can imagine. But a picture in the *Times* might still be over the top." Cliff had an idea. "Steve Lanning and Milt in the story might work and they'll be all about it. They understand publicity better that anyone."

Cliff motioned for Steve to join him.

"The reporter wants to use you and Milt in a wedding story. She said it might be the only time the two of you are together looking respectable and sober."

"Now you're talking. How much?"

"How much what? She won't pay you."

"No, how much are you gonna charge us?"

"Listen, Mr. Lanning. There are some people who do things for no money, for the intrinsic value of the act."

"The what? What the hell does intrinsy mean?"

"Intrinsic. It means the act itself has value."

"Oh, like sex?"

"Like sex. Or dancing, or singing, or talking to an interesting person, or training elephants because you want to and can, and not just for money."

"Writing? Is that why you want to write?"

"Yes, for the most part."

"Then get your ass on with it."

"The reporter said she'd help me work for the *Times*."

"Will you do it for free?"

"If you help Seamus with his AA plan."

"I'm going to."

"To get the ten grand?"

"No other reason. None of that intrisy crap."

"Did the attorney say you could have it?"

"Seamus is talking to him, thinks he will agree."

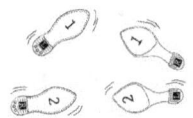

Cliff rolled a clean sheet of paper into the typewriter and snapped his fingers on the keys:

Dance Like You Don't Need the Money
By Cliff Walker

Franklin Acton and Cliff Walker waited by the old Pennsylvania Railroad Station in Morganport, Indiana, for the arrival of a carnival train hauling rides and shows, dancers and freaks, salt water taffy machines for the entertainment and salvation of the citizens of Capp County attending the annual Fair and Exposition.

When the train stopped the first person they saw was Steve Lanning, the elephant trainer, holding to his head a white towel soaked with red blood.

A former rodeo star, Milt Hinkle, told them, "Don't get blinded by the money, makes you march to the Man paying you, makes you miss the glory in your heart, makes you miss the joy of writing it, of riding the wild train."

Are the games on the midway fixed? You guess they are, but even so, you play the game anyway, hoping against better judgment that somehow you'll beat the almost-impossible odds and win the prize.

But you can't win or lose if you don't play the game.

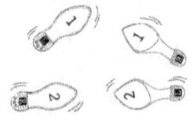

Wedding pictures were a Sunday feature of the *New York Times*: Celebrities, billionaires, senators, famous authors, rock and roll singers, mafia leaders, Olympic gold medalists and on this Sunday, the featured picture was from the Flannigan-Walker wedding.

Cliff had asked Katie what she thought about using the pictures, with Joan in them.

"We'll ask her. It isn't my decision."

"Will you ask her with me? She trusts you more than me. I'm just a reporter trying to sell newspapers. But I'm not. You know I'm not. Carol Fraley isn't either."

Joan surprised them. "I'd like that, all of us in the newspaper. Mom and Dad will be surprised."

Cliff listened, *all of us in the newspaper, all of us. She isn't alone anymore. She isn't trapped. She doesn't need a mask. Does she understand what this will do for thousands of people? That it will free them? Probably not, not now, maybe later, maybe never, but now is the key for Joan, now is all we've got. And all of the prior wedding pictures and all of the wedding pictures to come are pale, washed-out flat images compared to the Flannigan-Walker wedding. The faces are priceless, beyond belief, over the top, a guaranteed Pulitzer, pictures that sell more papers than ever before except for the pictures of the first man to orbit the earth.*

They bought the papers to see the freaks. Even the regular readers of the New York Times: *the intellectuals, the Wall Street Barons, the premier artists, star performers, the world's leading statesmen, the spiritual gurus, the presidents of the nations of the world—they bought the paper to see the freaks, just like the rag-tag marks who patrolled the midway with cotton candy stuck to their cheeks.*

Cliff reviewed his notes. He added comments to what Seamus had told him, some of the action he had taken in the short time he'd been with the show. When he had his notes organized, he wrote a rough draft and for the first time, he felt joy in his writing.

His excitement moved him to go over the draft several times until he thought he could give it to Carol Fraley.

She told him it was fair work. "Not ready for the *Times* but it's getting there. I can hear your excitement, keep going, damn it, just keep going—*please!*"

Pushing the keys was effortless. Letters turned words into sentences. Cliff's thoughts made it to the blank pages, one, two, three, four—as many as were needed to tell this story.

Seamus Flannigan is a force of nature, a child of God: influencing how church congregations are getting better at helping others. His example is inspiring. One man doing what he can to change the world.

His trek from Ireland to California to New York has spawned dancers, supported seekers on their quest for meaning, fostered loving groups who spread their love, one soul at a time, and presided over the wedding of his daughter, Katie to this hopeful writer, bringing me the mate I have been seeking, a partner who is teaching me how to dance like I don't need the money, the dance I've been born to dance.

And Seamus doesn't stop. It's what he does every day. He told me to write from my heart. He told me it was Thoreau who said 'How vain it is to sit down to write when you have not stood up to live.' They don't know it yet, but Steve Lanning and Milt Hinkle are going to be part of his process; the Seamus Flannigan Mobile Mission, always open for business.

Inspiring is one description; it works for me. He inspires me to step out, to love everyone I meet, to love them joyfully and thank them for sharing their joy, even the mixed-up contradictory, addicted, lying, cheating, loving, laughing, dancing band of carnies who are part of a tradition and the show never stops: twenty-five cents, one quarter of a dollar takes you all the way through and it's all alive on the inside.

CHAPTER 51

"For Ten Grand, I'll Quit." Milt Poured the Vodka on the Floor

Steve opened the door to the Pie Car and looked for Milt and saw him sitting in a booth, leaning against the wall with his stiff legs propped on the seat. Steve gripped the seats to keep his balance as the train made its way through Long Island.

He said, "Just the two of us. The kid's gone; Jack's gone. I'll be gone if you start talking."

They sat in the silence ordered by the elephant trainer because he said his half ear couldn't hold anymore of Milt's chin boogie. "I'm done listening to you. How many times have I said that?"

Milt sat with his head against the wall, looking through the window, and waited until he could talk again. He was wearing a dark blue jacket with Boston College embroidered in gold across the chest, a new coat given to him by Professor Cameron, a gift from the school, and Milt would wear it for the rest of his life, a medal of honor.

Steve ran his finger over a long paragraph, closed the book *On The Road*, then opened it again, trying to make sense of the convoluted words strung together like an abstract painting.

"Karac had to be stoned out of his gourd when he wrote this. I guess I can see why Cliff wanted me to read it. Not sure I can finish it."

Milt ran his fingers over the front of his jacket and felt the stitches spelling *Boston College*. "I didn't used to think much of reading until we went to Boston College."

"*We* didn't go to Boston College. *NO TALKING!*"

"You were there, too." Milt had to include Steve.

"I don't know what you want, but saying I went to Boston College with you ain't doing shit to come up with a plan that lawyer will buy."

"Hear me out. We're close to getting serious money, bless Jack's soul. I got another idea. Like we told him before, we change it to *The Sheriff from Boston College* with a picture of me holding a book on the front."

Steve twisted his head. "We *already* ran that one past him. He didn't go for it."

Milt forced himself to keep his voice down. "We get Duke to make it look like a library, books on shelves."

Steve stared at Milt. "Why do you think a library is any better than a jail? He already said no! We got to come up with something better. Neither one of us is smart enough to zip up our pants."

Milt filled his coffee cup with vodka and downed it in one swallow. His eyes glistened.

"We got our pictures in the *New York Times,* don't that help? Seamus says we should do something to help the drunks, what about that? He says ex-drunks can help better than anyone. We can do that."

"I didn't know you'd quit."

"For ten grand, I'll quit." Milt poured the vodka on the floor; the clear alcohol glistened and puddled into the worn carpet. "Seamus can help us. He's going to help us. He wants us to use the money to help the drunks, says we're the best ones out here to do it, start one of them AA meetings. Jack might still be alive if we did."

Steve closed his eyes, head down. "That damned Jack done it on purpose. He knew we'd never get the money. He's laughing his ass off, wherever he is. He knew if we tried to do what we always do, we'd end up with the same thing—nothing."

Steve looked at Milt and thought it was time to listen to someone else.

"No doubt, Seamus has got something different…might work. That lawyer can't say no to Seamus and his AA club. For ten grand, we'll give it a shot… What Cliff said—the *intrinsy* value, what it's all about."